D0201664

About the Author

Lilly Bartlett's cosy romcoms are full of warmth, quirky characters and guaranteed happily-ever-afters. Lilly is the pen-name
of Sunday Times and USA Today best-selling author, Michele
Gorman, who writes best friend-girl power comedies under
her own name.

The Big Little Wedding in Carlton Square

Michele Gorman writing as
LILLY BARTLETT

A division of HarperCollins*Publishers*
www.harpercollins.co.uk

Harper*Impulse* an imprint of
HarperCollins*Publishers*
The News Building
1 London Bridge Street
London SE1 9GF

www.harpercollins.co.uk

A Paperback Original 2017

First published in Great Britain in ebook format by
Harper*Impulse* 2017

Copyright © Lilly Bartlett 2017

Lilly Bartlett asserts the moral right to
be identified as the author of this work

A catalogue record for this book
is available from the British Library

ISBN: 9780008226589

This novel is entirely a work of fiction.
The names, characters and incidents portrayed in it are
the work of the author's imagination. Any resemblance to
actual persons, living or dead, events or localities is
entirely coincidental.

Set in Birka by Palimpsest Book Production Limited,
Falkirk, Stirlingshire

Printed and bound by CPI Group (UK) Ltd, Croydon, CR0 4YY

All rights reserved. No part of this publication may be
reproduced, stored in a retrieval system, or transmitted,
in any form or by any means, electronic, mechanical,
photocopying, recording or otherwise, without the prior
permission of the publishers.

To my friends Ben and Ting, proof that love
blooms gloriously across cultures, and whose
DIY wedding inspired this story.

This is a work of fiction, which means that any corruption
of government officials or questionable market activities
comes purely from the imagination of the author, who is
sure these things don't happen in real-life.

Chapter 1

Breathe, Emma. Pretend this is just a perfectly normal walk, like the time we went rambling all over Hampstead Heath and even though it started to drizzle and Auntie Rose had spent ages getting my hair straight, I acted like I'd been wishing for a clammy mist to come along and soak me through.

No, wait, that's when Daniel told me he loved me. With water dribbling off my nose, frizzy hair and all. Oh god.

The important thing is to be cool and calm and not to act like some crazy person about to be proposed to. That's how I'll want Daniel to think of me whenever he remembers the day we got engaged. His cool, calm girlfriend who answered with something clever and nonchalant but still genuine and emotional.

Because I'm sure that's what this is. In the entire history of the South Bank, the only people who've ever come here to walk along its wide Thames-side promenade are tourists and lovers.

It's not only the location that's alerted me. There've been clues, though I'm sure Daniel thinks he's been subtle. A few months ago as we cuddled on his sofa with a bottle of wine and a film neither of us was very interested in, out of the blue he asked, 'Do you ever wear rings? I just wondered because Mummy does.'

I should explain about the Mummy thing before we go any further, otherwise you'll be picturing someone not very appealing. Daniel is very appealing. He's not a mama's boy (or a mummy's boy). That's just what posh people call their mums. It's why he speaks like his jaw is wired open and loves red trousers, even though he's only twenty-five. He might be a bit hard to understand sometimes because he slides over most of the syllables in words but lands on the letters at the ends. Isn'T thaT amaahzing? I'm getting pretty good at translating him into normal, though, so I'll do my best.

Anyway, that one little question was the biggest clue that he might be thinking in the long term. There were other things too – mentions of future plans, including what sounded like a Christmas invitation to his family's next year, even though we've just passed Valentine's Day. But he asked about the ring months ago and, forewarned, I did shave my legs nearly every day after that (and definitely for Valentine's Day, just in case), though lately I've reverted to my normal shaving-twice-a-week-if-I'm-lucky stubble.

All of which is to say that I'm not as prepared for today as I'd like. My hair's got a weird kink and instead of a killer outfit I'm in my usual jeans and trainers and my winter wool coat that I should have replaced last year when it started to pill. It's too warm for a wool coat anyway. I can feel my face sweating. Just to complete that marry-me look.

Daniel, I now notice, is dressed up. He's wearing his tan brogues with his red trousers, and the stripy scarf I got him for Christmas is looped over his navy jumper.

I have to catch my breath when I sneak a glance at him. In the early spring sunshine his hair and complexion are golden, even though we haven't been away all winter. He's got the kind of skin you see on gorgeous Scandinavians in those adverts selling extra-healthy yogurt, with pinkish lips and just the right amount of stubble for a Saturday afternoon. He catches me with his bright blue eyes, edged with the longest, thickest brown lashes this side of a Rimmel advert.

'Everything all right?' His arm tightens around my shoulder, which fits perfectly into his armpit as long as I'm in trainers. Which I am, as previously explained.

'Everything's perfect.' And I mean it. I've been in a near-constant state of happiness since the day we got together.

'I think so too,' he says. 'This is perfect.'

Something about the way he says it tells me this is the moment. Even if I hadn't had the clues first, I would have known.

Gently he steers me to the stone wall at the edge of the river. The tide is going out and it smells a bit fishy, but I wouldn't mind doing this on top of a rubbish tip. 'I know we haven't been going out very long,' he says. 'But—'

'Nearly a year,' I remind him. Shush, Emma. Let the man speak.

'Yah, nearly a year.' He envelops my hands in the warmth of his. 'And I've known for nearly that long how much I love you. You aren't like anyone I've ever met before and I feel like I could spend the rest of my life learning more about you. And the more I learn, the more I love, so ...' When he drops down on one knee I'm aware of people starting to stare. 'Emma Liddell, will you please make me the happiest man on earth by marrying me?'

My eyes are so glued to his hopeful face that I almost don't notice the box he pulls from his pocket.

But I notice the ring when he pops open the box.

'Daniel! That's—' Huge. It's a square-cut diamond whose sparkles could do permanent retina damage in this sunshine. 'I can't let you go into debt like this.' He only works for a charity.

'I'm not in debt. It's a family ring.'

'Which family? The Queen's?'

His face reddens. 'They have a bit of money. I didn't like to mention it because it doesn't matter. It doesn't, does it?'

He looks like he's just confessed an infectious disease. 'No.' I laugh. 'I think I can manage to love you anyway.'

'Is that a yes, then?'

'It's a yes! Of course it's a yes, I love you!' We fling our arms around each other to the enthusiastic applause of the tourists, and maybe even a few of the lovers, on the South Bank.

'I cannot wait to marry you, Emma Liddell,' he murmurs just before he kisses me.

Two weeks later...

When Daniel said his family had a bit of money he failed to mention that he grew up in a mansion. Not a mansion block but an actual bona fide mansion – four floors high, white stucco-fronted with black-and-white chequered tiles in the doorway under the portico and an ornate wrought-iron fence to keep out the riffraff. Not that any riffraff probably comes to this part of London.

I can't stop staring up at the façade. My feet don't want to move and the rest of me is taking orders from them. If the neighbours catch sight of me, they'll be straight on the phone to the Old Bill about someone casing the place.

The last time I was inside such a grand home I'd mopped its floors with Mum. She's never going to believe this.

Huge topiary trees flank the black front door, which is so shiny I can almost see my reflection. I pinch a leaf from one of the trees. Real. Of course it is. The heavy lion-headed knocker makes an echoing boom inside.

Daniel didn't let on about any of this, not the huge family house or the topiary or the knocker. He was so uncomfortable when telling me about his family having money that I felt bad bringing it up again. He's right – we're marrying each other, not our families.

I've met Daniel's parents and sister several times before, but they've never mentioned any of this either. I'd assumed we always met at restaurants because his mum doesn't cook, but now I suspect he's been keeping this dirty little rich secret from me. It's hard to get too cross about that.

The slender blonde woman who opens the door is about my age. She smiles her greeting and steps aside for me. She's wearing black trousers and a white blouse, which makes me feel better. I was worried I hadn't dressed up enough for this do.

'Hiya, I'm Emma Liddell.' I stick out my hand, but she just looks confused.

Maybe I should have cheek-kissed her? Daniel is always kissing people he's just met.

'May I take your, erm, helmet?' she asks.

We both glance at the duck-egg blue helmet under my arm. It's not exactly a Louis Vuitton. Now I've got a second reason to wish I hadn't driven my scooter. It had looked so little and careworn parked out front amongst all the Rollers and Audis.

'Sure, here. Sorry, I didn't get your name?'

She takes my helmet, ignoring my question. 'The guests are through there.'

I turn away quickly so she won't see my cheeks flush. She's not one of Daniel's friends who happens to be dressed in black and white and answering the door. She's their maid.

That's a great start.

I can hear loads of people in the room where she's pointed. It seems like about a mile between there and the front door. Possibly because Daniel's hallway is bigger than my entire house. Wide stairs run up on one side and the ceiling must be fifteen feet high. Everything is painted either boring pale grey or white, with a huge silver mirror on one wall and tall vases of lilies on the long black table underneath. The only interesting thing I spot is the giant copper and glass lantern that hangs from the ceiling, like the ones you find outside pubs. I hold on to that tiny little slice of home comfort as I make my way towards the noise.

I should have asked the maid to get Daniel for me so I wouldn't have to walk in alone. What if I don't see him right away? What if he's not here yet? I only know his parents and sister, and I definitely can't talk to them without Daniel here.

Not that they're rude. Just in a different world.

The world I'm about to join. If they'll have me.

There aren't as many people in the room as I'd feared and of course Daniel's mother, Philippa, sees me straight-away. So much for hiding in the corner. 'Emma, darling!' she cries. 'It's so wonderful finally to have you here in our home. We've been bothering Daniel for months to invite you and now, finally, here you are with us.' She hold my hands out, which she's got grasped in hers. 'Don't you look lovely?'

'Thank you. And thank you for this party.' I say this to both Philippa and Daniel's father, Hugh, who's standing beside her. Hugh doesn't usually make an appearance unless Philippa makes him, so she's clearly making him. I'm not surprised he stays in the background with a force of nature like Philippa around. She's a take charge kind of woman, whether you like it or not. Daniel told me she even orchestrated Hugh's marriage proposal. But they seem to rub along okay, so maybe he'd have got around to it eventually on his own.

Philippa waves her hand at the room. 'Oh, this is nothing, just something I cobbled together so we can celebrate!'

I glance at the silver and the sparkling champagne glasses laid on blue linen tablecloths, the stacks of cocktail napkins that look like real linen too. She's even got matching waiters, and I don't mean they're dressed alike. They're clones of one another.

Philippa looks perfectly put together as usual. She's got on a navy wool dress that probably cost more than I earn in a year, though if I compliment her on it she'll say, 'What? This old thing? It's been in the back of my closet for ages.' And then she'll try to give it to me, even though she's about a foot taller than I am. Because she's very gracious like that.

She's not classically pretty – more handsome. And tall, like I said. Her big booming voice matches her personality and she's exactly what you'd picture if I told you she's a hearty woman. She's somewhere north of fifty, but how far north is anyone's guess. Could be Manchester, could be the Orkneys. She's got a few lines around her mouth and a few around her eyes, but she hasn't tried to Botox or fill them. Too much bother, she claims. She probably colours her hair too, but the dark blonde looks completely natural. Daniel says she used to have it all the way down her back when she was young, but now she wears it in a bob like nearly all the other women in the room. Something about giving birth seems to make women cut off their hair.

I doubt I'd ever do that. Not that my hair is overly long now. If I tip my head back, it reaches my bra strap. It's naturally wavy, but Auntie Rose did me a blow-dry this morning.

I'll never be able to subtly hide the grey like Philippa can, though. Not that I need to reach for the L'Oréal yet. I'm only twenty-four and my hair's nearly jet black, thanks to a great great (great? I forget) grandfather, imaginatively known as Blacky all his life. I'm the only one in the family who's got his hair. Mum's even got a natural ginger tinge, or so she claims. Auntie Rose has done her colour forever – it's always red but veers between Amy Adams and Prince Harry.

'Right, you must come meet our dear, dear friends,' Philippa says, leaving Hugh standing on his own with his drink. I catch his wink as his wife drags me off. Better me than him, it says.

'May I introduce you to George and India, Lord and Lady Mucking? George's parents were lifelong friends of

Hugh and me, and we've known George since he was born!'

Lady Mucking is pretty and plump, with the requisite blonde bob. Her nose is slightly big but nothing compared to her husband's. I could stay dry in a hurricane under that thing. But his face is friendly and they both smile when Philippa introduces us. They're older than me – probably in their late thirties – but not nearly as old as I imagined lords and ladies would be. Though for all I know the upper classes might give birth to fully grown lords. Or maybe they sprout like tulips every few years in the Queen's garden.

'India, George,' says Philippa. 'May I introduce Emma Liddell, Daniel's fiancée!'

I can hardly believe I'm marrying into this lot. I had no idea it was this bad. I mean good. Of course I mean good.

'Very pleased to meet you both,' I say as I shake their hands. I've never knowingly touched a lord before. His hand is sweaty. Maybe he's never knowingly touched a commoner.

'Hellair! Lidl, you say?' asks George. 'As in the super-market? I knew it was family-owned. Are they Lidls?'

I nearly guffaw at the idea that I'm part of some

supermarket dynasty, till I catch on that he's serious.

'No, no, not related. L, I, double D, E, double L. I think Lidl is German. We've been in East London forever. Dad's traced us back to the eighteen-eighty census.'

'Yah, our family was in Burma then,' George says.

'You're a cockney?' India asks. Her hands twinkle with jewels as they fly to her chest. 'That's delightful! Let me see, yah, I remember. Did you come up the apples and stairs just now?'

I smile indulgently. Anyone west of Farringdon thinks we all talk like the cast off *Lock, Stock and Two Smoking Barrels*. 'I did and I'm Hank Marvin for one of those.' I snatch a tiny sausage roll from a passing tray.

India looks confused. 'I mean starving. Is Daniel here?' I ask Philippa, trying not to sound as panicky as I'm starting to feel.

'Oh yes, he's just gone to check on the kitchen. They're being awfully slow with the rest of the canapes.'

Sure enough, Daniel wanders in, amiably chatting with a waiter who's carrying a tray of what might be miniature pancakes.

'Em!' He scoops me up in his arms for a gentle kiss. 'You look gorgeous.'

'Not too …?' Market stall? I want to ask. It's a plain

little black dress with lace on the short sleeves and down the front, but I wonder if Daniel's crowd can tell it's not designer. It feels wrong wearing lace when the rest of the room is in wool and silk, and nobody aside from the staff is wearing black.

'It's just right,' Daniel says. 'You're beautiful. You haven't been here long, have you? I got caught up talking with Pavel in the kitchen. We were in the same village in Laos in the same month, isn't that amazing?'

Pavel seems to be the waiter that Daniel walked in with. Sure enough, when Daniel waves at him, Pavel waves self-consciously back.

Daniel's got one of those naturally friendly faces that means strangers are always stopping him for directions, and he's so nice that sometimes he even walks them to their destination. I love that he's always striking up conversations like this. If he didn't, we'd never have met.

'I'm awfully sorry I wasn't here when you arrived,' he murmurs as we edge out of earshot of Lord Mucking. 'You're ever-so brave to face this mob on your own.'

I think it's kind of brave too. But then I'm going to have to get used to it sooner rather than later. 'You didn't mention that you're stonking rich,' I say. 'I thought you took our course because you were interested in the historical architecture of stately homes. Not because your family lives in one.'

His expression is slightly bemused, like he's seeing his family's lounge for the first time. It's about the size of one of the galleries at Tate Britain, and if I'm not mistaken, the painting on the burnished panelling over the fireplace is a Constable. They could have put velvet ropes around Lord and Lady Mucking and charged an entrance fee.

'But I did tell you what Father does,' he says.

Something for Lloyds, he'd told me. We used to have a Lloyds branch not far from us, but it closed down. Nobody working there looked like they could afford all this, even if they were the manager.

But I've got it wrong. It's not Lloyds the bank but an insurer by the same name, and Daniel's father is a lot bigger than a branch manager.

'He helps underwrite their insurance.' Daniel catches my expression and shrugs. 'It means he provides the money to pay out when insurance claims are made.'

'Like when someone wrecks his car or gets his phone nicked,' I say. 'What's in it for him if he's fronting all this money?'

'They give him a percentage of the insurance premiums

and he hopes there aren't too many claims. They're specialist insurers so they underwrite bigger things than stolen phones. More like military coups and earthquakes. Or Michael Flatley's legs or Bruce Springsteen's vocal chords or ...' He clasps his chest. 'Dolly Parton's breasts.'

'Dolly Parton's breasts are definitely bigger than a mobile phone. And your dad gets a cut of these premiums.' My head swims as I take this in. 'I see. Is this his only job? I only ask because keeping up a gaff like this must be expensive. My dad had the same problem with our council flat, so he was a taxi driver *and* a trader down the market, as you know.'

He laughs at my lame joke. 'He's got his own investment portfolio too. I've told you, it really doesn't matter.' Pronounced rahly. He looks worried that I might bolt at the news that he's genuinely minted. 'You're marrying me, not my family.'

'I know, it's just that I'm not used to a house quite like this.' That's the understatement of a lifetime, considering that I share a bedroom with Auntie Rose at home.

He runs his fingers through his blond thatch. 'Right, darling, I haven't been completely honest with you, but please promise you won't judge me.' He waits for me to nod, though my tummy is starting a series of forward rolls that doesn't feel nice. 'I did mean to tell you about my family. I don't usually have to say anything when I meet people in our circles. Everyone knows everyone, at least by reputation. But we met and I liked you so much and it's just that you're so ...'

'Poor? Working class? Not like you?'

'Normal. I was going to say normal, Em. And we got along so well that our backgrounds didn't seem to matter. Or at least I hoped they didn't. You can see why I didn't mention anything at first, can't you? Then as time went on it got harder to say "Oh, by the way, my family is wealthy" without sounding like a tosser. Besides, that's them, not me. I only work for a charity, remember?'

He looks honestly anguished about his family. 'You make it sound like they're criminals,' I say. 'So you're a rich boy done good, eh? Breaking that horrible cycle of wealth?'

That makes him laugh. 'I sound like a spoiled twat, I know, I'm sorry. It sounds ridiculous no matter how I explain it, but wealth does seem like a crime to some people.'

'And you were worried that I might think so too?'

'I was too bowled over by you to take a chance like that, even though I should have known you wouldn't judge. I'm rahly sorry my family is wealthy,' he says. 'There's nothing I can do about that.'

So he did shield me from the worst of it. I mean the best of it. I've got to stop saying that. 'Don't worry, I'll get over it,' I tell him. 'Somehow I'll manage to overlook your bank account.'

'My bank account only has my salary in it ... and not even much of that these days.'

'There you are!' Abby bounces toward us. It's a welcome interruption, to be honest. I'm not wild about the idea that Daniel kept all this from me, but I have to admit I see why he did it. It's been tricky enough breaking the news to my side that I'm in love with a public school-educated bloke who shops organic. I'm not going to be the one to tell them that the prime minister is probably on his family's Christmas card list too.

Abby is Daniel's little sister and could have been cloned from their mum, except she's a few inches shorter with longer blonde hair, the same shade as Daniel's. Watching them together always makes me think of golden retrievers. 'How long do I have to stay?'

'Are you not enjoying our engagement party?' Daniel asks.

She rolls her blue eyes. 'It's the same people we always

see. Besides, nobody does engagement parties anymore. Not since Mummy and Daddy were married back in the dark ages.'

I feel the flush creeping up my neck as I think about the do Mum wanted to throw for us.

Daniel remembers it too, because he says, 'Do try and keep up. Everyone's doing them now.' He puts his arm around me. 'Come along, Em, duty calls. We'll say hellair to all the bores and then we can relax.'

It's not easy keeping track of who's a lord and who's a sir, so I just end up nodding and smiling at everyone as Daniel lets his mother drag us round the room. Every so often she pulls my hand in front of one of her friends for inspection.

I haven't been able to stop staring at the ring since Daniel put it on my finger. Mum nearly fell over when she saw it.

Frankly, I'd have been just as happy if he'd stuck a Foster's pull tab on my ring finger. I can't wait to marry this man.

'Emma works for a Vespa dealer!' Philippa volunteers to the group I've just met. 'You know, those darling little Italian scooters that are so fun.'

I thought she was just being polite when I first told

her where I work, but for some reason she thinks selling scooters is interesting. Maybe it's because everyone else she knows is busy running boring old banks or funding coups or whatever Daniel's dad does.

'Do you know that Anna Green got them for her grandchildren at Christmas? To ride round the estate,' says one of Philippa's friends.

If anyone rode a Vespa round the estates near me, it'd get nicked before it turned the first corner. I'm guessing Anna Green's estate is a bit different. It would be, if she's handing out five-thousand-quid scooters to her grand-kids.

'And not only that,' Philippa carries on like nobody has mentioned Anna Green and her grandchildren, 'she's about to graduate from uni! Working *and* studying, clever girl! I couldn't do both.'

'You've barely done either,' says one of Philippa's inter-changeable friends, though Philippa doesn't seem to hear her. 'When's the big day?'

Everybody's eyebrows rise towards the ornately plas-tered ceiling when I tell them we're doing it in three months.

'There's no reason to wait,' Daniel explains. 'I'd marry Emma next week if Mummy wasn't so set on the party.'

Everyone asks us this question and believe me, we've looked at it from all angles. No matter how we do our sums, we won't have much more money in a year than we've got now. Sure, we could save a bit if we moved in together, but then my rent would go to a landlord instead of my mum and dad, and that would cause a whole other set of problems. They don't like to talk about it, but my parents can really use that money. So if anything, it's not the approaching wedding that worries me but the dent that my moving out is going to put in their household budget.

'It won't be a big wedding, though,' I say. 'Maybe sixty people? Just our families and close friends.' We could go over the top and take an age to plan a big do, but we're not bothered about the groomsmen's bowties matching the serviettes or making photo montages of Daniel and me drooling through our childhoods. We just need someone to marry us. Throw in a bit of food and lots of drinks and everyone will be happy.

'Sixty!' Philippa laughs. 'We've got more than that just from our side, darlings. It'll have to be bigger, but don't worry, I've got lots of ideas.'

My mouth feels a little dry.

'What kind of ideas?' her friend asks as Daniel's godfather, Harold, and his wife join us. There was a slightly awkward moment when Daniel first introduced me to Harold and I said, 'So you're *The Godfather*,' making Italian hand gestures and talking like I had a mouth full of cotton. Everyone stared at me and I had to pretend I hadn't just done that. Harold is a lord too, but I don't curtsy or anything. The less attention I draw to myself, the better.

'I thought that as it will be summer we could have the whole thing under arched trellises that make a roof woven with flowers. Yah, and hang them with crystal chandeliers!' Philippa beams. 'Or even build a structure to suspend an entire hanging garden!'

The assembled crowd all nod, murmuring yah, yah. Philippa's got a feverish glint in her eye that's making me nervous. Hanging gardens? Where are we – Babylon?

'I'm not sure—'

Bless her, she picks up right away on my discomfort. 'Oh, darling, I don't want to step on your toes, not at all! Maybe chandeliers aren't your style. Of course we could use whatever you'd like. Maybe something more modern, like those gorgeous exposed lightbulbs that Heston has at his restaurant in the Mandarin. Only we could have hundreds of them lighting up the night. Wouldn't that be romantic? Imagine!'

Yeah, imagine. Imagine the cost. I bet Heston didn't get his lights from the B&Q sales bin like I'm planning to do.

And imagine Mum and Dad's reaction if I tell them we're building hanging gardens so we can suspend chandeliers. They'd send me straight to the GP to have my head examined. No, they wouldn't need to. I'd make the appointment myself.

But Philippa looks perfectly serious. 'If you want something more traditional, we could do crystal, yah, for the tables, and silver cutlery. Or gold? Does anyone do gold anymore? I can't keep up with all the trends! And a gorgeous vintage pattern for the plates. We could even use my pattern if you like it, though you'd need to hire since I've only got place settings for forty-eight.'

Who has actual china for forty-eight people? The only time I've sat down to eat with that many people was at Uncle Colin's fundraiser for the RNLI. We ate off the Tesco Value range.

Now's probably not the time to tell my future mother-in-law that Mum and Dad suggested a casual do in Uncle Colin's pub after the wedding. Actually, it's probably not the time to tell Daniel, either. He looks pretty excited about his mother's ideas. We'll need to talk about this.

'What do you think of fish?' Philippa asks.

'I like fish.' Though I wasn't thinking of a sit-down meal. Maybe some snacks. We could push the boat out and get them from M&S.

'You could have enormous tanks of the most beautiful fish!' Philippa says. 'We could give them away in little bowls to the guests after the party. Wouldn't that be fun!'

Yah, yah, everyone but me says.

'Couldn't we just return them to the pet shop after the wedding?'

Listen to me. Like I'm actually considering aquariums at our wedding.

'Oh darling, you are hilarious. We'll need favours for the guests anyhow. This way we can double up. Although maybe you'd rather do jewellery or key fobs? Aspinal have beautiful things.'

'We'd like to keep the costs down,' Daniel says. Finally, the voice of reason. 'We're only a young couple!'

Right. The last thing we want is to end up twenty grand in debt.

'Of course, darlings. You just give me a budget and tell me whatever you want. I'll find it for you.'

'You'll marry in St Stephen's?' asks Philippa's other

friend. Daniel's father and godfather and the other men have stood silently while their wives fire off the questions. They're probably mulling over football scores, or whatever rich people think about when they're not counting their money.

'Erm, actually we were thinking of a registry wedding. In a nice registry, though.'

'Not church?'

'My family's not really religious,' I say.

'Right. St Stephen's is only C of E,' Philippa's friend assures me. 'It's not religious either.'

That still wouldn't go over well with Dad, but I'm not going to be the one to argue with Philippa's friend.

Somehow I've got to get the discussion away from gold cutlery and chandeliers or next they'll start demanding swans. With Aspinal jewellery.

'Have you been to East London at all?' I ask everyone.

Harold, Daniel's godfather, comes to life suddenly. He cuts an imposing figure in the room with his tall, broad-shouldered physique and thick white hair that streams, mane-like, from his head. 'Yah, when I worked in the City, before we moved to the wharf,' he says. 'We used to go to Brick Lane quite a lot for a curry.'

'And probably to Shoreditch for a lap dance!' I add.

Whoops. Perhaps I shouldn't have accused Lord Godfather of stuffing notes into G-strings.

But he roars with laughter. 'Indeed, yes!'

His wife smiles indulgently. 'Oh, Harold.'

This is truly another world. If Dad ever confessed that in front of Mum, she'd knock his teeth out.

Don't get me wrong, I like Daniel's family. They've been nothing but kind to me and I'm sure all their friends are nice too. It's just that I'm not exactly up to their usual standard, am I? It's so constantly apparent that they can't help but notice it. So far they've been too polite to say anything, but it's just a matter of time.

I'm dead on my feet when we get back to Daniel's, and pleased to see that his flatmate, Jacob, isn't home. Not that I ever feel like the third wheel even when he is. I know technically he should be the extra wheel, not me, but since he and Daniel have been mates since school, there was potential for some tension. Far from it. Jacob made me feel completely welcome despite my crashing his lad's pad. In fact, at first he acted like I was the first girl Daniel had ever brought home. Needless to say I like him all the better for that.

It probably helps that even though it's not a big flat

it never feels cramped. Its layout is all nineteenth-century higgledy-piggledy, with the front door all the way down a winding set of stairs at the bottom of the building, the high-ceilinged eat-in kitchen at the opposite end to the cosy lounge and Daniel's bedroom set under the eaves up in the converted loft.

It's teatime, but I feel a little sick from all the canapes. I've had to get used to eating like this since meeting Daniel. His family and friends like to have what they call 'nibbles'. Philippa laid on enough canapes to feed an army. So don't blame me for eating like a cadet. *Emma Liddell, reporting for eating, Sir!*

'God, I'm glad that's over,' Daniel says as he throws himself down beside me on the lumpy old settee and offers to rub my sore feet. My shoes might look Fendi-esque, but the blisters are pure Primark. 'Now that you've been properly introduced, Harold said you'll have to come along for supper with me next month.' His thumb finds the spot in the middle of my foot that he knows I love to have massaged.

'I had to be properly introduced first?' Maybe I should have curtseyed.

Daniel laughs. It was that laugh that I first noticed when we met. He throws himself into it with his entire body. I dare anyone not to at least smile when they hear him. 'He's old-fashioned,' he explains. 'I hope you weren't awfully uncomfortable today. Mummy does like a party, and I know those social engagements can be tedious. I've always hated them. But now it's just us again.' He leans over to kiss me. 'So, formalities finished, we can focus on our wedding.'

'Aw, have you been dreaming about being a bride ever since you were a little girl?' I tease.

'Who do you think you're talking to, Emma Liddell? I've always thought of myself as an independent woman,' he says. 'No man is going to tell me what to do.' He snaps his fingers, then laughs at his own joke. 'In all honesty I never imagined myself being married.' His eyes meet mine. 'Until I met you.'

This should be cheesy, right? But Daniel says things like that a lot, and with such feeling that I have to bite down my urge to take the piss. That's just my nerves anyway. I'm not used to being loved so obviously. Okay, I'm not used to being loved at all. I've had exactly six boyfriends in my life and two of those might not even agree with the title. Still, not such a bad track record for a twenty-four-year-old living at home who's known ninety per cent of the men in her neighbourhood since she was in nappies.

I've never been in love with any of them like I am with Daniel. Sometimes that frightens me, but then I see him and know he's in just as deep. 'I've never wanted to marry anyone else either,' I say. 'There's just one thing ...'

His thumb stops its rubbing. 'What is it, Em?'

'Nothing bad! It's just that your mum has a lot of ideas about the wedding.'

He starts working on my other foot. 'She's ever-so excited. It is the first wedding in the family.'

'I know, and I want her to be involved. It's just that everything sounds kind of expensive.' Kind of expensive? I've already calculated what it would cost to give all our guests a cheap necklace from Accessorize. It's about half my savings. 'Like you said, your parents might be able to clear the UK national debt, but we don't have a lot of money ourselves and we really shouldn't be going in to debt for a party, right? Would you mind very much if we keep it really low-key?'

He gathers me into his arms, shifting till we find the lying-down position on the settee that doesn't make my arm go numb. When we first figured out that this was possible, it seemed like the universe telling us that we really are perfect together. 'I don't mind,' he says. 'I just want to spend the rest of my life with you. My side can pitch in as much or as little as we want. Besides, I'm sure a wedding doesn't have to cost that much.'

'This is based on what, your vast amount of wedding-planning experience?' I say, as I spot a crumpled bank statement peeking out from under the settee. Who knows how long it's been there? Daniel and Jacob really need a cleaner. Snatching it up, my eye falls on the balance. And on the account owner's name.

'Daniel?'

Suddenly we're sitting up staring at each other with the bank statement between us.

'Don't worry,' he says. 'I'll pay it off. I needed a new suit, that's all.'

'Made of what, solid gold?'

He laughs. 'You'd be proud of me, actually. I channelled my inner Emma and found a rahly good deal. That's not all from the suit.'

'That's not making me feel better. Daniel, we've talked about this. Why don't you just wait until the money's in the account to buy what you want instead of always playing catch-up?'

'But you know I'll pay it down, darling. I always do, don't I?'

I know he does. He is very good at tightening his belt when he's spent too much, and he'll get that overdraft down just like he's promised.

'This is all the more reason not to go overboard with the wedding,' I tell him. 'Your family won't need to pitch in. We'll do something nice that we can afford. Mum and Dad have some money for us.'

'Em, your family shouldn't have to pay for everything when we're more than happy to contribute. After all, it's my side that wants a blowout and Mummy has already offered. Your parents will let us help, won't they?'

'We'll see. Let's look at our options first, okay?'

But I already know what Dad's going to say about the idea of Daniel's family paying for his only daughter's wedding because he can't afford to.

Chapter 2

'Bollocks!' Dad's already got his arms crossed. His re-crossing is just for emphasis. I've got more chance now of winning the EuroMillions than getting him to change his mind. I didn't even want to have this conversation again. But Mum, being Mum, wouldn't stop going on about the wedding plans. Like I haven't worked out for myself that most decent places are already booked up. We'll probably end up paying over the odds for a garage under the arches.

I really don't want to have our wedding in a garage under the arches.

'I'm just saying that they can afford it.' The words are out before I can stop them.

Mum closes her eyes and sighs.

Why can't I ever quit while I'm not too far behind?

The set of Dad's jaw tightens. 'Don't get me wrong,' he says. 'You know I think Daniel's a good lad, but you don't need a big fancy wedding to get married. You're committing to each other and you can do that just fine at the registry with a little party after. Your mother and I were married—'

'"In the town hall not ten minutes from this house,"' I finish for him. He's trotted out the same lines ever since I first dared to ask for Dr. Martens when I was ten. Real ones, not the Junior Dr. Martens rip-offs they had down the market. What's good enough for my parents is good enough for me. I've heard it a million times, and quite a lot recently. '"We had our do at the Cock and Crown,"' I continue, '"with our family and friends, and everybody was happy."'

'"We stuffed ourselves on prawns from the prawn man till we were nearly sick,"' Mum finishes. '"We didn't need to spend a lot of money and it served us just fine."'

Mum and I grin at each other.

'Exactly,' Dad says. 'So you know the story, Emma.' His voice grows as soft as his expression. He's a handsome man, my father. He's usually got a sparkle in his eye and a cheeky grin for everyone, but he can be a pit bull if you push him. 'Why not have a simple wedding?'

he says. 'The important thing is that you love each other.'

When I hug him his beefy arms squeeze me tightly. 'I know that, Dad. We do love each other, and I don't want anything fancy. I'm going with Kell to see some places tomorrow. We'll find something that works.'

I just hope it won't cost the earth. Mum and Dad are really stretching to give me two thousand quid for the wedding. I know it's draining their savings, but whenever I protest they change the subject.

So I'm not about to tell Dad that my future mother-in-law is probably expecting ice sculptures and a synchronised dove release. Our parents haven't met yet. The last thing I want to do is make Mum and Dad even more preoccupied with Daniel's family than they already are. When I told Mum about the engagement party she asked me to take photos of Philippa's bathrooms. As if rich people don't poo the same way as everyone else.

I had to explain that no, they don't have fancy quilted loo roll or one of those hand soap pumps – just a plain old bar of soap in a dish. And drapes on their windows – no nets.

Maybe that's what the great social divide really comes down to: the haves versus the have nets.

Our parents will need to meet before the wedding, as soon as we figure out the best way to do it. It was hard enough introducing Mum and Dad to Daniel. The fact that he's from West London is enough to make them uncomfortable. As soon as I mentioned Chelsea, Mum started going on about redecorating before he came over.

Our house is perfectly fine. Maybe it's a bit dated, but we have lived here my whole life, and Mum hasn't exactly got an interior design budget to work with. It's a typical sixties council house on a red-brick two-storey terrace where most of the gardens are kept up pretty well. We've got wood floors all inside and tile in the kitchen and bathroom. The suite isn't new, but Mum doesn't let anyone eat their dinner on it so it's not too stained, aside from Dad's chair, and there are stacks of coasters everywhere so there's not a water ring on any of the tables. When I was little I wanted a bay window like Kell has at her house, but other than that I haven't really wished for anything different.

'Do me a favour,' Mum says. 'Go get Auntie Rose with your dad. She's at the pub with her ladies. I'll get the tea on and then I've got to be to work for seven.' When she leans down to kiss my dad, the curtain of thick straight ginger hair that she wears in a long bob covers their faces.

'Right, to the pub, Dad?'

'Ready when you are.' He awkwardly pats his pockets. 'I've got me money. Off we go.'

'One pint, Jack, and then come back. I mean it. Otherwise the tea'll burn. Half an hour.'

He waves over his shoulder as I grasp the handles of his wheelchair and carefully manoeuvre out the front door and down the ramp.

We had the ramp installed on my twentieth birthday. I remember because Kell joked that it was for when I came home pissed from the pub. We all made out like it was the greatest invention in the world. Now Dad could come and go as he pleased, we said. He put on a brave face, but everybody knew he'd have preferred not to need it in the first place.

If he wasn't a taxi driver, he would probably have realised a lot sooner that he was ill. But, like he said, sitting on your arse all day is bound to cause some pins and needles. It was when his vision started going funny that he finally admitted his symptoms to Mum. She had him down to Helen at the GP's surgery almost before he'd finished telling her.

The doctors did loads of tests that Dad got pretty sick of by the time they told him he's got multiple sclerosis. That was over ten years ago. It's the kind that comes and goes and gets worse over time, which is why we had to get the ramps fitted on my twentieth birthday. He'd had to stop work a few years before that, though. He can walk with crutches if he has to, but he doesn't usually have to with the wheelchair and all of us to push him around when he gets bad. Their bedroom's on the ground floor now, in the old dining room, and we had an en suite added so he doesn't need to worry about going upstairs at all.

Of course, Kell was worried about me when it all first happened. At fourteen everything is a huge deal anyway, so when it really is a big deal it seems catastrophic. But she didn't really need to worry because my dad is still my dad; he's still with us and he's still himself. He can't drive the cab anymore and it's pretty bad when he relapses, and Mum's gone down to part-time work, what with looking after Dad and Auntie Rose, but that's why I'm working. It's lucky I'm here.

But once I get married I'll have to move out. Imagine the row if I try to keep giving them money then. You've seen how Dad reacts when Daniel offers for his parents to pay for our wedding. I'll have to hide tenners down the sofa cushions or something.

Auntie Rose is doing a victory lap around the pub when we get there, shouting, 'Persimone! Get IN!'

'She's winning, I take it?' says Dad to Uncle Colin once he's finished nodding his hellos to the half-dozen men sitting round the battered tables.

'Insufferable!' Auntie Rose's friend, June, shouts from the big square booth by the door. 'Take her home, Emma, she'll only be a dreadful winner again.'

'Sour grapes,' sings Auntie Rose as she throws her ample frame back down in the booth, jostling the Scrabble board on her landing.

'Mind the game!' Doreen adjusts the tiles. 'Don't spoil it for the rest of us. Next week we're playing cribbage.'

Auntie Rose takes a sip of her lime and soda. 'Where's your fighting spirit?'

'I'm about to fight,' Doreen grumbles. She will too if they let her have too much sherry. She might look like a sweet old lady, but you'd do well not to cross her. There was once a husband, but he disappeared after getting caught playing away once too often. Maybe he's living with his mistress out of town, maybe he isn't. That's all I'm saying.

So all's well at the Cock and Crown. Nobody's surprised to see a seventy-five-year-old woman fist-pumping her way round the bar. Technically she's my great auntie, my Gran's younger sister. She's been meeting her best friends here every week for about the past forty years for a game of cribbage or cards or, when Auntie Rose gets to choose, Scrabble. No matter what else happens in their lives, they wouldn't miss a week unless they're in the hospital, like when June broke her hip, or one of them dies, like my Gran did seven or eight years ago. That's when Auntie Rose came to live with us. She's not so good at being on her own.

'We've got to be home in half an hour for tea,' I tell my auntie, who's gone back to studying her tiles. Her lips move as she considers her next play. She's got an impressive vocabulary considering she left school so young. She credits that to my great grandad being a newsvendor. He let her do the crossword from *The Telegraph* every day, as long as she never creased the page and ruined it for sale. She used to trace out the crossword onto a sheet of paper and fill it in.

'You all right?' June asks me in her twenty-a-day voice

as everyone shifts round to make room for me and Dad. I catch a waft of June's Mentos. 'How are the wedding plans coming along?' Her pale blue eyes are lined with life and worry.

'We're really just getting started.' June and Doreen nod their bright blonde heads. Auntie Rose does their hair too. She's got a very limited colour palette. She figures if it looks good on her, it'll do for everyone else. 'But it's less than three months away so we really need to make a start.'

'That's plenty of time,' June says, rolling up the sleeves on her knock-off hoodie. She always dresses in a range of nearly-Nike and almost-Adidas, like she's on her way to aerobics. 'Your parents did it in less time than that.'

Looks shoot between the older women as Doreen fidgets with the little gold cross nestled in her cleavage. You wouldn't catch her out of the house in trackies. She's always in a wrap dress. The wrapping job's a bit hit and miss, though, given the shape of the package inside.

'In those days things weren't so formal,' Auntie Rose says. 'Nowadays everything is so fancy. I saw in the news about couples who spend a million quid on flowers! I bet the Queen doesn't spend a million quid on flowers.'

When Auntie Rose says the news, she means *The Sun*.

The Telegraph is good for the crosswords, but she gets all her information from the tabloid.

'Oh, I know!' says June. 'My Karen's youngest had two hundred people at her wedding. They had to get a second mortgage to pay for the whole palaver. Those payments'll probably last longer than the marriage.'

'We're not taking out any loans,' Dad says. 'We've got a bit of dosh saved. We'll do right by you, Emma.'

'I just wish you'd let Daniel's parents give us money,' I say, even though I know I'm pushing my luck. 'They won't even miss it.'

His fist slams on the table, making Auntie Rose's lime and soda jump. 'Goddammit, Emma, why can't you get it through your head that I don't need your in-laws' charity! Isn't it bad enough–?' He shakes his head. 'Don't be fooled by the wheelchair, girl. I might not be able to do most things anymore, but I can look after my own family. Now that's the end of it, Emma. I mean it, this topic is closed. We're doing this for you, and that's the end of it.'

His pride will never let him accept help from Daniel's parents. 'All right, Dad,' I sigh, 'and I'm really grateful for everything you and Mum are doing. Incredibly grateful. We'll keep it very low-key, like you suggested.'

I don't want to cry here in the pub. The very idea of Mum and Dad draining their savings for me when they've got so little as it is.

'Aw, you're a good girl,' Doreen says. 'You've got your head on straight, don't she, Jack?'

Not necessarily. I just know when I'm fighting a losing battle with Dad. And it's not like I want an extravagant wedding anyway. I just don't want Mum and Dad using all their savings for it.

But I'll never budge Dad now, so the least I can do is spend their budget wisely. We'll have a nice little wedding and everyone will love it. They might not get gold necklaces or exotic fish, but they'll still have a laugh.

It is just one day out of the rest of our lives. We don't want to go into debt like June's Karen's youngest, do we?

I know Uncle Colin would be really touched if we asked to have the party here. He's rightly proud of his pub. But as I stare round, trying to see it as an outsider would, my heart sinks. I love a fruit machine as much as the next person, but their blinking lights don't exactly give off the right ambiance for a wedding party. The chairs and booths that I've sat in my whole life look clunky and tired, and there's no getting round the faint odour coming from the swirly green carpet. Even if we could turn off the machines and take down all the football paraphernalia that Uncle Colin has collected over the years, it's not the Ritz in here.

But it is home. Plus it's where Mum and Dad had their party, though Uncle Colin was only a barman then, not the landlord.

'When do I get to meet your bloke?' Uncle Colin asks as he empties a rack of pint glasses on to the shelf behind the bar. 'You can't keep him from me forever, you know.'

'I've only met him once myself, Colin,' pipes up Auntie Rose from the booth, 'so you're not the only one.'

Dad and I exchange a look. Auntie Rose has met Daniel four or five times at least, but we smile at her indignation. It's better than correcting her. She only gets upset when we do that.

'I'm not keeping him from you, Uncle Colin. I'm planning to bring him round next week to meet everyone.'

'Barbara's still up north,' he says, pulling a pint of ale for one of the men sitting at the bar. 'The week after would be better. Or you could always bring him round twice. We'll have to get used to him eventually.'

'He'll have to get used to you lot, more like,' I say. 'I'll bring him the week after next then. That way he can brace himself to meet everyone at once.'

I haven't been keeping Daniel away. He's met Mum and Dad several times, and my best friend Kell, of course. It's just tricky trying to entertain when you're still living at home. There isn't exactly room for romance in our house. There's barely room for the family.

We have to pry Auntie Rose away from her friends, as usual, to get home in time for tea. She's won at Scrabble again, but I don't think they let her. She may be losing her marbles, but she's still a dab hand at board games.

Later, in bed, just when I'm about to drop off to sleep, Auntie Rose's voice floats over from the other bed. 'I don't have to tell you about the wedding night, do I?'

What am I supposed to say to that? First off, the idea that my old auntie might explain the Kama Sutra to me makes me shudder. Secondly, she's not technically even supposed to know about that, since she's never had a wedding night. And even if she does have some inside knowledge, I'd definitely rather not hear it. 'No, I know what happens, but thanks all the same,' I say, really hoping she'll fall asleep quickly.

'Well, I should bloomin' hope you do, with a man like Daniel around.'

She's quiet, but I know her. She's not finished. If she

asks me any intimate questions about Daniel, I'm going downstairs to sleep on the settee.

'Then you also know you're going to be too tired to do anything after the wedding, so my advice is, find a quiet spot during the do and get your leg over. Got it, girl?'

I stifle a laugh into my pillow. 'Yes, Auntie Rose, thanks for the advice.'

The walk to Kelly's fish van the next afternoon is as familiar as my walk to the corner shop each morning to pick up Auntie Rose's *Telegraph*. Long before Kell became the reigning fishmonger in her family business empire (if a single van can be called an empire), we used to come together after school to beg spending money off her dad. Going bass fishing, that's what we called it. We'd get some coins, or not, depending on whether he'd shifted the sea bass – a big ticket item that only the people in the houses on Stepney Green splashed out on. So Kell's pocket money was dependent on who wanted fancy fish for tea.

We've been inseparable since childhood, except for a terrible two weeks in year six when we stopped speaking over something neither of us can remember, so Kell knows everything there is to know about me. Which should give her hours of material for her bridesmaid's speech.

I tell her about Auntie Rose's advice after making her swear not to mention it at the wedding. She reminds me a lot of her dad when she's working, and not just because she wears the same white coat and white mesh trilby hat that he always did. They've also got the same relaxed, efficient way that makes it seem like they don't mind when customers take all day to make up their minds. Her dad, Mr McCarthy, doesn't come to the market as much now, preferring to take care of the buying and the restaurant deliveries, so Kell does most of the retail trade. She ends up covered in fish scales, but it's better than getting up at 4 a.m. to haggle over the day's catch at Billingsgate.

She's slicing a trout from gills to tail and stripping out its guts. 'You want me to take the heads off, right?' she asks the customer standing next to me.

'Yeah, but I'll keep 'em,' says the woman. 'Don't throw 'em away!'

'You're here every week, my love. Have I ever thrown them away?'

'Well, don't.'

Kell wipes her hands on the apron over her coat. 'She's probably right,' she says to me, meaning Rose about the wedding, not the customer about her fish heads. 'Give me five minutes to pack up, okay? I've got a change of clothes in the van. I can close up and move it when we come back. Sorry, my darlin', I'm closing,' she tells the grey-haired black man who's just arrived. 'Unless you want the fillets. The snapper, yeah? Okay, give me a minute.'

I wander down the row of market stalls to wait till Kelly's ready. Not that there's anything new to see since I was here a few days ago. It's busy, as usual, with mostly women shopping. I like to think I know my way around a kitchen, but I haven't got a clue what some of the fruit and veg is on the Asian stalls. If you promised me a hundred quid, I couldn't cook it for you. Mrs Ishtiaque next door buys it all the time, though. She's definitely the best cook in our road, but I'd never admit that to Mum when she needles me. It's just different food, I tell her. Of course curries are more interesting than plain old roasts when they've got all those spices in them.

Auntie Rose won't eat any spice at all. She's even suspicious of basil and won't touch garlic. 'I like me food good and plain,' she says. It's definitely plain, but I don't know about good.

Stacy Boyle is at my favourite shoe stall, on her phone as usual. 'All right?' I ask her, because I know she can carry on at least three conversations at once.

'Yeah, all right,' she answers, pushing her silvery pink fringe off her face. 'How were the shoes for your party?' Then, to her caller she says, "e's got no right. Well, tell him to fack off.'

I don't have the heart to tell her they killed my feet so I tell her everyone loved them instead. Stacy's grandad was a cobbler. Her dad was too till it got cheaper to buy new shoes than fix old ones. Like Kelly's dad, he comes to the stall sometimes, but mostly it's Stacy who works here now. When my parents were my age the Boyles had a tiny shop just behind the stall. It's like that with a lot of the market traders. Take Kelly, for instance. She's a fourth-generation fishmonger. But instead of a stall, she has a repurposed ice cream van, with a big window in the side. Mr McCarthy had that converted into a fold-down display area to hold the fresh fish on ice. He also wanted to turn the giant ice cream cone on the roof into a sea bass, but Kelly didn't think that painting scales on it would fool anyone. They sold the cone, which is a shame.

''e's always saying that,' Stacy says. Then, to me, 'Anything else for you today?'

'Nah, I'm just waiting for Kell to finish, thanks. We're going to look at some venues for the wedding.' Just saying it is exciting!

'All right for some,' Stacy says, either to me or her caller as Kelly approaches. 'Good luck!'

Kell's been working on a list of places to check out for the reception. Not that she's telling me anything about her ideas.

She's not the only one with ideas. Philippa barely waited for me to leave the party before she started firing off emails. Wouldn't it be amazing, she'd written, to have it at Kensington Palace? Yes, *the* Kensington Palace, where the future king of England lives. Like we're the Middletons or something.

'I don't suppose we're going to West London?' I ask Kelly as we shuffle down the bus to make room for a lady with a double pram.

She gives me the same look she's done since we started school together. To me, she doesn't look that different than she did then. She's got the pale round face and upturned nose of her Irish ancestors, and her eyes turn into crescents when she smiles. She says her thick straight brown hair just hangs in her face to annoy her, which is why she wears it in a ponytail with a heavy fringe.

'We don't need West London,' she says. 'We've got better.'

Kelly's always been suspicious of anything that's outside our postcode. It may as well be France as far as she's concerned. She's not interested in going there, either.

I used to think the same thing till I started taking courses in Central London. It's no use trying to convince Kelly that there's a world west of the City, though.

The bus lurches past grand stone buildings that are tall enough to block the sunshine from the narrow streets weaving between them. It's easy to imagine men in bowler hats hurrying from their clerking jobs instead of the office workers who're all walking with their mobile phones out.

She pushes the button to let us off near a tiny lane. There's a low arch between buildings leading into a big square. 'Holy shit, Kell, this isn't for us. It looks like a church. You know Dad—'

Her eyes crinkle. 'Keep your wig on, it's not a church.

It's for your party. You wanted something to impress Lord and Lady Muck.'

'Mucking.'

'Whatever.'

Its Portland stone façade and huge arched windows look official, like a town hall.

'It's Stationer's Hall,' she explains as we look around outside. 'You know, one of the guildhalls, for stationers and newspapers, publishers and the like. It's as close to books as I could get and still be posh. I figured you wouldn't want your wedding at the newsagent's and you're such a booky swot that I thought you'd like this.'

I love it. Plus, I know my great grandfather was only a newsvendor, but I like this slight connection to my family. 'How'd you even know it was possible to have a reception in a place like this? I figured it'd have to be in a hotel.'

Kelly nods. 'I know. That's why you made me your bridesmaid.' She taps her forehead. 'Lateral thinking.'

'I thought I made you my bridesmaid because you threatened to kill me otherwise.'

'I only threatened to kill you when you made Cressida bridesmaid.'

'Don't start on Cressida, please.' Her feelings about

Daniel's friend are a whole story that's not worth getting into just now.

She pretends not to hear me. 'With me you get your life, and you get your lateral thinking for free.'

'A two-for-one offer.' Once a market trader, always a market trader.

She leads us down some steps to a big wooden door that swings open as soon as she presses the bell.

The man standing in the doorway might be around our age, but he's got about nine strands of blond hair left on his head, which are swept back with some kind of unfortunate gel that makes it look like the raked sand in a Japanese zen garden.

We just about keep straight faces when he calls us Miss Liddell and Miss McCarthy and introduces himself as Mr Thompson-Smythe. He'll make a perfect head teacher if this job doesn't work out.

'After you, Miss,' Kell says to me.

'No, after you, Miss,' I say back.

Mr Thompson-Smythe smiles blandly.

He leads us down a corridor lined with oil paintings of old men who all look like Margaret Thatcher, asking about my wedding plans so far. I feel his disappointment when I say there aren't many. *Emma must try harder.*

'We're keeping it small,' I offer him. 'Maybe around sixty?' As long as Philippa doesn't go overboard with the invitations.

'Terrific,' he says. Sixty is obviously the perfect number for a wedding in his opinion. 'Well, this is the Stock Room. It can seat up to sixty guests or have a hundred guests standing. Are you thinking of dinner or just a drinks reception?'

'Erm, I don't know,' I say, looking up. Giant brass chandeliers hang from the lofty ceiling, which is painted white, gold and blue. It's not a huge room, and with the walls all clad in dark wood and covered in livery shields, it feels a little oppressive.

'Terrific,' says Mr Thompson-Smythe again to reward my indecision. 'The oak panelling dates from the seventeenth century and we do allow candlelight in this room.'

Seventeenth-century panelling! I wouldn't let anyone light a candle near it.

Mr Thompson-Smythe pushes through the wooden double doors at one end of the room to let us into a huge hall that's panelled like the one we just came from. It's a lot brighter, though, thanks to an enormous stained-glass window at one end.

Henry VIII banqueting tables are pushed up against

the walls and a few colourful flags hang high up to round out the medieval feel.

Mr Thompson-Smythe watches us take it all in. 'The floors and panelling in this room are oak and date from the sixteenth century. The original liveries are on the carved shields above the panelling and candlelight is allowed in here too. Would you have candles?'

He's really pushing the candlelight. Maybe they're trying to keep the electricity bills down. 'I don't know.'

'Terrific.'

I'm starting to suspect he's not really paying attention to my answers.

'What do you think?' Kelly whispers as Mr Thompson-Smythe scurries away to pretend not to listen.

It's definitely right up my future mother-in-law's street. 'I like it, but … it just feels a bit formal. That's not it, exactly, but do you know what I mean?'

'Too posh for us? It's like royals would have a party here.'

'Mmm, no, just not our style.' I smile at Mr Thompson-Smythe, who creeps back to our side.

'Do you have any questions?' he asks. 'Miss McCarthy checked and the hall is free on your proposed wedding day.'

'Oh, good,' I say, not wanting to reject his sixteenth-century décor and hurt his feelings. 'It's very beautiful. And there'd be plenty of room for us. What's the cost to hire it?'

'The hire fee is four thousand and seven hundred pounds, plus VAT. We'd require a small deposit to hold the booking.'

'Terrific,' I say, casually leaning on one of the banqueting tables to keep my legs from going. 'And does that include ... food?'

'No, it's the hire fee only. We can supply you with a list of caterers, though.'

Unless they supply me with a bank account to pay them, this is never going to work.

'The fee does include the whole building,' he continues, 'so you'll have use of all the rooms, and the garden as well. You could have a pre-dinner drinks reception outside, for example, if the weather is nice, then dinner in the Livery Hall and dancing in the Stock Room. We're very flexible.'

For nearly five thousand quid they should be more flexible than a circus contortionist.

Kelly can see I'm having trouble breathing. 'We've got more venues to see, so can we get back in touch in a few days?'

'Of course. Would you like to see the Court Room?'

He can tell he's losing his audience.

'Nah, that's okay, thanks,' she says. 'We'll ring you, okay?'

I can't get out of there fast enough.

Four thousand seven hundred quid to hire a room for the day? They must be insane. All that panelling and candle wax has addled Mr Thompson-Smythe's brain. I'm trying not to panic, but it's hitting me just how hard this is going to be.

'I thought Daniel's family offered to help,' Kelly says. 'Do you need to sit down? You don't look good.'

I sigh. 'They did offer, but Dad's adamant that he doesn't want their help. He says he should be able to take care of his own family.'

'That's so sad, with everything he's been through,' says Kell. 'I feel sorry for him.'

A lump wells up in my throat. That's been happening a lot lately when I think about how Dad must feel. 'At first I thought he was just being his usual stubborn self, but it's really important to him that he and Mum do this for me. He'd be crushed if he thought someone else had to pay for my wedding. I've got to figure out a way to do this.'

Kell puts her arm around me as we turn our backs on the Stationers' Hall. 'You don't have to do it on your own. I've got some savings that you could have if you need it.'

'Thank you, but even all our money together won't cover the cost of something like this. And it's just the start. We'll need food and drink too.'

Kelly purses her lips. 'What if we did a takeaway, fish and chips or a curry or something? That'd only be six or seven quid a head. That's not too expensive.'

I nod. 'It's a bargain. Then we'd just need another five thousand quid to have somewhere to eat our takeaway. No, this is going to have to be on a shoestring. And by shoestring, I mean the flimsiest piece of thread you've ever seen.'

The problem is, Daniel's family is expecting those shoestrings to lace up a fancy pair of Manolos. I've got the sinking feeling that a curry and a can of lager isn't going to cut it for them.

'There is another place closer to home,' she says as our bus pulls up. 'It's the library at Queen Mary. You could even walk there on your wedding day. Save a few bob on bus fare.'

'That one pound fifty will come in handy, but it doesn't really make a dent in the hire fee, does it?'

There has to be another option that's within our budget and, since I can be as stubborn as my dad, I'll just have to find it.

Chapter 3

Kell and I did go see the library at Queen Mary's, but my heart wasn't really in it. Or at least, my wallet wasn't. It would have been perfect, grand and Victorian and stuffed with books – two soaring balconies surrounding the huge and airy octagon-shaped room with sunshine streaming through enormous windows to light the elegant vaulted dome high above. It was slightly less expensive than Stationer's Hall, in the way that sirloin steak is slightly less expensive than a fillet. No matter how many places we've visited, and it seems to be all we've done for the last two weeks, Kell and I can't find a nice, cheap burger of a venue. At this rate we really are going to end up under the arches. Won't Daniel's mother just love that?

This is turning out to be so much harder than I imagined. I can't concentrate on my coursework with the wedding hanging over me. I've been rereading the same page for the last twenty minutes. Anti-social behaviour, looting, blah blah blah.

But my final exams start in two weeks and I haven't gone to uni for the past five years to bungle it now. It's been hard enough getting this far.

Just try telling everyone you know that you're studying criminology when everyone you know has at least second-hand experience with the Old Bill. The mistrust of authority round here won't go away just because one of their own has enrolled at the Open University.

People only tolerate our neighbour, PC Billy Bramble, because he gets them out of scrapes and drinks in the Cock and Crown.

Dad still suspects I'm going to end up working for the Met like Billy, that one day he'll see me walking the beat in a Kevlar stab vest and one of those hats with the checkerboard bands. And Mum wishes I would for the pension, as long as I find a nice, safe desk job.

Dad doesn't have to worry, though, and Mum shouldn't hope. I don't want to be the one catching or punishing the kids who go off the rails. I'd rather be the one making sure they don't derail in the first place. I'm not exactly sure yet where I'll work, but I can imagine what the job will look like. It'll be something that keeps kids in school and out of prison or gives them interesting things to do so they don't feel so hopeless.

A couple of do-gooders, that's what Kell calls Daniel and me. She's right. Daniel's kids walk miles for clean water and, once I find my job, I'll have to keep mine from nicking stuff.

I knew all about Daniel's kindness streak by the time we had our first date, so I shouldn't have been surprised when he took me to a fundraising gig that his charity was doing. I was tempted to ring Kell when we walked into the venue and I saw who was playing. She'd head-lined at Glastonbury and won Grammies. And there she was sitting on a stool, in a jumper and jeans, with her voice floating over the piano that accompanied her. I'd never been that close to someone so famous.

'We don't need to stay long,' he'd said into my ear. 'I've just promised my boss I'd stop by, that's all.'

'You didn't tell me your job was so glamorous.' As far as I knew, he was just a lowly staffer at a water charity.

He'd laughed and grabbed my hand, shifting our month-long flirtation up a gear. My tummy flipped. 'It's usually very unglamorous. I talk about drilling and well specifications with engineers a lot,' he'd said. 'This fundraiser has been a treat. She even came into the offices to see what we do. I was completely tongue-tied when I met her.'

'You met her?! Wait, are you trying to impress me by basking in reflected celeb glory?'

'Yah. Is it helping at all?'

I'd nodded. What I didn't add was that even without the eye-wateringly famous connection I already knew I was nuts about Daniel.

Auntie Rose stirs. 'You're up with the birds,' she says.

'Just revising before work.' I close my book. There's no chance of getting anything done once the house starts to wake. 'I'll do more later.'

She sits up with a grunt. 'I don't know where you came from,' she says, not for the first time.

I play dumb. She loves having this conversation. 'What do you mean?'

'I couldn't abide school, neither could your mother or your Gran. Your mum bunked off every chance she got. And there's no Einstein on your father's side, either. Must be some rogue gene making you so bookish. I've never seen another like you.' I can hear the pride in her voice, like I always do.

'That's good,' she continues as I pack away my books. 'Look at you, about to graduate from university! You're the only one of us who didn't quit by sixteen. You're going to do good things, Emma.' She smiles. 'You might even get out of here.'

'I don't want to get out of here!' I say.

'But you will, and there ain't nothing wrong with that.'

Her words echo in my head as I make my way to work. I know every single shop, school and business along the route, and quite a few of the people too. Some of them wave when they see me – there aren't that many powder blue Vespas about. The rhythms of the street and its characters are as familiar to me as those in a little village would be to someone from the countryside. There might be more buildings and pollution and graffiti and crime, but this is home. Why would I ever want to leave?

My colleague pulls up at the same time as me. 'All right?' Zane asks. I'll smooth out his accent for you, which is Jamaican courtesy of Hackney Wick. If I were to spell it out, it'd have only vowels. He likes to lean and gurn when he talks too. He thinks it's street.

I pull up the shutters on the Vespa dealership while Zane starts wheeling the bikes out front. 'Where's the golden boy?' he asks as he brings out my favourite scooter so I can motorhead all over it. It's the Vespa of my dreams, the one they've put out for their seventieth anniversary. It's top of the range with a 300cc engine, front and rear disc brakes and all the glamour of the old bikes.

I don't bother answering Zane's question. It's not really a question anyway. It's an accusation aimed at our boss, Marco. The golden boy is his son, Ant – it's short for Anthony, but he hates when anyone uses his full name.

Our boss has a few scooter shops so he doesn't spend much time at ours. Neither does his son, even though he's paid to.

I don't mind that much. We're not usually very busy anyway, and since the scooter sales are commissioned, the less competition the better. It bothers Zane, though. Which is why he asks every morning.

I crack open my criminology book and Zane pulls a tattered paperback from his bag. This is the perfect job for me, really. It's steady money – not much but steady – and I can do it with my eyes closed. I should be able to by now. I've worked here since just after my sixteenth birthday. It was either work in a shop or start The Knowledge to get my taxi badge. And Dad really didn't want me doing that.

'Why not?' I'd asked. 'Because I'm a girl?'

He'd shaken his head. 'Don't be daft. It's because I want more for you.'

'Dad, I hate to break it to you, but working at the scooter shop isn't exactly climbing the corporate ladder.'

'No, but you won't work there forever. It takes years to do The Knowledge. Once you do it, you're not gonna want to change to something better.'

I hadn't known what to say to that. Dad never complained about being a cab driver. He had lots of friends in the business and it kept the roof over our heads.

Now I know what he meant. Cab driving would have made me just comfortable enough to be stuck. Why give up a bit of comfort to start all over?

Dad was right. As usual.

I try to study, but it's no use; I can't concentrate. And Zane's frustrating disinterest in my wedding plans means I have to wedge it awkwardly into conversation myself. Lucky him. He's stuck with me till we clock off at five.

'Zane, your sister got married, didn't she?'

'Both of them did,' he says, sucking his teeth. Tall and slender with baby-smooth warm brown skin and cheekbones that are wasted on a guy, he's good-looking when he's not pulling faces. He's got a tattoo all up his neck that I know for a fact made him cry when they did it, but maybe people who don't know him are impressed when they see it.

'Where'd they have their receptions?'

Teeth suck. 'Eyeono.'

'How can you not know? Didn't you go to them?'

'Aw, yeah.' He thinks, nodding his head, which is covered in little braids that stick up in all directions. 'We had a party at the Jam Club, in the room at the back.'

I know the place. It's a reggae bar that makes Uncle Colin's pub look like Hampton Court Palace. Imagine Daniel's family toasting our nuptials with cans of Red Stripe while everyone twerks to Bob Marley on the sound system.

Daniel is outside the Overground station after work, watching the market's ebb and flow as he waits for me.

The fish traders are starting to clear up, emptying their styrofoam crates of ice and water and stacking them. If it swims, they sell it. Technically they're Kelly's competitors, but in reality they're not. Everyone's got their place in the market. They know their customers, and there's an unwritten rule that nobody steps on toes, so everyone has enough custom.

That's not to say that tempers don't flare with everyone living cheek by jowl here. But the shouting today is just the vendors trying to draw the punters' attention, especially now it's nearly the end of the day and they want to flog the perishables before going home.

If I change my point of view, I can just about see what Daniel is seeing, though it's not easy. Everything is so familiar to me. I see my neighbours in the veiled faces of the Asian women and old schoolmates in the lairy hoodies out-boasting each other next to the camera and phone stall.

Daniel isn't sticking out too badly in his navy V-neck jumper and jeans. The guys around here do wear V-necks, though not usually over button-down collared work shirts. And definitely not tied over their shoulders. For his own good I had to put a stop to that the first time Daniel tried it here.

It's the rest of the area that doesn't quite fit with Daniel. The market isn't neat and neutral like where he's from in Chelsea. There you know you'll see manicured trees and grass, shiny black railings and white-fronted houses, well-dressed people, clean cars and designer shops. The sounds will be of traffic and, in quiet corners, birdsong.

Just as Daniel sees me, two of our neighbourhood

junkies reel by with their cans of Strongbow. Daniel jams his hands in his jeans pockets.

'Don't worry, they won't nick your wallet,' I call as I approach for a kiss. 'They never bother anyone.'

He drapes his arm round my shoulder. 'Yah, I wasn't worried.'

'Then stop looking like you're about to face a firing squad. We're only going for a walk before the pub. It's perfectly safe.'

He's already worked out that this is Jack the Ripper territory, though he doesn't know that one of the murders happened right behind the train station he just came from. The less grim local history that he and his family know, the better, I think.

'Am I that obvious? It's not rahly my milieu, is it?'

Who says *milieu* in normal conversation? 'Not if you talk like that, it's not. You know, Chelsea is just as hard for me to get used to as this is for you.' I look round at the older women in colourful sarees and young ones in trendy hijabs. Two Caribbean women sweep by in brightly embroidered caftans and matching head wraps. This is my milieu, as long as we're being poncey about it. 'It's intimidating seeing all those people walking around your neighbourhood wearing expensive clothes.'

I'm only half joking as I lead him away from the station.

'East End girl meets West End boy,' he says.

'There's a song in that.'

He laughs. 'The Pet Shop Boys beat you to it.' His humming is so off-key that at first I think he's joking. I only know the song because he's just said what it was.

'Wow,' I say. 'I've never heard you sing before.'

'Rahly? I'm sure you have. I love to sing.' Off he goes again. Cats up the road start mewling in protest.

'No, I'd have remembered.'

But really, who am I to tell him his voice qualifies as torture under the Geneva Convention when he clearly loves it? I don't always see him being this unselfconscious. Daniel is one of those people who never seems to put a foot wrong – jumpers tied round his shoulders notwithstanding, although in his world everyone does that, so maybe it's not a good example. My point is that I feel like I'm special when I get to see him totally at ease. Though I know he works hard to look that way all the time.

We take a turn off Whitechapel Road, leaving the hustle, bustle, noise and fumes of the main thoroughfare behind. 'Here's what I wanted to show you,' I tell him proudly as we turn into the narrow cobbled road. 'Welcome to Stepney Green.'

'Gosh, this is unexpected. It looks a bit like Hampstead. Do you remember?'

'How could I forget?' We both smile.

A few days after the charity gig date we met again in Hampstead village and made our way to the swimming ponds on the Heath. Before Daniel, my dates invariably involved drinks in a pub somewhere or, at a stretch, a film before drinks in a pub somewhere. This felt different, and not just because there were no beer mats. We already had that comfortable certainty about each other that usually comes after months of going out. We got a running start at it during our course together.

I'd been at the Open University four years by the time I took our architecture class, up to my back teeth in criminology courses, so it felt pretty decadent to take something so unrelated. But that was the point of Kell and my family giving me the City Lit voucher for Christmas.

Daniel signed up for the same reason. On the other side of London he'd been up to *his* back teeth in the water charity where he worked. So we were both branching out. It just so happened that our branches intertwined perfectly, first as study friends and then as something a lot more exciting.

That didn't mean I was crazy about the idea of swimming with Daniel in a duck turd-filled pond, though. It's hard to be alluring when you're trying not to drown.

For the record, I can swim. I just don't like putting my head underwater. But with Daniel going on about how much he loved the weekend swims he'd done there with his dad since he was a teen, I couldn't very well tell him that the only time my swimsuit came out of the drawer was to sun myself in the back garden.

I sneaked glances at his lean torso and muscular just-hairy-enough legs as we made our way to the dock. 'Jump straight in?' he asked, reaching for my hand.

'Or go down the ladder?' I said, snatching it back.

'Yah, of course, if you're more comfortable that way. Do you mind if I jump in?'

He sliced easily through the water with hardly a splash, emerging several yards away to grin at me. 'It's lovely!'

Slowly I lowered myself down the ladder, not showing Daniel my best side.

I managed to swim with him to the other side of the pond, all the while imagining what might be living in the murky water. The more I imagined, the more I was sure there were things, live things, dangerous things, swimming just out of sight under the water.

So nobody should have been surprised when Daniel's fingers on my leg unleashed such blood-curdling screams. I stopped swimming, naturally, and dove for my date.

Reader, I climbed him.

'Emma, it's okay!' he said, between gasps as I pushed him underwater. 'You're all right, just relax. What's wrong? Here, hold on to my shoulders. That's it. I'll swim us in.'

As I floated on Daniel's back to reach the ladder, he calmly suggested that we dry off in the sunshine and then have a picnic on the Heath. My hysteria hadn't fazed him.

Daniel found my attempt on his life perfectly understandable. That's a sign of true love. Though we haven't swum together since.

We walk over the blue cobbles of Stepney Green to peer through some imposing wrought-iron gates at the tall red-brick house. 'It was built in the late sixteen hundreds.'

Daniel nods. 'Yah, Queen Anne style. As you know.'

'I do know.' We grin at each other. I'm not just showing him this to prove it's not all market stalls and junkies round here. It's a nostalgia trip. And actually, we nearly didn't meet. I would have taken an art history course instead if it hadn't started during my exam week. 'Imagine if one of us hadn't signed up for that course.'

'My life would be quite literally unbearable,' he says, 'without you.'

'You are such a kiss-arse.' I love when he says things like this. 'You wouldn't know about me, so you wouldn't know what you're missing.'

'Right, but I do know. Unbearable.' He turns me to face him and plants a soft kiss on my lips. 'I know I tell you this all the time, but you're rahly not like anyone I've ever met, Emma. You never take anything for granted. It's so rare and I love you for it.'

I squeeze his hand. 'You don't take things for granted, either.' There isn't a silver spoon anywhere near Daniel's mouth. It's not even hidden in his cutlery drawer.

'I do try not to,' he says, 'but sometimes I catch myself. Then I've got to remember that I'm where I am because of everything my parents gave me. This charmed life of mine is an accident of birth. People love to say they're self-made when that's bullshit. Excuse the expression, but when you're born into a family that has the time to read to you instead of working day and night jobs to make ends meet, or that can afford to send you to a good school or even just properly feed and clothe you and put a roof that doesn't leak over your head, then you're not rahly self-made, are you? People congratulate themselves when they've benefitted from small classes and motivated teachers and tutors to help with revision, when they haven't had to worry about paying tuition or working through uni or parents who can't pay their bills. That's why I admire you so, Emma. You haven't had any of the privilege that I've been handed and yet here you are, about to graduate from university.'

'I see what you mean, but that's not really true, Daniel. I had most of those things too. I've had the supportive family who read to me, despite working multiple jobs, and teachers who believed in me and I had enough money to go to uni. We might have had to work for those things, but I've had a lot of help too.'

He shakes his head. 'You're right, I'm being too literal. Privilege can mean more than one thing. So we're both wealthy.'

I do feel pretty rich as we walk hand in hand from Stepney Green to Uncle Colin's pub where I know everyone is waiting. It's best not to tell him what I suspect: that it's probably not just my family inside. 'Just remember not to mention Uber. My dad'll go spare.'

Dad may not drive a cab anymore but a lot of his

friends do. You want to start an argument, try telling one of them you've got an Uber account.

He's about to push open the door when he hesitates. 'Should we get a bite to eat first?'

'There'll be seafood later,' I tell him. 'Go on, don't be a coward.'

I run into the back of him, though, when he stops dead in the doorway. Everyone in the packed pub is staring at us. 'Erm, welcome to my side of the wedding,' I whisper, giving him a gentle shove.

'Hi Daniel!' they all chorus over and over as they fall about the place laughing.

Shyly he raises his hand in greeting.

Mum waves us over to their table, where Daniel kisses her cheek and shakes my dad's hand.

'Mum, this is cruel!' I say. 'The Inquisition ended in the Middle Ages, you know.'

'Don't blame me. Everyone wants to meet Daniel.'

Mrs and Mr Ishtiaque are sitting opposite my parents. They have smiles plastered to their faces. I can't remember the last time I saw them in a pub. Don't blame Mum, my arse. 'I suppose you just fancied a pint tonight, Mrs Ishtiaque?' I tease. She's never drunk anything stronger than prune juice. 'Mrs Ishtiaque, Mr Ishtiaque, this is my fiancé, Daniel. Daniel, the Ishtiaques are our next-door neighbours.'

Mrs Ishtiaque clasps Daniel's hand in her tiny ones. 'We've known Emma since she was coming home from the maternity ward,' she says in her sing-songy Bangladeshi accent. 'She is like our daughter.'

'How d'you do?' he says. 'Emma's told me all about you. I gather you make the best curries in East London, Mrs Ishtiaque.'

Mrs Ishtiaque blushes at the compliment.

'The best,' Mr Ishtiaque confirms. He's a man of few words.

'Let's get this over with,' I tell Daniel when he's finished trading smiles with the Ishtiaques.

'Yah, now I know how you felt at Mummy's drinks,' he murmurs as we make our way to the bar.

Uncle Colin is pretending not to notice us. If he was in one of those old-timey westerns, he'd be polishing a glass and whistling.

He does a comedy double take as we approach. He's destined for the stage, honestly.

Hands are shaken across the bar. 'Barbara'll be down in a minute,' Uncle Colin says as he spritzes the shandies. 'You're very welcome here, Daniel.'

When Daniel visibly relaxes I feel like kissing my uncle. But he'd only get embarrassed if I did.

The ladies at Auntie Rose's table aren't backwards in coming forwards when we join them with our drinks. They've been looking forward to this for weeks. June's even traded her tracksuit for trousers and one of those silky printed tops with a pussy bow that office workers liked to wear in the eighties.

'Do you like East London?' Doreen asks, doing her trademark cleavage cross-twiddling.

'Yah,' he answers politely.

'What do you like about it?'

'Oh gosh, yah, I like that Emma was born and raised here amongst so many people she loves. And once I've spent more time here, I know I'll love it as much as she does.'

'Lor' love a duck, 'e ain't half charming!' says June.

'She likes you,' I tell Daniel.

He flashes them all his killer smile. I happen to know that those teeth took two and a half years to straighten out. I never had braces, so my own overlap a tiny bit. 'Thank you. I was just telling Em that it's not my natural milieu, but I hope I don't put my foot in it too badly!'

I cringe. Must get him to stop saying milieu. 'It's not his usual part of town.'

My family and friends don't seem to know what to make of Daniel. His poshness would normally set their teeth on edge, but their curiosity at this exotic specimen overcomes any ingrained mistrust. Before long they're showing Daniel how to play cribbage, firing questions and answers back and forth, and even though I'm sure they don't completely understand each other, they're laughing like old friends.

Doreen meets me at the bar. 'Your Daniel seems nice.' She doesn't bother keeping her voice down, so half the bar can hear her. 'Can't play cards worth a damn, though.'

'He's probably just letting you win,' I say.

'You and your auntie, both too cheeky by 'alf.'

'How is she? With you all, I mean?'

Doreen puts a leathery hand on my arm. 'She's all right, my love, not much more forgetful than the rest of us. She's been all right at home?'

'Usually. She's wandering more lately, though.'

'She's safe here.'

Most of the time you wouldn't think there was a thing wrong with Auntie Rose. She never gets muddled up and she doesn't forget words. She just gets into her head sometimes that she's got to be somewhere else. If someone's around when she grabs her coat or handbag and announces 'Right, I'm off', then we can go with her. But every so often she makes her announcement to nobody, and we have to send out a search party.

So far she hasn't left the neighbourhood, but you can't turn her around once she gets going, either. It might be the laundromat or the café or a specific shop. No amount of coaxing will get her to turn back. It doesn't matter that she never has laundry to do or a shopping list to tick off. She's going wherever she's decided to go, and that's all there is to it.

She doesn't seem distressed or frustrated that she can't tell you why she wanted to go in the first place. Whenever we ask her she just shrugs and says, 'One of life's mysteries.'

But what if she decides one day to go to Heathrow, or Downing Street via a rough estate? That's what I worry about.

I hear Barbara behind me as I'm carrying the drinks back to the table. 'So where is this young man I keep hearing about? Hello, my love!'

'Uncle Barbara!' I throw myself into his waiting arms. 'Come and meet Daniel. He's heard all about you.'

Of course I've told Daniel about Uncle Barbara, but

nothing prepares him for meeting my uncle in the flesh. First of all, he's Uncle Colin's identical twin. All six foot three hairy inches of him. Secondly, he's built like a railway siding. And thirdly, he's wearing a swingy red and white dress and shiny black knee-high boots.

He claps Daniel on the back with more force than someone in a frock should have. As everyone shifts round to make room for him I catch Daniel's eye. He's grinning like he can't imagine anything more fun than being surrounded by old ladies and cross-dressers.

Uncle Barbara used to be Uncle Mark, but I haven't called him that in a very long time.

'You've picked bridesmaids and groomsmen now, yeah?' Uncle Barbara asks us. 'They need some warning, you know. And you need time to find outfits. Once that's set, everything else can work around them.'

Of course he'd know all about it. I don't often think of him that way, but when he was Uncle Mark he was married. His wife took off with their two boys after finding him in one of her frocks. They moved away up north, and it's only in the past few years that his sons have even started talking to him. He goes up every few months, and I have to give him credit for that because it doesn't sound like it usually goes very well.

'Kelly's my bridesmaid,' I tell him, 'and Daniel's sister and one of his best friends.'

'And my flatmate, Jacob, will be my best man, along with three of my school chums as my groomsmen,' Daniel adds. 'It's going to be an awful lot of fun!'

'An awful lot!' croaks June as smirks dash round the table. I can tell they're not making fun of Daniel. Only his odd figures of speech. I can't blame them. He does talk like Bertie Wooster sometimes.

'You'll need another bridesmaid, Emma,' Uncle Barbara says. 'It's bad luck to have an odd number. We had three at my wedding and look what happened.'

'It made you queer,' Auntie Rose chips in. 'Only joking. I know the difference between a queer and a trannie.'

But not the difference between being offensive and not, clearly. 'Mum,' I shout over to their table. 'How many bridesmaids did you have?'

'Four,' she says. 'Why?' She gasps, throwing her hands over her mouth. 'Have you got only three? Oh *no*, Emma! You're doooomed.'

'You're all taking the piss,' I say. 'Hilarious.'

'It does look better for photos to have an even number on each side, though,' Uncle Barbara points out. 'If you're looking for another, I'd be willing to step in.'

He sounds jokey, but he's blushing under his beard.

Aside from my parents, Uncle Barbara is my closest relative under seventy and I'd love for him to be one of my bridesmaids, but can you imagine the looks on my new in-laws' faces seeing him come up the aisle? 'Thanks, Uncle Barbara, I'll let you know, okay?'

'Just don't wait too long, like I said. I'd have to get me dress. And shoes, accessories ...'

'There is such a lot to think about,' Daniel says, turning to me. 'So many decisions to make. How would you feel about chocolate?'

'I'm all for it!' Auntie Rose says.

'Is this another question like your mother's about fish? You're not going to suggest making the entire reception out of seventy per cent dark, are you, or have a Kinder vicar filled with toys?'

He laughs. 'Mummy mentioned a chocolate fountain, that's all. Guests can dip fruit in it. She thinks it will be such great fun.'

Of course she does. She'll probably want fruit that has to be airlifted in individually by private jet and chocolate sourced from some remote Aztec civilisation and made with leprechaun's tears.

'Mmm, maybe.' The reception would look like there'd

been a massacre at Willy Wonka's factory five minutes after this lot gets into a chocolate fountain. 'Let's see where we find for the reception first.'

Daniel grimaces. 'Right, it's just that she's got an image of the wedding in her head now,' he says. 'Of course we'll do what we want. It is our wedding. It's only that I wouldn't want to disappoint her if we don't use any of her ideas.'

'The last thing I want is a disappointed mother-in-law, so of course we'll use some,' I say. Just don't ask me how.

The pub has thinned out by the time Kelly nudges me later. 'The prawn man's here.'

'Told you we'd eat,' I say to Daniel, who can't take the grin off his face. 'What is it?'

'I've read about them,' he says.

'What, prawns? They swim in the sea.'

'You sometimes eat 'em with Marie Rose sauce,' Kell adds.

'Cockle men,' he says. 'Or prawn men. I didn't think they were real.'

'Aw, bless, he looks like he's seen a unicorn,' Kell says, waving the man over.

'All right?' the prawn man asks, tipping his basket of seafood toward us so we can have a look. We politely glance into the basket even though he always sells the same things. He's getting on a bit now and I've been eating his prawns since I was a little girl in here with Mum and Dad. He never says more than he has to. He just tips his cap as he goes from table to table, passing out snacks and collecting money.

We get three pints of prawns, which we demolish in about a minute. As I watch Daniel go to the bar to get his round in for us all, I get a little misty watching everyone's smiling faces. That's my fiancé, the most popular toff in East London.

Chapter 4

The window of the chic Sloane Square shop only has two dresses in it, and I can't see myself wearing either of them. Philippa and Abby are already inside, though, waving me in, so I can't just leave. Steeling myself, I crash into the glass door as I push to open it. What the hell?

The only shops around me that keep their front doors locked are the pawnbrokers. What shoplifter in her right mind would go round nicking wedding dresses? Just try stuffing one of those down the front of your jeans.

'Sorry,' I say to the forty-something woman who unlocks the door. Her smile is radiant, but it doesn't reach her perfectly made-up eyes. Everything about her says elegance, from her pale grey shift dress and high heels to her sleek blonde chignon and the simple gold necklace and earrings she's wearing.

'Won't you make yourself comfortable?' she whispers.

'Okay, thanks,' I whisper back. The deep-pile carpet muffles my steps, but we all hear my charm bracelet tinkling.

Philippa and Abby rise from the cream velvet sofa for kisses. 'Darling! We're having champagne.' My future mother-in-law's booming voice shatters the peace in the shop. 'Do have some.' She glances at the woman, who hurries over with a crystal glass. 'Isn't this going to be marvellous fun?'

I catch Abby rolling her eyes at her mum. She's only twenty and probably has better things to do than come wedding dress shopping. She knocks back the champagne and holds out her glass for more.

'We've just been chatting about designs,' Philippa continues. 'Yah, do you have something special in mind, darling?'

'I figured I could just try some on and see what looks good.' I never know what I'm looking for when I shop. I just go along the rails and pick out whatever catches my eye.

Only there aren't any rails in here. It looks like a miniature Versailles, all gold and mirrors and dangly crystal chandeliers.

There aren't any other customers, either.

'Right, absolutely,' Philippa says. 'But if you tell Sarah what kind of thing you have in mind, she can bring some dresses out for you. Or she could bring them all out. Sarah, could you bring out all the dresses you have in Emma's size?'

Sarah looks flummoxed by this notion. 'We do have quite a few dresses. Do you have a preference for lace, silk or chiffon? Pearls, beading or plain? White, off-white, cream or we have some other neutral colours?'

I'm in so far over my head I think the lifeguard has just blown his whistle. What I need is Mrs Delaney from next to the dealership to translate all this for me. She might not know anything about the champagne they're knocking back, but she's been a tailor her whole life. She knows her silk from her rayon. 'I've always liked lace,' I say.

Sarah seizes on this snippet and holds on for dear life. 'I'll choose some dresses,' she says, going through a mirrored door at the back of the shop.

'Abby was telling me about the wedding her friend's sister just had,' Philippa says as we wait for Sarah to come back. 'It sounds absolutely dreadful. Paper plates. One can't imagine!'

'Mummy, they were being ironic. Everybody's doing

peasant weddings now. It's all hay bales and paper streamers. I think it's a hoot.'

'Hoot or not, darling, isn't the point,' says Philippa. 'If one can't afford a proper wedding, then have a small one, by all means. But don't skimp. Paper plates aren't ironic, they're tacky. To think how their parents must have felt. And a falafel cart at a wedding? They may as well have just ordered Domino's and been done with it. I'd be absolutely mortified.'

It obviously doesn't cross her mind that a *proper* wedding might be a stretch for us too. I can feel my cheeks burning.

'It's such a shame your mother couldn't come today,' Philippa says to me as she finishes her champagne. She's oblivious to my cheeks.

'She's gutted, but she says she's looking forward to meeting you soon.'

That's a total lie. She has no idea I'm here. I practically wore dark sunglasses and a trench coat to the Tube so no one would see me. I'm cheating on my mum with my future mother-in-law and not even Kelly knows about it. I couldn't bring Mum with me, though, could I? She's nervous enough about meeting Philippa. I couldn't make her do it on Philippa's home ground.

This way I can make both Philippa and my mum happy. Mum and I'll go with Kell later this week to look at more dresses. Nobody needs to know about today.

Sarah returns wheeling a golden rail hung with a dozen or so frocks and leads me through a mirrored door.

This just got real.

She hangs three dresses on what look like solid gold hooks. 'Erm ...'

We're staring at each other.

'Thanks very much,' I say.

When she smiles I realise she means to stay in here while I get changed.

'Do you have your bra with you?' she asks.

'Right here,' I say, pointing to my chest.

'Oh, that might not work with the dress, but never mind, I can get you one to try.'

She opens the door just as I'm hopping out of my jeans. Philippa waves when she catches my eye.

'Mummy, don't be awkward,' I hear Abby scold as I yank the door shut.

Sarah gets me into the first dress and buttons about a thousand tiny pearls up my back. Now I know why she didn't leave me alone to do it.

Everyone gasps when I step from the changing room

and Sarah leads me to a platform with a wraparound mirror.

I can hardly believe it's me. The white sleeveless lace top of the dress hugs my torso perfectly, plunging to a narrow waist and then flaring over my hips. Suddenly I wish I had brought Mum. I can go through the motions again with her, but I'll never again have this exact feeling of seeing myself in a wedding dress for the first time.

I shove the unwelcome thought aside and slowly twirl on the platform.

'It does swamp you a bit,' Abby says. 'Because you're short. A less poufy skirt might be better. Can we have some more champagne, please, Sarah?'

I was thinking the same thing. About the dress, I mean. Sarah's never going to trust me with a drink in one of her dresses.

She shows me some simpler designs till we find one that I have to admit I sort of love. It's got a lace overlay all the way from the neckline to the hemline, but it's not poufy. The cap sleeves and straighter cut even makes me look a bit tall.

'Yah, that's it,' Philippa says. 'You may have found your dress. A column dress isn't easy to wear, but it looks beautiful on you.'

'It rahly does,' Abby says.

It really, really does, I think. I'd wondered if so much white might wash out my pale skin, or be too much contrast against dark hair, but it looks fantastic.

'You'll need something for your head, of course,' Philippa says. 'Is there a family veil that you'll wear?'

'No, no family veil.'

'Oh good, because actually I had another idea. A fresh floral crown! Wouldn't that be darling? The florist could do it in the most beautiful summer blooms and make simpler ones for all the guests. Imagine the photos. Isn't this going to be the most beautiful wedding?'

I doubt she's thinking of simply weaving daisy chains like Kell and I used to do with the dandelions that grew on the verge in summertime.

When Sarah tells us that for a fee we can expedite the eight-week lead time to order the dress, Philippa starts yah-yahing like it's a done deal.

Hold on, I can't buy this dress! Mum doesn't even know I'm here. Besides, I've got no idea how much it costs. I searched in vain for price tags when Sarah went to get me a bra.

'Oh good,' I find myself saying. 'And the price of the dress?'

When she tells me I nearly fall off my borrowed high heels. 'Mum will want to see it first, of course,' I say to their triumphant faces.

'Of course,' Philippa and Abby chorus.

'Send her photos!' Abby says.

I could do that. If she knew I was here.

Abby uses my phone to snap a dozen pics of me in the dress while Philippa keeps saying, 'This is such great fun!'

I feel a little sick as I pretend to wait around for Mum's response. 'She's not answering,' I say. 'Sometimes she doesn't have her phone with her. I can always bring her back here, right?'

'Absolutely,' Sarah assures me.

Her smile doesn't falter as we all say goodbye, but I think Sarah knows she'll never see me again.

As I walk to where my scooter's parked I delete the dress photos and the unsent text to Mum. There's no sense tormenting myself with that dress when I'll never afford it.

I wonder how Mum managed to buy a dress for her wedding. I know she and Dad had even less money than I do, though they did get married during the nineties recession. Things were probably cheaper then.

I nearly have a heart attack when my phone buzzes with a text just as I'm getting on my scooter. It's Mum. She knows I'm here. I glance at my phone. Mum doesn't know I'm here. It's Daniel.

Hope you're surviving the bear pit of wedding dresses. Want to meet the gang for a drink? Dxoxo

Pure hell drinking champagne and trying on gorgeous dresses. Let's meet! Emx

Daniel's friends always go to the same pub in Chelsea. It's pretty, atmospheric and comfortable and they usually manage to get a table even when it's full, like now. It's not miles different from the Cock and Crown, except for the people.

Daniel's flatmate, Jacob, waves when he sees me and nudges Daniel who, judging by his flapping arms, is in the middle of telling Cressida a story. I've no idea where he gets it, but he's practically Mediterranean when it comes to hand gestures.

He jumps up when he sees me. 'No dress?' His lips find mine.

'No, not yet, and I wouldn't bring it here even if I did

get one. You're not allowed to see it till the wedding.'

'Seven years of bad luck,' Jacob says.

When he speaks his pronounced Adam's apple bobs up and down. You couldn't call his skinny face, receding chin and giant beak attractive. He looked familiar when Daniel first introduced us. It took me a few meetings to realise why. Dad once took me to see the old Disney film, *The Legend of Sleepy Hollow,* and Jacob is the spitting image of cartoon Ichabod Crane. He's super nice, though, which is why he's usually seeing someone, despite looking like a caricature.

'That's for smashing a mirror, you berk,' Cressida tells him, unfolding herself from the booth. 'Mwah, mwah.' She kisses the air above my ears. I can smell the perfume in her long, straight chestnut hair. It's something sharp and citrusy, almost like a man's cologne. I air-kiss back without the sound effects. She'd know I was taking the piss.

Cressida comes standard as part of Daniel's friends and family package. I met her within weeks of our first date. As she's his good friend Seb's little sister and a regular fixture on his nights out, I think Daniel was keen to put my mind at ease. Just because Cressida is gorgeous and they're nearly best friends who've gone away on exotic holidays together their entire lives doesn't mean I should be concerned. You get the picture. She sounds like a nightmare, right?

I was all set to pretend to like her, so no one was more surprised than me when I actually did.

'Daniel says you've been summoned to the great Godfather's for the next supper,' she says.

'Should I be worried?'

'Yah, no, Harold is richer than Croesus, but he's not too big a bore. Besides, you're with Daniel and Daniel can do no wrong. He's the golden boy.'

'What would you like, Em?' Daniel asks. 'It's my round. Cressida?'

'Here, try this first,' she suggests, grabbing a bottle of pink wine from a sweating ice bucket to pour me a glass. 'We got them to stock it and it's finally warm enough to drink.' She means the weather, not the wine. 'Maybe your uncle would like it for his pub.'

'Mmm, that's good!' I say, trying to imagine Uncle Colin serving rosé to the Cock and Crown regulars. He won't even have Chardonnay. 'This is fine, Daniel, thanks.'

I slide into his spot beside Cressida as he goes to the bar.

Even if Daniel hadn't so obviously loved her – and

platonic or not, love is love – I'd have obsessed over Cressida, especially since I suppose I've let my mum's opinions about the la-di-das, as she calls them, cloud my view. They speak differently and have double-barrelled surnames and all come from the same schools.

But Cressida has been nothing but kind to me and I really, truly was happy when Daniel asked if she could be one of our bridesmaids.

'We drank cases of it last summer when we were in Saint-Paul-de-Vence, remember, Jacob?' she says. 'It's such a shame you couldn't come with us, Emma, you'd have loved it there! Nothing to do for two weeks but drink wine by the pool. It was divine. Which reminds me. What if we did something similar for your hen do? Or even hire the same place. I'm sure we could get the villa again, and you can have all your friends and family there under the same roof! It'll easily sleep twenty and it's so much more personal than having hotel rooms on some city break. I think your Auntie Rose would love it. There are a few steps down to the pool, but we could always help her up and down.'

Her deep brown eyes dance with delight at the idea. She's never met Auntie Rose and thinks she's a genteel East London Miss Marple.

'Well, I did only know Daniel a few weeks when you went away,' I say. 'It was a bit early to crash his holidays.'

'We'd have loved having you there,' she says. 'You're such a breath of fresh air for us.'

She's always saying things like this and they sound like compliments, but I could also be the cut-price flavour of the month. I never feel like I know for sure.

There's no doubt we're different, a fact that she's either hyper-aware of or seems to completely forget.

Take my hen do. She's got completely bonkers ideas about where to go. I'm not sure whether staying in a French villa would be more or less pricey than the long weekend at the spa in Baden-Baden she suggested last week, or going to see the Bolshoi Ballet in St Petersburg. That's St Petersburg, Russia, not some theatre in Kent, in case you wondered.

It's these kinds of ideas that make Kelly hate everything about Cressida. And they haven't met yet, so Kell doesn't even know that they might be coming from her good, if misguided, heart.

Something tells me that introducing them in a villa in France won't be the best idea. 'I think Kelly will plan something low-key and local,' I say.

'Oh, of course. Just tell me to shut up, will you?' She

waves away my objection. 'There's nothing worse than an interloper barging in on an old friendship. I just get overexcited sometimes because Daniel loves you so much.'

'Who do I love?' Daniel says as he comes back with pints for him and Jacob.

'You're such an arsehole,' Cressida says fondly. 'You know who.' She stares at him pointedly. Then, taking a sip of her wine, she says, 'What about your stag do? Or is it secret?'

Jacob's face splits into an enormous grin. 'I can tell them, yah? Anyhow, Emma should know in case she needs to post bail or something. We're starting with stuntman training at Ealing Studios,' he says. 'The name's Bond. Jacob Bond.'

'You chaps? Stunt training?' Cressida laughs. 'It sounds more like an Ealing comedy than a Bond film.'

Jacob ignores her barb. 'Then we're going paintballing in tanks and then on to Scotland on a whisky-tasting tour.'

'Where's all this manliness suddenly coming from?' I ask. Daniel gets manicures and he and Jacob like to meet for afternoon tea. He's not exactly Bear Grylls.

'The usual stag locations won't do for my chum,' Jacob

says, clapping Daniel on the back and making him spill a bit of his pint. Carefully he mops it off the table with one of the cocktail napkins. 'We looked into deer stalking, but we'd have to go in half-term, which is after the season ends.'

'Yes, well, naturally you need to plan your hunting around the children,' Cressida says. 'As any self-respecting caveman would do.'

Jacob is a geography teacher at one of London's exclusive public schools. Like Daniel, he decided to break with family tradition and do something that doesn't involve making squillions of pounds.

'That sounds like a nice weekend,' I say.

Daniel pretends to be shocked. 'Nice? Nice?! You can't call a stag weekend nice, Emma. That takes all the fun out of it.'

'Sorry. I mean it sounds really dangerous. Are you sure it's safe? You might get a little stiff from the stuntman training and not be able to sit in the armoured tank shooting at each other.'

Actually, I know all about the stag plans already. Daniel hasn't been able to keep them to himself. He made me promise to act surprised when Jacob told me. 'What about you?' Jacob asks me. 'What's your big idea for the hen do?'

'Emma's still deciding,' Cressida says. 'Whatever it is, it'll be fabulous and a lot more fun than driving tanks and getting whisky hangovers.'

'Kelly's got some ideas,' I say. I'm sure Cressida's right: it'll be more fun than driving tanks and sipping whisky. I'm not so sure it'll be more fun than sitting by the pool in the South of France, though.

Chapter 5

It's Groundhog Day. If I see my wedding dress today, I won't have to deal with six more weeks of looking.

Mum doesn't know I've been here before, of course. Well, not here, exactly.

Philippa's boutique was about as far from here as I can imagine.

We're driving round a dire trading estate in Kent trying to find some trace of a wedding dress warehouse.

'Sorry. This way's definitely not a dead end, though,' says Kell, signalling another turn in the completely empty car park. 'I'm really sorry about this.'

Her voice sounds small even though I'm wedged between her and Mum across the front seat of her cramped van. The windows are down to air it out, but we'll probably go into the dress shop smelling faintly of mackerel.

'It's okay,' I tell her again. 'The map from the website was useless. They should have better directions if they want people to buy their dresses.'

Even if it takes all day to find this place, I'm not about to do anything to make Kelly feel bad. Today is too important to her.

Mum too. I sneak a sideways glance at her as we circle again around one of the warehouses. 'You okay, Mum?'

'I just want this to be a nice day for you,' she says. She sounds as wobbly as Kelly.

'It is a nice day!' I grab both of their arms. 'I'm with you two, what could be better?'

'Finding the bloody shop,' Kell mutters as we circle the warehouse again.

But it's not a shop, at least not the way Philippa would imagine it. And it's not on that trading estate we've been circling for twenty minutes but the one across the road.

'Well, if you can't find something here ...' says Mum over the echoing clamour of our footsteps on the concrete. We've climbed three sets of steps that remind me of a dangerous parking garage you shouldn't risk after dark. '... you're not trying.'

We're adrift on a sea of white. Rail upon rail of dresses run the length of the warehouse, harshly lit by the strip-lighting in the ceiling. I guess if a dress looks good under fluorescents, it'll look good anywhere.

Kelly's already halfway down the first row. 'Gawd, will you look at this?' She holds a spangly strapless dress to herself. It's got layer upon layer of ruffles. With ribbons. 'You'd look like Little Bo Peep. Baaaa. On the Vegas Strip.'

'Or this?' I say, pulling another one from the rail. It has no skirt in front. The many layers – which remind me of the nets in our lounge – sweep away from a pair of white satin short shorts. 'For the exhibitionist bride.'

We don't need champagne or whispering sales clerks. Even without the drinks, this is more fun than the shop with Philippa. We rush to find more horrible dresses.

'Girls.' It's Mum. 'We're not here to have fun. We're here to find Emma a dress.'

Chastened, Kelly returns to where Mum is standing.

'Do you have any idea what kind of dress you might want?' Mum asks.

Both their faces light up as I describe the perfect dress back in Chelsea – the soft material and cinched-in waist. The tiny buttons up the back and the not-too-high-but-not-too-low neckline. I've been thinking about that dress all week. Dreaming about it.

But no amount of searching – up one row, down the

other and back again – uncovers anything even close to my dress. 'I can't afford these anyway!' I don't mean to well up, but even the gaudy fire hazards are too expensive.

Kell smothers me in a hug. 'You git, stop snivelling, will you? We'll find your dress – we just have to look harder and be smart. Do you definitely want a standard wedding dress? What about something less traditional?'

I wish I'd never gone with Philippa and Abby to that boutique. I can't miss what I've never seen. Ignorance really would be bliss. Instead, I've got a vision of me in that flowing wedding dress and it's not going away. 'I really do want a traditional dress,' I say.

'Then we're going to find you one,' answers Mum as she walks off toward the front, tucking her ginger bob behind her ear. She means business.

'Pardon me,' she says to one of the bored-looking women sitting on plastic chairs next to the till. 'Have you got a sale rail?'

The older of the women cocks her head. 'Everything is discounted.'

'But do you have a sale rail?' Mum persists.

'Some are marked down. You'll have to look.'

There's no chance of getting a glass of bubbly off these two.

'Right, then that's what we'll do. Come on, girls.' She heads for the first row again. 'We're finding you a sale dress that you'll love.'

This is one of the biggest reasons that my mum is such a star. If it takes her pulling each dress out to find the price tag hidden in its hideous folds, that's exactly what she's going to do, and I wouldn't want to be the one to try stopping her.

I know she's doing her best to keep our spirits up, but revisiting every dress in the warehouse just makes me surer that I don't want to wear any of them on my wedding day.

But I can't disappoint Mum. 'I'll try these,' I tell her as we reach the last row. I just hope nobody lights a match or I'll go up like Guy Fawkes on Bonfire Night.

Kelly comes into the fitting room with me while Mum stands around outside, waiting for the big reveal. Neither of the women near the till offers her a seat. That woman, Sarah, back at Philippa's shop would have made herself into a human bench to give Mum somewhere to rest her feet.

The first dress that Kell puts over my head has an underlay that crinkles. I'll walk down the aisle sounding like an empty packet of crisps. She does up the back and we both stare at my reflection in the full-length mirror.

'Hmm,' she says.

'Yeah. Hmm.'

It's not that the dress is horrible. It fits, generally speaking. But my waist looks thick and there's no escaping the glare from the fluorescent lights reflecting off the fabric.

'At least your boobs look good,' says Kell. 'Massive, in fact.' She frowns at her own rather flat chest.

'That's not what I'm looking for in a wedding dress, though.'

'Is it on?' Mum calls from outside. 'Let me see.'

I walk through the curtain knowing Mum's eyes will well up when she sees me, her only daughter, in a wedding dress for the first time. Her little girl, who she nursed through chicken pox and scarlet fever, scared the monsters from under her bed and watched grow into a young woman about to start her own independent life. I'm getting a little choked up myself just thinking about it.

So I'm not prepared to see her wince and shake her head. 'You look a bit ... un-slim in that,' she says. 'Try one of the other ones and see if they're better.'

'Thanks, Mum.' So much for the emotion of the

moment. Now I don't feel so bad for not having her with me the other day.

I go through the motions, but it's no use. The strapless ones all make my chest look too big, and the material is either too itchy or stiff or slippery.

We're pretty quiet in the van on the way back home. The cheapest dress Mum found was still too pricey. It was a size four and had a big lipstick smear up the front.

'Do you remember where you got your dress, Mum?'

'Your gran made it for me,' she says. 'She was an excellent seamstress till she got cataracts. She used to do the alterations for one of those Savile Row tailors, as you know. We always had the most beautiful suits hanging in the house.'

'Can you sew?' I ask her. I've never seen her do it, but then I didn't know she could tile a bathroom till she ripped out the old suite one weekend. Mum is full of surprises.

Mrs Delaney at the tailor shop near where I work mostly just alters men's suits nowadays, but she used to make some gorgeous clothes too. Not that I could ever afford to pay someone to make my dress. But maybe Mum could do something for me? It could start a tradition in the family, with mothers making dresses for their daughters' wedding day. Except I can't sew, so I'd have to have sons.

'No, I never really got the hang of it,' she says, deflating my handmade bubble. 'It was the last thing I wanted to do anyway. All that fine work would've ruined me eyes too.' She laughs, rubbing her knees. 'Like cleaning houses is so much easier.' She thinks for a minute. 'None of us followed her, though your Uncle Barbara's ex-wife sews. I know she's not related, but she used to make beautiful dresses. Still does, I imagine.'

'Maybe she'd make your dress!' says Kell.

Mum laughs. 'I doubt that. She caught Uncle Barbara wearing something she'd made. I think that got up her nose more than his cross-dressing did. We haven't really spoken to her since she left.'

'So she probably wouldn't want to sew me a free dress.' It was a nice idea anyway.

'Speaking of Uncle Barbara, have you thought any more about having him as a bridesmaid?' Mum asks. 'He's dying to be included, you know.'

'I know, and I really want him to be. I'm just not sure that Daniel's side would be open to the idea.'

She gives me one of her looks.

'So shoot me if I'm not sure I want a bearded man in

a dress walking up the aisle at my wedding!' I say. But then I feel bad. He's not just any man in a dress. He's my uncle and I love him. 'Have you still got your dress?' I ask Mum to get her to stop looking at me like that. 'I'd love to see it.'

I'm sure I've seen photos of their wedding day. They were all just snapshots, though, and I don't remember Mum's dress very well. I do know that she didn't have to grapple with the question of a cross-dressing bridesmaid. Uncle Barbara wore a suit like everyone else in those days.

'Oh, it's somewhere in the house,' she says. 'In one of the cupboards, probably. It would still be dear to get the fabric, you know, even if the tailoring was free. Those silks and laces don't come cheap. A ready-made dress would be better.'

Suddenly we're all thrown forward against our seatbelts as Kelly slams on the brakes. Car horns sound off behind us. 'What the hell, Kell?!'

'Oxfam!' she says, throwing on her signal to pull over. It's no use mentioning that she could have done that before hitting her brakes. 'Why didn't I think of it before?' She pulls out her phone. 'Here, look. I'm sure— Yes, look. Oxfam has wedding dresses. And … there's a shop in Leatherhead. Let's go look!'

She's about to pull out into traffic again when I say, 'Hang on. A donated dress? I'm not sure.'

I don't know why this idea bothers me, exactly. I love a good charity shop find as much as the next person. It's where I get a lot of my clothes. People get rid of some really nice things.

But why would someone donate her wedding dress? Because she'll never wear it again? Maybe, but everyone has clothes in their closet that'll never see the light of day. Why get rid of your wedding dress? Unless you weren't happy in it.

'I don't want someone else's bad karma,' I say. 'Happy brides don't get rid of their wedding dresses.'

'Some must.'

'But how will I know whether mine's from a happy bride or a divorced one?'

'Yeah, I see what you mean,' says Kell as she eases back into the driving lane. 'We'll have to come up with something else. We will, though. We'll find something.'

As soon as we get back from Kent, Dad says, 'That came for you,' pointing to a large flat box.

'I haven't ordered anything.'

'Something from Daniel?' Kelly asks as she throws herself down on the settee. 'Open it!'

I need a knife from the kitchen to get the box open. Whatever it is, it's well packed.

'I don't get it.' I pull out stacks of fabrics in every shade of white, cream, pale yellow, blue and green you can imagine. 'What are these for?'

'Serviettes,' says Auntie Rose, rubbing one of them between her fingers. 'This is top quality linen, by the feel of it. Why would Daniel send you serviettes?'

'I'm sure he didn't, Auntie Rose.'

'His mum?' Mum asks, picking up a few that have faint patterns on them. 'Damask,' she murmurs.

'I guess they're from Philippa, though she didn't mention anything.' I'm not sure what I'm supposed to do with them. There must be fifty.

Kelly picks one up. 'Is this what she wants you to have at your wedding?' She pulls out her phone to google the company. 'Holy shit, look at this! These are a tenner *each*.'

We all crowd round her phone to look as she scrolls down the page. 'A few are cheaper but not by much. This one's fourteen quid. Emma, you can't afford this.'

'Tell me about it,' I say. 'Ten quid for a serviette? Imagine how much she expects us to pay for the plates and cutlery.' I reach for my phone, then put it away again. I want to ring Daniel, but I feel like all I've done lately is moan about wedding expenses. Instead, I go in to the kitchen so I can ring Philippa without my family pulling horrified faces at me.

'Hellair, darling!' she says when she answers. 'How did your dress shopping go?'

'It was nice, thanks, Philippa. We're still looking.' I don't mention that the boutique we went to today ends in the word 'warehouse'.

'Yah, yah, wonderful, just let me know when you'd like to go back to Sarah's.'

'I will, thanks. Did you happen to send me a box of serviettes?'

She's quiet for a second. 'Right. The napkins, yah. I'm awfully sorry, I think I probably got carried away, but they had such delicious things that I couldn't stop! I thought they might give you some ideas for colours for your tables. Anyhow, see if you like any of them. They can order them in within two weeks, so there's no rush. You'll want to have a head count anyway before you order them.'

'The head count will be sixty,' I say.

She laughs. 'Well, these things do have a way of creeping up. I'm sorry, darling, I'm just about to have my massage. Can I ring you back after?'

'No, no, that's okay. I just wanted to say thanks for the serv– napkins.'

I know she just wants to help, but Philippa's suggestions feel like more than suggestions.

When I return to the lounge, Kell says, 'We've got a great idea. There are forty-two serviettes here. You can use them for the wedding and make up the rest with normal ones.'

'They're all different colours and patterns,' I say. 'I'm supposed to choose one.' Though nobody I know would care that they're mismatched. They'd be impressed that they aren't paper.

'Well, that's a waste,' says Auntie Rose. 'What will you do with the rest of them?'

'It's more than a waste. It's four hundred quid's worth of linen!' Kell says. 'I bet we could sell them down the market.'

But I shake my head. 'Nobody wants to buy mismatched serviettes. Philippa didn't even sound like it was a big deal when I rang. Maybe she spends this much on serviettes all the time.'

'Maybe she does,' Auntie Rose says. 'All right for some.'

Mum starts packing them carefully back into the box. 'Put them away, Emma, we don't want to get them dirty.' She stops to look me in the eye. 'My love, you're not really thinking of spending this much on serviettes?'

'Of course not, Mum.'

She nods, looking as worried as I feel.

Chapter 6

Four hundred quid on serviettes. I feel like I've slipped down the rabbit hole and emerged in the middle of Harrods. Daniel wasn't surprised about his mum's suggestion, but he agrees that it's ridiculous to shell out that much on serviettes. Though he'll probably want something besides kitchen roll on the tables.

Philippa's suggestions made me uncomfortable at first. Now they've got me completely panicked. What is this woman expecting for her only son's wedding?

My tummy rumbles as I throw three tins of on-sale tuna in my basket along with a loaf of sliced bread. I've been eating so much tuna lately that I may grow gills by the wedding. *Do you, Daniel, take this cod to be your lawfully wedded wife?*

But homemade sandwiches fill me up for lunch and

that's the main thing. I can splurge on takeaways again after the wedding.

Mmm, takeaways. I stick my face into the carrier bag, inhaling the scent of Mrs Delaney's fried fish, vinegar and chips.

Actually, that makes me feel a bit sick on an empty stomach. The quicker I deliver Mrs Delaney's lunch, the quicker I can eat my own.

Her shop's been beside the Vespa dealership for over a hundred years, though neither she nor the Vespa dealership have been around that long. It looks like it hasn't changed its window display since it opened. Swathes of faded lace drape the window and bolts of silks and velvets stand upright in a crate in the middle. The glass is sparkling clean, though, and there's not a speck of dust on the display floor. Mrs Delaney climbs in there every week with her vinegar and newspapers and dusting cloths.

No easy feat for someone in her seventies.

'I'm back, Mrs Delaney!' I call through the curtain into the back of the shop. Even though I've been in here dozens of times it never seems right to just barge in back there.

Mrs Delaney slowly emerges from the curtain in a

cloud of Crabtree & Evelyn rosewater powder. I can't pass a garden in summer without being reminded of her.

She does everything slowly because of her arthritis. It hasn't crippled her hands yet, but everything from the waist down creaks with effort. 'Thank you, my love,' she says, reaching for the carrier bag. 'Would you like some?'

She asks the same thing every time I deliver her fish and chips. I can't accept her offer, though, when I know that order feeds her for a few days. 'No, thank you. I've got my lunch right here.'

As she unwraps her fish I stare around the shop. It's long and narrow, with floor-to-ceiling shelves for all the bolts of cloth that a tailor needs. I guess when Mrs Delaney had a thriving business those shelves were full. Now there's lots of empty space. It's dark in here, but she doesn't turn on the lights unless she's got a customer.

Now most of her work comes from the big shops on Oxford Street and in West London. Every time one of the fancy retail shops offers to hem your trousers or take in your skirt, it's someone like Mrs Delaney wielding the needle.

She does still get a few commissions, mainly for hand-made suits, but I hardly ever see anyone in here. Which is a shame, because Mrs Delaney loves company. That's why I come in whenever I can to say hello or, like today, to deliver her lunch.

Her wide blue eyes dance with excitement as she asks about the wedding plans. She's a very elegant lady, with a trim figure that's always in a dress, and a salt-and-pepper pixie cut she's had since the sixties, because she loved the way Mia Farrow looked with it. 'Have you found your dress?'

If I'd found my dress, then the whole neighbourhood would have heard about it already. Good news travels almost as fast as bad news round here. 'Not yet, and Mum says that having something made would still be pretty expensive.'

Mrs Delaney nods, deflating the tiny hope I'd harboured that Mum was wrong. 'The fabric alone can run to several hundred pounds. Plus the tailoring. Of course, I could do you a deal on that, but even so, it wouldn't be cheap.'

I can feel my shoulders slump. 'We've got a tight budget.'

That's an understatement. Our budget's in a Vulcan Death Grip.

'I take it eloping's not an option?' she asks, dipping a chip into the little pile of salt she's made. 'Then it seems to me you need someone else's dress for free. I'd ask my

Patty, but you wouldn't want a twenty-five-year-old dress.'

I smile. 'Does it have big puffy sleeves and satin on it?' I'm imagining Princess Di on her wedding day.

Mrs Delaney returns my grin. 'And a bustier neckline and all-over lace and a bustle. I made it myself and it was gorgeous, though no one would be caught dead in it now!'

That makes me think of my mum's dress. 'Could you alter a dress like that, though? I don't mean Patty's but if I got another one? Could you alter it into something more up-to-date?'

'Of course, girl. I could put together a whole new dress for you from the scraps of the old one.'

'You're incredible, Mrs Delaney. Would it be expensive? To update one instead of making one from scratch?'

'It might be just a few quid for an easy job. We won't know till we see what needs doing.'

Then I'm definitely going to make sure Mum digs out her dress when I get home after work. It might not be my dream dress, but it'll be my mum's, and that might be even better.

Back at the dealership, my mobile rings just as I'm hovering behind the counter about to bite into my sandwich. If it wasn't Dad, I'd ignore the call.

'Auntie Rose has left,' he says before I even say hello. 'She was here for *Homes Under the Hammer* but gone by the time *Bargain Hunt* started.'

'Pretend I use a regular clock, Dad, not the *TV Guide* to tell time.'

He sighs. 'She'd escaped by twelve-fifteen.'

I check my phone. Quarter past one. 'I'll check the pub first. Did she say anything before she left? Anything that might give us a clue where she's gone? Where was *Homes Under the Hammer* this time? Anything that could have sparked a memory?'

'No, it was up north somewhere. Wait. They did an intro where everyone was dressed up like the sixties, dancing to psychedelic music.'

I find Auntie Rose half an hour later wandering the cramped aisles of the Jiffy Mart on Mile End Road. 'Auntie Rose? What are you looking for?'

'Oh, nothing in particular. I'm just waiting for everyone.' She picks up a tin of dog food.

I'm never sure if she really knows who I am when she's wandering. Part of me doesn't want to ask. 'Are you going somewhere?'

She nods. 'You know we are, if the others ever get here!' She laughs. 'I've never seen such a crowd for turning up late.' She sets the tin down to check the dainty silver watch at her wrist. 'We'll miss the first act if we don't hurry.' Her worried look pulls at my heart.

'That's okay, they're going on late,' I tell her. 'We've got time.'

I feel guilty when I see her expression relax, but what else can I do? I don't want my seventy-something auntie in distress because she's afraid of missing a gig that probably happened back in 1967.

The young guy behind the till catches my eye. I answer his mouthed 'Okay?' with a nod. It's not the first time Auntie Rose has been in here. I didn't understand why she kept coming back here until I noticed the old pub sign on the wall outside. She and my gran used to come here to dance to the latest cover band hits.

'Have you got everything you need, my love?' she asks a few minutes later, consulting her watch again.

'I've got everything I need. Have you?'

'I don't need anything,' she says. 'Shall we go home?'

And just like that, Auntie Rose is back in the twenty-first century.

It's not Alzheimer's or dementia, according to the GP. This time-hopping streak apparently runs in Mum's family and she's not worried about it, so I usually try not to worry either. Who knows? I might enjoy popping back a few decades myself when I'm her age.

Daniel flings his window open when I pull up outside his flat. Of course he's heard me arrive. My old Vespa sounds like angry bees.

'Supper's almost ready,' he calls down. 'Though my panna cotta might not be wobbly enough.'

That's the kind of thing I'd never have expected to hear before meeting Daniel. Having a guy cook for me is unusual enough. But having one who's concerned about the wobble in his pudding? 'I'm sure your wobble is perfect,' I say, making my way upstairs.

Of course it is. Everything he cooks tastes delicious, and I'm not only saying that because I'm not the one doing the work.

He says Harold taught him to cook. Godfathers, it seems, instruct on recipes as much as religion.

I love being in Daniel and Jacob's flat. It feels grown-up sipping a glass of wine and talking about our days while he stirs his pots and I set the table in the kitchen. Sometimes I pretend it's ours and we'll get to live here forever.

It's only wishful thinking. Jacob's so nice that he probably would move out if he didn't own the flat. And so far the only alternative in our price range is a narrowboat where we'd have to chop wood for heating and dispose of our own toilet waste.

This all seemed so easy when Daniel asked me to marry him. Everything fell into place in my head. We'd have a simple ceremony surrounded by loved ones and then live happily ever after. Friends would come to our gorgeous new flat for meals that we knocked up together and we'd spend weekends on the settee feeding each other toast and marmalade and generally being in love.

Instead, we're living on opposite sides of London, trying to find somewhere to live that doesn't need life jackets, while planning a wedding in ten weeks that's fit for the aristocracy.

Meanwhile, I'll take every second of time alone with Daniel that I can get. Even when Jacob is in the flat there's more room to be a couple here than at home with my family.

That never bothered me growing up. When my gran was alive she was at our house every day. It's normal to have family all around, all the time. There wasn't even any conversation about Auntie Rose moving into my bedroom with me after Gran died. Though it's understandable for an eighteen-year-old not to want to share her bedroom with a snoring pensioner, it would have felt weirder to say no than yes. Most people I know have aunties or grandparents living with them.

'Auntie Rose wandered to the Jiffy Mart again,' I tell him as he throws some salt into boiling water.

He stops what he's doing. 'Poor Auntie Rose. Is she okay? She's back safe at home?'

Daniel was really close to his granny on his mum's side. He even lived with her during summers when his parents were travelling. She only died two years ago and he still mentions her a lot. So he understands how much Auntie Rose means to me.

'Yeah, she's fine,' I tell him. 'I found her waiting for her friends to listen to a band there. She never seems upset when she gets confused, so I guess that's good. I'm just grateful that she's got us to look after her.'

She moved in with my gran to keep her company after my grandad died, but they were really company for each other. They bickered like crazy, but they were close. 'That's the problem with being an only child,' I warn him. 'You can try pawning me off on Kell, but you'll probably have to look after me if I start wandering when I get old.'

He reaches for my hand. 'I'll wander with you. We'll be old and doddery and get lost together.'

I don't want to rush us into incontinence pads and free bus passes, but I am looking forward to growing old with Daniel.

I get to be young with him first, though. 'I really didn't think one little wedding would be so expensive,' I tell him over dinner.

'It would be easier if you'd let my parents help.'

'It's not me that's stopping them, Daniel, it's my Dad. Can't you understand how he feels to go from supporting his family to being out of work and in a wheelchair most of the time? He feels helpless enough as it is. He hates that he's not bringing in a pay cheque anymore, even though it's not his fault, it's the stupid disease. He doesn't want to accept any handouts.' I put up my hand at Daniel's objection. 'I know it's not really a handout, but that's how he sees it. Someone else has to step in and pay for what he can't. Being in his situation with the MS has made him really sensitive about that. You should have heard him when Mum first talked about applying for the disability allowance. He acted like she was telling him she was going begging in the street. Even if I could sneak some money past him, I can't lie to him. He's proud, Daniel, and it would seem like a betrayal, even though he'd probably never find out. I'm afraid we'll have to make do with a small budget. I'm sorry about that, but can't you understand why?'

Daniel leans over the kitchen table to kiss me. 'Don't ever be sorry about that, Emma. You're the most loyal person I know. And honest and very caring about people's feelings. We'll just have to figure this out together. I don't suppose you've got any rich uncles waiting to give you your inheritance?'

I think of Uncle Colin and Uncle Barbara. We come from a very long line of un-rich people. 'Unfortunately not. But if you can take care of the rings and the suits for your side, I'll worry about my dress and the dresses for the bridesmaids. Everything else needs to come out of Mum and Dad's budget.' I study his face. 'I really am sorry that we might not have the big fancy wedding your mother wants. You should have fallen in love with a rich girl.'

'That would never have worked, because she wouldn't be you. I'll take a perfect life with you over a—' He makes air quotes with his fingers. '"—perfect wedding" any day.'

He grabs some paper and a pen from the worktop to make a list. 'Right, yah, what we need is a dose of practicality, and we'll find ways to save money. I've already found a bargain, just today, in fact. The car that takes you and your wedding party to the ceremony can also drive us to the wedding breakfast after we're married. That's two journeys for the price of one. My colleague said his driver could do it.'

I kiss his expectant lips, since he seems to think this kind of economising deserves a reward. 'Daniel, I hate to break this to you, but there's nothing practical about a chauffeur.'

He looks honestly surprised. 'Well, how will you and your family get to the ceremony, then?'

'A bus or taxi, or maybe we could walk if our heels aren't too high. And Dad's already got wheels.'

He laughs like I'm joking. 'Seriously, Daniel. A chauffeur will be too expensive. Maybe you should leave the bargain hunting to me. You're not very good at it.'

But he looks so disheartened by my rejection that I want to take the words back. It's not his fault that he didn't grow up worrying about spending. Besides, we shouldn't be having rows over money already. Hopefully we'll have fifty years of marriage for that. I find myself saying, 'Okay. We should keep track of all the expenses in one place. If you give me the chauffeur's details, I can look at booking him.' The lie slips out before I can stop it. There's no way we can book that car, but I don't want to hurt his feelings when he's only trying to help.

Half an hour later our list covers both sides of the paper. 'There's a lot to do,' I say.

'Yah, but if we prioritise,' he says. 'We can do this.' He scans the page as I pull my kitchen chair round to sit beside him. 'Right, most important is—'

'The ceremony,' I say.

'Definitely number one, and it's all I rahly care about, marrying you.'

'Me too. Everything else is a bonus.'

Of course we have to have a snog to seal the sentiment.

'The town hall is cheaper than a church,' I say when we've definitely finished snogging. 'We could do it at Bromley Public Hall. It's close to us and it's where my parents were married.'

His expression goes all mushy. He is possibly even more sentimental than I am. 'I love that we've already got a connection to it,' he says.

'Then I guess the party venue is next most important.'

But Daniel shakes his head. 'What about your dress? Isn't that next?'

'I have an idea for my dress. I might wear my mum's.'

'You'll be beautiful,' he says.

I just have to get Mum to find it. She's been very vague

every time I've asked her. Maybe Dad knows where it is. 'Next is the party.'

'Is there somewhere we could use for free?' he wonders. 'If only my parents hadn't put in the pond, we could have used their garden.'

Ha, pond. More like a lake. They've got ducks. Migrating swans would fit back there.

'I don't suppose your back garden ...?' he asks.

I picture the washing lines that crisscross the small patches of grass behind our houses. That wouldn't work, unless we could string tarpaulins between them like Kelly and I did with blankets in our lounge as children. 'I don't know what the council rules are, but I'm guessing they wouldn't like us throwing a huge party on their land.'

He takes my hands into his. 'One step at a time then, darling. We're going to figure it out together.'

Sitting there with Daniel holding my hand, I do feel like we can pull this off.

I don't get home from uni till late the next afternoon. I don't often spend the night at Daniel's, but I have to make an exception when I've got exams. Auntie Rose raises the roof when she snores, and that's one time when I need my sleep.

That's what I tell myself, and my parents, and we all pretend it's not just an excuse for a sleepover at Daniel's.

The exams went okay. I didn't have a panic attack or anything when I read the questions. I'll be married by the time I get the results, but honestly, my coursework doesn't seem nearly as important as this wedding right now. Even though passing means I'll officially be a university graduate. First in the family. Sometimes it feels like everyone's counting on me.

To be honest, I never thought I'd get to this point. Back when I signed up for the first class I promised myself that I would do my very best to finish it. I didn't dare look beyond that single course.

Dad's home when I get in. His keys are hanging on the low hook by the door, so he can grab them even when his hands aren't working properly.

'There's another package for you,' he says, wheeling in from the kitchen. 'It's on the table.'

'Not more serviettes, I hope.'

'It's smaller than the last one,' he says.

He's right, it's only a titchy little box, but it's heavy, and the smell hits me in the face as I open it. What has Philippa done this time? There must be thirty bars of chocolate wrapped in beautifully printed paper, some milk chocolate and some dark. 'It's chocolate,' I shout to Dad. 'There's mint, coffee, sea salt. Vanilla ... Olive oil, smoke! Thyme, lemongrass, basil!!'

'Auntie Rose?' I shout. 'There's chocolate down here.' Auntie Rose doesn't like to miss out on chocolate.

But there's silence instead of thundering feet.

'Is she here? Where is she?' I ask Dad.

The alarm flashes on his face too. 'I don't—She was here.'

I'm just about to head for the stairs when Auntie Rose rushes down. 'Pass me a Cadbury Roses.'

'I'm afraid they're not Cadbury's, but there's a plain milk chocolate bar. Do you want to try that? Where were you?'

Her jowls jiggle when she laughs. I used to love stroking them when I was a child. She was less fond of the practice than I was. 'Fat lot of good your education is doing you, considering I just came down the stairs. Where do you think I was?'

She sniffs at the chocolate as I go to ring Philippa from the lounge. There's no note in the package, but it's her MO, all right.

'Yah, hellair!' she booms. 'I thought for wedding favours, chocolate would be a fun and inexpensive gift for everyone. I've found a chocolatier based in Shoreditch. That's local to you, yah?'

I'm touched that she's done this.

'Do try them all,' she says. 'I got through several samples in the shop. Have you tried the goat's milk one?'

'Not yet, but I will. Thank you so much, Philippa, that's very thoughtful.'

'Yah, no, yah, it's nothing. A little local flavour is just what you should have at your wedding. I've got to dash now, darling. Friends are coming for supper and the cook's just arrived.'

Dad's wheeled himself in while I was on the phone. 'Philippa strikes again, then? Pass one here.'

'Sure. Sheep's milk or lavender?'

'Don't be cheeky,' he says. 'Give me a regular one.'

'There aren't any regular ones.'

'What about you, Elaine?' calls Dad as she lets herself in the front door. 'Do you fancy some goat-hair chocolate? They're from Philippa.'

'What's all this?' Mum picks over the chocolate bars. 'Does she really eat these?'

'I have no idea. She seems to have bought one of everything in the shop. She's ridiculously generous to keep sending us things like this.'

Mum gets a funny look as she hands something to Dad. 'Actually, your Dad and I have something for you too. Jack?'

He clears his throat. 'This is for your wedding.'

There can only be one thing in the envelope he's holding. 'You've already given me money.'

'Emma.' The way he says it silences me. 'Your mum and I want to give this to you.'

I count eight fifties in the envelope. 'I know you can't afford this!'

As soon as I see Dad's face I wish I could take that back. 'I mean, thank you very much, but this is a lot of money. You need it.'

'It's extra money, Emma,' Mum says. 'We aren't going without.' She puts her arms around me. 'Please take it. Your father and I want you to have a bit more for the budget. Please. We're not going without, believe me.'

'Where did it come from, then?' I know my parents' situation. There's no extra money just lying about.

Mum's rubbing her hands. No, not her hands. Her fingers. 'Not your ring!'

'I want to do it, Emma. Your dad and I want to do it for you.'

'No way!' I nearly shout. 'You didn't sell it!' Dad bought

135

her that ruby and diamond ring for their fifteenth wedding anniversary.

'We wanted to,' Mum says, sounding less sure in the face of my anger.

'Where did you sell it?'

'Calm down, Emma,' Dad says. 'It's not sold. It's at the shop.'

The pawnshop. In other words, as good as sold.

'Which one?'

'Never mind which one,' Mum says. 'Will you just accept it and say thank you?'

But I've already got my bag over my shoulder. 'I'll be back.'

'Emma, don't!' shouts Dad.

That ring represents fifteen years, no, nearly twenty-five years of a happy marriage. They're nuts if they think I'd let them pawn it so that I can hand out chili choco-lates to a bunch of wedding guests.

My neighbourhood has no shortage of pawnshops, so it takes me a while to find the right one. I go blurry-eyed more than once, but I can't wipe my eyes with my scooter helmet on.

The pawnshop owner, Steve, starts speaking as soon as he sees me coming through the door. 'You're so predictable,' he says. 'I told Elaine you'd be in here.' He hands me my mother's ring. 'I don't blame you.' He takes the envelope back and puts it under the counter. 'I wouldn't have sold it.'

'I appreciate that. Do you want to count it?'

He laughs. 'Emma, I've known you since you were in nappies. I know it's all there.'

'Thanks,' I say. 'I don't know what they were thinking.'

'They're thinking they want their daughter to have a nice wedding. I'd do the same for my two.'

'And they wouldn't let you, either.'

'No, probably not. I'd still do it, though. You'll under-stand someday when you're a parent.'

I've calmed down by the time I park my scooter back at home. Mum's face appears for a second in the window. I smile at her, but I don't know if she sees me.

They're only doing what they think is best for me, but I don't want them to have to. I don't want to cause anyone any trouble over a stupid wedding.

'Mrs Ishtiaque, hiya.' She's cutting back some flowers next door in her front garden. Her saree is the same shade of pink as the hyacinths that run along one of the borders.

'Ah, hello, I was wanting to talk to you,' she says,

coming to the low brick wall that divides our properties. 'Please will you tell me how to help you, for your wedding? We've had three, you know, and I know how hard it is to do.'

'That's very kind, Mrs Ishtiaque, thank you. We're working out some of the details now so I can let you know what we need, okay?'

'Okay, dear. Anything you want, you'll be asking me, yes?' She raises her fingers. 'Three weddings. Three. I can help.'

'Yes, Mrs Ishtiaque, thanks.'

Mum and Dad are waiting for me in the lounge. 'You understand why I can't let you do this, don't you?' I ask when I hand Mum back her ring. 'I know how much you want to help. Just not like this.'

'We'd do anything for you, you know,' says Dad.

I kiss the thick brown hair on top of his head. 'I know you would.'

If I didn't understand before why Dad won't let Daniel's family give us money for the wedding, I do now. It's horrible to feel like someone else has to do something for you because you can't do it for yourself.

Chapter 7

I f I squint my eyes and pretend the noisy four-lane
road isn't here – with its buses and the drunks arguing
over their cans of lager – then the Bromley Public Hall
could look beautiful. Or it would have a hundred years
ago before all the characterless council buildings grew
up around it.

'It's rahly nice,' says Daniel, taking in the two-storey
white stone building's Corinthian columns and the
wedding cake balustrade running along the rooftop. I
could be wrong, but I think he's squinting too.

'Not exactly the leafy square where your parents'
church is, though.'

We both look over our shoulders at the enormous
building opposite. It's an interesting piece of thirties

architecture when you notice the sculptures and mosaics that decorate it, but it does hulk over the road.

At least the Bow Bells is just next door, so I've got a better chance of getting my side to the ceremony on time and hopefully not too drunk. I can always send Mum and Auntie Rose over to round them up if I need to.

The registry is busy filing life's paperwork. A few other couples are there, some with tiny babies that need the council's official stamp of approval.

My parents would have registered me here after I was born. And my grandparents probably registered my parents and their parents registered them.

I wasn't very curious about my ancestors before meeting Daniel. He can practically trace his family back to the Dark Ages. We haven't got a family bible like he does, that records all the marriages, births and deaths through the centuries, so what history I know comes from hearsay. Someone from Mum's side was transported in Victorian times for being on the wrong side of the law, so technically our family has travelled across the world. I haven't mentioned this to Philippa.

The fifty-something registrar who deals with us has the resigned air and dress sense of a lifelong civil servant, with his nondescript suit trousers and pale blue shirt and his slightly too-fat yellow striped tie. He takes us into the Vestry, where their weddings are held.

Big brass chandeliers hang from the high vaulted ceiling and the sun shines in through large arched windows. It's got a really sumptuous feel, from the pale yellow walls to the deep blue carpet. It reminds me a little bit of Daniel's parents' house in its grandeur, though it's missing their priceless artwork. 'I can see us getting married here,' I tell him.

'Me too. It's perfect.' He kisses me.

'As you can see, it's set up for a wedding today. We can move the chairs around to accommodate your guests. How many will there be?'

'Around sixty,' I tell the Registrar as Daniel smirks. 'What?'

He shakes his head. 'There'll be more than sixty.'

'We can seat up to a hundred and twenty with the partition open,' the registrar says. 'There's an extra fee for that, so you'll need to let us know before the final balance is due. Would you like to go ahead and book the room?'

We look at each other and smile. 'Yes please,' we chorus. 'I can pay you now,' I say, drawing out my purse. I've got Dad to thank for my intense fear of debt. *If you can't pay for it right now, then you can't afford it and shouldn't have it*, Dad always says. It comes from all his years driving a taxi when he was only paid in cash.

'Though not the extra fee,' I say, carefully counting out the money for the registrar. 'We're only having sixty guests.'

Daniel looks like he's about to contradict me but kisses me instead.

When we step back outside on to the busy road, it looks the same – minus the drunks – but it feels different. It feels like it's a little bit ours now.

'So, July fifteenth,' says Daniel. 'It's officially official.'

I can't wipe the smile off my face, though I'm starting to sweat. Now the clock really is ticking. In eight weeks and three days we'll say 'I do'. That's fifty-nine days to pull together the perfect wedding for all our family and friends. 'I feel a bit sick,' I say.

Daniel puts his arms around me. 'It's a lot to organise, but don't worry, we'll do it.'

He's making me feel claustrophobic. 'No. I mean I really feel sick.' All I can smell are the bus fumes from the road. My head feels light and my saliva glands have gone into overdrive.

A look of worry crosses his face. 'Come, sit here.' He

leads me to a picnic table in front of the Bow Bells. 'I'll get you some water. Will you be okay sitting here for a minute?'

'I think so—'

My lunch hits the pavement beside the table. 'I'm so sorry.'

'Oh bugger, that's vile. You poor thing. Right, stay there, I'll get you some water.'

As if I'm in any state to run away.

I don't usually vomit from excitement, but then I've never booked my own wedding ceremony before. Taking deep breaths seems to help.

'Maybe you've overheated?' he says, returning with the water and a cool wet bar cloth for the back of my neck. We both stare up at the cloudy sky. If anything, it's a little chilly.

'I'll feel better in a minute,' I tell him. 'I'm sorry. It's not exactly how I imagined this moment.'

'There's nothing to apologise for, Em. If we're going to spend the rest of our lives together, eventually we'll throw up in front of each other. Think of it as a milestone. Tick.'

Weakly I smile. 'I'll feel better if I don't think about it.' Deep breaths.

143

'Mind over matter, right, okay,' he says. 'Let's think about our honeymoon, then. It's going to be my parents' wedding present to us, so please promise me you won't say no. We'll go somewhere amahzing, somewhere incredibly beautiful to be completely pampered. You deserve to be treated like a queen and not have to worry about money for once.'

'No arguments here,' I say. Unlike my Dad, I've got no problem accepting money from my future in-laws. 'We should go somewhere new to us both. Where haven't you been? I've been to Blackpool and Southend-on-Sea. Don't be too disappointed.'

'Those were my top two choices,' he says. 'I'm devastated.'

Maybe we'll go somewhere exotic and islandy, like Tahiti. Not Thailand, though, since Daniel was there on his gap year and might have drunken memories of snogging girls on the beach. 'Have you been to Polynesia?' I'm already imagining the way Daniel's skin goes golden in the sun. With his blond hair, he'll practically glow.

'If that's where you'd like to go, then I'll look into it,' he says. 'Should we go straight after the wedding or wait?'

I hesitate. 'Can I get back to you on that?'

'That's a cryptic answer.' He's frowning at me.

'Sorry, I don't mean to be. It's just that I'd like to go when ... *I'm not on my period*,' I mouth in my best Les Dawson impression. If you want to see my parents crease up, watch them when the old Les Dawson sketches are on the telly. 'I'll just check the dates later, okay?'

It would be one thing to have my period crash the party unexpectedly, but it's crazy to walk into that crampy bloated line of fire on purpose. Especially if we'll be on a beach.

I'm feeling normal again by the time I get home. The house is locked up and the keys are off the hook, which means Dad and Auntie Rose are at Uncle Colin's and Mum's working. There's no one to tell that our wedding is now official. I'm just about to ring Kelly to meet me at the pub when my glance falls on the calendar hanging over the bin in the kitchen. It's got Dad's various doctor's appointments and Mum's work schedule. It's not where I keep track of my monthly cycle. My family's close, but we're not that close.

I never used to bother keeping track, but I've had to since meeting Daniel. Otherwise, invariably, I'm reaching for the tampons and complaining of headaches just as we're about to do something romantic together.

That's what happened the first weekend that we went

away together. He'd turned up at the dealership just as I was pulling down the shutters. 'What are you doing here? Is that my bag?'

'I'm taking you away.' His kiss coincided with the shutters clanking shut.

'But I'm working tomorrow. And Kell—'

'Kell knows. Your boss does too. You've got the weekend off. I've got us an Airbnb in Brighton and an eight o'clock dinner reservation. Are you surprised?!'

I'd laughed. 'Shocked! Happily shocked, thank you.' I'd looked at my bag. 'You've packed my bag?'

'With Kelly's help, so you don't have to worry.'

Uh-huh. I bet she didn't pack tampons. 'We'll just need to stop at a Boots on the way,' I'd said.

It was a gorgeous weekend. Crampy but gorgeous.

That's why it's best to plan these things.

Thumbing through the little diary that's in my desk drawer upstairs reminds me how much time we've spent together since we got engaged. I flip back to the last set of tiny Ps in the margins (ingenious system, I know) to count the weeks forward to our wedding day. It would be just my luck, wouldn't it?

One week, two weeks, three weeks, four weeks … five

weeks. One, two, three, four, five days more brings me to today.

That's not right.

I recount. I'm feeling sick again.

Is it the consequence of what I'm seeing in my diary?

Or maybe the cause?

'Kell, come over,' I say as soon as she picks up. 'Now.'

'What's wrong?'

'Possibly everything.'

She's at my front door in five minutes. She hasn't even changed out of her tracksuit. She's got a bit of pasta sauce on her chest. That's a good friend. 'You're scaring me. What's happened?'

'I've missed my period.' There's no use being coy about it.

'Have you got a pregnancy test?'

I bought two double packs the last time I worried that I was late. That's right, I did, didn't I? This is probably just another false alarm.

'Have you taken it?'

'Without you? You are joking, right?'

She clasps her hands to her chest, unwittingly covering the pasta stain. 'I'm so touched that you'd wait to let me watch you wee on a stick.' She looks at me. 'Seriously, you don't want me to go in with you.'

'No, I can manage to hit the stick on my own, but thanks for the offer.'

She's not crazy about me waving the stick in her face when I come out. 'Two minutes. Time it on your phone?'

They're the slowest two minutes of my life. What will I do if I'm pregnant? I mean, it's not the absolute end of the world since I'm getting married in two months. But it's not ideal. We haven't even talked about children yet. And I know Daniel's not expecting to have one for our six-month anniversary. I still need to find a proper job after graduation and I definitely can't afford to stop working to have a baby. That would be months away, though.

More immediately: will I have to waddle up the aisle? 'When do you start to show?' I ask Kelly.

'God, don't put the belly before the horse, Emma! You'll jinx yourself.' She checks her phone. 'One more minute. Do you want to look?'

I'd laid the stick face down so the little window doesn't show. 'Not yet.'

But then maybe I'm not pregnant. It's possible that all the stress of trying to throw a wedding is messing up my cycle. Stress does do that. Besides, we're careful when it comes to birth control. We're young, but we're not stupid.

'Two minutes,' Kell says.

I flip over the stick.

'Well, that's good,' she says.

'What's good?' I ask.

'The test definitely works. Congratulations.'

We stare at the big pink cross.

I'm going to be a pregnant bride.

Chapter 8

I can't tell my parents about this. I may be almost twenty-five and engaged to Daniel, but every time I think about breaking the news, I morph back into a teenager. As it is, Dad gives me a look whenever I say I'm staying over at Daniel's. And I always make the excuse that I need to sleep without Auntie Rose snoring in my ear, or that I don't want to drive back across London after a night out. I know it's incredibly old-fashioned for them to be so protective, but I am their only child.

I used to wonder why I had no siblings. They were only a little older than me when I was born. Whenever I asked them they laughed and said that one was enough. Apparently I wasn't an easy child.

'Colicky,' Mum says now when I ask again as she searches for her wedding dress. 'Oh my God, you were so colicky. And you didn't just grizzle. You wailed constantly. I thought I'd go mad. Your gran used to take you to her house just so that I could get a few hours of peace and quiet in the afternoons. You woke every two hours in the night screaming the house down too.'

'Are you honestly telling your only child that she put you off children forever?'

'And toilet training,' she adds. 'You wouldn't even start till you were three.'

'Thanks, I get the picture. I wasn't the delight I am now.' I wonder if colic and delayed toilet training are hereditary. 'Is that it?' I point to a blue plastic carrier bag at the back of the shelf.

She reaches in to open the bag, pulling out a huge ball of satin, lace and sequins.

'You know, Mum, for someone who's always on at me about taking care of my things, you didn't treat this very well.'

'Well, I was never going to wear it again, was I?'

There are acres and acres of material. 'They went for full coverage in the olden days, I guess?'

'That was the style,' she says, gently fanning the dress out over the back of the settee. Its skirt spans the four-seater. 'And I loved those sleeves.'

The shoulders are the size of bowling balls, mushrooming from long sleeves of floral lace. It's got a narrow white satin collar at the throat and sheer white netting covering the neckline. And sequins sewn in to the satin brocade. A lot of sequins. 'Did you wear some kind of hoop skirt or something underneath?'

Mum smiles. 'I didn't need to. You filled it out nicely.'

'Me? How—What?'

'I was pregnant when your dad and I married.'

She says this like she's telling me she picked up more loo roll while she was at the shop.

'Four months by the wedding day. Your gran had to take the dress out twice!' She points to the panels at the sides of the dress. 'See? Here.'

Now looking at it, the waist does look a bit big for her. Mum has always been slender and fit from her cleaning jobs.

'You never thought to tell me this before, Mum?' Not that it really matters, but it's the kind of thing you like to know.

She shrugs. 'We didn't tell anyone before the wedding. Only your gran. People knew after because of the timing when you were born, but we never broadcasted it.'

A sense of foreboding creeps up my spine. 'Why not?'

She vaguely waves her hand. 'I guess it was because people judge a pregnant bride. Not for getting pregnant – it was the nineties so nobody cared about having children out of wedlock – but for some people it puts a question mark over the wedding. Did we get married just because of the pregnancy? Was that the reason, not because we really loved each other? "Elaine was pregnant, you know. She must have trapped that nice Jack into marrying her." Especially Jack's mother, who acted like he was abdicating the throne to marry me. I wasn't havin' her spoil our wedding day.'

I'm no mathematician, but even I can count to nine. 'Your anniversary is in January and my birthday's in November.' If she tells me I've been celebrating the wrong birthday all my life, I'm going to be seriously cross.

She nods. 'Our wedding anniversary is in April. The date we met is in January. Your dad took me away to a B&B in Whitstable our first year to celebrate and we just carried on with it after we married. It always seemed like the more important date anyway. His mother knew as soon as you were born, of course, and the old cow never let me forget it. But at least we got our wedding day without her going around telling everyone I'd trapped her son.'

154

I hadn't even thought about that. Possibly the only thing more awkward for Daniel's family than him marrying a girl off a council estate would be knowing he was about to marry a pregnant girl off a council estate.

Sometimes I don't know what I think I'm doing, marrying into that family. I know it sounds crazy, backwards, to wish they were more like me instead of wanting to be more like them. But I do. This would all be a lot easier if they weren't so damn posh. Because they might be giving me the benefit of the doubt now while everyone's on their best behaviour, but what about later when the normal disagreements break out between us? Will our differences really not get dragged into it then?

And now this. Talk about stacking the cards against myself.

'Mum? I'm pregnant.'

Her face goes very still. 'Oh, Emma, no,' she whispers.

That's not the reaction I was hoping for. I feel tears prick my eyes.

'You're too young! You and Daniel should have years together before you start thinking about havin' a family. You've got your whole life in front of you. And now ...' She looks like she's going to cry too.

'Well, it's not like we planned this. And for the record, I just found out, so we were already engaged. Daniel doesn't even know yet, so this isn't a shotgun wedding.'

Her hug is fierce when she gathers me in. 'Sweetheart, I know how much you and Daniel love each other. Dad and I both do. I'm sorry for my reaction. It's because I love you so much. I just wanted you to have an easier life than I've had.' She holds me at arm's length. 'You're finishing university when your dad and I left school at sixteen to work. You've got the chance to have a career, not just jobs like we've had. You won't have to worry all the time about money like we did. There's so much that I want for you, Emma. You shouldn't have the same life I've had.'

'You make it sound like it's been terrible. That's not fair on Dad.'

'It's not your Dad's fault, I love him to the ends of the earth! He and I have had a wonderful life. We are having a wonderful life. But it's been a hard one too, because of the choices we made.'

'You mean because of me.'

'No! Because of you it's all been worth it. But we didn't better ourselves like you're doing and it's meant dead-end jobs. Sweetheart, I clean up after people for a living and your dad was a cab driver.'

'Being a cab driver isn't dead-end.'

'It's not secure, either,' she says. 'It's fine as long as you're working, but there's no pension, no safety net. Look at us now that Dad can't work. I want more for you. Emma? Promise me you won't give up your dreams. Will you promise me that?'

'Of course I promise, Mum. I haven't worked this hard for five years to give it all up just because we have a baby. I can do both. Daniel and I can do both, together.'

'We'll all do it together,' she says.

She helps me into the dress and buttons up the back. It's still got a bit of room at the waist but not much. I hardly recognise myself when I look in the full-length mirror on the back of the bathroom door.

'It's bloody awful!' Mum laughs.

'It looks like a fancy-dress costume,' I admit.

'Oh, Emma, I know you want to save money, but you can't wear this. It's so out of fashion. Look at those sleeves!'

'Yes, but what if Mrs Delaney can alter it? Imagine it without the sleeves. She could just take them off, right? It'd be a nice sleeveless dress then.'

'And that neck. She'd need to take off the collar and netting.' Mum traces her fingers over the satin of the neckline underneath. 'It might not be so bad then. But are you sure? Don't you want your own dress, not some hand-me-down?'

I think about the gorgeous dress I first tried on with Philippa and Abby. It made me feel like a princess. 'It's not just any old hand-me-down, though, Mum, is it? It's your dress, and you married Dad in it and you're still going strong after twenty-five years. That's good karma. I'll have Mrs Delaney alter it and it'll be lovely. I'll be proud to walk up the aisle in it.'

She smiles. 'And your gran put extra material into the side panels, so you can still take it out if you need to. I guess she's given you a little something for your own wedding.' She shakes her head. 'Heirloom jewels would have been better, but that's never going to happen in our family. Maybe hand-me-down pregnancy dresses are our tradition.'

'Just promise you won't tell Dad?' I say. 'We can tell him after the wedding, but I don't want him to know now.'

'You'll always be his little girl, you know.'

Yeah, his pregnant little girl. 'Just don't tell him, okay?'

'Don't worry, it's your news to tell, not mine,' says Mum.

Daniel is nervous when I meet him at his flat. I didn't mean to sound ominous when I said we had to meet, but I can't tell him about his impending fatherhood over the phone, can I? And I've got to do it before we get to Philippa's for dinner. Especially now that Mum knows. That just slipped out when I heard that I was actually at my parents' wedding. I'd wanted to tell Daniel first.

He's not the only one who's nervous. I have no idea how he's going to take this. It's definitely not in our plan. We don't even have a place to live together yet, and now I guess we'll have to look for two bedrooms.

I don't think it's really hit me yet. I mean, now that I know, the symptoms are so obvious. So physically, yes, but emotionally, no.

'Is everything okay?' he asks when I get to his door. 'You sounded odd on the phone.'

I kiss him instead of answering. 'I've seen Mum's wedding dress.'

'Brilliant! How is it?'

'It's bloody awful, but I'm going to try to get Mrs Delaney to alter it for me so it'll be nice.'

He takes my overnight bag from me. 'Would you like a drink?'

'Just some water, please.' My mouth has gone dry.

I follow him into the kitchen. 'I learned something interesting about the dress.'

'Hmm?' He pours my water from the filtered jug on the worktop.

'I've been in it before,' I say.

'I can imagine you dressing up as a little girl. You'd be adorable.'

'I guess it was a little me. Embryonic, in fact. Mum was preggers when they got married.'

'Didn't you know that already? I mean, I'd have assumed you'd know.'

'Well, I might have if they hadn't been lying about their anniversary all these years.'

'That's odd. It's not exactly a shameful secret. People have sex before they get married. Not that I'm thinking about your parents having sex. Oh. Now I am. Sorry.'

'Let's sit down.'

His worried frown deepens.

'There's no easy way to tell you this, and I have no idea how you'll react, but honesty is the best policy, right?'

He clasps my hands. 'You're worrying me. What is it?'

I can feel my eyes start to sting. What if he freaks out? What if it's all too much? We're only young. He didn't bargain for this when we met. We're supposed to get years of fun before we have all the responsibility of having a family.

But I've got to admit it: it's been less than twenty-four hours since I've known and I'm already getting broody. I want this baby. As difficult as it'll be. 'I won't be the only one in the wedding dress when I walk up the aisle, either.' My hand goes to my tummy as his eyes widen.

'Are you serious?' he whispers. 'Are you ...?'

I nod, watching his expression. 'It's a shock, I know.'

His eyes fill with tears. They spill down his cheeks as the smile spreads across his face. 'Too bloody right it is,' he chokes out. 'Wow. Just ... wow.' He puts his hand over mine. 'Our baby is in there? You're sure?'

'I took two tests with Kelly to be sure.'

'Of course Kelly knows.' He smirks. 'I'd have been surprised if she didn't. How do you feel?'

'Like throwing up!'

'That's why you—'

'Vommed on the pavement.'

'And why your—'

'Boobs are huge, yep. I guess I'll need to go to the doctor for the official test, but it does seem like I'm going to have a baby.'

'We're going to have a baby. Are you pleased?'

I nod. 'Are you?' I think I know the answer.

His grin is nearly splitting his face in two. Yes, I know the answer as he kisses me.

'There's just one thing,' I say. 'Can we not tell anyone until after the wedding?'

At first he thinks I'm nuts, old-fashioned and nuts, but he understands when I explain my reasoning. Neither of us wants anyone to suspect that we're only marrying for the baby. Some of his mum's friends have already been snidey about how fast our wedding is approaching.

So this is going to be our secret. Ours and Mum's. And Kelly's.

Every light in the house is glowing when we get to Daniel's parents' for dinner. 'Do you feel okay?' he asks as he opens the door.

'Mmm. A bit delicate, to be honest. I'll be okay, though.'

'Just say when you want to leave. You need to rest.'

'Hey,' I say as he takes his shoes off in the hall. 'I love you.'

'I love you too,' he says, kissing me deeply.

'Get a room,' Abby calls when she sees us. 'God, you're rampant. Hellair!'

I smirk, as always, at her pronunciation. I shouldn't

really. I know I sound as funny to them. 'Hiya. Are there many people in there?' I whisper. Better to know how big a crowd we're in for before we're amongst them.

'Just George and India, Lord and Lady Mucking, you remember. He's got that huge nose. And Harold, of course.'

Philippa is the first to notice us come in. 'Darlings, I was just talking about you!'

Daniel grabs my hand. I'm not sure if it's for his support or mine. 'Hiya, Philippa.' I kiss her ruddy cheek. 'Hiya, Hugh.'

'Emma, my dear, come in. Nice to see you as always.' Hugh doesn't hug me, exactly. It's more of a fleeting wrestling hold, but I appreciate the gesture. It's Philippa I've got to thank for Daniel being so tactile.

Lord and Lady Mucking are as interested in me as they were when we first met. I don't feel like a performing monkey, but I definitely get the feeling they're amused by me.

Hugh drifts off to talk to Daniel's godfather, but George, Lord Mucking, stays near his wife. Their business talk is probably too boring even for him.

'We must get the invitations out soon,' says Philippa to me. 'Otherwise people will be booked up already.'

'Yah,' George says. 'Everyone will jet off once the holidays start.'

He says this like having to jet off is a great bother. 'You don't have to worry about that with my lot! They all know when the wedding is.' Plus hardly anyone goes away outside the M25.

'Yes, dear, but our side hasn't been notified.'

'But I told you, Mummy, it's the fifteenth of July. You have been notified.'

'Yes, but we haven't *told* people, Daniel. Officially. We can send out a Save the Date card if you'd like to wait a few more weeks to send the invitations, but rahly, it must be one or the other.'

'We're not sending out a card to say we're sending out an invitation, Mummy. We can send out the invites soon, I'm sure.' Daniel looks at me for confirmation.

I shrug. 'As long as we have all the names and addresses then it shouldn't take very long. I was thinking of something simple. Maybe even an email. Nearly everyone has an email address, right?'

Philippa looks like I've just offered to invite people by loudhailer. 'Oh no, that won't do at all. We have to have proper invitations.' She goes to one of the sideboards. 'I've been looking at some options for you, and here's an idea that I think is just darling. Open it!' She hands Daniel a long flat box, about the size and shape of a Thornton's Continental collection. But something tells me it's not.

He unties the ribbon and lifts the lid as I squeeze in for a look. Inside is a pair of gaily patterned gardening gloves and some seed packs and cardboard labels.

'Open the note on top!' Philippa urges me.

It reads: *Plant these seeds wherever love may grow.*

'Now look under the gloves,' she says.

There's a piece of stiff card decorated with pen drawings of flowers and pots. In calligraphy is a sample wedding invitation.

'It wouldn't have to be exactly like this, of course. I only thought of this as an idea because, you know, I have my gardening consultancy, but you might like a theme that ties in with your family instead. We could put anything inside the box you'd like, but wouldn't this be a divine way to invite guests? So romantic!'

Yeah, right. I imagine putting in a Mum-themed pair of Marigolds, a few dusting cloths and some Dettol.

'It is really marvellous,' Daniel says through his smile.

Marvellous? Marvellous?! Of course it's bloody marvellous, if we want to spend a fortune on each invitation.

Sure, Daniel, I want to snipe, *who would you like to invite to sit and stare at each other for the day, because there'll be no money left over to actually have a wedding?*

'It's a clever idea, Philippa,' I say out loud. 'But I think a simpler invitation will be better.'

'Right, yes,' Daniel says. 'Definitely simpler.'

'Whatever you want, darlings, it's your wedding. Just be sure to order them soon so they don't go out too late. I've started a guest list for our side, though I'm sure I've forgotten someone. There are bound to be a few stragglers, yah? Right, shall we eat?'

'I'm Hank Marvin!' India says. 'Is that right, Emma?'

'Perfect.' I have to give her full marks for effort, though something tells me she wouldn't last long in East London.

'Darlings, I've been meaning to say,' says Philippa when we've sat at the long dining table. 'Wedding favours. Why don't we give everyone sterling silver frames and have a photo booth set up with rahly funny props and they can take pictures to fill their frames? We could engrave each frame with the person's name. Wouldn't that be amahzing?'

'Mummy, the engraving's a bit over the top, don't you think?' says Daniel.

Right, it's the engraving that's over the top, not buying

sterling silver for your wedding guests. Dear Daniel is trying, but he hasn't got the hang of economising yet.

'Will you have a band?' Daniel's godfather, Harold, asks.

A black-clad waitress sets a plate before me. The smell of the sea nearly floors me.

'Mmm, I love oysters, thanks Mummy!' says Abby. 'You must have a band, Emma. They could play covers, but a DJ is just too naff.' She squeezes lemon juice over the oysters, picks up a shell and slurps down the slimy bit of snot.

Everyone else is slurping away.

I wouldn't eat one of those with a gun to my head. I'm not even sure that I can. Can pregnant women eat raw animals? Raw *living* animals? I can feel my mouth start to sweat.

Daniel catches my eye. 'Sorry, Mummy, I should have mentioned that Emma once had a bad reaction to oysters.'

I shake my head like this is devastating. 'I'd better not risk it. Would anyone like mine?'

'Me, me!' Abby says.

'Don't be greedy, Abby,' Philippa admonishes. 'Share them. Would anyone else like one?'

Abby looks heartbroken when five of my six oysters

end up on other diners' plates. 'There, and one for you,' Philippa says to her. 'So, darlings, a band, then?'

'We haven't decided yet,' I say. 'We could look for one, I guess.' Though I was hoping we could set up Kelly's iPhone with a couple of speakers and use her Spotify account.

'Miriam found a cracking band for our wedding, do you remember, Philippa?' Harold says. 'The bassist got so drunk he fell off the stage and broke his shoulder.'

'And Pips split the back of her dress, remember?' Hugh adds. 'If anyone should have been wearing knickers ...'

They all laugh like hyenas over Pip's backside and the bassist's broken bones.

'We were thinking we might just do a playlist,' Daniel says. 'On iTunes or something. That way everyone can have a few of their favourites.'

The table falls silent.

I know he's trying to be supportive, but the less they know about our cheap plans, the better. 'But we'll go listen to some bands too,' I say, smiling at my fiancé as more dishes come out from the kitchen.

What's the worst thing for someone with a delicate constitution to eat? I mean the most vomm-inducing thing you can think of? Maybe a big plate of stinky sprouts. Or super-runny eggs, or that fermented herring that crazy Swedes eat.

No, I can tell you that it's definitely stir-fried chicken with oyster sauce. Just looking at the gloopy, slimy sauce glistening over pink-hued chicken makes my head swim. They're putting big serving bowls of it all over the table, and spooning out rice to everyone.

Then, without asking, the waitress ladles the goo all over my plate.

The sight alone is bad enough to make me retch. The smell that hits me tips me over the edge. 'I'm sorry!' I shout just as I throw myself over the side of my chair.

At least my splash manages to miss the rug under the table. I crawl closer to the edge of the room where giant vases sit (probably Ming, if I know Philippa). I'm vaguely aware that everyone starts talking at once.

Suddenly Daniel shouts 'Oh no!' and pitches himself off his chair. Before I know it, he's joined me. The two of us must make a pretty sight, retching into his mother's silk plants.

'What on earth is wrong with you two?' Philippa demands.

Taking a deep breath, I take my head out of the plant pot. 'I'm so sorry. I felt sick all of a sudden.'

'Me too,' says Daniel. 'We must have food poisoning.'
This is news to me.

'I'm sorry, Mummy, we had bacon sandwiches earlier.
The bacon must have been off.' Daniel shoots me a look.

'We're definitely never going back to that caff!' I say.

'I think we'd better go. I'm so sorry, Mummy, everyone.
I hope we didn't ruin your meal.'

'You bloody ruined mine!' Abby says. She's just cross
about the oysters.

'Abby, shush. Can't you see that they're ill? My poor
darlings. There's some bread in the kitchen, and take
some of the steamed rice with you in case you can eat
anything later. You will ring if you need anything, won't
you?'

Meekly we nod. Understandably, nobody kisses us as
we depart.

Outside, Daniel asks, 'Feeling better?'

I nod. 'Much, thanks. I'm sorry, it was the sheen on
that chicken.' Just saying it is making me woozy. 'Why
did you get sick? Do you really think you've got food
poisoning?'

Daniel grins. 'I couldn't let you be the only one.
Otherwise they might suspect.'

'You *faked* being sick?'

'I didn't fake anything. I stuck my finger down my throat. I have a very sensitive gag reflex.' He looks proud of this.

'That might be the most disgusting thing I've ever heard.'

His face falls. 'You're not angry, are you?' He raises his fist in a salute. 'Solidarity.'

'I've never loved you more. Thank you.'

He pulls me into an embrace before rethinking the kiss. 'We're in this together, Emma. You, me and our baby. Even if it means throwing up with you in my mother's dining room. Now, you may not feel like eating but I'm actually starving. Do you mind if we get something on the way back?'

'I bet I could stomach some pizza,' I say. 'I am eating for two.'

We chatter together all the way to our favourite pizza place.

Chapter 9

It's only a blood test. I expected more fanfare somehow – you know, for a rabbit to be involved.

'Do you have any questions?' my GP, Helen, asks after she's made our heads spin with everything that's coming our way in the next nine months.

'When will the nausea stop?' I ask.

'Is it safe to have sex?' Daniel wants to know. 'Sorry. Inappropriate.'

I can't meet her eyes. Helen's known me since I was in nappies.

'Sex is perfectly safe,' she says. 'You can't harm the baby, and most women feel better after the first three months. Congratulations, both of you. How're wedding plans coming along? Colin says you've booked Bromley?'

That's the good and the bad thing about everyone

knowing everyone around here. It's great when you're a quid short for your shopping, for example, and your GP happens to be walking by with her purse. But it would be embarrassing if you had to explain about some suspicious itching to the woman you see every week in the pub.

'I guess we'll sort some more out this week,' I tell her. 'Our parents are meeting for the first time.'

'Oh, good luck!' she says. 'I hope it goes better than when my parents met Jimmy's.'

'They get along now though, right?' I ask hopefully.

'Uh, yeah, sure.'

What if our parents hate each other, like Helen and Jimmy's do?

We've both got to go back to work after the appointment, but I'll see Daniel later anyway, when I bring my parents to his flat to meet my future in-laws. That should be fun.

Zane's with a customer when I get to the dealership and our boss is behind the counter, which almost never happens. 'What time you call this?' he shouts when he sees me come in.

Marco is a small Italian man of about fifty with a curly head of salt-and-pepper hair and the ruddy complexion of a drinker. I never see him in the pub like everyone else, though. He likes his wine at home over dinner with his wife. Like a lot of our neighbours, being born in another country doesn't stop him from feeling like an East Londoner.

'I call it time off for a doctor's appointment. Hello to you too.' I throw my bag behind the counter.

'I don't pay you to go to no doctor's appointments.'

'You hardly pay me to work, but it's no use going over old ground. I was gone forty-five minutes. I won't take lunch.'

'Right you won't.'

'That's what I said.'

'I'm saying yes, you won't.'

Marco loves getting in the last word. He might sound like a twenty-first-century Dickensian Fagin but he's not bad to work for. He just blusters a lot.

'Where's Ant?' I ask just to wind him up. 'Is he not working today?'

'He's busy,' Marco murmurs.

'He's going to have to learn the business soon if you want him to take over for me when I go.'

Marco's red face turns redder. 'When you're going?'

'I've told you, as soon as I find a job that uses my

degree. My exams are finished, so I should have my certificate in a few months. I can start looking now, though.'

'It's a hard job market. Takes time.'

'I know. I'm giving you time to train my replacement.' That's supposed to be his son.

'Might take longer,' he says.

'I've told you I'll give you a month's notice, but, Marco, when I go, I go. You can't make me keep working, you know.' He sometimes confuses employment with indentured servitude.

I do feel for him. None of his sons want to take over his business. It's the same story for a lot of people we know. Our parents are in trade, but my generation wants something different. You can't blame us, really. Times have changed. I'm lucky that Dad never wanted me to do The Knowledge, and what would Mum have handed down to me anyway? Her buckets and mops? Like she said, I can do something else.

Kelly's not so lucky. I wonder if she'd choose being a fishmonger if it wasn't in her family, or if she wasn't her parents' last chance to pass it down. Her two sisters were always clear that they wanted nothing to do with the business. Kell made the mistake of letting her dad teach her to clean fish. Now she's stuck for being a soft touch.

After work, Mrs Delaney is just shutting up when I stop in with Mum's dress. She likes to keep regular hours despite not having regular customers. 'All right, Mrs Delaney?' I ask as she locks the door behind me.

'Can't complain. Well, I could, but who'd listen?'

She always says this. I always laugh like it's the first time. 'I've got Mum's dress for you to look at. Do you think you could alter it for my wedding?'

Her fingers work over the fabric and seams with the concentration of a forensics expert looking for clues. 'Your mum's dress? Your gran did a fine job on this.'

I feel immensely proud when she says this, like one pro footballer is praising another. 'I'd want to update it, though.'

Mrs Delaney laughs. 'Of course you do, it's not a fancy-dress party! Oh, I did love all the lace back then, though. So feminine.' She sighs. 'I suppose you want these off.'

'Yes, please. And the collar. I haven't got much money for alterations either, so maybe you could just let me know how much it'll be to do that. I think the fit is nearly all right.'

'Girl, I'm not about to let you walk up the aisle on

your wedding day in a dress that fits *nearly all right*. All you really need me to do is take off those sleeves and the netting at the bust. It's a very quick job. If I make other suggestions, that'll be my doing, not yours, so stop worrying about the money and go try on the dress.'

Later when I'm back in my normal clothes and about a million pins are holding together Mum's dress, Mrs Delaney and I sit in the back of the shop with our cups of tea.

I can't stop smiling at her. To have a professional tailor rework Mum's dress is beyond a dream. She'll only take twenty quid from me to take off the sleeves and the top. 'Look, girl, you could do it yourself with a pair of scissors,' she'd reasoned.

I haven't mentioned my expanding waistline, but I did ask her not to take out the extra material at the sides, in case I eat too many pies between now and the wedding. If she's got her suspicions, she's keeping them to herself.

Mrs Delaney talks about tailoring while we sip our tea. She learned from her parents, who learned from their parents. It must have been nice knowing she always had a skill she could get paid for, and a lot more stable than regular shop work. She never imagined that people wouldn't always have their clothes made but times moved on. She's got a real grudge against Biba for starting a mail-order business that made ready-to-wear cheaper than having something run up by a dressmaker.

'Now everyone buys those disposable clothes. When fashions change, people chuck out the old and buy the new. But I suppose that's progress and one little woman ain't gonna stand in its way.' She looks impish when she smiles because of her pixie cut and the way her eyes crinkle up. 'I just wish I had something to pass on to my Patty and her girls like my parents passed on to me.' She looks around. 'I'll hate to see this place turned into a bleedin' Starbucks.'

'We all would. Do you own this building?' Mrs Delaney and her Patty could be in for a nice surprise. The shop is run down and her flat above probably hasn't seen a renovation in my lifetime, but even derelict buildings round here are going for a packet these days.

'I wish I owned it! Do you know what this building is worth? I'd already be living on the Costa del Sol.'

Of course Mrs Delaney isn't naïve about that kind of thing.

It's always had a long-term lease, she says, signed between her family and the Goldings for three generations. There's twenty years or so left on the lease, but if she closes her business, they could re-lease it to some big corporation.

We both stare round the narrow shop. 'All right, maybe not a big corporation. But it won't be a tailoring shop anymore and that would be a shame. I just wish people still made clothes by hand.'

'But they do! Mrs Delaney, loads of tailors and dressmakers are making clothes now. Everyone wants vintage dresses, and there's that *Great British Sewing Bee* on telly.' I tap my phone. 'I'm sure I read something about it. Here, that's right. A new breed of tailor.' I show her the article on my phone. 'It's all about how the tailors on Savile Row have started training apprentices and how it's rejuvenating their business.'

'This ain't Savile Row!'

Nobody would argue with that. 'But maybe you could sell your business instead of just closing up. You've still got the connections to the big shops and all the alterations coming from that. That's got to be worth something. If you did want to sell the business, instead of just closing, then you'd have a bit of money for yourself and Patty. I'm sure there's a dressmaker or a tailor who'd love to make this their shop. It's vintage.'

'You mean old.'

'Vintage sounds better. It just needs some zhuzhing up.' I run my hands over the burnished countertops. 'All this antique wood. It's got so much character with these shelves and old brass hooks.'

'You mean vintage brass hooks, not old,' she says.

'You're getting the idea. If you want me to help you, I could. Really, Mrs Delaney, we could make the shop look great.'

She rubs her bony knees. 'I'd love to give it up, to be honest. I've only kept on this long to have the money coming in, but if I could sell the business then I wouldn't need to keep working. My bones are tired.'

'Let me get Kelly over one afternoon, okay? She's got a great eye for this kind of thing, and you can start to look at how to sell a business. I guess you'd need to transfer the lease too. I don't suppose you know anyone who might know? Like a solicitor or an accountant?'

'The only solicitors I know are the public defenders who keep our lads out of the nick.'

We both laugh, but it's completely true.

I definitely feel like I might throw up as I make my way to Daniel's flat later for dinner, but I can't blame the baby. It's my parents' fault. They've been asking me weird questions about Daniel's parents since we got into the Tube. Mum's on about their breakfast. 'I bet their cabinet's not full of Family Size Frosties, that's all I'm saying.'

'Is that how you're judging them now? By their cereal choice?'

'What about his lordship, Harold?' she wonders. 'What does he eat?'

'Commoners,' Dad murmurs. 'They probably all eat bran. People like that do.'

'What, regular people?' I snap, smirking at my own pun. 'Seriously, they're normal. Stop making them out to be from another planet. You know Daniel. Imagine him with boobs. That's his mother. Grey hair, that's Hugh.'

But Mum shakes her head. 'They're not normal. You said Hugh owns an insurance company. The prime minister doesn't even own an insurance company.'

'He doesn't own it. He owns a share in it. That's different.' But even I know it's not so different. 'Please don't embarrass me.'

Mum glares at me. 'This coming from you, who used to tell strangers in the supermarket that I'd abducted you. I had to carry round a photo album to prove I was your mother.'

It takes forever to get from the Tube station to Daniel's

flat because Dad's on his crutches. He says it's because the Tube isn't so good for wheelchairs, but I know he doesn't want to meet Daniel's parents in the chair. 'Dad, do you want to rest?'

His face is red from the exertion. He sets off down the pavement.

'Are you in pain?' Mum asks, tucking a lock of hair behind her ear. 'I've got painkillers.'

'Stop fussing over me like old women. I'm fine. Let's go.'

Dad is still pretty fit, even with the MS. He was always sporty and never missed a run, sometimes doing it late at night after his taxi shift. He can't run now, but he's at the gym a lot working his muscles. The doctors say that's probably why the disease hasn't progressed as fast as they expected.

Daniel didn't want to make Dad climb three flights of stairs to his flat. Our discussion got quite heated about that. But I know my father. He's got an independent streak the width of the Channel. He hates that we sometimes have to push him around in his chair when he has a relapse. He'd rather crawl than let someone help him so, as much as I hate watching him gripping the banister as he lurches up the stairs, I have to let him do it.

'Do I look all right?' Mum asks when we get to Daniel's door.

'Twiggy would be proud,' I tell her. Her dress is gorgeous, from Twiggy's M&S summer collection, a swingy sleeveless navy A-line dress that shows off her legs. 'I like your new colour too.' Auntie Rose did her hair in chestnut red this time.

Philippa and Hugh are on their feet behind Daniel when he opens the door. I can tell by his expression that he's probably been fielding weird questions from his parents too. 'Darling!' Philippa booms, clasping me to her when we get inside. 'And these are your wonderful parents. Hellair!' She grasps Mum's hands, pulling her in for air-kisses. Mum doesn't seem sure how to react in the face of this Chelsea hurricane. 'And you must be Jack. Hellair!' She pumps his outstretched hand.

Hugh's and Harold's greetings are more subdued, though still friendly. Daniel reaches for my hand.

'You're awfully kind to come all the way across town to see us,' Philippa continues as we pile into the lounge, which doesn't look small until you try cramming four parents and a godfather into it. 'We did say to Daniel that we'd be perfectly happy to come to you. Next time!

Shall we sit?' Tactfully she steps around the seat closest to Dad so he can sit there.

Hard as I try, I just can't imagine what Philippa and Hugh would make of our council estate. Or what our estate would make of them.

In seven weeks we'll all find out.

Mum and Dad keep sneaking glances at Harold. He may be a lord, but he's not one of those stuck-in-aspic types. He doesn't smoke a pipe or ramble around in a draughty mansion surrounded by his faithful dogs. He and his wife live in a townhouse in Chelsea and watch the *Game of Thrones* box sets just like everyone else.

Daniel is hovering in the lounge doorway. 'I'll get us drinks. Elaine, Jack, what would you like? Beer, wine, gin, water, juice, something else?'

'Beer for me, please,' Dad says.

'Me too,' says Mum.

'Yah, let's all have beer,' Philippa says, talking over Hugh, who's just asked for gin.

'Water for me, please,' I say.

'But you're not watching your weight are you, darling?' asks Philippa. 'You have a lovely figure.'

I blush, remembering too late that only Mum and

Daniel know. 'Well, actually I thought I'd stop drinking to be sure I fit into my wedding dress. I'm going to wear Mum's!'

'Right, that is marvellous!' Philippa says. 'What a lovely tradition.' She turns to Mum. 'You must be rahly thrilled. I doubt I could even find mine. It's probably in one of the closets somewhere. That's such a lovely dress, Elaine.'

Mum blushes. 'Thank you, it's Twiggy's design from M&S.' She smooths the skirt. 'Have you seen her collection this year?'

'Yah, no, I'm afraid I haven't. I detest shopping. I wear my clothes until they fall apart.'

We all look at her cream vintage bouclé jacket. It's still got a few good centuries left before it falls apart.

'Hugh,' Dad tries, 'Emma says you're in insurance.'

'That's right,' he says, adjusting the legs of his brick-red chinos to try to cover up the blue and green stripy socks he's wearing. 'Commercial risk, mostly.'

The silence stretches as we listen to the faint clink of glasses in the kitchen.

'Football fan?' Dad asks.

'Rugby. I was a scrum half at uni. Harold is keen on Chelsea, though. You?'

'I'm a Spurs supporter,' says Dad.

'If you'd ever like to come to a match, Jack, I've got season tickets,' Harold says. 'Though they're in the Chelsea end, so probably not when they're playing the Spurs.'

Mum's just worked out that Philippa's jacket is designer. *Chanel*, she mouths.

Talk peters out again.

Finally, Daniel returns with a tray. I nearly tackle him to help, just to have something to do. 'Jack, glass,' says Mum when he tries to wave it away.

'Cheers,' says Daniel once everyone has their drinks. 'To our families.'

'Weddings are always such a good laugh,' Mum says. 'I remember ours like it was yesterday.'

'Yah, me too.' Philippa smiles. Then she goes on about how it poured with rain and they had to move the entire wedding breakfast into the house. That's what she calls it: the wedding breakfast. Her mum was furious to have everyone tramping all over the Oriental rugs. Mum's eyes get wider and wider as Philippa explains how they set up a band in their lounge. Their drawing room, she calls it.

'Was it a big wedding?' Mum asks, recovering slightly.

'Not very. A hundred and ten. Luckily there was plenty of room in the house. Where did you have your wedding?'

'Oh, just round the corner from my parents. It wasn't nearly as grand as yours, I'm sure. Everyone just went to the pub after the ceremony.'

'How quaint!'

Philippa might mean that in a good way, but I can tell Mum thinks she's taking the piss. 'Well, we didn't have much money for a fancy party.' Mum's twisting her ring round and round her finger. They haven't said anything more about pawning it, but I don't think it'll leave Mum's hand again.

'I wish we'd gone to the pub,' Hugh says, pushing his hand through the same thick hair that Daniel has, though his is grey. 'Bloody nightmare, weddings. Everyone gets so worried about all the silly minutiae when none of it really matters. Good booze and friends are all you need.'

'Hear, hear!' says Harold.

Dad raises his beer glass to that, but Philippa tells Hugh he's full of shit – not in those words exactly. Then she rubbishes his mother by calling her precious, which seems a bit out of left field, but I suppose they must have a history. I haven't met that gran yet. It sounds like Philippa wants to keep it like that. Nobody uses the word precious in a good way to describe an adult. Her own mother was wonderful, according to Daniel, though dead, as I mentioned, so she won't be coming to the wedding.

'Jack's mother is a nightmare too,' Mum says, and while I'm pleased to see her bonding with Philippa, I wish she'd do it over something that didn't make Dad squirm. She's right, though. We hardly ever see his parents, even though they live only a few streets away. Now I know it's not just because of how badly they reacted when Uncle Barbara became Uncle Barbara. The senior Liddells are about as tolerant of differences as they are of pregnant brides.

I suppose I shouldn't complain, as long as our parents are finding something to talk about. It's not like they'll have to spend a lot of time together. Just the wedding. Maybe they can exchange Christmas cards after that.

Just as I'm starting to relax over dinner, Dad says, 'You should come out to ours some time. I think you'd like our pub.'

'Oh, yah, that would be marvellous,' says Philippa. I catch Mum's terrified look. 'Name the day and we'll be there! Only not on Tuesdays because that's my spa day.'

I just know Mum's going to want to redecorate now.

It's nearly last orders by the time we get to the Cock and Crown to pick up Auntie Rose after dinner. There are a few regulars in and Dad says hello to them all.

'How did it go?' Uncle Barbara asks me. He leans closer, whispering, 'Your auntie's been dying from curiosity.'

Auntie Rose is sitting with her ladies and doesn't look like she's dying from anything. 'Oh, *she's* been dying from curiosity? I suppose you're not at all interested,' I tell Uncle Barbara. 'It went okay, but I'm glad it's over. Dad's offered to have them round here and Mum's panicking about it.'

He looks around, at the worn carpet and the gaffer tape that Uncle Colin had to use to cover a crack in the fake leather on one of the benches. 'In 'ere? I don't blame your mum,' he says, oblivious to the impression he'd make on my future in-laws, with his strawberry-printed dress complementing the week-old stubble on his chin. 'Did everyone get along? What did they talk about? How'd Jack do on the crutches?'

I wince, remembering. 'He was okay, but I think he's in more pain than he's letting on.' We both look across at my dad.

'He usually is,' Uncle Barbara murmurs.

'Was Auntie Rose put out that we didn't take her with us? She said no, but I didn't believe her.'

He shakes his head. 'Nah. She said she didn't want to eat your uppity muck anyway.'

I sigh. 'That's what she told me. She knows it was just roasted chicken and rice.'

'You'll never get her to eat rice. It's forrin,' he says.

I wander over to where Mum is telling the ladies about Philippa. 'She goes to the spa every Tuesday, don't you know,' she says to their chorus of jeers. 'And she wore a Chanel jacket. To tea at her son's house!'

'Mum, don't make fun of her, she was perfectly nice to you.'

'Perfectly nice, pffftt. She called our wedding quaint.'

'I think she meant that as a compliment.'

'*Oh, how sweet it must be to be poor,*' she mimics. '*We rahly must try it some time. Rahly, yah.*'

The ladies all laugh, and I know it's no use trying to defend Philippa against this crowd. I'm not a hundred per cent sure I should defend her anyway. For all I know she's making fun of our accents right now.

Chapter 10

At least they don't completely hate each other. Not like the grudge Mum still holds against that Sheila Larkin, who lorded it over everyone when her husband started driving a Merc. She came down a peg or two when we found out it was only leased, but Mum still blanks her if they pass each other at the market, and that all happened before I hit puberty.

So it may be some time before Mum gets over Philippa's quaint comment.

The Cock and Crown has lost some of its sparkle now that I'm not drinking. On the bright side, everyone seems to accept that I want to lose a few pounds before the wedding. On the less bright side, it makes me wonder if I've been eating too many takeaways lately.

Urgh, just thinking about takeaways is making my

tummy churn. Morning sickness, my arse: it's nearly 9 p.m. I sip my lime and soda. It's not just the sickness, either. I never thought I could be this tired. 'I'm just glad I've finished my exams,' I tell Daniel. 'I couldn't keep my eyes open to revise.'

'You can relax now that you've finished,' he says.

He and Kell know where this exhaustion is coming from and it's fun having the secret to share. Though Daniel is no locked vault. I have to keep stopping him from rubbing my tummy in front of people. They'll either catch on that I'm pregnant or think I've got trapped wind.

'Sure, total relaxation,' I say. 'Except for the wedding. And finding a job.'

Daniel frowns. 'But you don't need to worry about the job. There's no reason to go through that effort now, right?'

There's something wrong about the way he says this, about which word he puts the emphasis on. He said 'There's no reason to go through *that* effort now', not 'There's no reason to go through that effort *now*'. Kell and I trade glances. 'No, not right this second while we plan the wedding,' I say, 'but I'd like to find something by the autumn.'

'Your days selling scooters are numbered,' says Kell. 'Lucky you.'

'If you want them to be,' Daniel murmurs. 'You should be relaxing now.'

It's not the time to get into a row about my job plans. Until now I didn't think there might be a reason to.

'Except that if we don't find a reception venue soon,' I say instead, 'we'll end up sitting on the pavement and toasting the marriage with cans of Stella.'

I've already thanked Uncle Colin for the offer to use the pub so he's not expecting to throw the party here. There's got to be a better option, something fit for Philippa and her crowd.

Even Mum agrees after meeting her that we need to step up our game. Pints in the Cock and Crown will never do for them. Mum knows better than to mention the ring again, though. We've got champagne tastes with a beer purse, that's what Dad says.

'I wish you'd let me find somewhere,' says Daniel. 'If I didn't know better, I'd say you didn't trust me.'

'Oh, I definitely trust you to find somewhere gorgeous,' I say. 'But let's be honest. Your idea of frugal is buying non-vintage champagne.'

He grimaces but can't really object.

'You'd find the perfect place that we definitely can't afford and then we'd row over it.'

'So you don't trust me,' he says quietly. Suddenly we're not joking. Fear creeps up my neck.

'I do trust you, Daniel, of course I do.' This is true. I would trust him with my life. It's his spending that I have to keep an eye on. 'I wouldn't be marrying you if I didn't trust you. You're just ...'

'What?' he challenges. 'What am I?'

'You have good taste, that's all I'm saying. See? This is what I mean. Now we're rowing.'

'Pssh, you amateur!' Kell says. 'That's not a row.'

'It is for us,' I say. When I reach for Daniel's hand he takes it.

'Like I said, you're amateurs. You should ask the brain trust in here for some ideas. Someone must know of space in an old building or under the arches.'

Of course! We've been looking in the wrong direction. I can't out-posh someone like Philippa, but I may be able to out-romance her. 'You know how I love a distressed look,' I say.

'How *we* love a distressed look,' Kell answers.

A few years ago, we gave our everyday bedroom furniture a French country makeover. It turned out okay on

Gran's reproduction Queen Anne table but not so good on Ikea's boxy veneer bed frame.

Now I'm picturing something whimsically, grandly derelict for our party, like a mini Taj Mahal with peeling paint. More likely it'll be a fume-filled garage where we'll have to hand out facemasks at the door.

'There's no question you'd get distressed under the arches,' Kell says, standing up to address the room. 'Right, hello. Hellooooo.' Nobody pays her any attention.

Sticking her fingers in her mouth, she lets rip with an ear-piercing whistle.

All conversation stops in its tracks.

'Lor', Kell, I'm deaf,' Doreen shouts.

'Sorry, Doreen. Right, you lot, our girl needs help. As you know, these fine people are getting married. So where can we throw a party cheap for what, sixty? Sixty people. Anywhere at all?'

The suggestions come thick and fast, starting with the pub – it's an obvious first option – to the hair salon next door if they can move all the chairs and hairdryers out of the way.

'What about the church?' Doreen asks. 'Vicar, couldn't they have a party there, in the hall where the Slimming World is? Or even out back?'

Our vicar, Del, sips his pint as he considers his answer. I say 'our' vicar like my family has ever heard one of his sermons first-hand.

'There'd be no libations allowed,' he says. 'Those in authority frown on our celebrations, no matter how wholesome, ever since our patriotic support of the Euro tournament last year.' He drains his beer.

'In fairness, there was a lot of damage,' Uncle Colin points out. 'And the neighbours complained about the noise.'

'The lads were just showing their support,' says Del.

I should explain about our vicar, since he's probably not what you're imagining. He came late to vicaring after a colourful career in football hooliganism. Tattooed from his fingers to the back of his shaven head, he'd terrify a person in a dark alley, but, now reformed and totally repentant, he's a giant marshmallowy pushover. As long as you don't cross him.

Uncle Colin takes Del's glass to pour him another pint. 'Just tell me how I can contribute to your day though, Emma,' Del says. 'Are you in need of my services for the ceremony?' Taking his beer, he moves to the upright piano that sits against the wall under Frank Lampard's signed West Ham shirt. It's Uncle Colin's pride and joy. The shirt, not the piano.

'No, thanks, Del, we've booked Bromley Public Hall,' I tell him. I hope this doesn't offend him. It shouldn't, since he's never known my family spiritually.

'Well, I'm happy to be of assistance any way I can,' he says, seating himself at the piano. The first few bars of 'I've Got a Lovely Bunch of Coconuts' starts everyone's toes tapping.

Our vicar plays beautifully, all the old-timey songs that everyone knows the words to. Even when he's seven or eight pints into his night, his playing is faultless.

Auntie Rose and her ladies love him. They can remember when most of the pubs had pianos and they're usually the ones to start the singalongs at Uncle Colin's. They like to recall when Del's grandad used to play.

'I'm afraid any place with a roof will probably cost some dosh,' Uncle Colin says.

Any place with a roof ... any place *with* a roof. 'What about somewhere without one?' I wonder. 'Maybe there's an outdoor space, like a park or a garden.'

Though Philippa will be expecting Kew Gardens if I tell her the wedding's outside. She won't like sharing a bench in the park with the local lads.

'That's not a bad idea,' Kell says as Del starts playing 'Itsy Bitsy Teenie Weenie Yellow Polkadot Bikini'. 'Too bad there's no beach close by. They're public, right?'

'The Queen owns them,' Auntie Rose says. 'Or she owns the sea, I forget. She owns something.'

'The swans,' Doreen says.

'Hey, Councillor,' Uncle Colin calls to the slender man nursing his pint at the end of the bar. He's one of our long-suffering elected officials. People are always complaining to him while he's trying to enjoy his pint. Given the state of the council, personally I'd drink at home if I were him. 'What about it? Could they do a party in a park?'

'You could,' he says, turning to us. 'You'd just need to apply for a license, fill in a form and pay the fee.'

He tells us the council decides the fee depending on factors like the size of the space and what's being set up. It's definitely more than a hundred quid, he says, though the exact amount is negotiable.

So much for that idea then, I think, just as Del ends his piano playing with an ominous Da Da Da Dum and walks over to the man. Clamping his meaty hand on his shoulder, he says, 'Well, Councillor, it seems to me that if it's negotiable, we should start negotiating, yeah?'

His words are friendly, but there's no mistaking his tone, or the grip he's got on the councillor's shoulder.

'But ... you don't even know where you want it.' The councillor sounds nervous.

'Let Emma and her fiancé work that one out,' Del says smoothly. 'You and I'll negotiate the terms, yeah? And remember, you're dealing with a man of God.'

Yeah, I think, *a man of God who's been inside.*

Everyone acts like we haven't just witnessed the extortion and probable corruption of a city official. Uncle Barbara scoots into the booth beside me, adjusting the top of his wrap dress as he sits. The clingy material isn't doing anything for his beer belly, but the bright blue suits him. I know what he's going to ask before he opens his mouth. My eyes shift away from his. They're so hopeful, so full of kindness. I do want him to be a bridesmaid. I'm just struggling to imagine what Daniel's family and friends will think seeing him walking up the aisle with Kelly, Cressida and Abby.

Daniel was totally fine about the idea of my uncle wearing a dress in our wedding party. I mentioned it to him back when Uncle Barbara first started hinting. 'Your family won't think it's weird?' I'd asked him.

'Oh, no, they'll find it completely bonkers, but who

cares? You should have whom you want at our wedding. We're supposed to be surrounded by the people we love, yah?'

That was easy for him to say when he's already in his family. They have to accept him. The jury is still out on me.

But our wedding party is uneven without Uncle Barbara and he knows it. Not that that's a reason to make someone a bridesmaid if you don't want to. Like I said, I really do want him there with me. 'Uncle Barbara.' I sit up straight. He does the same. 'Will you be one of my bridesmaids?'

'Oh, love, it would be an absolute honour!' he says like my offer has come out of the blue. 'You're like me daughter, Emma. You know that.' He reaches for his hankie.

Daniel grasps my hand and Barbara's, looking like he's about to go off too. This is going to turn into a real snotfest in a minute. Luckily Kell recognises my delicate condition because she says, 'Good. It's about time you got around to asking him. Barbara can come dress shopping with us.'

'Of course,' I say, 'We're meeting the others on Oxford Street to get some ideas. But you will shave on the day, won't you?'

Uncle Barbara beams as tears glisten in his soft brown eyes. 'I'll do anything you want me to, Emma, me love. Thank you.'

The next morning I get Philippa's guest list, but there's a mistake. I ring Daniel at work. 'Have you seen your mum's email?'

'Right, yah.' He sounds distracted like always at work. He's probably busy thinking about all the poor African children who need wells built. 'Finally, now we can send out the invites.'

'Well, yes ... to about half the list. Did you open the attachment?'

'Yah, why?'

'Did you see both pages?' I can hear his keyboard clicking.

'Yah, Emma, I saw. I do know how to open an attachment, you know.'

'I'm glad to hear that. Do you also know how to count? Because I tallied seventy guests from your side and that doesn't include all the "and families" she's put on there. You know we're planning on sixty guests in total.'

He laughs, but there's nothing funny about this. 'I told you it would be more. We'll have to pay the extra fee and open up the whole room at the registry. We can't not invite people to our wedding, can we? We'll just have to stretch the budget.'

He's treating this all like a bit of a challenge, like it's fun pretending to be poor. He has no idea what it's like when there really isn't more money.

'The important thing is that we can send out the invitations now,' he goes on. 'And, we're saving money by not having to do Save the Date cards first.'

'That's beside the point, Daniel. We can't afford to fund a party for all of your mother's friends!' When I say I'm going to call her, suddenly he gives me his full attention. 'Don't worry, I won't insult her. I'll just find out how close all of these people really are. We need to keep the invites to close family and friends, Daniel.'

'And we will. Why don't you let me ring her? You shouldn't have to do it.'

I *would* like to save my debut as the bitchy daughter-in-law until later if possible. And I think I can trust him to fight our corner. 'Yes, please. Ring me back as soon as you've talked to her?'

'I'll ring her right now. Will report back.'

He does ring back, more than an hour later, but his

news isn't good. 'I'm afraid there rahly isn't anyone we can take off that list,' he says.

'Do you even know who everyone is?'

'Right, I knew you'd ask me that, and I do now that I've asked Mummy. Go ahead and quiz me. I know you're dying to.'

I just so happen to have the list printed out in front of me. I start reading from the bottom where Philippa probably put the random guests she thought of last. 'Who's Dame Edwina Hislop?'

'Mum's boarding school chum,' he says. 'They ran away from school in Switzerland together. Mum was her bridesmaid. Her son is Mummy's godson.'

'Fine, they can stay. Professor and Mr Henderson?'

'They've been our next-door neighbours since I was a child. She's a heart surgeon, not a uni professor.'

'Abdullah Sharaf?'

'The Jordanian ambassador. Or consulate general, I forget. He's an old chum of Father's from Oxford.'

'The Crawford-Blacks? Sir Renwick? The Meyer-Mannings?'

'My cousins, Abby's godfather and Mum's best friends, respectively,' he says. 'You met the Meyer-Mannings at the party.'

I'm starting to see that this is a pointless exercise. 'There really isn't anyone we can cull from this list?'

'I don't see how without offending my parents.'

And I definitely can't do that if I want to be in Daniel's family. 'So we're throwing a wedding for dames and sirs and ambassadors.'

'And lords and ladies, I'm afraid. Shall we just elope?'

'Can we??'

'Emma, I was only joking. You and I can do this. Having the party outside is an inspired idea. It doesn't have to be expensive. We'll just get a big tent.'

'Maybe we won't need one if the weather is good.'

He laughs. 'I don't think we can take that chance. Leave it to me. Didn't I find a bargain on the chauffeur? I'll find us a reasonable marquee.'

I doubt that, but he sounds so pleased to be helping. He's still touchy about what I said last night and I don't want to row again. 'Great, thanks,' I tell him. If we blow the budget, then the marquee company can always lose our booking.

'I suppose we should ring the town hall about that extra room?' Daniel suggests.

'All right, I'll do it.'

'No, Em, let's ring him together. Just give me the number and I'll conference call us.'

This wedding is officially going to be bigger than I imagined.

Uncle Barbara is clean-shaven, wearing jeans and a jumper and Dr. Martens when we meet outside Debenhams on Oxford Street. I've never asked him where he gets his outfits. He doesn't shop down the market and anyway, Stacy Boyle probably couldn't find shoes in his size.

I was ten when Uncle Barbara's wife left and we started noticing some changes. He didn't pop out of the back room of the pub one day with a 'Ta-dah!' and a prom dress, though. He started wearing silky blouses when he came for tea or a dangly necklace with his polo shirt. His socks got louder and his clothes got softer. Clip-on earrings and cardigans eventually found their way into his ensembles, but it happened so gradually that nobody was completely sure if he was making a transition or just having a crisis from the divorce. Then one night he turned up in flowing wide-legged trousers and a wrap top and the penny dropped. Uncle Mark didn't look like Uncle Mark anymore.

Over the years his wardrobe has suffered mission creep and now he's almost always in a dress. There came a point when he stopped being Uncle Mark. Even now in his man-clothes he's Uncle Barbara to me.

Abby and Cressida smile warmly when I make introductions. They've been briefed, of course, about why Uncle Barbara is dress-shopping with us, just to avoid any awkward questions. Not that he'd mind answering them.

He doesn't usually dress up outside the neighbourhood. That's what Mum and Dad call it: dressing up. He's safe with us, but it would only take one intolerant gobshite to turn Uncle Barbara's world into a very scary place.

'Nice to meet you,' he says, kissing their offered cheeks. 'It's been ages since I've been on a shopping spree. Thank you for letting me come along.'

'It's our pleasure,' Abby says. 'The more the merrier when it comes to shopping. Personally, I hate it, so any distraction is welcome.'

I warn them again that we're only looking for ideas today. Under no circumstances must we come home with dresses. But as I walk towards Debenhams' door, Cressida and Abby turn the other way.

Cressida's forehead furrows. 'We're going in there?' She says this like it's a brothel.

'What's wrong with Debenhams?' Kell demands, squaring her shoulders.

'Nothing at all! I just thought we were starting at Selfridges. I mentioned to Emma – they've got all the same concessions plus the designers upstairs. Honestly, though, let's go here.'

'No, let's go to Selfridges,' says Kell, as if Cressida has just challenged her to a duel.

Selfridges! I'd wanted to start at Primark and work my way up to H&M. Debenhams *is* upscale for my purse.

'It won't hurt to look,' Kell murmurs to me as we walk further along the pavement to Selfridges. 'Like you said, we're not buying today. She's just showing off anyway. "Ooh, the designers are upstairs." She's probably going to say she knows them personally.'

'Kelly, how can you call going to Selfridges showing off? Get a grip on yourself.'

Kell's never been the jealous type before. If anything, I was the one who didn't like to share when we were growing up – attention, affection or the last custard slice – being an only child and used to having my own way. Kell has three older sisters who literally knocked the selfishness out of her. So I don't know why she's acting like I'm her exclusive property now. She practically cocks her leg to wee on me whenever Cressida's around.

'Have you got anything in mind?' Abby asks as we make our way through Selfridges' wide glass doors.

Something for under a tenner, I want to say. But I don't, of course, because she doesn't know I can't afford their dresses. 'I thought we could get some summery ideas that suit everyone.'

'We all have such different figures,' Kelly says, pointedly looking at Cressida's big chest. 'I can wear anything.'

'You have a lovely figure,' Cressida says, reaching for a flowy coral Grecian-style dress.

Kelly ignores the compliment.

'I wouldn't mind something shorter,' says Abby. 'My legs aren't bad.'

'They're gorgeous.' Uncle Barbara's agreement makes Abby grin. Somehow it doesn't sound creepy for him to say this about a twenty-year-old's legs. 'Might's well make the most of them. And maybe something loose-fitting to be kind to tummies.' He pats his.

'We'll have a butchers,' Kell says. 'How boracic are you really, Ems? Could you spend a Godiva? A pony?' She smiles. 'A monkey? Those are upstairs.'

'What's a monkey?' Cressida asks.

'It's slang,' I say, 'and it's rude to leave others out of the conversation, Kelly. We're only looking for ideas, right? Don't worry about the prices now.'

We fan out across the sales floor, gathering armloads of frocks as we go.

'She's picking some minging dresses,' Kelly says to me at one point when Cressida is out of earshot.

'They're not minging, she's got good taste.'

'Better than me?'

'I'm not having this conversation. Go try your dresses on with the others.'

Kelly's got to get over this pettiness soon because I do like Cressida a lot. And that's why Kelly can't stand her.

'Ta-dah!' Kelly swoops out of the fitting room after the fifth or sixth wardrobe change, this time wearing a flowery pastel chiffon dress. 'This is the one.'

Abby emerges in a pale green tutu-inspired dress. 'Cressida?' Abby calls. 'Hurry up.'

'Erm, this one doesn't fit very well.'

'Never mind, you can get another size, let's just see.'

She emerges holding her hand over her cleavage. The dress only has tiny spaghetti straps. It's a flowy candy-striped chiffon with a handkerchief hemline and it's gorgeous. Or it would be if the top was about two sizes bigger. 'I think more coverage might be better,' she says.

'But the style is nice,' Abby concedes. 'And it shows off your legs.'

'Oh, Kelly, yours is fabulous,' Cressida says. 'What do you think, Emma?'

'I agree. I like yours and Kelly's.'

'But which one do you like better?' Kell asks.

'I like them both,' I tell her pointedly. 'Let me find them in your sizes so everyone can try them on together.' Then I remember something. 'Not that we're buying them, but it's good to get an idea.'

By the time I find the dresses on the sprawling sales floor I've nearly convinced myself that they'll be a bargain.

Then I look at the price tags. Of course they're not.

'I like Cressida's better,' Uncle Barbara says when they've gone back inside to change.

I agree with him. 'Would you like to try one on in your size?'

He looks sad. 'I can't really, can I? It's a ladies fitting room.'

'I'm sorry, Uncle Barbara.'

'Don't be, my love, I'm just happy to be here with you.'

Kell's sense of humour has completely failed by the time we're done in Selfridges, but I feel like we should at least have a drink together to celebrate the fact that we've found a dress idea that everyone likes.

'There aren't any good pubs round here,' Kell says when I suggest the drink.

'I have a better idea than a pub and we don't even need to leave the shop!' says Cressida. 'The champagne bar is right through here.'

'Erm, well ...' I start to say. Champagne? 'I'm not really drinking till the wedding.'

'My treat. Please, I insist. Won't you let me buy everyone a little glass?'

'You can buy me a big one,' Kelly says. 'As long as you're offering.'

Cressida smiles. 'I'm offering.'

The waiter pushes two small tables together for us. 'So this is how the other 'alf lives,' Uncle Barbara says, staring around the room with its dove-grey upholstery and mirrored chandeliers. 'Do you come here a lot?'

'Not often, but it's nice after a bit of shopping. Emma, are you thinking of having bubbly at your wedding?'

'She's not made of money, you know,' Kell snaps.

'I do know. She's told me.' She points to the menu as the

waiter takes the order. 'But you don't have to spend a lot. Look, this prosecco is twenty-nine quid. If we were downstairs in Harry Gordon's, the cheapest bottle would be about fifty. We've saved twenty quid just by being here instead. And these are restaurant prices. In a shop you could find drinkable prosecco for under twenty pounds a bottle.'

'She does know what she's talking about,' Abby offers.

'Yes, it's always important to economise on the champagne,' Kelly says.

I glare at her. 'Kelly, if I didn't know better, I'd say you were taking the piss.'

'Well, I mean, come on! She's congratulating herself for saving money on champagne, Emma. Champagne. Tell her how we've had to look down the back of settee cushions to find twenty pence for the gas meter.'

'You're exaggerating, Kell. It was never that bad.'

'Speak for yourself.'

'I am speaking for myself and I'm saying lighten up, please.'

I can't meet her eyes, though, because it was that bad after Dad couldn't work. I don't actually remember raiding the settee, but I do remember Mum's creativity at teatime. It kept us from going hungry, but it put me off tinned beans for life.

My parents couldn't really blame me for not taking up the chance to go on with my education then, what with the situation at home. They howled about it for weeks, but how else were we supposed to live when most of Dad's disability allowance went for rent and Mum's carer's allowance didn't come close to making up for the cleaning jobs she had to give up to look after him when he had a relapse?

We made an ironclad deal, Mum, Dad and I. I could work for two years, but then I had to go back to studying. Which I've done. I wasn't about to break their hearts twice.

When the waiter brings the bottle and glasses to our table, nobody questions my excuse to have water instead. I don't know what I'm going to do on our wedding day. I guess I'll have to spit out my toasts so I don't get the foetus drunk.

Kelly raises her glass. 'To Emma and Daniel and their wedding.'

It could be my imagination, but she seems to clink her glass against Cressida's harder than necessary.

'Don't forget about Emma's graduating after the wedding,' Abby adds. 'That's a bigger deal than marrying my brother anyway. One only has to say "I do" on the wedding day, but getting through uni takes years of effort.' She contemplates her champagne glass. 'I can't wait till I finish and get out into the real world to work instead of having to rely on Mummy and Father for everything. That's awfully depressing.'

Abby's at uni at UCL. Her parents wanted her to go to Oxford like Daniel did, but she doesn't usually seem to do what her parents want.

'Sounds a nightmare,' Kelly says, but she's not hostile to Abby like she is to Cressida. 'Don't be too keen to leave your cushy position, work isn't all that great.' When Kell tells her she's in the century-old McCarthy family business, Abby says, 'Oh, my friend's father's in seafood too. He owns the Caviar Chateau, maybe you know him?'

Kell and I exchange glances the split second before we crease ourselves. 'Abby, you are priceless!' I say. Her question is totally innocent and completely devoid of pretension.

'I don't think our paths have crossed, no,' says Kell. 'But I'll keep my eye out for him at Billingsgate.'

'It's lovely that you're keeping your family's business going,' Cressida says. 'I rahly admire you for choosing that as your career.'

Kell spins her finger. 'Woop dee doo. It's my destiny

to be elbow-deep in fish every day. It's just a job. A career is for people who can already afford to do what they want. We're in the first camp, right Em?'

But I'm thinking about what Mum said about me having more than she had.

Cressida turns to me. 'Now that you've finished school you can find something that uses your degree. Something fulfilling and fun.'

Kelly scoffs. 'Work isn't meant to be fun. It's meant to let you live. If it was something you loved doing anyway, they wouldn't have to pay you, would they? It'd be a hobby or volunteering.'

'I love what I do,' Cressida says.

'Yeah, well, not everyone can arse around in a museum all day.'

I wouldn't call Cressida's job at The National Portrait Gallery arsing around. If anything, she's working her arse off.

But instead of rising to Kelly's bait she says, 'No, that's true, but you may as well enjoy what you have to do for a living. It sounds like that's what Emma wants too.'

'You don't know what Emma wants, Cressida. You can give an opinion when you've been her best friend for twenty years.'

Her foul mood washes over the table. Even if the champagne bottle wasn't empty I doubt anyone would want to continue this conversation.

Just when I think Cressida is about to suggest we leave – and I don't blame her – she says, 'I've got a surprise for you all. Please don't make any plans for this Saturday because I've booked the day for us all at the Berkeley Spa. It's my treat, and Emma, Daniel has already invited your mum for me. She's been dying to tell you! And we rang your work and arranged the day off with your boss. Kelly and Barbara, I hope you'll be able to take the day off too.'

I can see that Kelly is struggling with her answer. If she wants to say no, first she'll have to get her inner freebie-lover to stop screaming yes in her head.

'I'd love to, thank you,' Uncle Barbara says. 'Well, I never. Me, going to a spa. What's Colin going to say about that?'

'He'll say you're a lucky bugger,' I tell him. 'Cressida, this is too much!'

But she holds up her hand. 'I love going there anyway and it'll be so fun to go with you!' She catches Kelly's scowl. 'With all of you!'

Chapter 11

I can't stop whispering as we all creep after the white-coated woman wearing Crocs. I've never been inside a spa before. The silence reminds me of the time I went to church with Kelly, only it smells better and doesn't echo so much.

Uncle Barbara keeps jabbing me in the ribs with his elbow and pointing as if I'm not taking all this in – the walls covered in white shingled boards and the reception desk made of pale river pebbles. Tall candles flicker, though it's bright in the reception area. The only real colour comes from the little green jars strategically placed on shelves, and a few lavender and herbs planted in pots. White pots, of course. Mum hasn't said a word since we met the others in the hotel lobby and she can't stop fiddling with her hair.

I feel like The Wurzels visiting Buckingham Palace.

'You can get changed through here,' the woman wearing Crocs whispers. 'There are robes and slippers. Your first treatments start in one hour, so you may like to relax at our rooftop pool beforehand.'

Uncle Barbara looks nervous when the Croc woman leads him off alone to the men's side to change.

'See you upstairs,' I tell him. 'Put your cozzy on under your robe.'

Philippa, Abby and Cressida head straight to the lockers like they own the place. Of course they do. They're here every week. Meanwhile, Mum is standing so close to me she's practically wearing my shoes, and Kell keeps squirting complimentary moisturiser on her hand to sniff it. To borrow Daniel's pet word, this is not our milieu.

'We couldn't be luckier with the weather!' Philippa says. Her voice ricochets off the lockers. 'You'll adore the pool. God, I need some sun.'

With that she peels off her top and unsnaps her bra as Mum and I whip round to give her some privacy. 'I'm just ... I'll only be a minute,' says Mum, hurrying off to find somewhere private to change.

Abby wriggles out of her jeans and pops off her pants

before digging around in her bag to find her swimming costume.

'The toilets are through here?' I ask, shouldering my bag to make my escape before I see any more of my in-laws than I already have.

'Your mum's found them,' Abby says. 'Just through there.'

'Wait for mc,' says Kell as she follows me.

Of course, we three have a lot to say under the toilet stalls.

'Well, I didn't expect that!' Mum whispers from one side.

'Rich people have no shame,' Kell adds from the other.

'I guess they're just comfortable around us,' says I, who wouldn't willingly get naked in front of my own mother.

'Are you changing in there?' Kelly asks.

'I'm about to,' I say. There might be changing cubicles but I'm not about to go out there to look.

'Emma, I think my swimming costume is too ...'

'Too what, Mum?'

'Common. It's only from the market. I should have got a new one from M&S.'

'How can a swimming costume be common?! You're

being silly. It's a nice suit and you look good in it.' As I pull my own on, I remember my worries the first time I went to Philippa's for the party. 'Really, Mum, don't worry,' I say more kindly. 'We're here to relax and enjoy ourselves.'

'Oh, I'll never do that,' she says, 'but you two have fun. I'll be happy knowing you're enjoying yourselves.'

She can be a real martyr sometimes.

Upstairs, Kelly rushes to one of the windows at the edge of the rooftop terrace. 'Holy shit, look at this!' She nearly bashes her face on the glass that keeps uninvited breezes from bothering the spa-goers.

We are so sophisticated.

'Isn't it the most marvellous place?' Philippa says, pulling one of the deck chairs forward from under the arched portico that runs all the way around the pool, so that the sun hits the end of it. 'The chairs will fit perfectly between the pillars,' she continues, pulling forward six more chairs. 'So there's room for us all in the sun.'

'Mummy's always rearranging things up here. The staff don't like it,' Abby says.

'The staff have to like it, darling, because we're paying them. Elaine, do please sit here next to me. You too, Barbara. I'm dying to get to know you both.'

Mum looks like she's going to her execution, but Uncle Barbara bounds to the chair Philippa is offering.

Mum's trying not to stare at Philippa as she takes off her robe. She's checking to see how uncommon her swimming costume is.

I should have known. It's plain, black and well-fitting. Nothing flashy or obviously designer about it. Which means it's definitely designer.

Abby's got on a gorgeous zigzaggy two-piece that makes her look like a girl from Ipanema Beach.

I've got on a two-piece too, but I get the feeling I'm more Brighton Beach than Ipanema. Suddenly I'm self-conscious about my tummy. I've always had a little one, but knowing there's a baby in there makes it seem more sticky-outy than usual.

With Mum and Uncle Barbara holding court beside Philippa under the neighbouring arch, I'm left to referee between Kelly and Cressida.

Abby takes herself off to a chair under the arch beside us. Out of the firing line.

'This is just like the lido near us, eh?' Uncle Barbara calls to me with a smirk as he settles down. He's not at all self-conscious and I love him for that. No matter that he's so hairy he could be Darwin's missing link – which is very striking when he's wearing a dress – or that his tummy surges gently over the top of his swimming trunks. He can't stop smiling at everyone.

Philippa's face lights up. 'Yah, we'll have to come with you one day! I adore a good swim.'

I can just see Philippa's reaction to the breezeblock entrance and the hospital-like corridor that leads to our lido's changing rooms. Not that you want to change in there, though. The outside rooms are marginally better, even with their soaking floors and occasionally cast-off swimming costumes balled up on the floor. Instead of cushioned deck chairs with freshly-laundered Egyptian cotton, everyone sits on the concrete-tiled pool deck on their own soggy bath towels. And there's no plinkety plonk of soothing music wafting from hidden speakers, or if there is it's drowned out by all the children screeching at the top of their lungs. It's like a crap Ibiza pool party but with more wee in the water.

'This is bliss,' Cressida says with her eyes closed.

Kell silently mimics her.

'It *is* bliss,' I say, shooting a dark look at Kelly. 'Thank you again for doing this for us. I can't imagine a better day!'

I should have known that saying that in front of Kell

would be like waving a red rag in front of a bull.

'It's very relaxing,' she says in a way that makes relaxing sound like the worst thing she can think of. 'But when we do our hen party we'll have fun.'

'I am having fun,' I say.

'It's relaxing,' says Kell again. 'But we'll have actual fun when we go out. I'm thinking of an epic pub crawl. With costumes.'

My hand goes to my tummy, but Kell doesn't notice. She's not reading her audience very well.

'That sounds like a blast,' Cressida says, 'but I thought you weren't drinking till the wedding, Emma?'

Kelly looks like it's Cressida's fault that getting pissed in a pub isn't exactly ideal for a pregnant bride. 'Okay, something else, then, but we'll still go out and have fun, right?' she says to me. Her look is defiant and hopeful all at once.

'Definitely.'

'What about a canal cruise?' Cressida suggests. 'Where you hire a private boat that goes around London and you can bring your own food and drink on board.'

'I like that idea!' I tell her. 'Then people could eat or drink whatever they like. Auntie Rose might even be able to come, and Mum and Philippa.'

Kelly is shaking her head. 'No offense to Elaine and Philippa but don't you want your hen do to be just your friends?'

'Everyone would be welcome,' I say.

'But then we may as well just go sit in your lounge and not have to pay for a private boat. Don't you want to get out there where everyone can see us? Otherwise it's not a laugh.'

Personally, I'm happy to skip the L-plates and rubber willies. 'I think I like the more relaxed idea,' I say.

'I think it's a shit idea.'

I swing my legs off the sunlounger. 'Kell, could you help me with something back downstairs? We'll be right back,' I tell Cressida.

I round on Kelly as soon as we get back out by the lift. 'What's wrong with Cressida?'

She shakes her head. 'I have no idea. She's got some really stupid ideas, doesn't she? Floating around on a canal boat. Bor-ing. Don't worry, though, I'll sort us out something fun.'

'That's not what I mean. I want to know why you're being horrible to Cressida and trying to wreck this day for me.'

'Me?! I'm not doing anything! I'm agreeing with you, she's really—'

'She isn't doing anything but being nice. Like she's always been to you. You're the one who's being a bitch. Why? What has she ever done to make you hate her like this?'

'See? I knew it. She's turning you against me,' says Kell. 'You can see that, can't you? You used to be happy just going to the pub and now it's all champagne and spas. You know, we never used to fight before she came along.'

'We're only fighting now because you're being so unfair to her. She's probably paid a huge wedge for us to come here today. Why can't you see how generous that is?'

'You call it generous. I call it manipulative. She's always throwing money at you. I'm surprised she hasn't offered to pay for the wedding. Then you'd be in her debt forever. That's fine for some, but if you'll excuse me, I'd rather not be bought. I've got more self-respect than that, thank you very much.'

Kelly has always been a no-BS kind of person, but this is harsh even for her. 'And I suppose you're saying I don't.'

'You seem awfully pleased to make her your new best

friend whenever she opens her purse, so you can draw your own conclusions. You know what? Actually, I'm not feeling very much like a spa day today, so I think I'll head off. I'm sure Cressida can get her fee back for me if she wants to.'

'Come on, Kelly, don't be like this.'

But she's already pushing the lift button. 'Maybe I'll see you later. Have fun with your friends.'

I could follow her downstairs and try to get her to change her mind, but to be honest it's easier when she's not around Cressida. 'See you later, then,' I say.

She stares at me till the lift doors close.

When I get back to the pool, Philippa and Mum are talking about the wedding. I'm still fuming from Kelly's accusation, but I force myself to listen. I'll tell them Kelly's not feeling well when they notice she's gone. It's best to let her burn off some steam. I can yell at her again when she's cooled down.

'A garden square – I never thought of that. How wonderful!' says Philippa. 'Was it hard to arrange?'

'We've got it covered.' Uncle Barbara taps the side of his nose.

'All right, Goodfella,' I say. 'We haven't picked the exact place yet, but we've found out that the council hires out

its public spaces, so we'll just need to fill in some paperwork when we decide. Daniel's meeting me later to have
a walk around.'

'It's going to be so fabulous!'

'But low-key, Philippa,' I warn her.

'Yah, no, yah, low-key, absolutely. Like Abby said, iron-
ically casual, I've got it.'

Something tells me she doesn't, really.

'If you need any advice about the plantings, just let
me know.' Philippa turns to Mum. 'I've been a gardener
for nearly thirty years. It's just a little business, designing
and planting gardens.'

'Mummy's being modest. She's won awards,' Abby calls
over from her sunlounger. 'She's ever-so good.'

Mum's brow creases. 'But you don't have to work.'
Implication: so why on earth would you?

'Right, but, Elaine, I *want* to. I love doing physical work
every day. I've been mad about flowers since I was a child.
I trailed around after our gardener like his shadow, so I
suppose that made me his apprentice, whether he wanted
one or not.' She smiles at Mum. 'Emma tells me you're a
professional cleaner, so we both work with our hands.'

I can see Mum redden, but Philippa doesn't seem to
notice it.

'There's something satisfying about it, don't you think? It frees the mind to wander. One couldn't do that in an office.' She reaches over to grasp Mum's hand. 'We *are* lucky!'

When Mum nods, her smile for Philippa seems genuine.

Somehow my future mother-in-law might be managing to bridge a gap that seemed wider than the Grand Canyon.

Daniel's hand goes straight for my tummy when I kiss him hello at the Tube station. 'You know it's only about the size of a kidney bean,' I tell him. 'It's not much of a baby yet. More of a legume.'

'It's got fingers and toes and a nose, though. Look.' He shows me an app on his phone. 'I'm keeping track. Something new happens every day. It's incredible. That's our baby.'

My hormones must be off. Looking at phone apps doesn't usually make me teary.

One glance into my eyes sets him off too. God, the pair of us!

As we walk from the station, Daniel wants to have a look at Victoria Park. One of his colleagues went to a festival there last summer and now Daniel wants to recreate it for our wedding. 'We could have stages and everyone wearing wristbands and—'

'Smelly Portaloos and mud and falafel trucks,' I finish for him. 'Sounds romantic. Your mother would especially love the falafel truck.'

'She does have the wellies already.'

'Which she's probably not planning as part of her mother-of-the-groom outfit.'

Smiling, he leans in for a kiss. 'Possibly a bit over the top?'

'Possibly a bit. I'm thinking of somewhere more intimate. I know it's got to be a public space but maybe a little less public than headlining at Weddingbury.'

'I don't care if the whole world sees us married, Emma. I can't wait to do this with you.' His gorgeous blue eyes bore into mine.

But it's not the well-wishers walking by who worry me. It's all the fancy handbags and jewellery on the West London guests. 'I'd like something more private,' I say. Secure, I mean. No reason to give the area's pickpockets a rollover jackpot. 'Maybe with railings around it.' A guardable perimeter, in other words. 'I've got an idea. It's not far.'

His guesses get wilder as we walk away from the Tube station, till he's convinced we'll have our reception at The Globe Theatre or the O2 Arena. I almost hate to disappoint him that we won't be swooping in from a cable car.

It's not a very inspiring walk, with a mix of council flats, industrial workshops and closed-up pubs flanking the road. Then we round the corner and the confusion of building styles gives way to two-storey workers' cottages built in London's yellow brick with white-trimmed windows and flanked by wrought-iron railings. 'So? This is Carlton Square. What do you think? Do you love it? I love it.' The square itself is also ringed with black railings and if it weren't for the smattering of cars parked alongside, we could be standing here in the mid-eighteen-hundreds when the houses around it were new. 'Look at the streetlights. They're like the old-fashioned gaslit ones. Imagine how pretty they'll be at night.'

'It's gorgeous,' he says. 'We could string fairy lights around the trees and in the box hedges too.'

The grassy little square comes alive in my imagination as we step inside. I can see all our friends and family wandering along the paths there. Pretty tables set up, draped with colourful cloths and dotted with fresh flowers. There's laughter and clinking glasses and music and love. So much love.

'This is rahly perfect,' he says as we stand with our arms around each other breathing in the leafy green peace of the square. 'And the company I found can put the marquee just over there.'

'Mmm hmm.' That's the marquee I cancelled after Daniel booked it. I'm not sure yet how to replace it for free, but I'll have to think of something. 'Let me ring our vicar now. It shouldn't take long to get permission.'

Just as I think it'll go through to voicemail, Del answers.

'Excellent choice, Emma, excellent choice,' he says when I tell him about Carlton Square. 'Leave the necessary arrangements to me. Congratulations, it will be a memorable event.'

There's no doubt about that. 'Thank you, again, Del. I guess you'll let me know the fee?'

'That's not necessary, Emma. There'll be no fee.'

'Oh, you've already talked to the councillor?'

'Not yet, but there'll be no fee. Speak soon, Emma, thank you for the call.'

'It's great that your vicar can organise this for us,' says Daniel as I hang up. Dear, innocent Daniel.

I nod. 'He's got a certain way with people.'

Chapter 12

'To make up for being a total dick at the spa, you're going to do two things for me,' I tell Kelly's answerphone as soon as I've opened the dealership. 'One. Meet me at Mrs Delaney's after work today. You need to help me remodel her shop. Two. Don't make any plans for after because we're baking a cake. I'll explain when I see you at Mrs Delaney's. I finish at five.'

She'll turn up out of guilt. She's already texted twice to test the waters for an apology. She knows her accusation was way off-base. As if I'd ever be friends with a person just because she was rich.

Kell only hurt herself by storming off like that. I loved every minute of the pampering. No wonder Philippa's spa Tuesdays are sacred.

Mum liked everything except the massage. She spent

the whole time tensing her buttocks, she said, in case the masseuse caught sight of her slack behind.

I couldn't care less about my slack behind or anything else. It was all hanging out by the time I'd done my facial, foot massage and the all-over body scrub that reached areas I've probably even missed in the shower. I've never been so polished in my life.

Our vicar rang back to say that he's booked the square for us. I'd never doubt the word of a man of God, but I did ring the council anyway just to see if there's anything else we should do to make it official. I'd hate to see my in-laws handcuffed for trespassing on our wedding day.

But Del did work a miracle because Carlton Square is really ours! I was sure to thank the councillor when I saw him in Uncle Colin's. He flinched a bit when I tapped him on the shoulder, but I'm sure that's just because I startled him.

I do a double take when our boss's son strolls into the dealership just before lunchtime. 'This is a surprise.'

'Pop thinks you and Zane are slacking off. He's sent me to check,' Ant says.

'Talk about the lunatic taking over the asylum. You slack off more than either of us.'

He shrugs. 'So I'm not really here to judge, right?

What're you doing for lunch? I'm starving.' He pats his stomach. He's totally fit. The problem is that he knows it.

'You only got here thirty seconds ago. Seriously, your dad's expecting you to take over when I go. Do you have any idea how the shop works?' He's been coming in here for over a year, and I'll bet he still doesn't know where the window shutter controls are.

'Pop is deluded,' he says. 'This is just a short-term gig till my music takes off. I don't want to get too comfortable or I'll lose my edge. You've got to be hungry to make it.'

'You'd better have a back-up plan.' I've heard Ant's music. He'll definitely go hungry without a back-up plan. 'I've already told your dad that I'm only giving a month's notice.'

'He should sell up anyway. He thinks it's still the eighties. Nobody wants to work here. You don't really, do you? Zane doesn't. We've all got better things to do.'

I can't really argue with him when I'm planning to quit the dealership as soon as I find something else. Still, it's sad to think of my boss's family business going down the pan. This place'll probably be a Nando's in a few years.

Kelly raps on the front window after work just as I'm wheeling my favourite scooter back to its spot inside. Usually I sit on it for just a minute, imagining that it's mine, but not with Kell watching me.

'Hey, how was work?' she asks when I meet her out front.

'I made a sale.'

'Good. Good.' She looks at me from beneath her fringe. 'Are we okay? I am sorry for the other day,' she says. 'Did they say anything about me leaving?'

'No, everyone was too polite. Unlike you.'

'I know. I'm sorry. You're right, I am a dick. You do forgive me, though, right?' She hesitates. 'Any idea how long it might take? Just so I know.'

'I'll let you know.' I smile.

She grins back. You don't throw away twenty years just because of one fight. We both know that.

Mrs Delaney takes forever to answer our knock. 'I hope she's not sleeping,' says Kell, listening for movement inside. 'Or worse.'

'God, that's morbid.'

'Well, she's like a hundred years old.'

'Oh, look, she's risen from the dead,' I murmur as Mrs Delaney comes to the door.

'Sorry, girls, I was just finishing up a hem. Come in.'

My heart sinks as I glance around. Somehow in the weeks since I first talked to Mrs Delaney about updating her shop, it's morphed in my head from a nearly-derelict room to one that was romantically antique.

It's just a nearly-derelict room. 'Kell, I've told Mrs Delaney that I'll help her update the shop so she can sell her business, and you're going to help me. Mrs Delaney, have you got a toolbox?'

She roots around under the counter to unearth a sewing box. 'Will this do?'

There's a little hammer, a few nails and loads of yarn in the quilted box. We could probably hang a picture, but not much more. 'That's okay. I can get whatever we need from home for next time.'

Mrs Delaney is perfectly happy to let us tear her shop apart as long as it's better than before when we're done. We gather at the front window where a raised wooden display area was added at some time in the past fifty years or so. It's only plywood and sticks out into the room. It needs to go. 'Then people can see directly into the shop,' I say.

'It ain't much to look at,' Mrs Delaney admits.

The casing is flimsy and already coming away from

the frame in places. As we clear the bolts of lace from the display window, they release a mushroom cloud that kicks off our sneezing fits.

'Those used to be some of my bestsellers,' Mrs Delaney says when she returns with a stack of gardening gloves for our demolition. 'That's handmade lace from Belgium.' She runs her fingers over the cloth. 'I haven't used any of this in years. Decades.' She sighs. She must miss the old days when she wasn't just hemming skirts and trousers.

'They might be worth something to a dressmaker who's interested in the shop.'

'Nah, there ain't enough to worry about on most of those bolts, just a few yards each.'

Still, they'll look pretty on the shelves behind the counter. I move them to one side. 'Kell, help me pry this off.'

'Careful, let me do it,' she says, shooting me a warning look.

Oh, right. Sometimes I go entire hours forgetting I'm pregnant. I nearly had a heart attack after the spa day when I suddenly wondered whether all that salt rubbing might have hurt the baby. It didn't, as it happened, but Google scared the crap out of me. I'm lucky I didn't have any essential oil massages. I've got to be more careful and remember there's a baby on board now.

As the first plywood board easily gives way with a squeaking crack, a chunk of light streams in through the window. We'll need a crowbar and maybe a saw to take the frame apart, but the other sheets peel away, exposing the shop to the road, maybe for the first time since the Blitz.

'I remember it opened up like this,' Mrs Delaney says, 'when my Gran and Grandad had it. Gran used to sit by that window with her old Singer. I loved it in here, though it was bleedin' cold in winter. Grandad didn't use the fire unless he had to.'

Kelly and I look at each other. 'Have you still got your Gran's sewing machine?'

'I don't throw much away.'

That's obvious from the state of the place.

Behind the faded curtain, the back of the shop is a treasure trove of tailoring paraphernalia. The old sewing machine sits on its wooden table with a cast-iron foot pedal to propel it. I spot two more machines, one with a flywheel hand crank and a more modern one.

Kell pulls a metal frame from a pile of papers and fabric cut-offs. 'Shoe rack?'

'Nah, girl, it's for holding bobbins.' She gets Kell to hold it up with the flat side against the wall. 'Keeps you from always searching for your threads. There's another one here somewhere, a wooden one for the smaller spools.' Slowly she makes her way around the perimeter of the room amongst about a hundred years' worth of tailoring debris. She lifts a large sheet covering a hulking cabinet. It's for trimmings, she tells us, a haberdashery cabinet for ribbons and buttons and whatnot. 'It's here somewhere. I wouldn't have chucked it.'

Kelly runs her hands over the cabinet's smooth wood while I peek into its two dozen glass-fronted drawers.

'Mrs Delaney, have you modernised at all since your grandparents had the shop?'

'No need to. Sewing's not changed. Sewing never changes.'

It's a practical answer from a very practical woman.

We find two dressmaker's dummies and old-fashioned irons and, eventually, Mrs Delaney's wooden spool holder. Ten or so little racks are attached to its frame, with small pegs every few inches to hold the spools.

'My grandad was given that when he finished his apprenticeship,' she says. 'It's not fancy, but it's always done its job.' She hunts around for some colourful spools to demonstrate. 'See? It goes on the wall. Tidy.'

Kell is thumbing through a large bound book with fabric pages. There are several more stacked on a bulky table. The cutting table, Mrs Delaney tells us.

'There ain't no market for them cloths anymore,' Mrs Delaney says. 'Nobody wants your ginghams and such. Too old-fashioned. It's a shame. I used to make some lovely summer dresses with them.'

She strokes the bolt of black and white striped cloth I've just picked up from a pile. 'Ah, that one. That was for a customer's daughter's Sweet Sixteen birthday party. Every time the girl came in for a fitting she had me raise the hemline and whenever her mother came she made me lower it. It was the sixties. The mother was fighting a losing battle.'

As she unwinds more fabrics I start to see that there are memories folded into every bolt of cloth in the shop. This is more than Mrs Delaney's business. It's her life.

'Come on,' she says. 'I'll make us a cuppa.'

As we sit in the back sipping our PG Tips, I look more closely at the fabric sample books. 'Mrs Delaney, would you use these for anything now? If not, I wonder if I could have them?' I pick a fabric sample at random, a sunny floral print. 'They'd work for serviettes, wouldn't they?'

'They're about the right size,' she says, 'but they'll need

hemming or they'll only unravel on you. You could use my machine.'

'But I can't sew,' I say.

Her look of disappointment makes me cringe. 'I guess I'd better teach you how, then, before your poor Gran turns in her grave. It won't take too long once you've got the hang of it.' She roots around under the cutting table. 'Here. Cut out the ones you want.'

Kell and I cut out dozens of samples as our tea goes cold – colourful florals, ginghams, stripes and some pastel solids. As the riot of patterns pile up, an idea starts coming together in my head.

What if we made the party décor a mishmash on purpose? Like an old-timey street party in the square. That might even work better than trying to do something formal. Finding cut-rate swans or free chocolate fountains would be tricky at this point, so maybe we can convince Daniel's side that it's all *meant* to look a bit chaotic and home-made.

It's got to be worth a try. We haven't got many options left.

Back in my kitchen later, after Dad has taken Auntie Rose off to the pub to meet the ladies, I hand Kelly an apron. 'I guess you're wondering why I've called you here today.'

'You know I can't cook,' she says. 'Unless it's fish.'

'It's not fish. And it's not cooking. It's baking.' I start pulling flour and sugar out of the cabinet. 'We're going to bake our own wedding cake.'

'You've lost your mind.'

It won't even need to be huge. We'll just cut it into tiny pieces so everyone gets a taste. I'm imagining three tiers with simple white icing and some flowers picked from the garden. Maybe some strawberries or something on top.

'You've never baked in your life,' Kelly accuses.

I gesture to my tummy. 'I've never done lots of things, but it doesn't seem to be stopping me. We just need to follow the instructions. That's why there's a recipe. It's not rocket science.'

Though it is science, and neither Kell nor I paid much attention in class.

'What does "cream butter" mean?'

'It must mean liquid, right? Cream is liquid. Pop it in the microwave. It says to use a cup. No, try one of the mugs,' I say when she reaches for a tumbler.

A mug of sugar goes into the liquefied butter. 'Dare you to eat some,' Kell says.

'Baking is very precise, Kell. I wouldn't want to mess up the quantities.'

'Sorry, Nigella. Does it matter that you don't have self-raising flour? Or do you think it's the same as plain, like flammable/inflammable mean the same thing.'

'It's just practice. I'm sure it'll be fine.'

While we wait for the cakes to bake, I fish one of the cards out of the box on the table. I wanted to wait till they're completely finished to show Kell, but this is the girl I trusted first with news of my lost virginity, pregnancy and everything in between. I can't keep a secret from her when it's staring her in the face. Together we keep secrets from other people.

I find her invitation. 'For you. You have to imagine it has an envelope.' They're just some blank cards I found at the market, really, with a wrapping-paper heart stuck to the front and a little flower collage inside. But at least they're unique.

Instead of regular invitations, which all started to look samey-samey after a while, we're writing a letter to each guest telling them what they mean to us and inviting them to the wedding. Kelly's is short and sweet.

Dear Kelly,

You're my best friend in the world, my soul-mate and my partner in crime. You've always had my back and I've had yours. We couldn't be closer if we were sisters and I can't wait to share my wedding day with you.

'You're not actually going to cry over that, are you?'

'No,' she says, wiping her eyes.

'Good, because if you fall to bits, you'll only set me off.' Her emotion makes me uncomfortable. It feels like the other side of the anger she unleashed at the spa. 'They're simple, but we like them. Did I tell you about Philippa's ideas? She expects us to send everyone gifts! I've told her we want to keep it low-key, but she doesn't seem to understand what that means.'

'They don't understand anything about us, Em.'

'Well, in fairness, we don't understand them either.'

'Who cares? I'm not interested in them. They're not our people.'

'But they're going to be mine, Kell, so I have to care. They're my new family.'

At that, Kell bursts into tears. I knew they were too close to the surface.

'It's just a matter of time before I lose you,' she says. 'You're here now but soon you won't be. You'll get a great job and move in with Daniel and like you said, those are going to be your people. Then I'll be lucky to see you when you come to visit your parents. I'm just sad about it, that's all.'

'It's not going to happen, Kell. This is my home.'

'Only until you move in with Daniel. Then that'll be your home and this is where you've come from. You can see the difference, right? And I guess that's the way it should be. You're moving on. You won't be stuck down the market for the rest of your life like the rest of us. You've got the chance for more, and I do really want to see you make a different life. But I hate it too. I know I can't hold you back because that's not what's best for you, but I hate letting you go.'

The only thing I can say is that she's wrong, so that's what I do. 'And you can make a different life too, you know. You're not tied to the business. You could do something else.'

'Nah, I can't. I don't have the same drive that you do. You've always had it, swotting up in school and reading all the time. Christ, you used to go to museums *for fun*. You're not like me. You're meant to have more.'

'I have enough with you and my parents and everyone here.' Now my eyes are filling up.

'I'll rephrase that, then,' she says. 'You should have more.'

I can't think too much about leaving here or I'll sob from now till the wedding. I know it's not like the olden days when girls went off to their husband's homes never to be seen again, but I can't shake the feeling that something important is changing and I'm not sure I want it to. I'm scared. Excited, but really scared, if you want to know the truth.

The timer dings on the oven and I'm grateful to pull my mind away from my thoughts. But when I slide the tea towel along the oven handle to peek at the cakes, I can't see them over the side of the tins. My sponges look more like J-cloths.

'But baking a cake is so easy,' Kell teases.

'Shut up.'

'We could stack up a few dozen layers to get a couple inches of cake.'

'Shut up.'

I need another plan for the cakes. And one for my married life, while I'm at it.

As soon as Kelly leaves, I ring Daniel. 'I'm sorry, but

I can't live in West London. We have to find somewhere East.'

'All right,' he says, 'but where is this coming from? Is it the hormones?'

'Piss off with your hormones!' I hang up and burst into tears.

Later I text him. *Yes, hormones. But I still want to look here. xxxx*

Getting a new job and marrying Daniel is enough change for one woman. Hormones or not, I can't leave my roots too.

Chapter 13

I've been too wrapped up in wedding plans to notice how tired Dad's looked lately. Mum has to tell me. 'He's relapsing,' she says, the worry etched on her face. I feel as if a knife is twisting in my tummy. 'As usual, the stubborn git won't admit there's anything wrong, but he can't hide the spasms when he's sleeping. They're worse than last time. It's not just his legs.'

Sometimes it feels like a losing battle with Dad. Even though the disease itself isn't usually life-threatening, it's getting worse. If it turns into the more aggressive type, then he'll be in serious trouble.

It's already hard for him to be stuck in a wheelchair most of the time and not able to work when all his friends are still out earning a living. And I know he's more uncomfortable than he lets on. He never talks about what it feels like having his symptoms. Our GP, Helen, told me, though. Her favourite cousin's got it too and she keeps a blog. It's a very honest view of the disease, but it makes for uncomfortable reading, knowing it's probably how Dad is feeling too.

'I know why he's keeping quiet,' Mum says. 'He's afraid he'll miss your wedding if they send him into the hospital again for treatment.'

'That's still weeks away and besides, he'll miss more than my wedding if he lets it get worse, Mum. What are we going to do?'

'I'm telling Helen,' she says. 'Your Dad's gonna kill me, but it's for his own good.'

Our GP is as tough as old boots and never lets angry patients faze her. I once saw her wrestle a man to the ground when he went to light up out front of the pub. She'd only given him his diagnosis that afternoon and – emphysema or no emphysema – she wasn't about to let him make it worse.

I wouldn't cross her and hopefully Dad won't, either. I'd hate to see him wrestled to the ground.

'Do we have to tell Gran and Grandad about Dad?' I ask.

'Not yet.' Her eyes slide away from mine. 'I suppose

I'll have to deal with them once we know more. Have you told them about the wedding? You really need to.'

'Not yet,' I mumble.

The cowardly apple doesn't fall far from the tree.

I might not see my grandparents as much as I should, but I see them about twice as much as I want to. 'I'll go round on my way to drop off the invitations.' I can't make Daniel come with me. I love him too much for that.

The Liddell family divide stretches much wider than the few roads between our house and theirs. We used to spend all the holidays together with Uncle Colin and my uncle formerly known as Mark, and their families. I've got happy memories of playing football in Gran's garden with my cousins, even though they always stuck me in goal. Then Uncle Barbara emerged, and so did my grandparents' 'true colours'. That's what Mum calls them. True colours are never a compliment.

'Who is it?' Grandad shouts through the door when I ring the bell. Even though he can see me through the peephole.

'Grandad, it's me, Emma. I've come to say hello.'

About twenty-seven locks clack and jangle before he opens the door. 'Beryl, company.' Our hug is awkward and he smells of Pot Noodles.

Inside it's oppressively hot. That's because their rent includes utilities. My grandparents aren't the type to pass up a freebie, even when it dries out their dentures.

'Well, this is a surprise,' Gran says from the kitchen doorway, and not in a way that puts me at ease. I've done nothing wrong, yet I feel like I should apologise.

Even before she was an outright bigot she was never one of those kiss-the-hurt-away, flapjack-baking grannies. Mum and Dad tried to get me to like her, but it was no use. Constant disapproval is written all over her leathery old face.

'Sit,' Grandad finally says, moving to his favourite chair. It's more burn holes than upholstery, but he won't get a new one. One day he's going to take a nap and go up in flames.

I've often wondered what they do all day. They eat only white bread sandwiches and the aforementioned Pot Noodles, so they're not cooking as such. Even when we used to come for Christmas it was Mum and my aunties who prepared the meal. They've never had a pastime or hobby aside from criticising, and the only visitors they get are the newly recruited evangelical door-knockers who don't know any better.

'So, I have some good news,' I say as Gran perches

stiffly at the far end of the settee and flaps the neckline of her sleeveless sundress to get a breeze stirring in there. As she does this her arm waddles swing merrily. 'I'm getting married. The wedding's in five weeks.'

Right away she wants to know what the rush is. I just manage to stop my hand reaching for my tummy. What a nightmare it must have been for Mum and Dad when they got married. No wonder they wouldn't tell anyone about me.

I lie and tell her we've been engaged for a year, just to let her wonder why I've kept it from her till now.

'Who's going?' she asks.

'His name is Daniel,' I say, ignoring her question, 'he's amazing and yes, we're totally in love. Thanks for asking.'

She tries on a contrite expression, but it doesn't fit well. 'I'm very happy for you. I suppose your whole family will be there?'

She might have been the one who cut herself off from the rest of us when she stopped talking to Uncle Barbara, but she hates that we've carried on just fine without her. I know what she's asking and I'm not giving her the satisfaction of an easy answer. Instead I ramble on about Daniel's family and all his friends. Grandad nods off when I start naming all of my side who'll be invited.

'And my bridesmaids will be in pretty floral dresses. We went shopping for ideas at Selfridges.' I'm totally name-dropping. Selfridges is the pinnacle of la-di-da fashion around here. 'Me, Kelly, Uncle Barbara and two from Daniel's side.'

It's the moment she's been waiting for. She pounces. 'Who?!'

'Do you mean Kelly? You remember, she's my best mate. Or Abby, Daniel's little sister or his friend Cressida? Or do you mean Uncle Barbara?' I pause for a second to savour this moment. 'They're all my bridesmaids.'

She looks like someone just spat in her shoe. 'That's a perversion. Emma, don't tell me you're seriously making a mockery of your marriage like that. It's disgusting.'

'Having people we love in our wedding party is perverse and disgusting?'

'Don't play the fool with me. You know. And I'll tell you something else for nothing. We won't be part of it.'

'I'm sorry about that. Then I won't send you an invitation.'

'It wouldn't do you any good if you did,' she says, folding her undulating arms. 'We're not coming.'

'Then that's all settled. You're not getting an invite, so you don't need to worry. It saves me the postage.'

Grandad wakes with a snort as I stand to let myself out. 'Thanks for coming, Emma,' he says, 'see you again.'

Uncle Barbara wouldn't like that I've taunted his mother like this. Even after the venomous old cow's treatment, he's always been respectful. Which proves he's a better woman than I.

But my Gran-standing will be for nothing if I can't find a bridesmaid's frock to fit him and – even if I could afford one – Selfridges don't stock dresses for a clientele of potbellied rugby player proportions.

I know exactly who can help me find the right dress, though. I go straight to the market to see Shahrzad, who runs my favourite dress stall. She's got a curator's eye, she knows her clientele coming and going, and trends hit her stall months before they're even on the high street. If not for her dad's heart attack during their usual Friday night fish and chips, which was mistaken at the time for bad indigestion, she'd probably be designing for the catwalk now. It was the last fish and chips her dad ever ate and she and her sisters were left to run the stall to support their mum. Being a real Anglophile, though, maybe her dad wouldn't have minded dying with the taste of battered cod in his mouth, all things considered.

Shahrzad was in the year below me in school, but

we're friendly through her best mate, Stacy Boyle, who runs the shoe stall. You'd never think they were friends to look at them. Stacy's all pink hair and piercings, where Shahrzad always wears her long dark hair in a loose bun atop her head and hasn't even got pierced ears. She's as demure-looking as Stacy is bold, but together they could kit out the nation.

Shahrzad listens carefully to my request, scribbling a few notes in a little purple notebook and nodding a lot. 'Could you find something similar?' I ask, showing her the photos on my phone.

'Of course,' she says. 'It's not a problem, just give me a few days. But your in-laws are never going to believe it's really designer. I can find you something decent, but it won't be the same quality.'

Well, maybe not at first, but I've got a plan. Shahrzad is well-impressed when I tell her.

But not everyone is as enthusiastic about my ideas as Shahrzad. Daniel might have joked about my hormone flare-up and refusal to live in West London, but now he's being awkward about it. What's worse, he won't just come out and *be* awkward. He's disagreeing by stealth.

Two can play at that game. Since he won't own up and

tell me he doesn't want to live in my neighbourhood, I've gone ahead and found us some flats to look at.

Hopefully they look better on the inside than they do from the road. Sixties ex-council flats don't have the same kerb appeal as Chelsea's white-stuccoed Georgian town-houses. A few geranium-filled flower boxes along the concrete external walkways can't overcome the flat-faced brutalism of central planning.

I purposely picked an estate agent who doesn't know me or my family, in case I have to disappoint him later with my opinion on his offering.

He's on his phone in front of the building, but there's no sign of Daniel. Avoiding anything that could be mistaken for eye contact, I throttle up past him and around the corner. I've made enough small talk with enough estate agents already to know it's best to avoid.

'Daniel, are you close?' I ask when he answers his mobile.

'Two minutes away. Are you there?'

'I'm around the corner. The estate agent is waiting out front. Text me when you get to him, okay?'

'Did you just do a drive-by? Coward.'

'I'm simply checking out the neighbourhood.' Like I don't know it by heart. 'See you in a minute.'

When I walk around the corner Daniel pretends he's surprised to see me.

The agent shakes my hand. 'Did you have trouble finding it?' he asks, not looking up from his phone.

'Nope, I looked at Google maps.'

'Didn't I see you drive past a minute ago? On a blue scooter?'

'Erm, I was just looking for parking.'

My eyes follow his to all the empty spots right in front. 'Scooter parking, I mean. Does this road not have scooter parking? That's a shame,' I say like it's a real deal-breaker.

Daniel reaches for my hand as we make our way inside.

The agent struggles with three locks on the flat's bashed up flat-fronted door and we have to walk single file down the short corridor into the main room. The walls are a dirty yellow and the carpet could have come from Uncle Colin's pub.

'It does have a lovely big window,' says the agent, gesturing to the single window in the tiny lounge. 'With a nice view.'

We both peer out the window at the buses on the main road. 'And constant traffic noise,' says Daniel to me.

'It's double-glazed,' the agent points out.

Which is fine, as long as we never open the window. 'The bedroom's at the back. It's quiet.'

And dark, I see as we tour the rest of the flat. Being the polite man he is, though, Daniel makes encouraging noises when the agent shows us the boiler cupboard (extra storage!) and the fact that there are two freezer drawers in the fridge (room for fish fingers *and* ice cream!).

'All right, I admit it. That was depressing,' I say as we walk hand-in-hand to my scooter. 'But we'll find better. I promise.'

'As long as it's close to a Waitrose,' he says. 'I'm not sure I can rahly cope otherwise.'

'Pah, Waitrose. We've got better. At the market you can just ask what's best instead of trying to poke at fruit through fifteen layers of packaging. There's the butcher for meat and Kelly for fish, and loads of bakeries. You could have fresh baked bread every day if you wanted.'

'Right, but would it be the seeded bloomer with honey that I like? You know how important my seeded bloomers are.'

And you know how important my family is to me, I think, even though he sounds like he's only joking.

But he won't get off the bloomin' seeded bloomer, and then he starts on the fact that there's no Costa Coffee or Waterstones. On and on and on he goes, till I start to think he really is serious.

Here I was, willing to pack up my entire life for him and move away from my family who, by the way, are ten times more important to me than his are to him, and he's grizzling about it being a little inconvenient to get his morning latte. 'Oh, for fuck's sake, Daniel,' I finally explode. 'Just get Ocado to deliver your bloody shopping and stop going on about it!'

He mistakes this for a joke too, saying they probably don't deliver to my postcode, and what about his favourite red-pepper hummus and kale chip snacks? Where is he supposed to get those all the way out here?

That's when I lose it. I mean, I really lose it and it all pours out. About my family being more important than his and what am I supposed to do, just swan off to Chelsea and let them starve so that he can have his flippin' red-pepper hummus and bloody kale chips?

It's a classic case of misreading your audience (from both of us), but I can't stop, even though he's doing his best to backtrack. It all tumbles out, about Dad being ill again and how all he cares about is his stupid Waitrose, and if he'll put kale chips in front of my family, then what does that say about us?

I mean, really, what does it say about us? We do come from different worlds. Here I am, scrambling to make sure my parents and Auntie Rose don't go without and he keeps spending huge sums on ridiculous things that we don't strictly need. Which I cancel and then he just goes and books something else, which I have to cancel again. Even if I do find a decent-paying job after the dealership, we'll always have different opinions on things like Costa Coffee and kale chips. 'I'm never going to value Waitrose like you do,' I tell him when I've calmed down enough to stop shouting. 'You deserve to know this now before it's too late.'

There's the whisper of a smile playing at his lips. 'And I'm sorry, Emma, but I might never want to shop at a stall in the road where people's hands have been all over the fruit. But this isn't a deal-breaker, is it, because I'd eat fruit off the pavement if it meant being with you.'

'We're just very different,' I say, 'and I'd never make you eat fruit off the pavement.'

'I love you, Emma. I'd give up Waitrose for you.'

I'm touched that he'll change his shopping habits for

me, but my ringing mobile cuts off the rest of his decla-
ration. Mum, I mouth, answering.

Auntie Rose is gone again.

'I'm coming with you,' Daniel says, taking the spare
helmet off the back of my bike.

'What about Harold's dinner?' We're supposed to be
there in an hour. I've already had to cancel once because
I felt so ill and exhausted. They must all think I've got
serious digestive issues.

'I'll cancel,' he says. 'We have to find Auntie Rose,
right? We're in this together. When we find her I can
bring her back home in a taxi.'

Not if. When.

But she's not at the pub and nobody there has seen
her. The clerk at the Jiffy Mart shakes his head when I
pop my head in. She's not in the laundromat watching
the dryers spin or at June's parents' caff. And she's not
at the cinema where she and my Gran sat through three
showings of *Jaws* back-to-back.

She's not anywhere.

I can't stop my hands from shaking as I ring Kell and
tell her what's happened. 'Tell everyone down the market,
Kell, will you?' I look up at the darkening sky. She won't

have taken her umbrella, wherever she's gone. 'She could be anywhere. We've got to find her.'

I don't find out till afterwards that Uncle Colin and Uncle Barbara left the pub to join the search, with only a promise from the regulars that they wouldn't abuse their trust. Stacy Boyle headed into the estate to knock on doors and more than a dozen of the other stallholders shut up to go look for Auntie Rose.

A couple of the phone stall boys spot her out walking along the verge on the A12. For such lairy lads they're touchingly tender with Auntie Rose, carefully helping her out of their car when they deliver her back to the house.

For the first time since she started wandering, Auntie Rose doesn't pass off her disappearance as a little adventure. She's as scared as we are.

Chapter 14

If ever we needed a family conference, now's the time. Auntie Rose might be sitting in the lounge as usual, happily munching her way through a packet of custard creams dunked in tea, but what about the next time she wanders, or the time after that? She made it to the A road when Mum turned her back. Given a few hours she could end up in Scotland.

I'm worried about her state of mind as much as her safety. She's always seen her wanderings as a bit of an adventure, dismissed with a knock on the temple and a cheery 'What am I like?!' She wasn't bothered that she couldn't explain them. This time it scared her. She keeps saying she doesn't want to go out, like walking through the door will trigger some kind of migratory urge that she won't be able to ignore. It's heartbreaking.

She looks so old now. Despite being solidly built, she's actually quite frail. I didn't notice that before, maybe because she's so gobby. She is in her seventies, the same age as my Gran when she died.

Gran had a heart attack in the middle of getting her weekly permanent wave. One minute she was moaning about our Eurovision entry and the next she was as flat as James Fox's ballad would be a few years later. To this day Auntie Rose won't watch the contest. Maybe if we'd had someone like Katrina and the Waves again that year, she says, her sister would still be with us.

Mum agrees about the family conference, but she thinks having Auntie Rose there will only make her feel bad, since she's the main agenda point. I say that's exactly why she should be there. Dad doesn't mind either way, as long as we settle things before Auntie Rose escapes again.

'To be clear,' I say to Mum the next afternoon when Auntie Rose is upstairs in the bath, 'this isn't the family conference and I'm not discussing Auntie Rose without her being here, because it's wrong. I just want to know what you're planning. Because, Mum, we can't put her in a home. She's always lived with her family and I—' I take a shaky breath. 'I can't let her be sent away like some unwanted old person in an institution. It's not fair.'

I couldn't live with myself if we sent her away, even if she went to live in one of those posh places where they do chairobics and have choices for pudding. The thought of her sitting there, without us, without the neighbourhood that she's known her whole life, sets me off. And it's not just hormones.

'We can't just chuck her out of her home because she's inconvenient, like she's the family dog who starts to wee on the floor. You wouldn't do it to a dog. I'm not going to let you do it to my auntie.'

Mum's hand flies to her cocked hip. 'I suppose that means you'd object to us putting her down too? The vet says it's painless.' She laughs at my expression. 'Well, get over yourself. What you're suggesting is just as mad. Nobody's going to send Auntie Rose away. She's our family.'

That makes me feel slightly better when Mum gets Auntie Rose to come downstairs after her bath. Everyone knows right off that this is serious. Mum even opens some packets of prawn crisps, so either she thinks we'll be here past teatime or that we'll need some kind of savoury distraction.

It's not a good start when Auntie Rose – who's been

walking around like she's waiting to be punished for something – bursts into tears when Mum says we all need to talk.

'I won't do it again!' she wails, reaching straightaway for the crisps. 'I'm sorry I caused you trouble, but I won't do it again. I don't know what came over me, but it won't happen again.'

It's awkward to get my arms round her while we're sitting round the kitchen table. 'This isn't your fault. You can't help when you wander. We all do silly things sometimes.' I want to reassure her that nobody's perfect, but the only thing I can think of is my accidental pregnancy and it's not the time to bring that up with Dad here.

She takes a great big sniff but can't quite suck up the drip at the end of her nose. Mum gets her a piece of kitchen towel.

'Maybe Auntie Rose should see Helen?' I say. 'If she can figure out why it's happening, then maybe there's a cure. Isn't that worth a try?'

'I know why it's happening, my love,' she says. 'It's from the strokes.'

She says this casually and Mum and Dad are clearly not surprised by this news. Unlike me.

'Strokes?! Auntie Rose, you need to be in hospital if you're having strokes.'

She waves off my protest. 'They're only little strokes, Emma, nothing to worry about.'

'And you've all known about this for how long? A decade? Great. Did you never think I might be interested to know?'

'We didn't want to worry you,' Dad says.

'I hate to break the news, Dad, but having to go find Auntie Rose whenever she wanders has been pretty worrying.' I've never thought of my family as particularly secretive, but first there was Mum's pregnant wedding day and now this. 'Anything else you'd like to tell me, before it comes out casually in conversation?'

Mum shoots me a warning look. She probably thinks I'm talking about Dad's relapse. 'Don't be so dramatic,' she says. 'Auntie Rose, you do get confused sometimes and it's not safe for you to be wandering all over God-know's-where. So how are we going to help this situation?'

'I don't know,' Auntie Rose says. 'Put a bell on me?'

'We could microchip you like Sheila Larkin's Pomeranians,' I say.

Mum can't resist. 'That Sheila Larkin! The way she

goes on about those dogs you'd think they'd won Crufts. It was only a titchy little show at the church. Honestly.'

'I'm only joking, Auntie Rose,' I say. 'And I don't think a bell would work.'

Dad holds up his hand. 'What we'll do is fit the doors with two-way locks that need a key going out and coming in. That way if you do forget and want to have a wander, one of us can always go with you. But Rose, would you be happy for us to do this? I don't want you to feel like you're a prisoner in your own home. We'll find an alternative if that's the case.'

But Auntie Rose is nodding her approval, so I guess she's not too bothered by her prison sentence.

Nobody wants to give up their independence, do they? Not when it's something we fight for from the time we're little. Dad completely lost his rag when he had to give up the taxi and start relying on Mum more. There he was in his mid-forties, having to get help from his wife to do up his flies. And worse sometimes, when his legs gave way and he needed the bog. So Auntie Rose is being cool about it, considering we're about to lock her into her own house. She's not blaming her gaolers, but that doesn't stop us blaming ourselves.

* * *

Kell's got everyone meeting at the pub to help us sort out the rest of the wedding details now that we've got someplace to throw the party. It's times like these that I appreciate my best friend's pig-headedness. It's useless saying no to Kelly when she wants something. And now she wants everyone's help.

Coming to the pub with Auntie Rose feels different now. We all try acting normal and she's pretending she's not been let out on good behaviour. But Mum is nervy and Dad's being a grump. He blames our fussing, but I know from the way Mum keeps tucking her hair behind her ears – which she knows isn't attractive with the way they stick out – that she still thinks he's keeping things from us. Her hair-tucking shifts up a notch when our GP, Helen, strolls in.

This isn't a night out, I realise. It's an ambush. In a second Dad is going to realise it too. 'I thought tonight was about our wedding?' I whisper to Mum while he's saying hello to June and Doreen at the table beside us.

'Can't it also be about your father?' she snaps back.

What am I thinking? Settle down, bridezilla. 'Yes, of course it can. Sorry.'

Daniel's glances dart between Dad and Helen and he

keeps doing cartoon-style eyebrow raises at Mum. It's lucky he doesn't play poker. 'Come help me with drinks,' I tell him before he unravels completely.

Poor Daniel. This is new territory for him. Not everyone's family gets quite so involved as ours. When I wonder aloud what Philippa would do in Mum's situation, knowing Dad needs the doctor, he says she'd leave Dad to it. That's when I have to tell Daniel that, even if it's uncomfortable, I'll never just leave him to it.

Helen's at our table when we come back with the drinks. Too late I remember that she knows about the pregnancy. And, more importantly, that Dad doesn't. 'Hi, Helen! Sorry, I'd have got you a drink. No alcohol for me, though. I'm off it till the wedding so I'll fit into my dress!' Dad gives me his what-is-wrong-with-you look. No wonder. I've delivered these awkward lines in a pitch so high the local dogs are probably howling. I sound like a lunatic. 'I'm getting my dress tomorrow from Mrs Delaney and I can't wait!'

She smiles easily. 'I don't blame you, I ate hardly anything before my wedding. That was the last time I ever fit into my dress, mind you!' She's ever the professional. She's probably got secrets about everyone in here. 'And how are you Elaine? Jack?'

'Fine, thank you,' my dad says, matching her conversational tone.

Her eyes bore into his. 'Are you sure? You look a bit tired, actually. And flushed.'

'It's warm in here. I shouldn't have worn a jumper. I'm fine,' he snaps, turning from her to sip his drink. The tremor in his hand is obvious. His pride breaks my heart.

'Jack, you're shaking,' she says. 'I can see your hand. Any other symptoms?'

'No,' he says. 'Just leave it, Helen.' But as he reaches for his pint again he misses at first.

'Jack, it's your vision too, isn't it? I'm sorry, but you know I can't ignore this, not as your doctor.'

'Then as my friend,' he murmurs. 'Please, Helen, not now.'

'I didn't notice the vision,' Mum says. 'Jack, why didn't you tell me? I knew you weren't sleeping well with the leg spasms.'

'Will you just leave it, Elaine!' Our drinks jump when he slams his hand on the table.

Auntie Rose scolds Dad from where she's sitting with her ladies. He doesn't usually shout.

'Will you please come see me?' Helen asks, ignoring his bluster. 'I can assess you and if it's a relapse, we need to start treatment as soon as possible. You know that.'

'Not till after the wedding,' he says, grasping one hand with the other to stop the shaking. 'First I'm walking Emma up the aisle.'

Mum retucks her hair. 'But you can have the treatment done before the wedding, Jack, and get it over with. Otherwise you may not be well enough to be there.'

'I'll be there, I promise you that. I'm not ending up in hospital again.'

So Mum was right. That's what he's worried about. The last time he let Helen put him through the course of treatment there were complications and he ended up in hospital for almost a week. He had to be on a drip.

'That won't happen again,' Mum says, even though none of us, not even Helen, can guarantee that.

'Helen, I'm walking my daughter up the aisle first. Walking, Emma, do you hear me? End of.'

When Dad says 'end of' it's pointless arguing with him. That's the phrase that killed my Dr. Marten dreams when I was ten.

But then again, I did eventually get those shoes.

At least he's agreed to go to Helen for an assessment, if not the treatment. I just hope his symptoms don't get any worse.

The atmosphere at our table lifts slightly as our friends and neighbours start filtering into the pub.

We all turn to look when PC Billy Bramble arrives. He's still in his copper uniform, which puts everyone a bit on edge. In jeans, Billy's the idiot we all know. In uniform, he's an idiot with the power to arrest. The phone stall boys greet him like the frequent friend he's become. Their stall trading doesn't always live up to the market inspector's expectations and Billy's been known to smooth things over for them. I wouldn't say he's corrupt – and neither would he, obviously. He helps the people he likes.

'Billy too?' I say to Kell. 'You're covering your bases.'

'You never know. He could come in handy,' she says. 'We need all the help we can get.'

Shahrzad and Stacy from the market are squabbling over which of them is better at doing make-up as they demonstrate on Doreen and June. Doreen's makeover is as understated as Shahrzad is, but, with Stacy's help, June could headline next year's drag queen awards. Uncle Barbara is sitting with them but won't let a mascara wand within ten feet. He wants to look like a man who enjoys a frock, not a man who enjoys looking like a woman.

When everyone's got their drinks, Kell raps her pint

glass on the table. 'Right, you lot. We're going to sort out all the wedding details for Emma and Daniel before we leave tonight.'

A few people start chanting 'Lock-in!'. Uncle Colin answers with 'Piss off!'.

'Who can cook?' she continues, wrenching the attention back to herself. 'Hands up if you can cook, anything at all. We need ideas for a few big dishes.'

June's hand shoots into the air. 'I'm a dab hand at chicken and mushroom pie,' she says. 'I can do a few big trays.'

I can't take her seriously now that she looks like an elderly white RuPaul.

Not to be outdone, Doreen shouts, 'Beef stew with dumplings!' She turns to June and says 'Everyone loves it', like June hasn't eaten her stew hundreds of times.

When Mum adds her lasagne to the menu and Kelly offers to help her make it, Daniel reaches for my hand. This just might work! Nobody can cook for a hundred people alone, but together we can do this.

Shahrzad and Stacy fight over who can make the most delicious green salads and finally agree to have a salad-off, which I hope goes better than their makeover competition, and Uncle Colin shyly offers to do a huge pot of creamy mash.

With every offer my eyes threaten to overflow. They're doing all this for us – Daniel, me and my family. Every dish is a little 'I love you'. I've never been so grateful for my tribe.

Then my colleague, Zane, raises his hand. 'You got a cake yet?'

'Emma made a corker the other day!' says Kell. 'Forget criminology, she's got a future in baking. Actually, it *is* criminal.'

'No, Zane, we don't have a cake.' Just to check I ask Daniel 'You don't happen to know how to bake, do you?'

'Sorry, no, my skills lie in panna cotta.'

'Panna what?' Auntie Rose says.

'It's an Italian custard,' I tell her. She rolls her eyes.

'I could make you one,' Zane offers. 'Actually, I need to tell you anyway. I'm starting catering college. Marco went spare today when I told him.' He's clearly pleased with this reaction. 'Don't look so shocked.'

I don't mean to, but Zane's the last person who comes to mind when I think of cake baking. Or cooking. Or college. 'Sorry, of course, yes, thank you, Zane. You'll wear a hairnet, though, right?'

He laughs, reaching for his springy dreadlocks. I hope that means yes.

Everyone's got ideas to help with the food and drink. June's Karen's youngest, who runs the family caff, is going to loan us all the plates and cutlery. Uncle Colin can get us a few barrels of beer if we can figure out where to put the taps, and the phone stall boys have a connection who can get us bottles of champagne for next to nothing.

'Your friends are incredible,' Daniel says as we kiss goodnight outside the pub later. 'They really pull together for each other. You're so lucky.'

'We're so lucky,' I say. 'You're part of the family now too.'

He nods. 'We are so lucky.'

A few days later Mrs Ishtiaque stops me on the way to Mrs Delaney's. As usual she's as colourful as her borders. This time her saree is electric blue. 'Emma, I am hearing everybody is helping with food,' she says over our garden wall. 'I would like to make you the curry you love. It is my gift to you and your Daniel.'

I shouldn't be surprised that our news made its way

round the neighbourhood so fast. And it's very kind of Mrs Ishtiaque to offer, but curry doesn't really go with the rest of the food. I can't get Philippa's fear of falafel carts out of my mind, and curry definitely won't impress Daniel's side. So I thank my neighbour but decline her offer. I just wish she wouldn't look so sad when I do.

'What did Mrs Ishtiaque want?' Mum asks as she locks the front door. The new bolts are taking some getting used to, but so far Auntie Rose hasn't complained about living inside Belmarsh.

'She just offered to make a curry for the wedding. I thanked her but told her she doesn't have to.'

'But you love her curry.'

'I know, but it's just not …'

'Good enough for your new in-laws?' Mum says.

'I was going to say right for a picnic theme.'

Mum purses her lips but doesn't say any more.

Chapter 15

Kelly is already at Mrs Delaney's and she's brought one of the phone stall boys with her. Jez was in our year while his brother, Gazza, was two years ahead of us. They used to be plain old James and Gary before puberty made them street. For a time all their friends walked around with nicknames like Fazza, Bazza and Razza. Most of them dropped the names and the bravado by the time girls actually started paying attention to them but not Jez and Gazza.

Kell and Jez did have a thing in sixth form for about a minute and a half. Kelly claims a lapse in judgement and I'm sworn to secrecy about the whole thing. It's not because Jez is a minger. He's actually quite fit, with a cheeky smile and nice brown eyes. But Kelly's sister used to be mad for him and she'd be gutted if she knew.

'He wouldn't lend me his tools, the git,' Kell says when she sees us. 'I don't know what he thinks I'm going to do with them. So he's come along as an extra tool.' She smiles at her own joke, which Jez either ignores or doesn't catch.

'I know what you'll do, you'll cut your arm off,' he says, picking up a hand saw. 'And then you'll blame me. Leave it to the man.'

Kell, Mum, Mrs Delaney and I watch Jez try to saw through one of the horizontal four-by-twos in the frame by the window. He's standing with his feet wide apart for leverage, his shiny tracksuit bottoms showing several inches of pants in the back. He gets the saw started, but then it keeps stopping every few inches and he has to start the cut again. 'What is this, Mrs Delaney?' he asks. 'It must be solid oak. We'll need a bigger saw.' He hacks at the support till the saw sticks again and bows alarmingly.

Finally, my mum steps forward. 'Jez, you're going to hurt yourself. Give it here.'

Jez doesn't want to hand over the saw, but he also doesn't want to go against my mum. And I wouldn't advise it anyway.

Mum squares up to the frame, places the saw at an

angle and starts cutting up the supports with swift easy strokes. 'Why don't you put some tea on? It won't take me long to get this down.'

Jez is mortified that my mum is more of a man than he is. He shouldn't be. She's always done the DIY in our house. But no one's surprised when he doesn't stay for tea.

While Kell brews us a cuppa, Mrs Delaney and I go into the fitting area that's curtained off at one side of the shop. 'I can't wait to see it,' I whisper as she unzips the dress bag.

'I just hope it fits,' she whispers back.

The satin is cool against my skin as I slide the dress up over my hips and get my arms through the sleeve holes. 'The moment of truth,' she says, buttoning up the back. She yanks the material with both hands, squeezing an 'Oof!' out of me. 'Good thing your gran left some room at the seams,' she says. 'I'll have to let it out. Hang on, let me get the top buttoned up so your mum can see it on.'

Not only has Mrs Delaney taken off the horrible puffy sleeves and satin dog collar, she's also calmed a lot of the pouf in the skirt. It's no longer a giant billowy toilet roll topper. She's put a few short pleats in at the top so that it fans out from my hips, but the miles of satin are gone.

When I step out from behind the curtain Mum does a little squeal. 'It doesn't look like the same dress!' she says. 'Mrs Delaney, you're a genius. You've even changed the shape.'

'And I added a train, but, Emma, if you don't like it, I can take it off.'

That's what's different about the back. There's a gorgeous lace overlay that swishes gracefully behind me. 'Is this the material from the window?'

Mrs Delaney nods. 'It was wonderful to get to work with it again, and with the pared down skirt I think it works. Luckily the satin is as yellowed as the lace. Do you like it?'

'I love it! It looks so vintage. I can't thank you enough.'

'There's no need to, girl. You're fixing up me shop and that means I might have something to grow old on. Course, that's years away.' She laughs. 'Now, get out of the dress so I can take it out.' She turns to Mum. 'That's gonna be a big baby.'

We all stare at her.

'It's obvious. At least, it is to me. Do you have any idea how many pregnant girls I've made dresses for in my lifetime? That's why I took out the volume and added the little pleats. More material will only make you look bigger. These darts hide a multitude of sins.'

'You won't tell anyone, will you?' I ask.

She shakes her head. 'I'm like a vicar,' she says. 'A woman of the cloth, if you will. I'm not telling nobody nothing.'

Mrs Delaney offers to show me how to use the sewing machine so I can stitch up the serviettes. I mean the napkins.

'Could I help you?' Mum asks. 'I'm not great at sewing, but I can use the machine if there's an extra one about.' Her smile is shy and most uncharacteristic. 'I'd like to do this with you, Emma, just you and me.' I spring a leak when Mrs Delaney says my gran would be proud to see us.

While I'm trying not to stitch my fingers together, Kell goes to the front where Mum has dismantled the frame. 'I'll clear up this wood before Her Highness arrives.' I know she's only doing it so Cressida can't look down her nose at us. Not that she would, but that's what Kelly's worried about. She didn't want Cressida and Daniel's sister coming out our way in the first place, but Mrs Delaney needs to take their measurements so she can pretend to make their dresses.

I'll be gobsmacked if we pull this off. The actual dresses are in a bag in the back in a variety of sizes – Shahrzad can send back whatever we don't use. She got an extra one that Mrs Delaney cut fabric samples off to show Abby and Cressida when they come in. She'll claim the cloth is being delivered in a few days.

Mrs Delaney wrinkled her nose when she saw the dresses, though luckily not in front of Shahrzad. She's going to take them completely apart, restitch the seams straight and alter them for each bridesmaid, with a custom lining. We've stacked up bolts of pastel green, yellow, pink and blue lining for Cressida and Abby to choose from when they come in. Kelly says she'll pick whatever Cressida doesn't.

'Am I interrupting?' the vicar calls from the doorway. 'What a pleasant surprise this is, eh, Mrs Delaney? We didn't expect a crowd.'

It takes me a second to recognise him. It's not that I haven't seen him loads of times, or that he's dressed any differently than normal in jeans and a V-neck jumper over his clergy shirt and dog collar. I've just never seen him here at Mrs Delaney's. Which begs the question.

'What brings you here, vicar?' Kell asks.

'I've come to play cards with Claire, as is my custom,'

he says. 'But I can see you're busy, Claire, so I'll come back at a more convenient time.'

'Thanks, Del, I should be free in an hour. I just need to do the fittings for Emma's bridesmaids.'

'Ah, the wedding. July the fifteenth, isn't it? I trust the plans are all underway.'

'There's still a lot to do, but I think we're getting there, thanks.' He might be a man of God, but I don't want to burden him, seeing as he's not on the holy clock with me. He is a very good listener, though, and I find myself listing all the details we haven't yet worked out.

'Music?' Kelly helpfully reminds me. 'You don't have that either, though I don't know why you don't use my Spotify account. I've told you I'll do you a playlist. It'll be killer.'

'But I can't.' I've told Philippa that we're auditioning bands. I've even sent her sample tracks I found online. 'It needs to be live music.' Mum and Dad might have enjoyed Kelly and the phone stall boys lip syncing and dancing to Beyoncé at their anniversary party, but that won't impress Philippa.

'Why not Del?' Mrs Delaney wonders. 'He's got a beautiful voice. And his playing ain't 'alf bad, either.'

The vicar graciously accepts this praise, adding,

'Emma, I would be greatly honoured to perform, should you require any musical entertainment. However, I am but a humble amateur music maker and I understand if you want instrumentalists of a higher calibre for such an important day. I bow to the superior talents of those classically trained, and await your judgement.'

At this he makes a sweeping bow. Despite talking like he's on stage doing Hamlet, I think he's just offered to play some tunes for us.

'That would actually be amazing, Vicar! Could you really?'

With his hand on his heart he could be a beauty queen who's just won the crown. 'I'll be delighted to do what little I can to contribute to your day. Will you have a piano in residence or should I make arrangements for mine?'

A lush vicar with a travelling piano at our wedding. I'll just have to spin it somehow to Daniel's side so it doesn't sound like we're getting a sozzled amateur belting out show tunes.

'What about tables and chairs, Vicar?' Kelly asks. 'Don't you have loads of them at the church?'

She shrugs at me when I protest that it's too much to ask. But Kell believes that more is more when it comes to favours. Del says we can take whatever we need from the church hall as long as we get everything back in time for the Slimming World meeting.

'That's music and tables and chairs sorted,' Kell says when Del leaves. 'Food is all set and Colin's doing the beer. Bridesmaid's dresses are in hand, thanks to Mrs Delaney. What else?'

'Serviettes will be done,' says Mum, stitching carefully along the hem of a piece of calico. 'And I think I can make bunting too, if Mrs Delaney doesn't mind us using the cloth samples. What about tablecloths?'

My eye falls on Mrs Delaney's bolts of lace piled on the shelves. 'Maybe we could borrow some of this?' I ask her. 'If you're sure you won't use them for dresses, that is.' Imagine how romantic the tables will look draped in Belgian lace.

She shakes her head. 'They're too yellowed for me to use, so you're welcome to them.' She nods approvingly. 'They'll be lovely with the serviettes.'

That's the tables done, then, with plates and cutlery from June's Karen's youngest. 'I can't believe this is really happening!' I squeal.

No sooner do I congratulate myself for pulling in every favour I can to throw this wedding, than I realise that it's never really been about the budget. Thank goodness for all my friends and family, but even without them we could have had a tiny ceremony and a drink at the pub after, like Mum and Dad did.

This is about Daniel's family. They can't know it's a simple affair on a shoestring, not with all Philippa's champagne and chocolate and hanging garden and chandelier and silver frame suggestions. I can't be the cause of her falafel cart shame. It's got to look as slick as Will and Kate's wedding, with all the pomp and glory that entails. Philippa and her lords and ladies are expecting the wedding of the century. We can't deliver anything less or I'll always be the daughter-in-law from the council estate. Of course it's all smoke and mirrors. Like the Wizard of Oz, I can't let them see the man behind the curtain.

Cressida and Abby are due at Mrs Delaney's any minute. I feel bad chucking Mum off the sewing machine when she's so carefully hemming the serviettes. 'They don't know we're making them ourselves,' I explain, collecting the squares of cloth. 'The less detail that Daniel's side knows about everything, the better.'

'I wish you weren't so worried about what Daniel's family think,' she says, gathering her bag up to go. 'I know you want to make a good impression. I just worry that you're trying to be something you're not, when you're fine just the way you are now.'

That's rich coming from my mum. My Twiggy-wearing, take-photos-of-the-bogs, redecorate-the-lounge mum. Instead of getting angry when I say this to her, though, she just looks sad, and then I feel bad. Sometimes it's not worth standing up, even when you know you're right.

Cressida and Abby turn up exactly on time for their fittings and don't seem to suspect any double-dealing. Kell and I have moved the old sewing machines and the gorgeous haberdashery cabinet out front along with the other props like the old irons, bobbin holders and dress-maker's dummies. Mrs Delaney has dressed one with an elegant gold evening dress that she made for her fortieth birthday party, and a beautiful pale blue fifties style one for the other. She's even got one of Mr Delaney's hand-made tweed suits – may he rest in peace – hanging from a brass hook on the wall. Hopefully it doesn't whiff too badly of mothballs.

'Such a gorgeous little vintage shop,' Cressida says to Mrs Delaney, who accepts the compliment with a regal nod of her head. 'Have you been here long?'

'My great grandparents were the first here,' she says.

I can tell Cressida is imagining an old East End full of chipper Eliza Doolittles selling posies and having hearts of gold. People often do that. There's romance in hindsight.

'Look at this suit!' Abby says, rushing to Mr Delaney's tweed. 'Wouldn't it look fabulous on me?'

Kelly laughs. 'You'd be swamped in tweed.'

'Yah, no, but I could have something like it made in my size.'

Mrs Delaney nods. 'Of course, if you'd like me to. I'll show you the tweed samples. First, though, let me get you both measured.' She hands them the fabric swatch that we cut from the dress. 'Emma has chosen this. So if you'd like to pick a lining, any colour here, I'll run it up for you.' She gestures grandly to the pastel bolts of cloth.

'I've only had handmade clothes once, when I was in Bangkok,' Cressida says as Mrs Delaney quickly measures her. 'Usually I just go to Harrods or Harvey Nicks, but this is so much better! I'm going to have you make all my clothes.'

Mrs Delaney nods before throwing me a look behind Cressida's back. She's trying to get rid of her shop, not find new customers.

Daniel and his groomsmen are waiting for us at the Tube after the fittings. 'And the Krays murdered their rivals in a pub just down there,' Daniel is saying, pointing in the wrong direction. He's obviously enjoying playing tour guide for his best friends, unfettered by historical or geographical accuracy.

'Actually, it was one Kray killing one rival, and it's not all murders round here,' I say, introducing Kelly to Daniel's flatmate and his best friend, Seb.

There's a slight chance that if Kelly can manage to get on well with Seb, when he's Cressida's brother and nearly identical in personality, it might be harder for Kell to hate her.

There's nothing to dislike about Seb. He's as friendly as Daniel and Jacob, and it doesn't hurt that he's tall and broad-shouldered with thick brown hair and green eyes that are fringed with dark lashes. Like the others he does like his coloured chinos, but then Kelly once went out with a goth so she's no stranger to awkward fashion. A pair of yellow trousers shouldn't faze her much.

The walk to the pub is loud and laughy and I'm the only one who knows that Kelly is being quieter than usual. She's still smarting over our argument earlier, which was a stupid one to have in the first place. You'd have thought I was rejecting our very way of life when I dared suggest somewhere nicer than the Cock and Crown to take everyone tonight. What's good enough for us should be good enough for them, she'd claimed. Maybe I'd rather just go out in West London and not even let them see where we live.

That hurt, to be honest. She's acting like I'm ashamed of where I come from when I'm just trying to make a good first impression. As any normal person would. You wouldn't turn up to someone's house for the first time without making an effort, right? That's all I'm doing: making an effort for our guests.

'There's not a free table,' she complains when we squeeze into the bar That Is Not Her Choice. It's a typical Victorian East London boozer with dark wood panelling and shiny brass fixtures. 'There's always a free table at the Cock.'

'There's a nice selection of ales, though,' says Jacob, scanning the taps. 'This is a great pub, Emma, thanks for finding it.'

Kelly can't say much to that.

'It looks like there might be a table leaving outside,' Seb says. 'Shall I go hover? It'll be a squeeze, but we're all friends.'

Abby goes with him to lend her five-foot-nothing intimidation, leaving the rest of us to tussle over the round. The men agree to split it, with Kell and I getting the next one.

'Leave me here, I could die a happy man,' Daniel says. 'I'm in ale heaven!' One of the few things he and his dad have in common is their avid support for the Campaign for Real Ale. Though I think most of their enthusiasm comes from drinking, not conservation.

He gets sad sometimes about not being closer to his dad. I can't imagine not being close to a parent, given how much time you spend together. But maybe that's part of the problem when you go away to boarding school. He's dead set against sending our child away. As if I'd ever let him anyway.

'I've found us an option for music,' I say when he's ordered the drinks. I've got to make this sound most appealing, so forgive me for what I'm about to say. 'I thought it would be fun to incorporate some East London traditions into the wedding, since we're getting married here. So I've arranged an authentic, erm, vocal pianist for the party.' My glance at Kelly begs her to back me up. I hope she knows I mean Del. Vocal pianist?! 'It's one of our wedding traditions. Everybody does it.'

Kelly nods. 'There used to be a ... vocal pianist in every pub in East London in the olden days, so I guess it was natural that we started having them at our weddings. All weddings have one ... they're good luck. I don't know why we didn't think of it sooner.'

Maybe we can pass off the entire wedding as an East London tradition. Would they believe that unmatched serviettes bring good luck too?

He's probably imagining a grand piano, top hat and tails, not a drunken vicar balancing a pint of lager on an upright.

We all sit outside at the picnic table sipping our drinks in the evening sun and chatting easily. Even Kelly is relaxing. She won't talk directly to Cressida yet, but at least they're at the same table.

Then Abby says, 'Mummy has an amahzing idea. Wouldn't it be fun if we all wore super glam false eyelashes for the wedding? She thought it would make Barbara feel comfortable.'

'I'm not sure super glam falsies would suit me,' Jacob jokes.

'That's very kind,' I say, 'but Uncle Barbara doesn't wear make-up. He's not trying to look like a woman. He just likes dresses.'

'Right, Mummy will be disappointed,' Daniel says. 'She thought he went all out with the wig and make-up and everything.'

'No, sorry.'

'Well, anyway, she had another idea that you're going to love,' he says.

'Even better than the chocolate fountain?' Seb says. I can't tell if he's taking the piss.

'I'm really sorry that didn't work out,' says I. 'Terrible to go out of business in the middle of the wedding season like that. And with the others already booked up.'

'I know, that was bad luck,' Daniel says. 'But this idea is even better.' He grasps my hand. 'Butterflies!'

'... butterflies what?'

'To release after the ceremony. Everyone can have a little box to open for when we come out of the hall. Instead of rice.'

I frown. 'You want our friends and family to throw butterflies at us?'

'Right, yah, no, they'd just flutter around us. Mummy can source local species for us.'

'Gorgeous,' Cressida murmurs. Yah, yah, yah, they all say.

I can just imagine the poor confused insects let loose

into traffic on the main road. They'll end up decorating everyone's windscreens. 'But, Daniel, practicalities aside, I'm not sure the budget is going to stretch to a live butterfly release.'

'Well, darling, there'd be plenty of money if you'd stop being so stubborn and let my family help,' he murmurs.

'You know why we can't do that,' I snap. 'We've talked about it and you agreed, remember? So indulging your mother in these impossible ideas isn't helping anyone.'

'What am I to do, Emma? She only wants to be involved, and I'm constantly having to disappoint her. Frankly, that's not nice for me or for her and I'm getting weary of doing it. I've been stuck in the middle between the two of you for months.'

And I've been stuck with a fiancé who just can't get his head around the fact that we have a budget.

Jacob raises his glass. 'Welcome to marriage. Isn't this fun?'

Everybody laughs while Daniel and I glare at each other.

Chapter 16

There are paint swatches taped all over the lounge wall when I get in from work. 'Mum?'

'They're coming,' she says. 'This magnolia doesn't work. What colour was Philippa's lounge? Have we got time to have Dad's chair re-covered? These covers don't zip off.' There's a butter knife on the seat. Has she been trying to pry the fabric off the chair? Her eyes follow mine to the bald settee cushions. 'I've sent Dad and Auntie Rose out to get those cleaned.' Her hand dives into the blue carrier bag she's holding. 'Is this the right bar soap? What kind did Philippa have?'

'How should I know, Mum?'

'Well, you used it. What did it smell like? You *did* use it, didn't you?'

'Of course I used it. I just didn't know that it was a

detail I'd have to recall later. I take it this is all about Philippa and Hugh?'

She's examining the table tops and muttering 'beeswax' to herself. 'Daniel rang here. They can come on Thursday. They want an authentic East London experience. I could kill your father for mentioning the pub. What are we going to do?!'

'Do you want me to ring Daniel and cancel them?'

'God, no, what would they think? Help me move this settee. It'll look less common in front of the window.'

'Mum, please, you've got to calm down. And you can't repaint the house. Philippa's not the Queen. They don't even have to come here. We'll meet at a restaurant or something.'

But Mum shakes her head. 'They're driving over.'

Now I get it. She isn't about to miss the chance for Sheila Larkin to see Hugh's Rolls-Royce in front of our house. 'Maybe they could drop off you and Dad after dinner instead and you could drive round and round the estate until Sheila looks out her window.'

'You wouldn't be flippant if you'd seen how that Sheila Larkin lorded her car over your father and me. She once offered to give us a ride, like we were street urchins. Well, she's not the only one with a flash motor.'

'Except it's not our motor, Mum.'

'They're your in-laws. As good as.'

I know better than to argue with Mum when it comes to that Sheila Larkin, and our settee could use a clean anyway, so I leave her to it.

My concern is for Dad, not whether our cushions are fluffed enough for my mother-in-law's inspection. He did go see Helen for tests, but we didn't need to wait for the results to know that he's relapsing. We can all see it. Both his hands are trembling now and though he still won't admit he's in pain, his gasps give him away when his legs spasm. 'Dad, we have to talk,' I say when he's returned from the dry cleaners. 'You need to go in for treatment. You know you do.'

'I'm not having this conversation.' When he starts to wheel himself away, something breaks in me. I throw one of the cushions at his wheels. 'No. You have to talk to me.'

He tries manoeuvring around the cushion, but it's stuck under his wheel. 'Emma. You're actually hindering a disabled man?'

'If you mean a selfish pig-headed disabled man who won't get the treatment he needs, then absolutely. Oh, yes. I did say selfish. Because that's what you're being. Stubborn and selfish. How am I supposed to enjoy my wedding day knowing you're in pain? Or not even there! How's Mum supposed to feel about it, huh, tell me that? Dad, you have to have the treatment now. It's the only chance you've got to be well in time.'

He runs his shaking hand through his hair, making it stand on end. 'And what if I end up stuck in hospital for your wedding? What about that? You know what happened last time.'

'I want to take that chance. And you should too. If you're in hospital, then at least I'll know you're getting the treatment you need to feel better. Dad, I love you. I don't want to see you hurting like this.'

'I hate this disease,' he growls. 'It's taking me away bit by bit.'

I kneel down beside his chair, pulling the cushion from under the wheel. I feel a little bad about that now. 'But it's not. You're still here. I need you here.' I put my head on his knee and he strokes my hair like he used to do when I was little.

'I'll do it,' he murmurs. 'For you and your mum.'

'Thank you, Dad.'

The house smells like fresh paint, the bar soap nestles in its new dish in the bog and the settee cushions never looked so good. Dad put his foot down when Mum tried to move his chair to the back garden, so she's filled it with throw cushions and is hoping for the best.

Dad's nervy but not because of Daniel's parents. He doesn't really care whether they're impressed with our fancy bog soap. He'll start his treatment tomorrow at hospital. He'll need an IV drip for the super-strong steroids they'll use to try to alleviate his symptoms. That makes tonight his last hurrah, hopefully for just a week or so. He's taking it awfully well, considering that Mum's making him hurrah with Philippa and Hugh.

Their arrival in the Rolls-Royce couldn't be more perfect. Sheila Larkin is out front watering her window boxes. 'All right, Sheila?' Mum calls across the road as she goes to greet the car at the kerb. All the closer to see that Sheila Larkin's face. 'I don't think you've met Emma's fiancé and his parents?' Mum's look of triumph is almost worth the two coats of definitely-not-magnolia paint she made me put on the lounge wall.

'What a lovely garden!' Philippa shouts, admiring Mrs Ishtiaque's borders. 'All the gardens look so nice.'

Mum deflates a bit, since Sheila Larkin's window boxes are obviously included in the compliment.

Daniel sweeps me up in his arms for a kiss. It didn't

take long after the pub for us to make up, but we can't kiss away the underlying problem. All this time I've blamed Philippa for having to put on such a flash wedding, but it isn't only her. She's trying to help, and she's excited about the wedding, but it's Daniel who keeps missing the point. He might say he understands about the budget, but I don't think he really does. When you're born with a silver spoon in your mouth, you don't expect plastic ones at your wedding.

And I'm not about to be the one to let our wedding be a disappointment. If Daniel, Philippa and the others want something special, then they're going to get it. Just as long as they don't look too closely into the details.

'You look gorgeous,' Daniel whispers in my ear as I bat his hand away from my tummy.

Right, gorgeous and fat. My jeans are undone under my top. There's no doubt now that I'm pregnant, though at least I'm only feeling sick some of the time. It's the need to sleep that's killing me. Zane covers for me at the dealership so I can kip on the floor behind the counter, but he's about to start catering college. Who's going to guard my nap breaks when he goes?

You'd think Philippa's never seen a ceiling light or a carpet before, the way she oohs and aahs over every little thing in our house. This delights Mum, naturally, who doesn't need any encouragement. If we don't get out of the house soon, she'll be opening her wardrobe for Philippa to show off her M&S dress collection.

At the chippy, we have to wait for a table that can accommodate Dad's wheelchair. He really didn't want Daniel's family to see him in it, but his leg spasms make walking too tricky even with crutches. He eats hardly anything when our orders come, claiming he's not hungry. But I can see his hands shaking. He's afraid he'll throw bits of fish and chips all over the table and embarrass us.

Despite having absolutely nothing in common except Daniel and me, our parents manage to keep the conversation moving. It's only when it turns to weddings that I feel my shoulders start to tense up. 'Our friends literally cannot wait for the wedding!' says Philippa. 'George and India were at a gorgeous do in Italy the other week, right on Lake Lugano. Have you been? Right, you must go, it's rahly spectacular. The guests all took speedboats from the ceremony to the reception!' She turns to me. 'How will we get to the reception, darling?'

Not by speedboat, I can tell you that. 'It's not very far between the two,' I say instead. 'Only about a mile. I guess everyone could walk.' Their faces are blank. 'Or ... the bus?'

'There'll be black cabs decorated with ribbons,' my dad says, 'to take the guests to the square.'

This is news to Daniel and me.

Philippa thinks this will be an amahzing touch of local colour and she wants to know about all our plans. She's been asking through Daniel all along, but I've fended her off with little details here and there. I can't very well pretend I don't hear her now when our knees are practically touching under the table.

The half-truths and lies trip off my tongue. By the time we're full of fish and vinegar and the bill arrives, we've got antique Belgian lace and bespoke hand-stitched napkins for the tables. Hugh is very impressed by the craft beer that's being brewed especially for the wedding. Well, technically that's true, since it *is* being brewed for sale to customers, and we are customers ... and we are having a wedding. Mum just manages to pretend her laugh is a cough when our vicar, Del, morphs into a concert pianist.

'What do you think about the butterfly release?' Philippa asks.

'Oh, the venue won't allow them,' I say. 'It's an environmental hazard.'

'But they're completely natural,' she says.

'I know. Health and Safety has gone mad, eh?' Daniel glances my way. Hopefully he assumes I'm just saving face because we argued over those damn butterflies. If he starts wondering about my other excuses, he might work out that the chocolate fountain people didn't really shut down because the world is running out of cocoa beans and the marquee hire company didn't actually double-book us with a country-and-western music festival. This wedding illusion is as much for him as it is for his family.

For the record, I will come clean with Daniel as soon as the wedding is over. Then we'll have a heart-to-heart talk about money, because we were clearly raised with different views about it. It's not a huge issue, especially when Daniel's family are so generous, but Daniel could definitely benefit from some down-to-earth common sense, just in case our future isn't always full of butterflies and chocolate fountains.

On our way to the Cock and Crown I manage to get Dad out of earshot of the others.

'Did you really arrange for taxis from the town hall, Dad?' It's a brilliant idea. I wish I'd thought of it.

'No,' he says, reaching back to pat my hand on the

push handles of his wheelchair. 'But I will. My mates won't mind doing me the favour. I could see the idea of walking wasn't going down too well. We can get Daniel's side there in taxis anyway. Walking's good enough for the rest of us.'

'Thanks, Dad.'

People turn curiously when we enter the pub, but it's probably only to get a look at Hugh and Daniel, who aren't at all embarrassed to be wearing matching green trousers. Philippa shouts a greeting to Uncle Barbara when she spots him behind the bar. She rushes over to kiss his cheeks like they're old friends. 'Lovely dress, Barbara! Oh, hellair,' she says to Uncle Colin. 'You must be Barbara's brother. You're the spitting image! I'm Philippa Billings.' She extends her hand. 'How d'you do?'

'Is that them, then?' Auntie Rose wonders, rather more loudly than she probably realises. 'Poshies, eh?'

I'm at her side so fast that it makes me slightly dizzy. 'Auntie Rose! Come and meet Daniel's parents!' It might be a squeeze getting everyone round the table, what with June and Doreen there too, but it's safer having them where I can keep an eye on them. And kick them under the table if I need to. But everyone is on their best behaviour and I'm starting to think that maybe our families aren't such chalk and cheese after all. They may not holiday together in the South of France, but they can manage the occasional drink.

Then Daniel goes and nearly ruins it for us.

I'm telling Philippa about my exams and upcoming graduation, and about the kind of job I want now that I'm qualified. I've been looking into a great charity that sets up youth activity centres around the country. Not only does it give bored teens something to do, it's got loads of support and educational services too. It would be the perfect job for me. 'I'd probably have to start at the very bottom,' I tell her, 'but it's exactly the kind of work I want to do.' I'm in the middle of excitedly telling her about how it's more appealing than social work since it gives the kids opportunities through the centres before they get into trouble, when Daniel decides to add that I don't have to find a job now.

The table falls silent.

'What do you mean, darling?' Philippa asks her son.

'Well, since she's getting married,' Hugh supposes, 'he means there's no need to rush into a job. Daniel can support them, right son?'

'That's a bunch of BS!' Doreen says. 'Our Emma hasn't gone to school for five bleedin' years not to use her degree.'

'Yah, that is BS, Hugh,' Philippa repeats. 'Daniel, darling, that can't be what you meant.' Her words are kind, but her tone is a warning.

Of course it's not what he meant. He meant that a pregnant woman doesn't usually rush off to look for a new job, but we can't say that, can we? I stare at Daniel. He'd better come up with something quickly.

The look of panic on his face slowly recedes as he shakes his head. 'Right, yah, no, of course not. All I meant was that with the wedding planning and the dealership, Emma has effectively been working two jobs. Three, if you count all the coursework and revising. She should take some time off afterwards to relax. She doesn't have to find another job right now. That's all I meant.'

Everyone seems to accept his explanation, but we're never going to keep this pregnancy quiet till after the wedding if Daniel isn't more careful.

Chapter 17

Despite Mum's manic cheeriness, the mood was sombre at home the day after Philippa and Hugh's visit, as we helped Dad get ready for his hospital stay. He's been in for three days now and is as grumpy as ever, so it seems that he's feeling more like himself. The steroids knock him for six, making him nauseated and giving him mood swings like a pre-menstrual woman (his words). I just hope they're also doing their job.

If I'd known Dad was going to be at the same hospital where we've come for my scan, I'd have rebooked it instead of having to creep through the corridors. If he catches us, I can always say we were coming for a visit, but then I'll miss the scan.

'Here, have some more water,' Daniel says, pushing the bottle into my hands.

'Please, no more. I'm bursting already. If they're running late, I might have an accident.' We check in at reception and trade smiles with the other couples sitting round the room.

This is getting very real. In six months, give or take (that's what the dating scan is for), we'll be parents. I have to give Daniel credit. He hasn't wavered once since finding out he's about to have a family. He's going to be an amazing father.

'So when *can* we tell people?' he asks as another couple is called in. 'I rahly can't keep it to myself for much longer.'

'No kidding. You're the worst secret-keeper I've ever met. But please wait until after the wedding. I just don't want your family to ... misunderstand. Please. This is important to me. Not till after the wedding.'

He kisses me. 'Then it's important to me too.'

In the examination room the sonographer starts sliding the wand around my gelled-up tummy. 'Hmm,' she says.

'Is something wrong?!' I can't quite see the screen from my position on the bed. 'Daniel, look at it, what's wrong?' What if our baby has a tail or two heads or something? It must be noticeable for the sonographer to react like that. I just know it's because I had a drink before I knew I was pregnant. I also had takeaways and not from the good Indian either. It was the dodgy Indian. Now I've got a dodgy curry-deformed baby.

'Are there any twins in your families?' the sonographer asks, digging the wand around some more. 'Because I'm seeing two embryos. It looks like you're having twins. Congratulations.'

It's a good thing I'm lying down because I feel faint. Daniel sits on the bed next to me. I guess he's not feeling so well, either.

Twins. Not a baby with a tail or an onion bhaji for a head. Two babies. That's twice as many to look after, to feed and change and house. Twice as many to carry and give birth to and worry about. And I thought we were just going to find out my due date.

Daniel is completely over the moon. He's got a list of names by the time we leave hospital. 'A ready-made family!' he keeps saying. But I've barely got my head around being pregnant, and now twins? I really wish my Gran was alive to talk to. She went through this with Uncle Colin and Uncle Barbara.

Then again, maybe I'd rather not know what I'm in for.

The next week is manic with everything we've got to do for the wedding, and I don't think I've ever been so tired in my life. Mum says she should have suspected twins with how dead on my feet I've been. I'm not even allowed to perk myself up with caffeine, only pure adrenalin and fear that this whole charade is going to come crashing down when Daniel's side finds out that our wedding is more Primark than Prada.

The one bright spot in the week is Dad's return home. The disease still has him in its grip, but the treatment has seemed to help, and hopefully his symptoms will lessen quicker because of it. He's adamant that the wheelchair will not come up the aisle with us, even though he's not able to walk very well yet. That sounds like he's back to his normal stubborn self, though he's also admitted that we were right to make him go for the treatment, which is most unlike him.

If Kelly didn't have her heart so set on my hen do, I'd beg off and go home to sleep for about a week. I really don't feel like squeezing into spandex to go to the pub.

'Maybe with a cardi?' I say to my image in the mirror. But Kelly is frowning at me. 'I told you the catsuits were a bad idea.'

'Well, if you weren't having twins it wouldn't be so noticeable.'

'I'm so sorry my egg split. How thoughtless of me. And twins aren't any bigger than one baby at this stage.'

'Then you're just a porker,' she says. 'You're right, though. You can't wear it like that. Try this over it.' She throws me a sparkly purple tutu from her bag. 'Pull it up a little higher. That's it. Problem solved.'

She puts her arm round me as we stare at ourselves in the full-length mirror. 'And just when I didn't think I'd ever find the perfect accessory for pink spandex.'

'Do you want the cape?' she asks.

'Think it's overkill? The outfit is so classy now, I'd hate for it to become tacky.'

'Give it here, then.' She ties the black cape round her neck and unzips her gold catsuit another inch. She looks like a slaggy superhero.

When Kell got so upset at the spa about Cressida's hen do suggestions, I thought she was just being petty. But now I think I get it. She's always made a huge deal out of our milestones. We've celebrated them all together and some of the best nights of my life have been with her. For her this is about us, about the fact that we're best friends. So I'll make an arse of myself in a stupid pink catsuit and a purple tutu that hides what looks like one of Mum's throw cushions stuffed down the front. What kind of person would I be if I didn't let my friend humiliate me in front of everyone I know?

'C'mere,' Kell says, pulling me back in front of the mirror. 'Ready? For posterity.' She snaps a dozen photos with her phone. 'It's only going to get messier from here.'

'Speak for yourself. I'm on the apple juice all night.'

'I am speaking for myself.' She grins at me.

Shahrzad and Stacy Boyle are already at the Cock when we arrive to jeers from the regulars. 'Gawd, this is mortifying!' Shahrzad says, shrinking further into her chair. 'At least you two turned up looking like twats too.' She's got on a shiny bright blue spandex mini-dress that she keeps yanking down to cover a few inches of thigh.

'Take the stick out of your arse and enjoy it,' says Stacy, lounging with her arm thrown along the back of the booth where she's sitting. She's got none of Shahrzad's qualms about form-fitting dresses. Hers is identical to her friend's, hugging every bump and curve. And Stacy has a lot more bumps and curves than Shahrzad.

As much as I want to curl up under the table and go to sleep, I'm starting to feel excited for the night ahead. I don't know what's in store, except that there's a pub crawl and we end up back here so that Mum, Auntie Rose and her ladies can meet us.

Catcalls start up from around the bar as everyone catches sight of Uncle Barbara, but they die down quickly as the men realise that whistling at their mate could be misconstrued as 'being a gay', as Auntie Rose puts it.

Uncle Barbara looks just as uncomfortable as they do. 'Too much?' He glances down at his outfit. 'I can change.'

'Well, that settles it. Barbara wins,' Kell says. 'You look fantastic.'

'You really do,' I say as he practically runs to our table. His black and white striped spandex dress isn't too tight or too short. It shows off his legs and disguises his tummy. Frankly, I wish I was wearing it.

Kell grabs her purse. 'So, now that we're all here, should we have a swift half? I'd like to propose a toast.'

'We're not all here,' I remind her. 'Abby and Cressida are coming. They are coming, aren't they? Kell?'

She sighs. 'Yes, they're coming. They're supposed to meet us. In fact, they're late.' She crosses her arms.

When they turn up at the Cock a few minutes later they're as surprised by our outfits as we are by theirs. Cressida's got on a really nice sparkly top and a pair of skinny jeans with her platform heels and Abby's in jeans too, with a flowy peasant blouse. In other words, they look perfectly normal.

'You didn't tell them?' I say to Kell. It's not so much a question as an accusation.

'Didn't I? I thought I did. Anyway, we'd better be going.'

'I'm so sorry we're not dressed up!' Abby murmurs as we follow Kelly along the road to the next pub she's chosen. 'Kelly must have told me and I just forgot, what with exams and everything going on.'

But I know the fault isn't Abby's, and she's only collateral damage. Kell will do anything to make Cressida feel unwelcome, even when it means she looks miles nicer than the rest of us.

Cressida pulls the neck of her top open and looks down it. 'Damn.' She notices me staring at her. 'I thought I had on a different bra. I could have just worn that. At least I'd blend in a little bit more. I rahly am so sorry!'

I'm about to assure her that she's not the one I blame when Abby grabs Cressida's arm and whispers something. 'We'll catch you up,' Abby says to the rest of us. 'Where's the pub, Kelly? I've just got to run in here first.' *Tampons*, she mouths to me.

Our arrival at the new pub causes the expected commotion. Unlike in the Cock, we're strangers here and

Kelly couldn't be more pleased with all the attention. It's exactly what she wants. Which just makes Abby and Cressida's arrival a few minutes later all the more irritating for her.

The punters cheer them into the pub too.

'What the fuck is she wearing?' Kelly says.

'It's a ... catsuit?' I say.

It is literally a catsuit, and not one of those sexy ones, either. Made of some kind of furry brown and white blotchy fabric, the baggy costume engulfs Cressida's slender figure and the hood covers her shiny dark hair. It looks itchy and horrible. Not to mention extremely flammable.

Cressida grimaces. 'Well, we're not going to let you look like a prat if we don't.' She links her arm in mine while Kelly scowls.

Abby is dressed as a panda. 'It smells. I don't think it's the first time someone has worn this costume,' she says. 'I need a drink.'

Everyone loves the costumes, which briefly makes Kell the odd one out till she gets over herself. Which only takes about half a pint. And then I couldn't really ask for a better night, even if I am the butt of most of the jokes.

Then Kell's banter starts to take on an edge. I don't think I've said anything to offend her, but it's hard to know with her being so sensitive lately. At first I'm the only one who notices it, until I make a perfectly innocent compliment about Daniel's local pub.

'Why don't you just go, then?' she says. Her expression is fierce. 'Go to West London and have a nice life with your ...' I gasp when she points at my middle. 'With your new husband and your new life and your new best friend.' Her finger aims at Cressida now. 'I can't compete with that.'

There's a second of stunned silence. Then Cressida nearly shouts. 'Oh, seriously, Kelly, even you cannot be that stupid.' I think Kell might hit her for that. 'You're not competing with anything. Or anyone. Can't you see how much Emma loves you? You're blind if you can't. Do you realise how lucky you are to have the kind of friendship that you and she have? It's unbreakable. I'm not a threat to you. I could never be. You've had a lifetime together. I'm thrilled that Emma wants to be my friend because she's an amahzing person and I'm rahly growing to love her. But I can't touch what you've got with her. I never will.' She shrugs. 'Lifelong friends are lifelong friends. You're not giving Emma much credit if you're threatened by the idea that you're not her one and only friend. And if you think a change in postcode is going to end that, then you really are a stupid girl.'

'I'm not going anywhere,' I say quietly. 'Kell, you're such a muppet sometimes. How can you lose me when you're the best friend I have ever had, and the best friend I will ever have?' I lean in to her ear to whisper, 'Who was the first person to know I was pregnant? I mean the very first person? You were. Even before Daniel.' Then, so everyone can hear, 'Look at me. Would I be dressed like this for anyone but you?'

Her smile is sad. 'I am a muppet. I'm sorry. I don't mean to bring everyone down tonight.'

'It's not me you need to apologise to.'

Kell shakes her head. 'No. It's Cressida. I know. I am sorry. You haven't done anything wrong. You're a nice person and I've been horrible. I can't promise I'll never be a bitch again.' She laughs. 'I seem to have a gift for it, but I'd like it if we could at least start over.'

'I'd like that,' Cressida says, and she seems to mean it.

'Group hug!' says Uncle Barbara. 'Come on, gather it in everyone.'

There's a half-hearted cheer when we get back to Uncle Colin's, but the joke loses some traction for the men the second time around. Mum, Auntie Rose and the ladies are waiting for us. Luckily they aren't in spandex. We've just managed to get everyone round one table when the pub door swings open. 'It's a policeman, for Emma!' Abby cries, pulling notes from her purse. 'Finally, the stripper.'

My blood runs cold at the announcement.

'A stripper!' June says, reaching for her own purse.

'Put your glasses on, for pity's sake,' says Auntie Rose. 'It's only Billy Bramble.'

If Billy is about to strip for us, then everyone had better keep their glasses off. 'Billy, please tell me there's not Velcro in that uniform.'

June starts thumping her fists on the table shouting 'Take 'em off!'. That should definitely be her last sherry.

'No, it's only that I've got a line on tents for you. Kell mentioned you need some.'

'S'cuse me just a sec. Boring wedding arrangements,' I say to everyone before following Billy to the bar.

I've been obsessing over the weather forecasts for weeks. Yes, forecasts, plural. Sometimes I have to look at eight or nine different sites before I find one that promises a sunny wedding day. That forecast better be right because otherwise Philippa can forget about silver frames or personalised chocolate bars. We'll have to hand out wellies and rain hats.

'I can get you all the tents you need,' Billy says, looking pleased with himself. His somewhat small eyes would look piggy if he didn't smile all the time. He always seems to be on the cusp of a joke that he never actually tells.

'That's such a kind offer, Billy, thank you, but we haven't got a lot of money to pay for tents. I'm just hoping it doesn't rain. I've been rubbing rabbit's feet a lot for luck.'

'There's no cost. Just let me know how many you need. I can borrow them from work. They're event tents.'

Of course! Police are always having fundraisers and such.

'A couple of us can set them up for you on the morning. I wouldn't risk putting them up in the square overnight unless there's someone to watch them. You're not thinking of setting up before, are you?'

Uncle Colin hears his question. 'We'll all do it on the morning. A load of us are going over first thing to take care of it all. Not you.' He points at me. 'Your mum said to make sure you're not running around on your own wedding day. We'll do everything. Have you sorted the bar? I can't have me taps gettin' half-inched you know. You need somewhere secure.'

I thought maybe a couple of the lads could keep an eye on them, but Uncle Colin's not so sure. They won't be much use after a few drinks. But there really isn't anywhere we can lock up if we need to. We'd need a shed of some kind for that, and we can't start putting up sheds in the square. Just a little stall of some kind – if it had solid sides – would do, but everyone down the market uses barrows and tables and tents. The barrows may look a hundred years old with their chipping red-painted wheels and warped wagon bed, but that's because they are a hundred years old. They do have a shabby kind of charm.

Could we rig solid sides on one of the fishmonger barrows? It's an idea. A rolling bar. And we could pile ice on the base, just like he does with the fish, only with lager.

A rolling fishmonger. Of course. Why didn't I think of it before? The fish van! 'Kelly!'

She thinks it's a wonderful idea and Uncle Colin is happy to let his taps, barrels and glasses be loaded into her van for the day. 'You've got the toilets hired, right?' he says as I'm congratulating myself on my ingenuity. 'All that beer needs somewhere to go.'

'Oh, shit.'

'A lot of wee too,' he says. 'And permits, I expect. Right, Councillor?'

The councillor confirms that we can't just park a Portaloo at the roadside. And we must have them. Philippa won't enjoy squatting behind the hedge.

But that's hundreds of pounds we don't have, and a stinky temporary toilet doesn't exactly scream luxury. I've got to find a better way.

When I drive over to the square the next day after work, it's even prettier than I remember. Everything is so lush and green and the little brick terraced houses surrounding the square are chocolate-box pretty. Even through my biased eyes it's an impressive sight – romantic, historic and perfectly London.

I hope the residents realise how lucky they are to live here. I think they must. All the houses look well-tended in this little oasis, tucked away from the hustle and bustle of the city. They've got everything they could want here – only steps from the main road, the markets, pubs, restaurants and cafés. There was even a café on the square, though it looks like it's closed down. I wonder why? I'd love to have a café just next door.

Peering through the scratches in one of the large

soaped-up front windows, I can see that it used to be a pub. The curved bar at the back is piled with boxes, and tables and chairs are still dotted around. Someone tried their hand at a shabby chic décor to turn it into a tearoom – china teapots and cups sit on antiqued white shelving and a chalkboard with a long list of teas leans against the bar. It would have been a cosy place for a cuppa. So what happened?

'Arrears,' the councillor tells me when I see him later in the pub. He shakes his head. I'm not sure if that's a reaction to the café's demise or because I've bothered him when he's trying to have his pint in peace. 'I worked with the owners for over a year. Even wrote off a chunk of their arrears, but they kept falling behind. You've never heard excuses like theirs. Their dog practically ate their rent cheques.'

'So what's happened to them?'

He shrugs. 'Gone to screw over another council, I imagine.'

'They're definitely gone? And the council owns the building?'

He starts to look like a hunted animal. 'Why are you so curious?'

'Well, I suppose they must have toilets in there? Ones

328

we might be able to use for the party? If we promise to clean up after?'

'More promises,' he says, noting that I'm not going away. He probably could resist me if the vicar wasn't listening to our conversation. He knows he can't resist the vicar.

'Well done on the loos,' Uncle Colin says later. 'We'll make a few signs so the punters know they can go into the café. So it looks like everything is just about ready. Barbara's shown you the flowers, yeah?'

'Flowers? No.'

Uncle Colin shakes his head. As the older brother by four minutes, he does this a lot to Uncle Barbara. 'Useless. Come out back.'

There's a decent-sized garden attached to the back of the pub. It used to be open to pub-goers, but Uncle Colin wanted space to grow his tomatoes, so he converted it to private after he took over and moved in upstairs.

He flips on the floodlight. Dozens of plant pots are neatly lined up on the decking next to the barbeque and Uncle Barbara's sunlounger.

'Barbara and Zane got them from the park.'

I gasp, looking at the riot of colourful flowering plants. 'They nicked them?'

He laughs. 'When has Barbara ever broken the law in his life? He ain't no tea leaf. They rang the ranger and asked to have 'em when they replanted the beds. He and Zane went over and dug 'em up. He's been tending them for weeks for you, so you'll have something for the tables.'

They must be full of pollen because I can feel my eyes begin to water.

Chapter 18

'I was beginning to think you were avoiding me,' says Daniel's godfather, Harold, stirring the risotto on his gleaming industrial cooker as we perch on the stools around the polished concrete kitchen island. It's a huge space, but Harold isn't diminished by it. Maybe his shock of white hair gives him the gravitas to fill it. It looks positively leonine against the black jumper and jeans he's wearing. Or maybe it's just his big personality.

His house might look like Philippa's from the outside – huge, white and imposing – but it couldn't be more different within. There's nothing traditional about Harold's gaff. He and his wife had it gutted when they bought it, he tells me. Having grown up in our fifties council house, where the only period feature was the avocado bathroom suite, it seems a shame to strip out all the character, but Harold is a man who looks to the future, not the past.

'It was the eighties,' he says, gesturing with his ladle around the kitchen. It's a giant white cube in the base-ment of the house, with a conservatory leading out to a long narrow garden. The kitchen table is black Formica and steel, the tall chairs clad in shiny black leather. It looks like Harold's wife – currently spa-ing in the countryside – might have tried adding a feminine touch here and there, but it's lost in all the leatheros-terone. I hope Daniel doesn't get his taste from his godfather.

'Nobody wanted overstuffed sofas or Edwardian tables,' Harold explains. 'All the old paintings felt oppres-sive when we were young, too much like the houses of our parents.'

'Mummy and Father didn't seem bothered by the old stuff, though,' Daniel says. 'Most of our furniture has come down through the family. I wonder if I'll be more traditional when it comes time to decorate our flat. I've never had anywhere to live with my own furniture.'

Somehow I doubt our children will cherish my dad's reclining chair or my French-Ikea bedroom set. 'I like modern things with a traditional twist,' I say. 'So maybe we won't fight too much about it.'

'I can't imagine you two arguing about anything,' Harold says.

I startle them both with my laugh. 'We didn't row before planning the wedding,' I explain.

'We haven't rowed very much,' Daniel objects. 'It's just that Emma's much better at budgeting than I am. But I'll learn, darling, I promise.'

'Miriam called off our wedding,' he says. 'Twice. Once over the guest list and another time when my mother cancelled the band without telling us. Philippa has been her usual helpful self, I take it?'

I can't be sure, but I think he's teasing.

'Silence from the future daughter-in-law says it all,' he says with a laugh. 'You're right. Discretion is the better part of valour.'

The more I talk to Harold, the more I like him. He's a big friendly man who doesn't seem to take himself or the world too seriously and it's easy to see why Daniel wanted to spend most of his school holidays here. The house might be black and white and sterile but Daniel's godfather is anything but.

Over dinner Harold catches me up on his life so far and by the time I'm yawning into my treacle tart – which has nothing to do with the company – I think I might love him a bit too.

He and Daniel's dad landed right into the start of the greed-is-good eighties when they finished university. 'That's out of fashion now, of course, but not then,' he says. 'Your father and I went straight into the City, as everyone did. It doesn't seem like that could be nearly forty years ago, but that's what happens. If you're not paying attention, you'll miss it.'

'You'll miss what?' I ask.

He shrugs. 'Everything that really matters.'

Even though Daniel must have heard it a million times, he looks as riveted as I feel as Harold recounts his early life for my benefit. His success was meteoric. Too fast, he admits, for a twenty-one-year-old with more money than sense. He was already with Miriam by the time he graduated and it was always on the cards for them to marry.

'Have you got children, Harold?' I ask.

He shakes his head. 'We had two choices. One can either get them out of the way early or wait till the fun gets old to have them. Daniel's father didn't meet Philippa till our late twenties and they weren't in any rush. I wasn't about to stop the party if Hugh didn't have to, so we waited. Miriam was just getting going in her career anyhow and it was no hardship jetting off every free weekend.'

'How old was your mum when she had you?' I ask Daniel.

'Thirty-five,' he says.

I knew she was at least sixty! Mum'll enjoy that fact.

'Our bet went against us, though,' says Harold. 'We got caught short, so it didn't happen for us.' There's a tinge of sadness in his voice. 'But I've got you. Best of both worlds. All the fun with none of the shitty nappies.'

Now I'm starting to see why Daniel is like a son to Harold. 'He's nearly toilet-trained now, though,' I tease.

Harold laughs. 'Your work has just started. Wait until you have to house-train a husband.'

'I nearly had Harold as my best man, you know,' Daniel tells me later as we make our way back to his flat. 'He is rahly the person I'm closest to.'

'Then why didn't you ask him? Or at least have him be co-best man with Jacob?'

'Yah, no, it wouldn't look right to have Harold standing

up with me when everyone knows he's like a second father. It's all right. Harold understands.'

'But if I can have Uncle Barbara as my bridesmaid, then surely you could have Harold as your best man.' Especially if that's who he really wants beside him when we get married. I hate thinking of him not being as happy as he might be on the best day of our lives.

His arm tightens around me. 'No, it's just not proper. That's all right. There's a right way to do things and my family will never understand if those rules are broken.'

My tummy lurches thinking about our wedding. We're never going to get away with this.

It's with this worry playing on my mind that I go to see the finished bridesmaids' dresses at Mrs Delaney's. They do look beautiful as she carefully shakes each one out to hang on a brass hook. Now that the front window display case is gone the light floods the little tailor shop and shows them off to perfection. But will the fabric hold up to scrutiny? It looks fine to me, but my eyes are calibrated for H&M, not Dolce & Gabbana.

But it would be insulting to tell Mrs Delaney that when she's worked so hard on them. 'In a way it's a shame I'm selling up,' she says, running her hand over the old sewing machine. 'I did enjoy doing these. It makes a change from hemming suit trousers. Though I don't suppose there's much of a market in hand-making knock-off dresses.'

'There's no rush to sell if you don't want to,' I say. It *would* be hard to give up something you've done for fifty years. Longer than that, since Mrs Delaney's parents had the shop first, and their parents before that. Actually, it's awfully

sad when you think about that. Mrs Delany has to close down her entire family business. It will disappear when she sells up.

I bet her grandparents never dreamed it would end like this. I hope she doesn't feel like she's failed them somehow just because the business is folding under her watch.

This could even be the end of an era in the neighbour-hood if another dressmaker doesn't take over the shop. Soon this might become the home of overpriced soya lattes and there'll be no trace left of Mrs Delaney's century-old business.

'My daughter's put the business package together for me and listed it with a few agents, so we may get some interest soon.'

'Are you very sad?' I ask her, fighting back a sniffle myself.

'Sad? Are you mad, girl? As soon as I offload this place I'm goin' to that Tenerife for a month! Ooh, it'll be so good for me arthritis. I might even find me a boyfriend over there. A nice Spaniard. Del keeps sayin' there's some life in this old bird yet.'

It's so nice to know that our vicar looks after his flock's sex lives as well as their spiritual ones.

Outside, I catch Stacy Boyle just as she's about to close up the shoe stall.

'All right, Emma? Not long now!'

'A week from this Saturday. I just saw the bridesmaids' dresses and the girls are going to love them.'

Of course she knows about the switch. She and Shahrzad have no secrets. They like the idea that they're helping pull one over on the poshies, as they call them. Though after meeting Abby and Cressida the other night, they're much kinder about Daniel's side. Robustly mocking, I'd say, instead of downright hostile.

'Stacy, I wonder if you can do something for me.'

'Anything, doll, just name it.'

I might not be able to give my bridesmaids Manolos, but I have a feeling that Stacy might know exactly where to find some Ma-nearlies. She's nodding before I even finish describing what I'm looking for. 'Tell me the sizes. I can have them for you by the end of the week.'

I feel like everything is in motion, creeping slowly toward me from all directions, and there's no way to stop the progress now. Everything I've done these past few months – all the planning, scrimping, wondering and worrying – has been for one day in just over a week. I'm struggling to put into words how much it means to me to pull this off. To have Daniel and his family and friends look around on the day and say to each other, 'We couldn't have done it better ourselves.' No matter what Philippa may think of me in the future, once she knows I'm pregnant, no matter how much I might somehow screw up Christmas or use the wrong fork at dinner parties or introduce myself to the maid, I'll have set the standard with our wedding.

I guess I do have the words after all. It means everything.

Which is making it a little hard to sit back and trust that everyone is going to do what they need to on the day. I can't very well be setting up tents and organising the food on our wedding morning. I won't be able to hop into Kell's fish van to pull pints or even see the wedding cake before the guests do.

Which means the wedding will be a surprise to me too. That's terrifying.

Chapter 19

I open my eyes to find Auntie Rose staring into my face. 'Are you awake yet?' she asks from about six inches away. I stretch my arms over my head, smiling as I see the sunlight peeking through the chink in the curtains that never quite shut all the way. No rain.

'I'm not sure. What's the time?'

'Half past nine.'

'Half past nine! Why didn't you wake me? I wanted to go over to check on the square before breakfast.'

'I just got up meself. I'm not your alarm clock. You'll just have to let it go. Everyone knows what they're doing. Let me give you some advice.'

I pull my covers up to my chin. 'This isn't about having sex with Daniel again, is it?'

She grins. 'You need a few more years before you're ready for my advice on that front.'

Where did my auntie get all this experience to hand out sex pot advice?

'Today is about you marrying Daniel,' she says. 'Nothing else matters. You don't need drinks or food or music or even a dress. You could turn up in your jeans and the only thing that would matter is marrying Daniel. He's a good one, Emma, and so are you. Just love each other. That's enough. The rest of us will get on fine no matter what happens.'

She lifts up the bedclothes and scootches in next to me. It's been a long time since we've had a cuddle like this. Way too long.

There's something extra special about living with Auntie Rose. She's my confidante and ally but also my sounding board and guide. I've talked to her about things I'd never tell my parents. She's a constant, as much as Mum or Dad.

My breath hitches when I realise how much things will actually change now. I'll have to leave my job. Even though that was the plan all along once I got my degree, now I'll have to do it to have the babies. Soon Daniel and I will find a flat and we'll move in together. Auntie

Rose's snoring will no longer wake me but neither will we talk late into the night.

I can hear Mum downstairs in the kitchen, clattering the dishes as she puts them away from the drying rack. She'll be inspecting the forks that Dad washed last night, and rewash at least half of them. Dad's stirring his tea in that frantic way he thinks makes the sugar dissolve properly. As if boiling water doesn't dissolve it anyway. Mum'll be wiping up after him because he always leaves his wet teaspoon on the kitchen table. She won't say anything. She'll just sigh to let everyone know she's being a martyr. Dad will tell her to go start getting ready, that he's perfectly capable of getting the breakfast on, and she'll say okay a dozen times while she takes out the eggs and bread and all the pans as if he hasn't lived in this house for twenty-five years.

I know when I go downstairs that Mum will have put out my favourite tea mug and that the teabag will be inside. She'll say 'Cup of tea?' and flip on the kettle without waiting for an answer.

I know all these things because they're part of the everyday mundanity that makes my history. I'm gaining something today, but I feel like I'm losing something too.

'Don't cry, love,' says Auntie Rose. 'This is supposed to be a happy day.'

Daniel rings me as I'm having my second cup of tea in the lounge, enjoying the brief peace and quiet as everyone gets ready in their rooms. 'I know I'm not allowed to see you, but I just wanted to hear your voice, and to tell you that I cannot wait to marry you today. Mummy is already driving me insane. Abby's run off to Cressida's. She couldn't take it anymore. How's everything at your end?'

'Mum thinks her dress is all wrong. She's got her entire wardrobe on the bed. Normal, in other words. Is it too late to elope?' I'm only half kidding.

'Unfortunately, I think so. But never mind. In exactly … two hours and twenty-seven minutes I get to marry you. That's all that matters to me.'

'Me too.'

It's only when Kell arrives that we realise Auntie Rose is gone.

'How did she get out?' Mum demands, as if one of us slipped her a key.

'Did you lock the door after you went out for the milk this morning?' Dad asks.

I thought I did but obviously not. Otherwise Auntie Rose wouldn't be on the loose. She's no Houdini.

I start putting on my shoes.

'Where are you going?' Kelly demands. 'Shahrzad is coming in a minute to do your hair and make-up. You can't leave. I'll go.' She digs out her phone. 'Colin? Where are you? Barbara too? Auntie Rose is out. Okay. Ring me back.'

'Today of all days!' Dad says. His tone is uncharacteristically harsh.

'Dad, she doesn't know what she's doing.'

His irritation deflates as quickly as it flared up. 'I know, love. I'm sorry. I just don't want anything to spoil your day.'

But Auntie Rose isn't going to spoil anything. She comes through the door a few minutes later, kicking off shouting from all sides.

'Well, don't blame me,' she says. 'If you want to keep me indoors, the least you can do is lock the bloomin' doors. Otherwise why'd you bother shelling out all that dosh on a locksmith? Waste of money if you're not gonna use 'em. This is for you, Emma.'

Carefully she pulls the bag from around the bouquet in her hands. 'I thought you could use this.'

'Oh my god, I completely forgot about a bouquet! Auntie Rose, you're a lifesaver!'

'I know you've got your something blue,' she says, shrugging off my thanks. 'I got this for another reason.'

I look between Mum and Dad. 'What? Why are you smiling?'

'You remember, do you, Jack?' Mum asks. He reaches for her hand.

'Hyacinths with lavender and sprays of daisies,' he says.

'Exactly right. I'm impressed.' Mum kisses him.

'I remember every detail of our wedding day. It was the best day of me life ... matched only by the day Emma was born.'

'Good save, Dad.'

'What a charmer,' Auntie Rose adds.

'Plus, Elaine, my love, you went on about it so much that it's drilled into my head for life,' he says as Mum chucks him a good one on the arm. Then to me, 'That was your mum's bouquet. Rose, you remembered?'

Auntie Rose nods. 'All the flowers came from Hazel's garden. Her old garden.'

'... You didn't just pick these from the old house?' Mum asks. 'But Auntie Rose, Mum doesn't live there anymore.'

My auntie withers Mum with her stare. 'I know that,

Elaine. She's been dead more than seven years. Her flowers are still there, though. You never heard such a fuss over a few flowers. The woman who lives there threatened to call the Old Bill on me. But I got 'em! So it's a bit of your gran in there too, I suppose. Not literally, of course, don't worry. We didn't bury her in the garden.'

My transformation from slightly scruffy to bridelicious is in the hands of Shahrzad and there's no one I trust more for the job. When she spins me round to the mirror I have to laugh. I've never looked this good in my life!

She's done my hair in shiny dark loosely pinned ringlets and given me dramatic eyes with flippy uppy eyeliner at the corners.

Kell and Mum help me step into my dress and Mum buttons up the back. With the panels let out and the little pleats it still fits and, most importantly, it hides the swell of my tummy. 'It's almost perfect,' Kell says as Shahrzad comes in for a look. 'But it needs something. Something ... something. I know. Here, try this.' The long veil slithers out of the box she's got.

'But I thought we were doing flowers for my hair,' I say. Kell found some gorgeous vintage roses and sweet peas that really stand out against my dark hair. I didn't ask where she got them. Hopefully she didn't raid my Gran's old garden too.

'Just try it. Here, it goes like this.' The comb nestles into the ringlets at the back of my head. 'The flowers go here like a tiara at the front. The veil was my mum's. It's a loan. Your something borrowed. God, don't cry. You'll ruin all Shahrzad's work.'

'It's okay, I know you two,' Shahrzad says. 'It's water-proof!'

Which is good because stepping into my pale blue suede Ma-nearlies sets me off again. They're gorgeous, and Kelly's, in pale green, are perfect too. Abby, Cressida and Uncle Barbara's are pale yellow and Abby has already said she wants a pair for one of her friends. I'm not sure how I'll swing that. I can't charge her more than what I paid for them, but then I can't tell her they're from the market, either. I'll worry about that after she's officially my sister-in-law.

'Photos!' Dad calls upstairs. 'Come down, Emma, but walk slowly. Elaine, girls, come down first.'

'He thinks he's flippin' Stephen Spielberg,' Mum murmurs, smoothing down her pale blue silk dress. Twiggy didn't do this one, though it is from M&S, and it's lovely with her cream straw hat.

But it's not just family waiting at the bottom of the stairs. Jez from the phone stall is there behind a handheld video recorder with two cameras around his neck. I can't stop grinning.

'I have an official photographer?' I ask him when I get to the lounge.

'It's Kell's idea. We've got all this kit anyway at the stall. As long as I get it all back in the boxes and don't drop anything ...'

It feels impolite to point out that the people who buy new camera equipment from Jez's stall don't expect it to have had a previous owner, no matter how careful he was with it.

'Let's get you to the church on time!' Kell says. 'Everyone's already at the pub.'

As Mum, Kelly, Shahrzad and Auntie Rose go out to the waiting taxi, Dad grabs hold of my arm. 'We'll be right with you, love.'

Mum smiles. 'We'll wait out here.'

Dad awkwardly gets himself out of his chair and on to his crutches so Mum can get the chair to the taxi.

'You know I'm not very good at saying things,' he says, with a serious look on his face. 'But I need to say something to you, and that's that I am so proud of you. Not just for everything you've done to get through school but for the person you've become. Even if you weren't my daughter, I'd be so proud to know you, Emma.'

'Thank you. I am who I am because of you and Mum.'

He nods. 'We gave you the basics, but you've become much more. Every parent wants better for their child than they had, and you're doing so much better. You're better than us, Emma, and I'm happy for that.'

'But I'm not better! I'm as good as you and Mum. You're as good as me.'

He shakes his head. 'You should never apologise for wanting more.'

'But that feels like I'm betraying you. I should be happy with all that you and Mum have given me. And I am. I'm so grateful.'

'It's not a crime to want more. I wanted more than my parents and so did your mum. And we had more. Believe it or not.' He looks around the lounge. 'My dad did piecework in the factory. I got to study The Knowledge and earn my living sitting on my arse. That's a step up. And you've heard Auntie Rose's stories. She and your gran didn't have an inside toilet. We should always be grateful for what we've got, Emma, but that doesn't mean we can't want more. You're smart enough not only to want it but to be able to study to get it. You're not destined to sell scooters your whole life. You and Daniel will make your home and maybe one day fill it with children who'll be grateful for all you give them but want more for themselves too. That's how we move forward.'

I don't think my make-up is going to survive this talk. We hold each other and cry. I'm crying because I know how much my parents love me. And I'm crying because I know they're right. I want more, and no matter what Dad says, it feels like a betrayal.

Shahrzad jumps into my taxi to fix me up as soon as Dad and I pull up in front of the town hall. 'Jez is outside. You can't have your photo taken looking like that. Now, please, try to hold it together! I'm good at make-up, but I can't work miracles.' She kisses my freshly smoothed cheek. 'Whenever you're ready, Emma. Good luck, Mr Liddell!'

With a monumental heave, Dad lifts himself from the seat and, with a control that must take every ounce of his ability, he steps confidently from the taxi. Holding on to the door with one hand, he holds out his other. 'Emma? Ready?'

I hold my Dad's hand, step out of the taxi and into a spontaneous round of applause. I look around at the dozens of people waiting in front of the town hall – both Daniel's side and mine – but it's hard to register everyone's faces. All I know is that I'm grinning from ear to ear and holding on to my Dad for dear life.

But my mind is perfectly calm. And it's filled with one thought. Daniel is inside waiting for me. I was wrong to think that everything we've done – all the work and worrying – is for the next few hours. It's really down to this, in the next few minutes, when Daniel and I will exchange our promises to spend the rest of our lives together.

'Dad, I didn't think I could ever be this happy.'

He kisses my cheek and leads me to where my bridesmaids are standing. 'Over to you,' he says, gently passing me off to them.

'But you're walking me up the aisle!'

He shrugs. 'You need to be fussed over by your bridesmaids. That's the tradition. I'll be there to walk you up the aisle. First I have to get everyone inside and check for stragglers at the pub.'

'And maybe have a swift half while you're there, Mr Liddell?' Kell teases.

'If you say so.'

We're led away to a little room. 'How's Daniel doing?' I ask Cressida. 'He is here, right?'

She laughs. 'He wouldn't stay for more than one drink next door in case it made him late. He can't wait to marry you.' Her eyes glisten with tears. '*We* can't wait for him to marry you.'

Time seems to slow in those few minutes before Dad returns to walk me up the aisle. So many smiles, so much laughter and so much love. Exactly as I'd imagined.

There's wedding music as Dad and I make our entrance, but I don't register the tune. I do see every smiling face now, though. And I'm conscious of my dad holding my arm, strong and sure of his steps.

But most of all I see Daniel waiting for me. The sun streaming through the tall window behind him makes his hair glow golden. His smile is as wobbly as mine as he fights back tears. 'You are so unbelievably beautiful,' he whispers to me.

The only time our hands unclasp is when it's time to exchange the rings. The ceremony is as short as we could make it and still be legally married. When the registrar pronounces us husband and wife a cheer goes up that threatens the foundations of the building. 'We're married!' Daniel says the second before he kisses me. We go up the aisle as everyone claps and laughs and they trail behind us out of the pretty room. Our footsteps echo on the town hall's marble floors and laughter bounces off the wood-panelled walls.

'Wait just a sec,' Kell tells Daniel, scooting in front of us and out the door. She comes back in. 'Okay.'

The huge wooden doors fly open and Daniel and I step out of the town hall, for the first time as husband and wife.

A roar goes up.

But our guests are behind us. So who's making all the noise ...?

The pavement in front of the hall is packed. Everybody is cheering.

Slowly I start to recognise faces. There's my favourite secondary school teacher standing beside ... all my teachers! And the head, and ... so many of my classmates. There's Stuart, my first kiss. That's Kevin, my first ... well, let's just say everyone I went to school with is here.

My boss, Marco, is waving madly as Ant looks mortified at his father's Mediterranean enthusiasm. Zane's family is beside them – his mum in her usual colourful African print kaftan and head wrap, and both his sisters in pretty summer dresses.

Mr and Mrs Ishtiaque's daughters – all three of them – are in beautiful pink, orange and blue sarees. When

Mr and Mrs Ishtiaque join them, together they look like exotic birds.

Even that Sheila Larkin is here, luckily not wearing a blue dress so Mum won't have more ammunition against her. The councillor is standing officiously beside PC Billy Bramble, who keeps talking into his walkie-talkie.

The couple from the Pound Shop are here, and the pet stall lady who's very nice but never knows when to end a conversation. Helen, our GP, grins happily beside the fish-stall man, who's standing with the lady who always does me a good deal on knickers and the bedding man with his twin sons and his wife. Pawnshop Steve is holding hands with his two little girls, who are doing a little dance. They're all here, every one of my tribe are here.

'Did you?'

Daniel nods. 'With Kell, obviously. It wouldn't be your wedding without everyone here.'

'Where are your parents?' I say, turning to find them. 'Get them, please, Daniel. And your sister and Cressida and Seb and Jacob. They're all part of this too.'

Kell rounds up Auntie Rose and Dad and Mum, Uncle Colin and Uncle Barbara, and we all stand together there in front of the town hall with Daniel's side. I don't know who grasps hands first, but within seconds we're all connected, Daniel's side and mine, our hands clasped together in the air, being welcomed by the cheers of my East London family.

Chapter 20

It's not till the crowd parts a bit that I see what's behind them. A queue of black cabs line the kerb, all festooned with white ribbons. 'Dad! They look fantastic!' Dad's grinning almost as insanely as me.

'I'd like to see Uber pull this off,' he says.

'Are you ready for the party?' asks Daniel. But he stops me as I go for one of the taxis. 'Not yet.' He nods at Kelly.

'Right, you lot!' she bellows. 'Pay attention. Hey, I'm talking here.' I just get my hands clamped to my ears before she lets rip with her signature whistle. 'Listen up. You all know the drill. Anyone who doesn't fancy a walk, please make your way to a taxi.'

'A walk?' I look at Daniel. 'We're walking?' I was totally bluffing about that. My Ma-nearlies will never make it.

He shakes his head and points. 'We're not walking.'

That's when I hear the clippety clop of hooves. Two huge white horses with matching plumes of feathers on their heads are walking briskly up Bow Road. The carriage behind them is streaming with a riot of silky cloths. The ramrod-straight old man driving the horses looks very officious in his black top hat and long coat. The carriage slows to a stop right in front of the hall.

'That's for us?!'

'It is,' says Daniel. 'Apparently it's an East London tradition.'

I shoot a look at Kell, who just winks.

Daniel kisses me while some of the guests make their way to the waiting taxis. 'You've done so much, everything, really, for our wedding, Emma. I wanted to do something for you.'

'He's been in on it all, Em,' Kell says. She catches my look of alarm and shakes her head so slightly that only I catch it. He doesn't know about our shortcuts, then. 'He's just acted like he was clueless. At least, I assume it was an act. You were so disappointed when the chauffeur fell through that when he asked me about getting a horse and carriage for you, it was perfect. Since, you know, it's an East London tradition anyway.'

The only East London tradition I know of that involves a horse and carriage is when someone dies. One of the Kray brothers notably came through the borough in one on his last tour, as it were.

'And here's the other tradition!' Daniel cries as people crane their necks to watch the commotion.

It's the vicar. He's wearing a top hat and tails and walking with his piano, which is being pushed along on wheels by four of the phone stall boys. 'Emma, darling, how marvellous!' cries Philippa. 'A mobile piano for our parade!'

Del is playing as he walks, a jolly tune that I recognise. One of the phone stall boys breaks off from his wheeling to hand out leaflets amongst the crowd, though my side doesn't need them. They're singing already.

'What's this?' Daniel asks, trying to get a look at the papers.

'Lyrics!' booms Philippa. 'We get to sing!'

'Excuse me, Mrs Billings,' Dad says in my ear. 'I hate to interrupt, but I think your carriage awaits.'

I let go of Daniel's hand to throw myself into his arms.

'What about your carriage? Will you take a taxi?'

'And miss walking with my daughter on her wedding day? Not a chance.' He gestures to Mum, who's got his wheelchair waiting. 'We've both got wheels.'

Everyone starts off, some in front of the horses, some behind or to the side. Daniel has to boost me up to the seat. We can just squeeze in beside the driver, who I now recognise as a regular at Uncle Colin's. 'Congratulations,' he says. 'I'm honoured to be part of your day.'

'Thank you.' Daniel has his hand in mine, but his head is swivelling around to take it all in. There must be nearly two hundred of us holding up the traffic all along Bow Road, but the police are redirecting the cars away from this impromptu parade. Loads of bystanders have their phones out to record the event. I don't blame them. I'd gawp too if I saw a horse-drawn carriage in the city. 'This isn't a wedding carriage, is it,' I murmur to the driver when Daniel's attention is on the crowd around us.

The gaily coloured cloths are carefully draped. Anyone who glimpsed underneath would soon realise that this peculiar carriage is only high enough for a person to lie down inside. And they might wonder why it's got windows on the sides and only opens from the back. It is meant to carry a person along one of life's milestones, but that milestone isn't a wedding.

The coachman shakes his head. 'I had a job this morning. Lucky they didn't want to keep all the flowers.' He gestures to the pile of arrangements on top of the carriage. 'Mrs Ishtiaque decorated it for you. I gather those silks are some of the family wedding sarees.'

'Where is she?!' I glance around looking for the Ishtiaques' bright clothes, but all around me is a riot of colour – sarees and summer dresses and African prints.

'What's the matter?' Daniel asks.

'I need to find Mrs Ishtiaque. I need to tell her something. Can you stop the carriage, please?'

'I'll come with you, darling. She's there next to the piano.'

'No, thank you, I need to do this alone. I'll be right back.'

I clamber down from the carriage and head toward our singing vicar. I can't let Daniel know how horrible I've been.

'Mrs Ishtiaque, thank you for decorating the carriage,' I say above the vicar's tune. 'With your wedding sarees!' She grasps my hands. Her entire face is smiling with such happiness for me. That makes me feel even worse. 'I've been unfair to you, Mrs Ishtiaque. I never should have refused your food. I ... I lost sight of what's important. I'm so sorry.'

'Emma, my love. I am understanding. I wanted to impress my mother-in-law too. It is natural.'

'But it's wrong! I acted like I'm ashamed of ...' I almost say 'you', but that makes me sound so awful I can't even say it. '... where I come from, and I'm not.' I look around. 'I'm so proud of where I'm from. I love your curry, and I love you. I'm sorry.'

She shakes her head. 'Do you think my feelings are changing for you with one refusal of my cooking? Your auntie is refusing me for years and I still love her. Now, go enjoy your wedding. We will be seeing you there!' She kisses me firmly on the cheek and pats my behind as I turn back to the carriage.

'Mrs Ishtiaque decorated the carriage,' I tell Daniel as I climb up so that we can make our way to Carlton Square. 'I just wanted to thank her. For everything.'

People come out of their houses and lean from upstairs windows as we turn off the main road and disturb the peace and quiet of their neighbourhood. It's not every day they see a horse-drawn carriage and a singing vicar on wheels. The wedding guests stream into the square under fluttering bunting, which festoons the gates and nearly every tree and box hedge.

When I thank the coachman he tells me that his next job today won't be as fun as ours. 'He'll be riding in back, I take it?'

The coachman nods. 'As soon as the food's unloaded.' He hoicks his thumb behind him.

I turn to look over the back of the carriage and sure enough, Doreen and June are directing the boys to pull out the big trays of food. I didn't realise we were a travelling buffet.

Our families are already inside the square, but I notice that everyone from the market is milling around outside. 'Please, won't you come in?' I say. 'I'm sure there's plenty of food and drink.' I feel bad now for not inviting everyone I've ever met in my entire life.

But there's a chorus of polite 'No thanks'. They all need to get back to the market. Saturday is a big shopping day and they can't lose the income. Which makes it all the more touching to think they took the time to meet us at the town hall and escort us here.

The square is beautiful as Daniel and I walk under the bunting to the cheers of everyone we love. 'You are quite amahzing,' Daniel murmurs in my ear. 'Look at everything you've done.'

But I haven't done all this. I'm as surprised as he is when I look around. We don't need the tent after all – there's barely a cloud in the sky – but it looks so pretty in the middle of the square. It's sitting over the tables that are set up for our dinner, and fluttering with dozens of coloured ribbons. I was afraid when PC Billy Bramble offered that it'd be a knackered old bit of canvas, or some horrific colour, but it's pristinely white. From a distance it looks like the side flaps are blue, but they're rolled up with the fine weather.

Billy has put his walkie-talkie away and is surveying the crowd with evident pleasure. 'That tent is perfect, thank you!' I tell him. 'If it gets cool later, I guess we could roll down the sides.'

A funny look crosses his face. 'I wouldn't do that. Keep them rolled up, okay? I borrowed them from work. The logo is on the side.'

'Well, no, I don't want you getting into trouble. Of course not.' I tap the side of my nose. 'Our little secret.'

'Yeah, plus it might freak some people out knowing they're eating in a forensics tent.'

'They're what?'

'Crime scene tents. Yeah, of course. Why else would the Met have tents? Just keep the sides rolled up.' He taps the side of *his* nose and strolls away.

I stare at the tent. It really is pretty. I'll just pretend it's never been erected over dead bodies.

Most of the crowd has drifted to where the vicar has set up his piano. 'This is so lively!' Lady Mucking says over the chorus of 'Whiskey in the Jar'. 'What great fun.'

'I wouldn't expect anything less from my daughter-in-law,' says Hugh, hugging me from the side. 'Do you know, that's the first time I've ever said that?' He smiles. 'Daughter-in-law. I like it very much.'

'Hello, isn't this great?' Kell says to Hugh and Lady Mucking as she comes over. 'What a day, eh?' Then in my ear. 'We have a problem.'

I keep the smile plastered to my face as a million scenarios race through my mind. 'Will you excuse us?'

'She's the woman of the hour!' Lady Mucking says, linking arms with Hugh to join in the singing.

'It's the champagne,' Kell says, steering me to where Jez is cringing behind the fish van.

'It's not right, yeah?' He pulls off another cork. It barely manages a gentle puff, let alone a pop.

It's definitely not right. It's supposed to fizz. That's why it's called fizz! I know I sound hysterical, but we haven't got anything else besides beer and soft drinks. I can't see the Dames and Ladies swigging lager from pint glasses instead. 'We can't serve that. It's got no fizz, Jez, no fizz!'

That champagne is supposed to be the one thing that's sophisticated about today.

'Calm down,' Kell says. 'It's still alcohol, right? There must be something we can do with it. Colin!' She waves him over. 'What would you do with shit white wine? The champagne's flat.'

'How flat?'

'Dead on arrival, mate.'

Uncle Colin hardly hesitates. 'You could add soda water for spritzers.'

I shake my head. 'A spritzer is just watered-down wine. It's got to look like it's on purpose. Jez? This is your fault. Can't you think of anything?'

'What's that Spanish drink me mum goes spare over? That's made with shit wine, yeah? Red, though.'

Sangria, of course! Colin sends Jez to the market for loads of fruit. 'Don't worry, Emma, it's your day. I'll mix up the batches as soon as Jez gets back.'

'Where've you been hiding?' Daniel asks when I find him again. 'Everyone is loving the shell game! Let's have a go.'

Shell game? I can't think what he means till I see the fishmonger's son standing behind a small TV table giving it all he's got with the cockney patter. 'Come on, mate, yer not spendin' yer in'eri-ance 'ere. It's only ten pahhnd, gehl, so 'ave a butchers and lay yer houses. All it takes is a tenner and twenty-twenty minces. Step up, step up.' He catches my eye and winks.

'It's a confidence trick, right?' Harold's wife Miriam murmurs to me as she watches him shuffle the shells.

'Yeah, it's just pretend.' Then more loudly, 'He's not keeping anybody's money. It's just a game for the wedding today. Otherwise we'll get the Old Bill round to nick 'im.'

He looks very disappointed to hear this, but the crowd loves it.

Standing there in the leafy square listening to our vicar on the piano and watching the bunting waving in the breeze, it's easy to forget we're in the city. It could be a sunny village green. 'This is so perfect,' I tell Daniel, leaning in for a kiss. 'And I think your side are really getting into the East London traditions.'

Jacob and Seb are leaning on Del's piano singing a duet while my mother-in-law throws down ten pound notes at the shell game like she's in Vegas. Cressida's got her arm linked through Auntie Rose's as she chats with her ladies.

We hear our names being shouted a few minutes later. Everyone is waving us over to one side of the square.

I clap my hands to my mouth when I see it.

'Emma, you did it!' Daniel says, hugging me. 'You said the chocolate display was impossible.'

But once again, I didn't do anything. Zane's standing beside the fishmonger's barrow, which is streaming with ribbons and laid out at one end with glasses filled with fruity sangria, a red-and-white stripy straw sticking out from each one. The other end is heaving with tiers of chocolate-dipped strawberries on a huge see-through tower, like a Christmas tree. It looks really familiar. It's not from our house … maybe the market? Shoes! It's Stacy Boyle's Perspex shoe tower that she uses to display her most wonderful finds.

I kiss Zane's cheek. 'This was you?'

'Me and your dad dipped 'em all,' he says. 'They couldn't let all those chocolate samples go to waste. There's some smack flavours, but they'll be good with the strawberries.' Turning to the crowd, he says 'Aaiight? Lucky dip! Guess the chocolate flavour.'

The crowd descends on the sangria and strawberries.

Even though things are buzzing all around us, it feels like Daniel and I are in a little bubble of calm. We're carrying on different conversations with our friends and family, but we're connected to each other. The peace flows between us through our clasped hands, a look or a smile. It's true what they say. This is the happiest day of my life so far.

'The bar is open!' someone shouts. Another cheer goes up when everyone catches sight of it.

'Isn't that clever!' Philippa says when she sees the two foot tall sign mounted on top of Kell's fish van. B-A-R is spelled out in white flowers, wrapped with fairy lights. The van has had a bunting makeover too, and the whole display window is filled with pint glasses nestling in ice.

'Wasn't that lucky?' Kell says to me, pointing to the sign. 'Your carriage's morning ride was called Barry.'

'Those are funeral flowers?!' I hiss so Daniel doesn't hear.

'Just the first three letters. The old gent pitched in by pitching over. Cheers.' She raises her pint when Cressida comes over with two of Philippa's friends.

'Where are you putting gifts?' Cressida asks as I kiss the blonde frozen-faced women beside her.

The women are clutching large wrapped boxes and cards. Those won't last an hour out here.

'This way,' Kell says smoothly. 'There's a table that's all set up in the tent. I'll show you.' She turns to me. 'It's all decorated.'

'Barry's surname wasn't "Gifting", by chance, was it?' I murmur to Kell.

'No such luck,' she murmurs back. 'This way, ladies!'

I grab Daniel's free hand – he has sangria in the other – and drag him to the tent to see what they've done.

The sight makes me catch my breath. Daniel throws his arms around me as we stand together taking it all in. 'Emma, darling,' he says, 'I'm really overwhelmed by all this. Well done!'

The vicar's long wooden tables are draped nearly to the grass with Mrs Delaney's antique Belgian lace. The patterns might be different on every table, but that just makes it more interesting. All the plates and cutlery sparkle and our mismatched serviettes add to the romance. But what's really spectacular are the little pot plants that Uncle Barbara and Zane got from the park.

Half a dozen sit on each table, tumbling riots of colourful blooms that couldn't be more perfect.

One of the phone stall boys is standing guard beside the gift table at one end. His dark suit is too big for him.

The guests eye him warily. 'Security, ma'am,' he says in a terrible American accent. I notice he's got an earbud in. He's probably listening to Capital FM, but it does make him look official. 'The rest of the detail is outside, ma'am,' he says to me.

'Roger, got it. Over and out.'

Kell smirks, but the guests are buying it.

One of the women says, 'Ooh, I see, they're actors! Is he the Secret Service?'

'No, dear, they're "protection",' says the other one. 'They're everywhere in the East End. Don't you remember the Kray brothers?'

'Then why has he got an American accent?'

They go off debating who he's supposed to be.

They seem to think this is all a performance. And I guess it is, in a way. As I scan the square, I try to see it through Daniel's eyes. The bar isn't Kelly's fish van. It's a vintage drinks truck like you see at music festivals. The tent's not covering a crime scene but a purposefully shabby chic dinner venue. And we rode here in a carriage fit for royalty, not a hearse.

We just might pull this off!

'Isn't that the prawn man?' Daniel gestures to the bar. 'Marvellous! Emma, you've thought of everything. I'll get us some. I'm Hank Marvin for some prawns.' He looks so proud of his cockney slang.

I didn't invite the prawn man. Word is obviously spreading that there's money to be made here today. But the guests are queuing to pay two quid for this slice of East London life and couldn't look happier. Everyone looks happy. Whenever I catch Dad's eye he raises his pint to me. He's in his chair now, thankfully. Mum's woven ribbons through the wheels. Dad thinks it's over the top, but he hasn't taken them off. Auntie Rose has started helping her ladies lay out all the food.

And Uncle Barbara is talking to his sons. I'm about to go over to say hello, but then I stop. Let them catch up first. I wasn't sure about inviting them. I didn't want to make Uncle Barbara uncomfortable, or sad if they didn't turn up, so I didn't tell him until they RSVP'd.

His eldest gestures to the bridesmaid's dress. 'Thank you,' I see Uncle Barbara say. Then my cousin smiles and nods. Uncle Barbara gathers his sons into a ferocious embrace.

I'll say hello later.

'Emma? You'd better come,' Stacy Boyle says. 'We may have a problem.'

I can see what she means from where we're standing. Lurking at the edge of the square are five teens that I don't know. They look like the phone stall boys do when they're not in their Crown Court suits pretending to be the Secret Service. But those aren't our boys. 'It's a public square,' I say. 'Maybe they're just neighbours.' Billy and the councillor knocked on all the doors in the area to let the residents know about the party today, and to invite them in for a drink if they fancied it.

'I don't know. They look like trouble. Where's Billy?'

'He had to go to work.'

'That figures,' she says. 'There's never a copper around when you need one. I don't suppose the muppets could run them off?' She gestures to one of the phone stall boys before answering her own question. 'I'll get Colin.'

My uncle is no stranger to persuading trouble to leave the premises. Just his hulking presence should be enough to scare them off. He looks positively enormous in his suit. But just as he starts towards them, I notice that they've drawn a crowd. Daniel's side has closed in on them in a semi-circle and they seem to be waiting for something.

'Uncle Colin?' I rush over to him. We can't make a scene.

'Will there be a show?' I hear Lady Mucking ask. 'I've seen these breakdancers on the South Bank. No, it was that *Stomp*, where they drummed on rubbish bins.'

My eyes are drawn to all the fancy handbags dangling from the women's arms. Those boys don't have drumming on their minds.

But the guests think they're part of the wedding. 'Uncle Colin?' I whisper in his ear. He nods and goes to talk quietly to the boys. They shoot menacing looks at the guests as he leads them out of the square. The guests are thrilled with the authenticity of their outrage.

I don't know who starts slow clapping, but soon they're all at it, and it's drawing more people over to see what's going on. Now everyone thinks those boys are performers. They're expecting a show!

Del's a good piano player, but I can't really expect him to be much good at beatbox and breakdancing.

But if they want a performance, we'll have to have to give them a performance. I've got an idea.

Everyone turns to me when I wave for attention. 'Ladies and gents, the dancers have just gone off to practice and they'll come on shortly. I'll be right back,' I tell Daniel.

It takes Kelly about thirty seconds to get her plan together. Sweeping the phone stall boys in her wake, she heads off. 'Give us fifteen minutes and make the announcement when I tell you, okay?'

Chapter 21

There's no way for Rasta Reg to make a discrete entrance with his waist-long dreadlocks and his yellow, green and black Jamaican-themed bicycle, but at this point our guests are expecting anything to happen, so it kind of fits with the day.

I grab Daniel's hand and lead the wedding party over to where the crowd is still milling around. There's a current of excitement now. Everyone knows something's about to happen. The phone stall boys have ditched their Crown Court appearance suits and are back in their usual jeans and hoodies. I doubt anyone realises they're not the same boys that Uncle Colin just led away. They're being their usual selves, ripping on each other, doing the swingy arm gangster walk and throwing made-up gang signs with their hands.

One by one they stride out behind one another, doing big arm claps to get everyone to join in while forcing them back into a big circle. Daniel is grinning for all he's worth.

'It's one surprise after another,' his dad says.

Tell me about it.

Music booms from Rasta Reg's sound system. He's a regular round our neighbourhood, blasting reggae tunes every afternoon from the back of his bicycle. His route never changes and nobody wants to tell him we don't all enjoy reggae as much as he does.

But it's not reggae this time. It's Beyoncé's 'Crazy in Love'. When the music starts up, our friends – Daniel's as much as mine – start head-bobbing. Love or hate the song, everyone knows it. When Kelly comes strutting into the middle of the circle in her own jeans and hoodie, even Hugh whoops his support.

The boys move to the back of the circle as Kelly starts to lip-sync the intro and, I have to say, the boys' twerking has lost none of its hilarity since they performed it as a surprise for Mum and Dad's anniversary party. Which I now know was four months early. Kell's moves are perfect as she struts back and forth singing and the boys wriggle behind her, and by the time Jez strides up to rap Jay Z's part, heads are sticking out of windows all around the square. Seb and Jacob have synchronised their overbite sliding head moves, to the envy of all dads in the crowd. Then, just when it doesn't seem like it can get any better, Auntie Rose and her ladies pop into the middle of the phone stall boys. Clearly they remember their choreography from the anniversary party too. Their moves are a little less exuberant than the other backing dancers – nobody wants to dislocate a hip – but the crowd goes mental.

There's a slightly tense moment when the audience demands an encore. Kelly and the boys only know one song. But the vicar soon distracts them with a full-throated rendition of 'I've Got a Lovely Bunch of Coconuts', drawing everyone over to the piano and leaving Daniel and I grinning at each other.

'This is amahzing,' he says. 'Look at our wedding day! The sun is shining, everyone is having the time of their lives and I'm married to you. It couldn't be more perfect.'

There's so much trust when he looks into my eyes. He has no idea that what he's seeing is a mirage, that the wife he adores hasn't been wholly truthful. I'm lying now by letting him believe this is all real. It's not exactly how I thought I'd start my marriage, even if it is only to make him happy.

Daniel trusts me. I've got to trust that he'll understand. 'Come with me,' I say, leading him by the hand. 'This is for your ears only. You can never tell your parents or their friends. Do you promise me?'

And then I whisper all my secrets to him, from Mrs Delaney's lace and serviettes to Beyoncé's backing dancers to Zane's wedding cake, Mrs Ishtiaque's clever hearse disguise, the bridesmaids' handmade market stall dresses and my Ma-nearlies, the impromptu sangria, chocolate sample strawberries and Victoria Park flowers. 'Oh, and that's from the funeral this morning,' I say, pointing to the B-A-R sign. 'It came off the hearse we rode here.'

'We really rode in a hearse on our wedding day?' he says. 'That's a bit morbid.'

'Yes, and, actually, there is one more thing. The marquee is a crime scene tent that Billy Bramble pinched from work. He may have to come get it if there's a big murder in the area today.'

As it all comes out, the enormity of what my family and friends have done together hits me. 'It's just that our budget was so small and your parents expected so much ... you expected so much—'

He kisses the end of my nose. 'Emma, darling. I knew you were incredible when I met you. This puts you into a superhuman realm. My god, the resourcefulness ... and I'm rahly so sorry. I got as carried away as Mummy did. You said from the start that there wasn't much money to spend. I should have heeded that. I promise that I will from now on.' He looks around. 'I rahly can't believe you've done all this. I love you more than anything in the world.'

And that's exactly what he says again later when he stands up after dinner to make his speech. He does a fantastic job of keeping up the illusion we've all worked so hard to create but cleverly manages to work in his thanks to every single person who's helped. 'And last but certainly not least.' He pulls me to my feet to stand beside him. 'I want to thank my wife for making me the happiest man in the world today. I can't imagine my life without you.' His hand seems to reach for my tummy in super slow motion, but even so, I can't stop it before it lands on the bump, where everyone's eyes are suddenly drawn. 'I can't wait for us all to start our lives together.'

His lips meet mine as everyone looks on in stunned silence. When I break off the kiss I glance down at myself. My bump is so obvious now. How could I have thought it was hidden?

Daniel realises what he's done a split second after it

sinks in with Philippa. My mother-in-law's face registers complete shock. Hugh puts his arm round her shoulder.

'Blimey, she's preggers?' Doreen says. Her comment rings out loud and clear across the heads of the guests. I can see Mum lean over to whisper urgently into Dad's ear.

When he looks at me I feel like I've let him down. I might not be able to read his expression, but I can guess what's in his heart. I grasp Daniel's hand harder.

Dad struggles to his feet. I think he's going to come to me, but instead he grabs a fork to ding against his glass. 'I didn't think anything could make me happier today than to see you two married, but I was wrong. To Emma and Daniel … and their family. Congratulations! We've got a lot to celebrate!'

The cheers and congratulations seem to loosen Philippa's expression. She manages a stunned smile as we make our way to her and Hugh. I want to talk to Dad too, but at least Mum's with him. This is obviously as big a shock to Daniel's parents as it is to Dad.

'We were going to tell you right after the wedding,' Daniel says. 'We only found out a few weeks ago.'

'How many weeks?' Philippa asks me.

'Thirteen, actually, so we can officially tell people now.

Though this isn't how we wanted to tell you. I'm sorry, Philippa.' I'm not sure whether I'm apologising for the way they've found out or for being pregnant in the first place. 'We had the scan last week. It's twins.'

Philippa's hand flies to her mouth. 'Twins? Hugh, it's twins.'

'THAT's why you chucked at dinner!' Abby says. 'You didn't have food poisoning.'

'Not now, Abby,' says Hugh. 'We've all worked that out.'

'You're having twins?' Philippa asks.

'Twins,' says Daniel. 'Mummy, are you all right? Say something.'

'All right? Am I all right? I'm marvellous, darlings! Twins, what fun! We'll have a party, of course, to welcome the babies. This is all so wonderful.' She gestures round the square. 'It's giving me the best ideas. I know ... we could have *live storks*!'

I shake my head. 'I think that's an amazing idea, Philippa. Whatever you want for the party, you just go ahead and do it. I'm sure I'll love it all.' The storks could serve the canapes, for all I care. My party planning days are well and truly over.

Dad said the right things, but I want to check whether

he's really all right. He shrugs when I ask him. 'I guess this might change your plans, at least in the short term, but you'll have your degree in a few weeks and no one can take that away from you. And there's a lot to be said for having your family when you're young. I didn't regret it for a minute. I'm sure you won't, either.'

He's never admitted that Mum was pregnant with me at their wedding. He probably assumes I'd mind. We don't always give people the credit they deserve.

It's late when Daniel's godfather pulls us aside. 'I didn't want to leave this on the gift table without an explanation,' he says, glancing around the square where the streetlights have come on, bathing the pretty houses in a gentle glow. I can see into the windows of some of them, TVs on, people living their lives. I like to think they're all as happy as I am tonight.

He hands a lumpy envelope to Daniel.

'Harold?' Daniel says, lifting out the keys.

'It's only a rental for now, but Miriam and I thought it was the best wedding present we could give you. And now under the circumstances ...'

Daniel's hand goes to my tummy. 'A flat? Harold, you've given us a flat?!' he says, handing me the keys.

'It's here!' I say, reading the key fob.

Harold smiles. 'Right there, in fact,' he says, pointing over our shoulders. 'It's vacant now. You can move in whenever you want. Like I said, it's a rental for six months, but the owner is looking to sell. There's an amount of money, Daniel, that's yours. You'd get it anyway as an inheritance. I'd rather you spend it while I'm still around to see you enjoy it. I know how much Emma wants to stay close to her parents, and you obviously like this square so ...' He shrugs. 'If you don't like it here, though, you can always find somewhere else. Go have a look. Not many couples get to look at their own wedding reception from their drawing room.'

Daniel throws his arms round his godfather. 'I love you, Harold.'

'I love you too, my boy.'

I'm in a daze as I walk with Daniel across the square. The house has a wrought-iron railing like its neighbours but no flowers outside. I bet Mrs Ishtiaque will know what'll grow best here. Daniel unlocks the front door. 'Come here.' With a heave, he scoops me up. 'I have to carry my bride over the threshold.'

'But not up the stairs, clearly,' I say as he sets me down inside the doorway. It's a narrow hall with stairs running up to the first floor and a wide doorway on the left leading through to the lounge. The large bay window (a bay window – my dream!) overlooks the fairy lights of our wedding party. We stand together with our arms round each other listening to the laughter of everyone we love.

'Thank you for coming into my world,' I tell him. 'My world here, I mean.'

He turns me to face him. 'Emma, darling, please get it through your head. It isn't about your world or my world. Together we're making our own world. It doesn't matter where we've come from, or where we live. Only that we're together.' He gently rubs my tummy. 'This is our world now.'

I look around the darkened lounge. This is our world now.

'You know,' I say, still staring out the window. 'Auntie Rose had some very good advice about the wedding night. Involving a quiet place where we can be alone.'

'I don't hear a sound,' he says, kissing my neck. 'Do you?'

'Definitely quiet here.'

It's nearly midnight when we all leave the square together to walk Daniel's side to the Tube and towards taxis. Dad and Hugh are making plans for a Chelsea match – though not when Tottenham are playing – and Mum's got her arm round Auntie Rose, who's singing 'When Irish Eyes Are Smiling'. No one had the heart to cut her off from the sangria. It might be forrin, she says, but it ain't 'alf bad. Philippa is still collecting compliments from her friends about the wedding and I think I just caught Seb holding Kelly's hand, but I'll have to have a debrief later to know for sure. I haven't told her yet about Harold's wedding present. I can still hardly believe it myself.

Now that everyone knows about the twins Daniel won't stop stroking my tummy. I have the feeling that's going to get old if he's still doing it in six months, but for now it feels wonderful.

'That was the best wedding I've ever been to,' I overhear one of Philippa's friends say as we reach the main road.

'Better than Lugano?' asks her husband, holding his arm out for an approaching cab.

'Sure. Anyone can have chocolate fountains and speedboats. This was rahly such awfully good fun!'

Return to Carlton Square with the next book in Lilly Bartlett's gorgeous Carlton Square series...

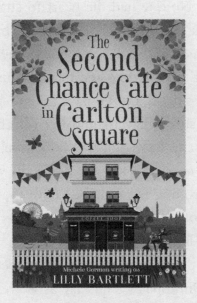

Read on for an exclusive look at the next book
in this heartwarming series,

The Second Chance Café in Carlton Square

Chapter 1

Stop the Convict Café!!

Concerned neighbours: Don't let our homes be overrun by criminals!

Are you worried about the untrustworthy people lurking around the
Second Chance Café day and night?

Do you want your children and grannies threatened and intimidated?

Would you like to have homeless people sleeping in *your* doorway??

HAVE YOUR SAY!!
Wednesday at 7pm
The Other Half Caff
Tea and cake will be served

I can't keep my hand from shaking as I reread the
crinkled notice. What a complete load of rubbish!
Criminals?! They're only children, for heaven's sake. Most
of them haven't even been to court yet. Intimidated grannies? Have you *seen* the old-timers around here? I
wouldn't fancy my chances against any of them down a
dark alley.

This really is the last straw.

All publicity might be good publicity, but the leaflet that's been pushed through every letterbox on the square won't exactly bring the punters in for a cuppa, will it?

'They were up all over the main road too,' says Lou, chewing on the end of her pale blue hair. She knows it's not attractive – or hygienic – when she does that, but who can blame her? She's only worried for me. For all of us.

'You want me to send the lads round to 'ave a word?' she asks. 'You know it's *her* behind it.' She punches her fist into the palm of her hand, like I wouldn't catch her meaning otherwise. Fat chance of that. Lou's about as subtle as an armed robbery. The last thing we need now is for her to go over there and prove everyone right.

Of course I know it's her behind it. It's been her behind it ever since we opened the café. But sending the kids around is only going to make the situation worse. And Lou knows that as well as I do.

I can feel tears welling in my eyes as I scan the leaflet again. It's not sadness, though. It's pissed-offness. I stare hard at the strings of calico bunting that criss-cross the ceiling until I'm sure I won't weep in front of my employees. Every single person in here, I remind myself – sipping their hot drinks, chatting, laughing or quietly enjoying the warm cosy ambiance – *loves* our café. So get a grip on yourself. Sticks and stones and all that.

One of the walkie-talkies crackles to life on the coun-tertop. 'Emma, Emma, come in, Emma.'

I'm not sure why I ever thought it would be clever to let the customers upstairs give us orders over those things. Most of the time they use them to ask the answers to stupid trivia questions that they're too lazy to look up on their phones.

I'm in no mood for trivia right now. 'What is it, Leo?' I'm sure my annoyance comes through loud and clear despite the static.

'We need you upstairs.'

'Do you actually need me to bring you something or is this your usual afternoon plea for attention? Because I haven't really got time right now.'

There's a pause. 'It's just my usual plea for attention. Sorry to bother you. Over and out.' The walkie-talkie goes dead.

Now I'm cross *and* I feel bad. I'm absolutely definitely not treating Leo any differently than usual. I'd have been just as short with him yesterday. It's the situation that's changed, not me. And definitely not my feelings.

Something tells me today should have been a duvet day.

Two months earlier...

I'm sitting at our solid old dining room table, oblivious to the fact that I'm about to make a mortal enemy. I don't even know Leo yet, or Lou or Joseph or most of the customers who will become my friends. Morning sun streams through the wide bay window in the front room, throwing a long rectangle of light along the floor. It'll reach my chair in another hour, but I'll be long gone by then.

That window is my favourite part of the whole house. It's where Daniel and I looked out over our wedding reception at everyone in the world we love. It's also where we took Auntie Rose's advice not to wait till after the party to christen our new marriage. While it's beyond mortifying to hear bedroom suggestions from your seventy-something great aunt, she was right. And there wasn't even a sofa there yet. We used to live life on the edge.

Now our edges are blunt and you don't really get any view from the window unless you stand up to look out over flower boxes – crammed full of colourful pansies and winter primroses – past the wrought-iron fence and over the quiet road into the garden square beyond.

I can't claim credit for the flowers. Mrs Ishtiaque comes

over every few months to plant new ones after I've killed the previous lot. It was involuntary plantslaughter, Your Honour.

Mrs Ishtiaque has lived next door to my parents my whole life. She looks out for me like I'm one of her daughters. She says that newlyweds should always have blossoms in their lives. Blooming flowers, blooming love, she claims. Though we're not technically newlyweds anymore. I'll have been married to Daniel two years in July. Sometimes it feels like two decades.

The twins are in lockdown in their high chairs, happily finger-painting stewed apples over everything. They're a couple of Picassos, those two.

It's a surprise to see them both painting, actually. They almost never do the same thing at the same time. If one is sleeping, the other's awake. One's breakfast is the other's playtime. The only things they seem to synchronise are tantrums and bowel movements.

I wouldn't believe they were related if they hadn't put me through thirty hours of labour.

'Mama! Mamamamamamamamamamama!' screams Grace, blinking fast to dislodge a bit of apple from her eyelid. She couldn't care less about the smears all over her face. It's the attention she wants.

'Have you made a mess, my love?' She squirms but lets me wipe her chubby cheeks. By the time I've got most of the stewed fruit off her, the cloth is filthy.

'Grab another wet cloth for Oscar, will you?' I call to Daniel as I spot him weaving his way towards us through the piles of laundry and strewn toys.

Changing direction, he calls, 'Clean-up in aisle six,' from the kitchen.

'Clean-up in aisles one through five as well,' I mutter, looking around.

No one would ever call me house-proud – Mum holds that title every year running – but even *I'm* getting fed up with the mess. 'Could you please fold the laundry while I get them cleaned up?' I ask Daniel. 'It's the pile on the sofa.' As opposed to the ones on the floor, the chair or the coffee table.

He plants a swift kiss on top of my head and plonks a soaking wet cloth into my hand. That'll need wringing out before I assault our child with it. I want to clean Oscar, not drown him.

'Can't I have my brekkie first? I'm rahly running late for work,' says Daniel.

My lips twitch when he says brekkie. And *rahly*. He's still trying to speak commoner like the rest of us do around here, but his posh accent really shows up the difference in our upbringings.

He didn't need to utter a word the first time I saw him for me to know he was different. Picture the scene: I'm twenty-five and it's our first day of class – an architecture course at City Lit in Central London – and everyone shuffles in to find a seat. The classroom is functional and bare aside from the battered plastic chairs and scarred desks – no oak-panelled walls, antique tomes or dreaming spires for us mature students. Most of us are huddled into wool coats against the bite of January, laden with satchels and rucksacks and nerves.

It wasn't Daniel's strong jawline or wavy blond hair that I first noticed, or his broad shoulders or long legs or the way his face crinkled into a friendly smile every time he caught someone's eye.

It was his vivid green trousers that I noticed first as he stood to take off his duffel coat. Then he pulled off his dark V-neck jumper to reveal a bright yellow striped work shirt underneath. By the time he'd tied the jumper around his shoulders, the rest of us – clad in T-shirts or sweatshirts and jeans – were staring at him.

Mistaking our curiosity for friendliness, Daniel did what no one ever did on the first day of class. He started talking to strangers. You'd think he was catching up with old friends the way he asked everyone how far they'd travelled and whether this was their first course. By the time the lecturer dismissed us that day, Daniel was on a first-name basis with everyone

And that sums him up, really.

It's not his fault he dresses the way he does. He grew up in one of those five-story white-fronted mansions in West London, with rooms stuffed full of masterpieces and precious artwork and a pond in the back garden. They had people who answered the door for them and made them their meals. They count most heads of state as friends and Daniel's godfather is a lord. It took me a while to realise that his parents are very nice people, despite sounding like the upstairs family from *Downton Abbey*. What a world away from the council house where I grew up with Mum and Dad. Our furniture is more Ikea than iconic and our friends drink pints, not Dom Pérignon. I don't run across many poshies in my day-to-day life, except for the ones who occasionally come this way to stuff fivers into G-strings at the local strip club. And I don't date them.

With such an upbringing, Daniel sounds like he should be spoiled or at least a bit of an arse, right? It's hard not to make assumptions when you hear about someone's giant house and their servants and gap year holidays. But like I said, he's kind and easy-going and generous, totally unflashy and not the least bit judgmental. It helped that I got to know all these things about him before I found out he was stonking rich. Otherwise, naturally I'd have presumed he was a wanker.

That doesn't mean we're not from different worlds, only that the differences are more about our accents and experiences, not the things that really matter. That's why I do give him full marks for trying to fit in, even if the slang sounds wrong with his plummy pronunciation. Besides, he totally ruins it with his next remarks.

'I'll just put the seeded bloomer in to toast, yah? It's the last of the loaf before Waitrose delivers again. I think we're out of hummus too.'

He sounds straight off the estate, doesn't he?

I stop wringing the sopping cloth into my half-drunk coffee cup. If I'm ever kidnapped, the police will be able to trace my last movements through the string of unfinished hot drinks I've left behind. 'Having your seeded bloomer toast before or after you fold clothes won't make a difference to your lateness, you know.'

When his face breaks into a cheeky smile, one dimple

appears on the left side. That dimple! It hints at a mouth that's usually lopsided with merriment. He can make me laugh at myself like nobody else. It's one of the things that's always charmed me. It would probably work now, but I'm too tired. 'I think I'll be more efficient, energy-wise, if I eat first,' he says, glancing at his phone. 'You're right as usual, though. Just let me answer this one email. I'll be quick.'

But he's not quick enough. By the time he finishes his toast I need him to change Grace while I do Oscar. Our children are messy at both ends. So the laundry will sit in a heap for another day as my award for Homemaker of the Year slips further away.

Daniel waits till he's at the front door to break his news casually to me. He thinks it cushions the blow to kiss me when he does it. Kisses or not, it feels like an ambush.

'I've got to meet with Jacob quickly after work tonight.' He nuzzles my neck. 'Are you wearing a new perfume? It smells so good.'

That would be the tea tree oil for the spot that's come up on my forehead. 'But you were out just the other night.'

'That was last week, darling.'

'Was it? Still, do you have to? I'll be working at the

café all day with Mum. I thought you could do tea for us tonight.'

'Yah, I could have if you'd told me before now, but I've already said yes to Jacob. He says it's rahly important, otherwise I'd cancel. I won't be late, though. And don't worry about supper for me. If it's easier, I can grab a bite with Jacob while I'm out. I love you!'

Yeah, sure it's easier. Easier for him. 'Love you too,' I say quietly.

And I do. I'm crazy about him. I just wish he was, I don't know, more helpful. No, that's not the right word, because he is almost always ready to help. It's his follow-through that needs work.

When the twins were tiny we were such a solid team: cuddling, changing, feeding, fussing, staring for hours in wonder and bewilderment. We did it *all* together. Even though he hasn't got the feeding equipment to be of much practical use, he'd sit with us while I nursed our babies so that I wasn't the only one awake.

But now that they're toddlers, he sleeps through the night even when we don't. He will do what I ask of him, usually without grumbles. But I've become more of a lead singer to his backing vocals and the thing is, I never wanted a solo career.

Grace raises her arms and mewls for a cuddle as soon as Daniel leaves, fixing me with the same long-lashed blue-eyed stare that he has. She's as irresistible as he is, with her golden hair and dimples. Oscar's got my family's red tinge, which thrills Mum. It would be nice, though, for one of my children to have my dark hair or even the cowlick at the front that I can't do anything with. Not that one should ever wish a cowlick on their children.

There's no time on the walk to my parents' house for a proper grizzle about Daniel getting to go out tonight. Even walking slowly, it only takes fifteen minutes, plus time to stop for the toys, dummies and shoes the twins jettison from the pushchair along the way.

It'll be no use whinging to Mum when I get there either. She didn't manage to hold our family together – raising me, making ends meet and looking after Dad while working her cleaning jobs – by being soft. She'll only be her usual sensible self and tell me that I'm over-reacting. It's not like Daniel is out every night or comes home pissed. You heard him. It's a once-a-week thing at most. And the world won't end because he didn't fold our pants. I'm just overtired. Looking after the children is a lot harder than I imagined.

Says every parent in the world. Still, I wouldn't trade them for anything. Well, maybe I would, just for half an hour so I could have a bath without an audience. I'd want them back, though, as soon as I was towelled off.

'Good morning!' I call into Mum and Dad's house as I let myself in with my key. 'You have a special delivery: two toddlers, fairly clean and ready to play!'

They're all in their usual spots in the lounge – Mum and Auntie Rose on the settees and Dad in his old reading chair that Mum has tried to get rid of for years.

Dad's face creases into a broad smile when he sees his grandchildren. 'Come 'ere, me loves!'

It's hard to unbuckle them with all the wriggling. They're in Dad's lap as fast as their little legs will carry them across the lounge floor. 'There's me angels,' he murmurs as he kisses the tops of their heads.

'Hah, you should have seen them at breakfast.'

'They're angels to me.'

He means it too. I don't know what happened to the strict father I had to deal with growing up. He's turned into a giant marshmallow of a man. 'How come you never spoiled me like that?'

'I would have if you'd smelled like biscuits,' he says.

'That's not what they smelled like an hour ago.'

You'd have thought Mum and Dad had won the lottery when I asked if they'd look after the twins for a few hours a day till I can get the café ready to open. Mum had the whole house baby-proofed, including Dad. She saw her chance with his chair, reciting a litany of child-hood diseases that might lurk in its nubbly striped fabric. But Dad offered to get it cleaned and she hasn't thought up a way around that. If she ever does manage to get rid of it, I just know Dad's going to go too.

He glances up. 'How are you, love?'

'Okay. Just tired, Dad.'

'She's burning the candle at both ends,' Auntie Rose says. 'It's too much, if you ask me. Not that anybody ever does.'

Auntie Rose likes to say that, but she knows how important she is in our family. We joke that that's why we keep her under lock and key. It's not really the reason. It's just nice to have a laugh about it with her. Otherwise it's a bit sad. 'You're right, Auntie Rose, but I can't stop now. Besides, it's not for much longer. Mum and I are stripping the tables and chairs today. We're nearly there.'

'You'll be just as busy after the café opens, you know,' Mum reminds me as she goes to tidy up around Dad's chair. She never sits still for long. 'You keep talking like it's all going to calm down suddenly. I just hope it's not too much.'

Of course it's too much, but Mum knows what it means to me to open this café. I didn't spend five years getting my degree not to use it just because my uterus decided it suddenly wanted to play host to a couple of embryos. There's a lot at stake. Not least of which is the wodge of my in-laws' money that's going into the business.

Being as rich as they are, they invest in all sorts of things, though Daniel doesn't like to rely on them. We didn't even accept help from them for our wedding. But that's another story.

When they offered to loan me the money for the café officially, there was a lot of discussion about it before Daniel and I agreed. I thought it would be better to borrow money from family instead of an impersonal bank. Now I'm not so sure.

They're not putting pressure on me or anything. I'd feel better if they did. But every time I promise to pay them back, Philippa waves me away with a cheerful 'Don't worry about that', like they've already kissed their investment goodbye. Now I think I should have risked the bad credit rating with the bank manager. At least I wouldn't have to spend every holiday at *his* house worrying that he thinks I'll never come good on the business.

I know I can do this. I'll have to, won't I? A year ago I wouldn't have thought I could handle having twins and look at me now. Frazzled, exhausted and barely managing, but I haven't screwed them up too badly yet.

When we hear the knock at the door, Auntie Rose says, 'That'll be Doreen.'

Mum opens it with the key from around her neck. I wasn't kidding about the lockdown around here.

'Where are the babies?!' Doreen exclaims, not waiting for an invitation inside. ''Ere, for elevenses.' She hands Mum a carrier bag full of biscuits. 'They were on special, two-for-one. Ha, like these two!'

Doreen is one of Auntie Rose's lifelong best friends. She smokes like a wet log fire and there are questions over exactly what happened when her husband disappeared back in the eighties, but beneath her over-tanned cleavage and lumpy wrap dresses there beats the heart of an angel. Just don't cross her or try cheating at cribbage.

There used to be four of them, till my gran died eight or nine years ago. She was Auntie Rose's sister. Now it's Auntie Rose, Doreen and June, whose husband hasn't disappeared, so she mostly does her visiting with everyone in the evenings at the pub.

Both twins scramble off Dad's lap to see what Doreen's got to offer. Oscar doesn't come empty-handed, though. Shyly, he holds his stuffed duck out for Doreen's inspection.

'He's just like you, Emma,' Auntie Rose says.

'Not Grace too?' I say, though I'm just fishing for compliments. Greedy me, wanting credit for all the best traits of my children. But Grace has Daniel's outgoing nature.

'Nah, she's a tearaway like your mother. It skipped a generation.'

Mum ignores my questioning smile. I love when Auntie Rose lets slip about Mum's younger days. When I was a child it gave me useful ammunition against her rules. Now I'm just curious to know more about my parents.

Auntie Rose gathers Grace up onto her ample lap while Doreen settles next to her with Oscar, and Dad tries not to look too jealous that they've got his grand-children. 'Off you go now,' Auntie Rose says to Mum and me. 'That café ain't opening itself. We'll look after the wee ones.'

'Okay, but we'll be back at lunchtime,' I say as Mum

hands me a bag full of paint stripper and brushes. 'I've got my phone if you need me. Mum does too.'

Mum manages to get me into the car after I kiss my babies about a hundred times and remind everyone about the nappies, bottles, extra clothes, extra nappies and the bottles again.

'It's only for a few hours, Emma,' Mum reminds me on the short drive back to Carlton Square.

'You were probably just as bad when you had to leave me.'

'I couldn't get away fast enough,' she says, smirking into the windscreen.

'Liar. I remember Gran telling you off for being a hover mother.' My gran was cut from the same no-nonsense cloth as Auntie Rose and my mum.

'Oh, she was a great one for repeating whatever she read in the *Daily Mail*,' Mum says, still smiling.

'The skip's arrived,' she notes as she carefully manoeuvres the car into the free spot just behind it. 'Let's take up those carpets before we do the furniture.'

Chapter 2

The café isn't much of a café yet, but it's perfect in my imagination. In reality it's still just the old pub that sits across the square from our house. It did have a brief life as a café before I took it over, but the owners never really got rid of its pubness. That's a blessing and a curse.

The waft of stale beer hits me as usual when I unlock the double doors at the front, though it looks better than it smells. There's a big wraparound bar at the back and shiny cream and green tiles running waist-high along all the walls. It's even got two of those old gold-lettered mirrored advertisements for whisky set into the walls at the side of the bar. When we first came to see inside, Mum climbed up the ladder to inspect the ceiling. It's pressed tin, though like the rest of the place, stained by about a hundred years of tobacco smoke.

She throws a pair of work gloves and a face mask at me. 'Put your back into it. Start in a corner where it's easier to get it up.'

That's easy for her to say when she's got muscles on top of muscles from all her cleaning jobs. She can even lift Dad when she needs to. Luckily that's not too often these days.

The carpet pulls away – in some places in shreds – setting loose a cloud of God-knows-what into the air. 'Open the windows, Mum!' I shout through the mask.

When the dust settles, there's no beautifully preserved Victorian parquet floor underneath. This isn't one of those BBC makeover programmes where gorgeous George Clarke congratulates us on our period features.

The floor is made up of rough old unfinished planks.

'That's even uglier than the carpet,' I tell Mum when she comes over for a look. 'We can't afford a whole new floor.' Even if we had the extra money, there's no way I'd hand that capital improvement to the council, who owns the lease.

'Let's have a think about this,' she says, leading me to one of the booths by the open window where, hopefully, the slight breeze is clearing away whatever was in that carpet.

The booths are as knackered as the rest of the pub, but at least they're wooden so they won't need re-covering. Unlike all the chairs piled in a heap upstairs. I don't even like to think about what's stained their fabric seats over the decades.

Suddenly Mum reaches into my hair. 'Hold still, you've got something– It's a bit of ... I don't know what it is.' Then she squints at my head. 'Is that a grey hair?'

My hand flies to my head. 'NO! It can't be.' I'm only twenty-seven.

'It's only because your hair is so dark that I noticed it. I started getting them at your age. Don't worry, it's only one ...' She reaches for my head again. 'Or two. 'Ere, I'll get them.'

'Ow, don't pull them out! You'll make more.'

'That's an old wives' tale. Let me just get—'

'Get off me!'

As I twist my head away from my mother's snatching fingers, I look out the window and straight into two strange faces. They look about as old as God and his secretary and as surprised to see us as I am to see them.

'Oh! Excuse us,' says the man. 'We thought we saw someone inside ...' He grasps the woman's hand. 'We're terribly sorry to disturb you.'

'No, no, don't be sorry,' calls my mum through the window. 'We're renovating the pub.'

The man hesitates. 'It's been decades since we've been inside.'

'It smells like it,' I murmur, then realise how rude that sounds. 'Since it's been open, I mean.'

'Would you like to come in?' Mum asks. 'You're very welcome.'

'We shouldn't bother you,' says the woman, but I can see that she's dying for a snoop.

'It's no bother, really, come in. Just a sec, I'll open the door.'

They're even older than they looked outside, but they come nimbly through the door like they own the place. They're both wearing long dark wool coats against the February cold snap.

'I always hated that carpet,' says the woman, seeing the pile I've made in the corner. 'It stank to high heaven. But then so did a lot of the men who drank 'ere.'

'Present company excepted.' The man removes his flat cap and bows, showing me the top of his balding, age-spotted head. 'Carl Brumfeld. Pleased to meet you. And this 'ere's Elsie.'

Their accents are as local to East London as my family's is. After I make introductions, Elsie asks, 'Are you the new landlord?' Her face is nearly unlined, but her hair is snowy white, spun into an intricate sort of beehive on top of her head. Auntie Rose would say she'd look younger with it coloured, but she says that about everyone because she does hair.

'It's going to be a café,' Mum tells them. As she relays this, her pride even tops her bragging about me going to Uni. And that was monumental.

'Oh,' they chorus. 'That's a shame,' Carl says. 'We were hoping to get the old place back. This is where we met, you see.'

'When was that?' I ask. Just after the dawn of time, I'm guessing.

'Nineteen forty-one,' says Elsie. 'We were children during the war. We used to sit together in that booth right there.'

'Wow, seventy-five years.' Mum whistles. 'What's that in anniversaries? Diamond is sixty. Of course you couldn't have been married so young!'

'We're not married now either,' Carl says.

'Carl is my brother-in-law,' Elsie adds.

Which does make me wonder why they're holding hands. 'You'll come back when we're open, won't you?' I ask. 'Maybe you'd like to sit in your old booth for a cup of tea.'

Where I'll be able to winkle their story out of them. A café is the perfect business for a nosey person like me to run.

'We'd like that, thank you,' Carl says. 'You're keeping the booths, then? It would be nice for someone to take account of history around 'ere instead of tearing everything down to build flats.'

'The booths are staying,' I assure them.

Carl's words stay with me after they leave. It would be a shame to strip the pub of its history if we don't have to. Except for the carpet. The history of spilled pints and trodden-on fag ends will have to go.

'Daniel's out tonight,' I tell Mum as we pull up the rest of the carpet together. Despite my promise to myself, the words are out before I can stop them.

She halts her ripping to glance at me. Her gingery bob has come loose from its hair tie and she keeps swiping it back behind her ears. She is pretty, though she doesn't usually wear much make-up. Only when she's doing things like trying to impress Daniel's parents. Then she goes for full-on slap, even though my mother-in-law doesn't bother with it herself.

'And you hate him a bit, right?' she asks.

Instinctively I want to deny it, even though I've just brought it up. 'I'm trying not to, Mum, and I know you're going to tell me I shouldn't.'

But Mum shakes her head. 'I was going to say that I understand. After you were born, when your father got to go out in his taxi every day, I wanted to puncture his tyres. I wanted to puncture *him* sometimes. He used to complain about how hard it was driving around all day. I would have bloody loved to trade places. Believe me, you 'aven't got the monopoly on resentment.'

Resentment. Is that what I've got? 'It's just so hard,' I say.

'I know, love, but it gets easier when they're in school.'

'Nursery?'

'University,' she deadpans.

I guess I shouldn't be surprised that Mum understands. She and Dad didn't wait long after their wedding to have me either. Everyone keeps telling us how lucky we are to be young parents. We've got more energy, they say. We'll still be youngish when the children are grown. But what about the decades in between? At the moment, it looks like a long time between now and then.

Mum gathers me into a carpet-dust-filled hug. 'It's always harder than you think it's going to be. Thank goodness I had your Gran and Auntie Rose. Your Granny Liddell was no help.'

'Thank goodness I've got you and Dad and Auntie Rose now,' I say.

Mum nods. 'Your Dad's a dark horse, isn't he? He's so much better with the twins than he ever was with you. He's got more confidence now than he did then. He was terrified of making a mistake with you.'

'Weren't you terrified?' I'm constantly worried that I'm doing it all wrong or that I'll damage the twins somehow. I could be feeding them too much, or not enough, leaving them to get too hot or too cold, smothering them with cuddles or not paying them enough attention, pushing them to learn new things or being too laid back, letting their faces get too dirty or wiping them so much that they'll end up with allergies. They might be underdressed or overstimulated, under-cuddled, over-coddled, disgruntled or disappointed. Just off the top of my head. I could give you another ten lists like that every single day.

'Of course I was afraid to mess up,' Mum says, 'but I didn't have a choice. You had to eat and be held and changed. If I didn't do it, who would?'

That's exactly how I feel. It's not that Daniel can't do it too. He's just not as good at it as I am. And lately he's seemed to leave more and more to me while he gets on with his life.

I always seem to have toddlers hanging off me when I try getting on with my life. Just try being glamorous with ladies who lunch when you're saying, 'Get that out of your mouth,' every two minutes.

Not that I've ever been glamorous. And my friends aren't ladies who lunch, but you see my point.

Today it's my turn to host everyone at the house, so despite having had to shove most of the toys under the sofa and the unfolded laundry into the closet, I've got the easy part. Just try going anywhere with the twins. Trying to move a circus is less challenging.

'Maybe if they didn't act like they'd invented nuclear fusion every time they changed a nappy, I wouldn't mind so much,' my friend Melody says, talking about husbands as she shifts her child to her other breast. Speaking of having children hanging off you.

Melody and Samantha, Emerald and Garnet – four women who at first had no more in common with me than leaky boobs and sleepless nights – are the reason I'm holding on to my sanity. But when your world has shrunk to leaky boobs and sleepless nights, that can be enough.

We're covering our usual ground – what we've done since we saw each other last week and who's aggrieved about what – and, also as usual, I've got to keep my eyes glued to Melody's face and away from her feeding daughter. Not because breastfeeding embarrasses me. Not at all. When I was breastfeeding my boobs came out anywhere the twins needed to feed, and we're only in my house anyway. When they legislate against boys wearing their jeans so low that you can see their bollocks from the back, I'll agree that we should be hiding feeding babies under tea towels and tablecloths to protect the public's sensibilities.

It would be perfectly normal for Melody to feed her toddler, Joy. Which she does. She just happens to also like to feed her five-year-old, who's not even sitting in her mother's lap. She's got her own chair. Her feet nearly touch the floor.

'Because it's such a huge favour to care for his own child,' Samantha throws in.

I'm not the only one who thinks that nearly school-age children really ought to be drinking milk from cups. Samantha doesn't bother trying to hide her eye roll. Melody doesn't bother pretending to ignore it. Samantha won't say anything with Melody's daughter here, though. She may be one of the toughest women I've ever met, but she's never cruel.

'Well, that's not really fair,' Emerald points out, brushing a non-existent speck of something from her pristine top. Not that a crumb could have come from any of the food on the table. She never eats the buttery croissants or packets of biscuits that the rest of us scoff. 'The men do work all day.'

I wince at her terrible choice of words. What is it that we're doing all day – and night – if not working? But Garnet, Emerald's sister, nods, adding, 'My Michael works late into the night sometimes.'

'Boo hoo,' Samantha bites back.

'Not to mention weekends.' Emerald ignores Samantha's dig at her sister. 'Anthony's a workhorse too.'

When Emerald and Garnet sit beside each other they look like someone has taken the same drawing and just coloured them in differently. Their eyes are almond shaped and they have identical long slender noses, angular faces and full lips. But Garnet's got nearly black eyes and her thick straight shoulder-length hair is cut in a heavy blunt fringe and coloured a russet red. Emerald has the same haircut but her colour is even darker than mine – almost a true black – and her eyes are nearly black too. It's very striking against her pale skin.

'Poor Michael has even had to cancel holidays,' says Garnet.

Melody covers her daughter's ears when she catches the look on Samantha's face. Samantha doesn't disappoint. 'Oh, for fuck's sake, at least they get holidays,' she replies. 'Not to mention sick days and bonuses and at least some bloody idea about all the hours they'll have to work. I'd trade places in a heartbeat. They're not sitting around with their friends feeling sorry for us, are they?'

When I first met Samantha in antenatal class I mistook her abruptness for rudeness, but she's just very honest and efficient. She used to be a high-powered consultant before her first child and she never really lost the drive. It was her job to go into companies and restructure them (efficiently, of course). Now she hasn't got anywhere for all that energy to go so she channels it into everyday life and her marathon yoga sessions. The rest of us might dress to camouflage the baby tummies we haven't quite lost yet. Samantha's got thighs that could crack walnuts.

Naturally, it gets Samantha's back up when Garnet and Emerald try excusing their husbands, which happens a lot.

It's not just Samantha's lack of employment that frustrates her. It doesn't sound like her husband appreciates her thighs, walnut-cracking or not, any more than all the work she does. Like I said, she channels a lot into yoga.

And Garnet and Emerald are very nice women once you get used to their rivalry. They only ever turn it on each other and have a long-running disagreement over which precious stone their parents think is more precious. That sums them up, really.

Not only were their first babies due within days of each other, but their husbands work for the same bank and their houses are one road away from one another. Both think theirs is the better neighbourhood. And the better husband.

Garnet was over-the-top smug about getting to the finishing line first in the maternity ward, pushing out her ten-pound daughter a day and a half before Emerald. But Emerald had the better time when her son was born in under six hours, and they've been competitively parenting ever since.

The sisters are closest in age to me, twenty-seven and twenty-eight, and both think they're the perfect age. Samantha is in her mid-thirties and Melody's age is anyone's guess, so of course we all do. I think she's well over forty because of her long frizzy brown and grey hair, but since I've got a few greys too (thanks to Mum for pointing those out), maybe she is younger.

'It will be all right, you know,' Melody says, fixing me with her pale blue, wide-set eyes. Combined with a longish face and big-toothed smile, they make her look a bit like a goat. I don't mean that in an insulting way. It's just so you can picture her. Because her hair is salt-and-pepper, though, instead of goat-coloured, the resemblance ends there.

Melody is even more of a tree-hugging yogurt-knitter than I thought when we first met, the kind of person who makes her own baby food and sews up holes in socks even though there's usually an uncomfortable lump in your shoe after, instead of just buying another pack of twenty for a fiver.

You won't be surprised to know that she gave birth to her daughter in an inflatable paddling pool in her lounge, with the sound of wind chimes and whale noises for pain relief. All her friends were there to see it and it sounds like it was a bit of a party between contractions. She claims it was the most magical three days of her life, especially when her then four-year-old cut the umbilical cord and her husband made an afterbirth smoothie for Melody. I imagine the other guests stuck to the hummus and kale chips.

I wouldn't have been much of a hostess at my own birth party. I cried through most of my labour because, holy hell, it hurt. Daniel did too, come to think of it, in solidarity and helplessness at seeing me. We were basically that nightmare couple in labour for the first time. But anyone who tells you it's not that bad is either lying or has had their memory erased by those post-birth hormones.

'I hate to be the one to break this up,' Samantha says, 'but I've got to pick up Dougie. It's been fun as always. Same time next week at my house?'

She doesn't need to ask because I wouldn't miss these get-togethers even if I ended up in hospital with appendicitis. I'd crawl on all fours with tubes hanging off me and a packet of biscuits clenched in my teeth. And to think that when I first had the babies I thought I didn't need the mums I'd met in antenatal class. Naïve, deluded Emma.

'Thanks for coming,' I say. 'Sorry we were out of milk.'

Everyone starts to shift as Samantha perfects her lipstick without looking and pulls out her hairbrush to give her chestnut tresses a swipe. Which reminds me that I forgot to brush mine this morning. At least I cleaned my teeth. I'm a winner.

'We should be going too,' Garnet says to her sister.

Their toddlers are already in day care, though that's not what they call it. 'It's pre-Montessori, like Eton is a feeder for Oxbridge,' they explain.

'I bet you'll be excited to start school in the autumn, Eva,' I tell Melody's five-year-old, who is busy drawing orange trees on her sketch pad. She's got her mum's clear blue eyes and long face.

'I can't wait for school!' Eva says, but Melody looks troubled. I'm not sure what she'll do then. Will she turn up at snack time in her nursing bra?

Chapter 3

Talk about putting the cart before the horse. Or the staff before the café, in this case. My glance falls on the stack of boxes leaning precariously beside the bar. One more thing to put away. It looks messy, unfinished and unprofessional. Ditto the half-painted walls, filthy window glass and stripped but yet-to-be refinished tables and chairs. It looks like a building site.

It *is* a building site. But in four weeks it needs to be a welcoming café. With staff.

So far none of this has seemed altogether real, despite the loan from Daniel's parents or the official two-year extendable lease from the council. Just paperwork, I've convinced myself. If it all goes pear-shaped for some reason, I can always find a way to pay my in-laws back and cancel the lease. No real harm done to anyone but me.

Until now. As soon as I put teenagers into the training positions they'll be depending on me for the job. And they deserve the chance to do something that could give them a leg-up in life. Lots of charities do after-school programmes and run youth centres and activity groups, not to mention everyone campaigning to get more funding. But training programmes are harder to come by.

I never imagined I'd set one up myself, yet here I am fidgeting over a stack of CVs and notes from Social Services, checking the door every two seconds for my first interviewee.

The lady at the council who has been helping me was uncomfortably vague about the applicants' details. I know they've all had reason to catch the attention of the authorities, which is why they're being put forward as potential trainees. But when I asked her what they'd done – just to know whether I'd be dealing with someone who's run red lights or run drugs – she went tight-lipped. And she wasn't exactly chatting like my BFF to begin with.

'We can't disclose any details about the cases,' she'd said, rapidly clicking the top of her pen. 'I'm sure you understand.'

I nodded like I did. 'When you say *cases*, do you mean their Social Services cases? Or their court cases?'

'Both,' she said. 'Either.'

'Uh-huh, I see. Would those be criminal cases or civil ones?'

She just stared at me over her reading glasses. 'Everyone we're referring has needed intervention by Social Services, and in each situation we feel that the opportunity to work, to get training, will benefit them.'

I felt like such a dick then. Here was this lady, working with troubled kids every day, probably for little pay and little thanks, and I was swanning in sounding like I only wanted the cream off the top of the barrel. 'Yes, of course, of course, that's why I'm here,' I said as my face reddened. 'To offer them that chance.' I took home every one of the files she'd prepared for me to consider.

Just the bare bones information I've got is enough to break your heart. A litany of foster care, school disruption and instability. I wanted to hire them all, so how was I supposed to choose between them to make a shortlist? I'm not exactly opening Starbucks nationwide. I've only got room, and money, for two trainees at a time.

I'm not looking for the *best* candidates, per se, like you would for a regular job. I'm looking for the ones who most need the help, and the ones who most want it. It's like going into a bakery and asking which cakes taste okay. No, no fancy decoration or mouth-watering icing. Someone else will gladly have those. I'll take the ones that are irregularly shaped or might have fallen on the floor, please. They're still perfectly good, just not as obviously appealing as the perfect ones.

A hulking form suddenly blocks most of the light from the open doorway. 'Yo. This for the interview?' his deep voice booms.

'Yes, in here. You must be Martin. Hi.'

He doesn't look like a Martin. He walks in with a sort of half-skip, half-lumber, as if he's got a bad limp on one side. 'Yo, I'm Ice,' he says, putting his fist in front of me for a bump. I must not do it right because he sucks his teeth at me. The kids are always doing this to me – when I don't get out of the way fast enough at the Tube station, or dither over the bowls of fruit at the market or hold up the queue in the local Tesco. Basically, whenever they judge me hopeless, which is a lot. 'Wagwan?' he asks.

He means what's going on. 'Well, we're renovating the café to get it ready for the opening, as you can see!'

He looks around as I look at him. His file says he's

fifteen, and his face looks babyish, but he's huge, man-size. There's a thick metal chain snaking into the front pocket of his jeans, which are so low they're nearly around his knees, and his mini Afro looks too old for his spot-prone brown face.

I know he's trying to be intimidating, but it's so clearly bravado that I just want to say '*Aww!*' and pinch his babyish cheeks. Though he might break my arm if I did.

He keeps looking around as I explain about the six-month training scheme and what would be expected of him. Eventually he says, 'Why you making it a café, not a pub? It'd be banging working in a pub.'

'Aren't you a minor? You can't work in a pub.'

He sucks his teeth again. 'True dat.'

'Maybe you could tell me why you'd like to work here?' He shrugs his answer. 'Can you think of *any* reason you'd like to work here?'

'It pays, yeah?'

'Right, yes. Any reason beyond the money?' Though at trainee rates he wouldn't really need that chain on his wallet.

'Nah, man, my social worker say I got to come.' He pulls a crumpled paper from his non-chained pocket. 'She said sign this.'

I take the short, photocopied statement from him and add my signature to the bottom.

Ice snatches it off the table and leaves without a backward glance.

By mid-morning my hand is starting to cramp from signing so many attendance forms. Some of the kids bother to sit down and a few even humour me by answering a question or two. Others turn up with their paper already in hand, waving it for a signature.

I'm in so far over my head that I should be in a submersible. I may have grown up in a tough part of London and be on first-name terms with PC Billy Bramble. I may have seen the fights break out down the market when the gangs kick off. But I've never lived that life myself. I like to think I'm street. I'm really just streetlight.

Take the kid who rumbled me for gawping at the purplish blood droplet tattooed on his arm. It had a triangle above it, like a gang symbol. 'You starin' at my tatt?' he'd said.

I could feel my face go red. 'Erm, sorry, I was just interested. Is it supposed to be blood, or a gang sign of some kind?' I couldn't sound more lame.

'Teletubby,' he said.

I'd never heard of them. The Teletubby Massive? I didn't want any gang members in my crew.

He pointed to the red blotch beside the drop. 'Tinky Winky.'

'You mean it's an actual Teletubby?!' I tried to bite down my smile.

'Joker blud did it to me.' He shrugged. 'I wanted a stopwatch.'

Just as I was starting to wonder if this boy with a children's cartoon character on his arm might be worth another look, I asked him why he wanted to do the training programme.

'Everybody likes coffee, yeah? I can drink that shit all day.'

'Well, yes, but you'd actually be working, not drinking coffee. And hopefully it won't be shit.'

'I can slip it to my bluds though, yeah?'

He really thought I'd pay him to hand out free coffee to his mates all day.

'I can let you know by next week, okay?' I said, scribbling my signature on his form.

Mum and Dad would have cuffed him on the side of the head for answers like that. I can hear Dad now. *Lazy sod.* My parents were working by the time they were teens, and not just making their beds for pocket money, either. Mum cycled all over London to pick up and drop off clothes for my gran's tailoring customers. 'Join a Union if you don't like the deal,' Gran used to say of the sweatshop wages she paid her daughter, but she bought Mum off by letting her keep any tips. Mum was slightly easier on me, and she'd never let me cycle across the city. She often took me with her to help when she cleaned houses, though. There was less risk to life and limb but the wages were still crap.

On his way out, my latest applicant passes a boy just coming in. 'Yo, Tinky Winky, 'sup?' says the boy.

'Fuck off, dweeb.'

'That's Professor to you,' he says.

I watch this brief exchange with interest. Not because the new boy, with his tall lanky frame, looks as if his brain has no idea what his arms and legs are doing, or that he doesn't seem frightened by his tattooed rival. His close-cropped wavy black hair and mixed-race complexion don't differentiate him from most of the other kids.

It's his three-piece suit and the fatly knotted blue tie round his skinny neck.

And his briefcase, which he sets on the table between us.

'I'm Joseph.' He sticks his hand out for me to shake. His long-lashed brown eyes are the first to look directly at me all morning. 'It's your lucky day,' he says. 'You can cancel the other punters because you've found your future employee.'

'Well, I hope I have, but I'll still need to ask you some questions, okay?' Who told him to be so cocky in an interview? I glance at his file. Lives with his mum and older brother, who seems to be mixed up with one of the local gangs. 'You're seventeen?'

'Yeah, but don't let that fool you. I can do anything you can, and I'm really *good*.'

His suggestion is unmistakable.

That won't do him any favours and the sooner he realises it, the better. Just to prove the point, I ask him if he can drive. No? What about buying alcohol legally? Are you registered to vote? No again? 'Then you can't quite do anything I can,' I say, 'so let's stick to the interview, okay? Why would you like to do this training?'

There's a scattering of hairs on his face where he's been trying to shave, and his suit sleeves cover his knuckles. I bet he's borrowed it from his big brother. He might have borrowed the razor too.

Joseph clears his throat. That doesn't stop his voice

from cracking. 'I see the position as a stepping stone for my future as a CEO.'

'A CEO ... here?' We both look around the pub. 'That's not really the position I'm recruiting for.' Unless CEO stands for Chief Egg-on-toast Officer.

'Well, then, what *are* you going to do for my career progression?'

'It's a six-month traineeship, so you'll learn all aspects of working in a café. Working with colleagues, serving customers, making coffee and tea...' I sort of run out of steam. It's just a café, not Microsoft.

He sits forward in his chair. 'Sales and marketing?'

I thought I might put up a few posters around the bus stops. 'Sure.'

'How 'bout customer complaint resolution?'

'I expect so. Tell me, Joseph, what would you like to be a CEO of?'

'A company with good benefits,' he says right away.

'Any particular kind?'

'Definitely stock options. And a gold-plated pension.'

'No, I mean any particular kind of company?'

'I'd be happy at Apple. Or Xbox.'

I like that he's dreaming big. My most ambitious goal at his age was getting a real pair of Dr. Martens. 'Well, maybe you'll get there. It would have been easier if you'd stayed in school, you know.' He finished secondary school but doesn't want to go on for college.

'I like to think of myself as a student of life,' he says. 'Steve Jobs dropped out. So did Bill Gates and Mark Zuckerberg, and they all became CEOs.'

'Mark Zuckerberg dropped out of Harvard,' I point out. 'If you get into Harvard, then you can feel free to drop out.'

'That's what my mum said.'

'I think I'd like your mum.'

Who can blame Joseph for not wanting to be in school? Not everyone is a swot like I was. I only left at sixteen because I needed to help Mum and Dad with the bills. And I went back to graduate from Uni.

If it hadn't been for the twins' unplanned arrival scuppering the job plans I had after university, I'd be the one on the other side of the interview table now, trying to get a charity to hire me and probably sounding as naïve as Joseph does.

There but for the grace of god, and my in-laws...

Joseph's heart seems to be in the right place, underneath the cocksure attitude. He needs a lot of help with his interview technique and he'll have to learn that people aren't just going to hand him a job as CEO because he asks for it.

He might not know a teabag from a tea towel, for all I know, but that's the point, isn't it? If he can already do the job, then he doesn't need the training.

'You've got the job if you want it,' I tell him. 'Congratulations. We'll open in four weeks.'

His face splits into a beaming grin. 'Yeah, that's well good! Are you for reals?'

'I'm for reals. You'll need to come in for training and stuff before the opening.' I consider my very first employee. My employee! 'Can I ask you a question before you go? Your briefcase. You didn't open it. What's in there?'

Joseph takes a second to answer. 'My lunch. Mum packed it for me.'

And just like that, the CEO-in-the-making becomes young Joseph again.

I've just finished putting away all the boxes piled near the bar when Dad turns up with Auntie Rose wheeling the babies in the pushchair. 'I'm glad the ramp works!' I shout to them as they come through the door. We just had it installed last week and it's only about three inches high, but it means Dad can come through in his wheelchair without having to pop a wheelie.

'I've actually hired someone!' I tell them.

'Wayhey!' Dad whoops, meeting me halfway for a hug. 'You're on your way now, me girl. Mind the wheels. This deserves a proper stand-up job.' Slowly he lifts himself from his wheelchair so I can throw my arms around him.

The twins stop their babbling to stare. They're not used to seeing my dad standing, and especially not without the crutches he uses to walk. 'Look at them,' I say. 'Astounded.'

'It's a bloomin' miracle, me angels.'

What a difference a generation makes. When Dad first came down with the multiple sclerosis that keeps him mostly in the chair these days, I was fourteen and mortified at having a disabled family member.

Typical teenager, thinking about myself instead of Dad, whose whole life changed in a matter of months. He'd had tingles in his arms and legs for a while but assumed it was from driving round in his cab every day. He might not have said anything if his vision hadn't started going funny, and the disease had already taken hold by the time he got the diagnosis. He stayed out of the wheelchair for a few more years – a few more years than he should have, really, but he's stubborn like that. Now he uses it most of the time, and it's completely normal for Oscar and Grace.

He sits down again. 'Let 'em loose, Rose. Emma, love, Kelly's right behind us with fish and chips.'

His announcement makes my mouth start watering. It's one of the advantages of having a fishmonger for a best friend. Kelly's worked a deal with the local chippy who fries up her leftover fillets sometimes. She throws the owners a few free portions of fresh fish to cook her tea for her, and they throw in the chips.

'Mum's gone to work?' I ask, reaching for my babies. I might have fantasies about child-free baths and cups of tea that I actually get to finish, but a few hours away from them starts the longing that pulls from my gut and makes me feel breathless.

That was a rhetorical question about Mum anyway. She cleans every weekday afternoon and evening. They're mostly commercial office contracts, with a few houses whose owners she liked enough to keep as clients over the years.

Just in case Daniel wants some fish too, I ring his mobile but it goes straight through to voicemail. He's probably in the Underground on his way home. I know Kelly. She'll have a portion for him when he gets here.

My best friend comes through the door, as usual, with about as much grace as a tipper truck. Kelly's not a big woman. She just makes big entrances. That sometimes tricks people into assuming she's tough, so they're not always as considerate as they could be. A perfect example is when her family decided she should be the one to take over the fish van instead of her sisters. They just assumed she'd do it, like a sixteen-year-old would naturally want to give up any chance of living a life that's wider than her local market.

'I figured you needed this after dealing with the little bleeders all day,' she says, clearing one of the booths to make room for our meal.

Kell takes a different view than me of the hoodies who hang around the market where she works. I can understand why, when she sometimes gets caught up in their skirmishes. She'd like to fillet them and I'm trying to save them.

'I've hired one of the little bleeders,' I tell her. 'You should see him, Kell, he's adorable. He wants to be a CEO.'

'Just watch the till. Rose, I got you extra chips.'

'That's kind, but I really shouldn't,' Auntie Rose says, looking up from where her hand is already elbow-deep in the carrier bag. 'I'm watching me girlish figure.'

Auntie Rose pats her hip with her free hand as she chews on a chip. She's a generously proportioned lady, in stark contrast to her sister, my Gran, who was always skinny like Mum. She's got the same smiling eyes and sharp mind, though. Except when she wanders.

That's why our doors are all locked from the inside and why we can't leave her alone anymore. For years, she's had little strokes that make her mind skip sometimes, which was okay when she stayed in the neighbourhood. But we had to take drastic measures after she turned up on the A12 with no idea how to get back home.

She's pretty relaxed about being incarcerated. She and Dad do everything together these days and she's as much a help to him as he is a minder for her. At least Mum doesn't have to worry about either of them when she's at work.

By the time we lock up the pub we're full of fish, salt and vinegar. Daniel's portion is soaking through the bag under the sleeping twins' pushchair. His phone keeps going straight to voicemail.

'Are you worried about him?' Kell asks, walking beside me.

'No, not worried,' I say, rubbing the phone in my pocket. 'More like disappointed. Don't get me wrong, Kell. I don't begrudge him having a night out. Lord knows, I wish I could do it any time I wanted too. It's just that, I feel like—'

'He's having his cake and eating it, the bastard,' she finishes for me. 'I'd be pissed off too.'

'Don't put words in my mouth, Kell. I didn't say pissed off. I said disappointed.'

'Really? Not pissed off when he gets to have these gorgeous children, the perfect family, plus you to look after it all while he goes out on the lash whenever he feels like it. Why does he get to be the only one? Shouldn't you get to do it too? I say hand the twins over to Daniel for a few hours and let him be the one to sit at home covered in sick, being jealous of you while you dance on the tables.'

'Kell, when have I ever in my life danced on a table?' She is right, though. He should be the responsible parent for once. At least for a few hours. 'You know what? I will.'

'Tomorrow. Do it tomorrow,' she says. 'We'll go out.'

'I can't tomorrow. I'm not sure what Daniel has on after work.'

'You mean like he didn't know what you had on tonight, yet just assumed you'd be there to look after the twins? Have I got that right?' Her stare challenges me to disagree.

'Fine, tomorrow night then. I'll tell Daniel.'